It takes love, patience, tenderness and courage to build a family. This Mother's Day we are proud to celebrate the joy, tears and sheer delight with…

To Mum, With Love

Two brand-new stories from two top romance novelists.

There's no one like Margaret Way when it comes to writing about Australia—or the passions of the human heart!

Wonderfully unique every time, Rebecca Winters will take you on an emotional rollercoaster. Her powerful stories enthral and leave you on a satisfying high!

To Mum, With Love

Rebecca Winters
Margaret Way

*First published in Great Britain 2006
by Harlequin Mills & Boon Limited, Eton House,
18-24 Paradise Road, Richmond, Surrey TW9 1SR*

TO MUM, WITH LOVE © by Harlequin Books SA 2006

The publisher acknowledges the copyright holders of the
individual works as follows:

To Be a Mother © Rebecca Winters 2004
The Cattleman © Margaret Way Pty Ltd. 2006

ISBN 0 263 85030 7

118-0306

*Printed and bound in Spain
by Litografía Rosés S.A., Barcelona*

TO BE A MOTHER

Rebecca Winters

Rebecca Winters, who lives in Salt Lake City, has been writing for Silhouette since 1989. Until very recently she also worked full-time as a teacher. She currently writes for Silhouette Superromance and for Mills & Boon Tender Romance. After an incredible nearly 100 titles, she's writing more books than ever, travelling, playing the piano, doing genealogy, looking forward to a second grandchild *and* enjoying life to the fullest.

Look for *Meant-To-Be Marriage*, Rebecca's new book coming in April from Mills & Boon Tender Romance®.

Dear Reader,

One of my children had a friend who as a teenager gave up her baby for adoption. It was no doubt one of the most painful experiences of her life. Even though it seemed the only thing to do under the circumstances, I have often thought about that courageous girl. Whatever happened to her? Over the years, how did she deal with her decision? Did the baby find a wonderful home? Did everyone involved find peace?

Those are questions for which I have no answers, so I wrote a story about a teenager who made the similar choice to give up her baby. I followed the lives of the characters involved to see what kind of impact such a decision had on them down through the years. From the first paragraphs I began to cry, and I cried all the way through their story. Some tears sprang from anguish, others from joy. Perhaps you, the reader, will have a similar reaction as you read their story and experience that emotional journey with them.

Rebecca Winters

PS If you have access to the internet, please check out my website at www.rebeccawinters-author.com.

This book is dedicated to all the courageous young women who have given up their babies for adoption.

CHAPTER ONE

Coeur D'Alene, Idaho
October 29

By some miracle I'm still here. It appears my cancer has gone into remission. I just heard the news this afternoon.

Maybe it's a coincidence, maybe it isn't, but tonight the pastor of my church came to see me. It was a comfort, rather than a shock, when he said that every person on this earth is dying, yet none of us knows the exact moment we'll be called home, not even me.

Instead of concentrating on the past, he suggested I think of my remission as permanent rather than temporary, and treat it as a rebirth.

Before he left my condo, he asked me if there was anything in my past that might be troubling me. He reminded me that matters of the heart have a strange and powerful effect on the body's ability to continue to fight disease.

The pastor's unexpected visit has left me haunted by thoughts of Nick and our baby to the exclusion of all else.

Memories are bombarding me. Memories, questions. Regrets.

Oh, the regrets...

Since the moment Nick walked out of my hospital room, not a day, not a minute, not a second has passed that I haven't yearned to be with both of them.

I could try to contact Jessica directly, but that would add cowardice to my list of sins. I have to do this the right way and approach Nick first.

My need to see my daughter is the height of human selfishness. Yet being given a second chance at life has caused me to search my soul, which has always hungered for both of them.

Nick will either tear up my letter or hang up on me. No matter. I have to try. Otherwise this life has made no sense at all....

SAMANTHA LET GO of the pen and buried her wet face in the pillow. "Nick—" she whispered in agony.

"NICK?"

Nick Kincaid glanced up from his field biology book. Everyone in the basement of the Lory Student Center at Colorado State was seated on couches or at tables studying for the last day of finals tomorrow. It was the place where Samantha had first met the rugged-looking twenty-year-old junior from Gillette, Wyoming. They'd been seeing each other since the beginning of fall semester in August.

"Hi," he said in a husky tone. Beneath dark-brown hair and brows, his gray eyes flickered with an awareness of the intimacy they shared. Hers probably did the same. "I thought maybe you weren't coming. Another ten minutes and I was going to phone you."

"I'm sorry I'm late."

"How did your last final go?"

"Fine."

"That's good. Have you eaten?"

They normally bought a hamburger in the center's Ramskeller Restaurant, but tonight food was the last thing on her mind.

"I'm not hungry. Could you leave now? I know you have your last final in the morning, but there's something important I have to tell you. It won't take long. I brought Mom's car."

Nick didn't own one. He worked as many hours as possible at his part-time job with campus security in order to support himself while he earned his undergraduate degree in biology. If he needed transportation, he got around on his bike.

He lived with a hundred other young men at the Hilan Apartments on Lake Street near the campus, and he had friends who helped him out and lent him their cars when he wanted to be alone with her.

His pride refused to let Samantha chauffeur them in one of her parents' cars, but tonight she wasn't giving him a choice.

He must have sensed her urgency. Without saying a word, he got up from the table and put everything away in his backpack. After shrugging into his sheepskin jacket he murmured, "Let's go."

She felt his hand slide to the nape of her neck beneath her parka to guide her to the stairs. He had a tall, powerful physique and was whipcord lean. Samantha was a curvy redhead who didn't stand much taller than his heart. She loved the way he made her feel feminine and protected.

In truth, everything about him appealed to her. It wasn't just the physical attraction, although the chemistry between them was explosive. What drew her to him on other levels was his innate maturity and intelligence.

She was counting on those particular character traits to help him cope with what she had to tell him. Though she hadn't really lied, there were some things she hadn't told Nick the truth about. For the last four months she'd managed to push those sins of omission to the back of her mind in the hope they would never have to come to light. What a foolish, foolish girl she was....

A cold winter wind buffeted them as they left the center and walked to the corner of the next block, where she'd parked her mother's Lincoln. It didn't take long to drive to the foothills near her home. Samantha parked the car at Horsetooth Reservoir overlooking Fort Collins.

By now the interior of the car was too warm. She started to turn off the fan, and Nick anticipated her movement, then pulled her into his arms. For the first time, she resisted him.

"We can't do this right now, Nick. I promised Mom and Dad I would be home by eleven. That gives us an hour."

She felt his reluctance before he relinquished his hold on her and sat back in his seat. "What's wrong?"

"Everything."

A grimace broke out on his face. "Why do I get the feeling this has something to do with your parents?"

"I—it's not just Mom and Dad."

"The hell it isn't," he said without raising his voice. "It's no secret I'm not from a wealthy, well-connected family like yours."

Samantha's hand tightened on the steering wheel. "You're jumping to conclusions about that, Nick."

"Then enlighten me!" he demanded. "If you've met someone else and want to break up, just be honest about it. Don't hide behind your parents' disapproval of me."

Nick's forthright personality fascinated and intimidated her at the same time.

"There's no one else. Surely you know that by now. As for them not considering you a suitable person for me to be dating, they'd feel the same way about any other guy. In all honesty it's *my* fault they've forbidden me to go on seeing you."

"Forbidden? How could they forbid you to do anything? You're in college and are able to make your own decisions."

She shivered. "You're going to hate me when I tell you."

A sound of exasperation escaped his throat. "That wouldn't be possible. Come on, Sam. Don't keep me in suspense any longer."

"I'm pregnant," she confessed. "I couldn't believe it when I found out, not when I know you took precautions."

To her shock, his eyes blazed with light. A smile lit up his handsome features. "We're going to have a baby?"

"Yes."

"What's the due date?" He sounded too happy.

"June twenty-fifth."

"That makes you almost three months along. Sweetheart—when did you find out?"

"Two days ago."

"Two days and you didn't say anything until now?"

"I've been too scared."

He reached for her and crushed her in his arms. "How could you be scared to tell me something so wonderful? You *know* how I feel about you."

"Do I?"

"How could you doubt it? I was going to surprise you with a ring on Valentine's Day so we could start planning a summer wedding. But with a baby coming, we'll get married over the Christmas holiday instead. I'll always take care of you and our children, Sam."

"Wait…" She pushed her hands against his chest to prevent him from kissing her. When he held her close and told her the things she'd been dying to hear before now, she couldn't think clearly. "There's more I have to tell you. I'm afraid it's going to change the way you feel about me."

"As long as we love each other, nothing else matters."

"I do love you, Nick, but—"

"But what?"

"I'm not old enough to get married."

"Of course you are!"

She shook her head. By now the tears had started. "No. I may be taking some college classes, but the truth is…I'm still in high school."

"High school?" he whispered, staring at her as if he'd never seen her before.

"Yes. Since I was in advanced placement and had

taken all the math and science classes my school offered, I started some college classes early on scholarship. But I—I won't turn eighteen until March.''

"Sam!"

"I knew you'd be angry,'' she blurted in panic. ''I should have told you the first day we met, but I was afraid you wouldn't ask me out, so I didn't say anything. After you started dating me, I never seemed to be able to find the right time to tell you the truth because...'' She hesitated. ''Because I wanted you to love me.''

He shook his head. ''Didn't it once occur to you I could be accused of statutory rape for making love to you? You're only seventeen!''

''The thought never entered my head until the doctor told me I was pregnant.'' She wiped her eyes but the tears kept coming. ''When he glanced at my chart, he said I wasn't of age yet and warned me he would have to tell my parents.''

Nick pursed his lips. ''How soon can I expect to be hauled into court?''

''At first Mom and Dad threatened to do just that, but I told them *I* was the one who talked you into making love to *me*. I also admitted that you didn't have any idea I wasn't eighteen. Dad said he wouldn't press charges if I agreed to break up with you and never see you again.''

''That's archaic,'' Nick retorted. ''You're younger than I thought, but it doesn't change the fact that we love each other. We'll get married now. It's as simple as that.''

''No, it's not,'' she cried. ''They won't give me

their permission. In their shoes, I wouldn't, either,"
she added in a quiet voice.

"What do you mean?"

"Let's be honest here, Nick. You never mentioned
marriage. I'm not at all sure you would have if you
didn't know I was expecting."

"It was always in my mind, Sam, but I wanted to
give you a little more time. In two months I would
have put a ring on your finger."

"That's easy enough for you to say now that you've
been told the news."

"Because it's true!"

"Maybe, but I'll never know for sure, will I?
You've sacrificed so much to get this far in college.
With only a year and a half to go before you receive
your degree, you don't need to be saddled with an
unwanted wife and baby."

"Those are your parents' words, not yours."

"Does it really matter? I don't want to hold you
back. After talking it over with them, I've decided to
give up the baby for adoption when it's born."

"No you're not!"

"Please hear me out. To avoid talk, they're going
to buy a home in Denver. We'll be moving there,
where no one knows me, over Christmas. I only have
two more high school classes to take to get my di-
ploma. I can go to a local school there as well as attend
Denver University."

He clasped her upper arms. "We're going to be
parents. There's no need to uproot you when I'll be
marrying you and taking care of you."

She shook her head. "No, Nick. Some other couple
has been praying for a baby because they couldn't

have one of their own. They'll raise ours. Years from now when we're both settled in our careers and have met someone we love, then it will be the right time to marry and have children."

"What career could be more important than being a mother and father to *our* child?"

"I'm planning to be an attorney, like Dad. It's been a dream of mine for a long time."

His brows furrowed. "You never told me that."

"You never mentioned marriage."

"Sam—"

"You might as well know everything. I was accepted at Harvard undergraduate school. It has been arranged since July, when Mom and Dad flew me back to Boston. I'll be attending there in the fall of next year."

His hands slid down her arms. He kissed the tips of her fingers. "I knew you had an exceptional mind. I just didn't realize how exceptional. Why don't we get married now and keep attending Colorado State? Next summer, after the baby's born, we'll move to Boston. I'll get a night job and help take care of our child during the day while you go to school. We'll make it work, Sam."

As much as she wanted to believe him, she couldn't be sure he wasn't saying that just because he knew it was what she wanted to hear. "What about your degree?"

"I'll get it. The important thing is that we'll be together raising our son or daughter."

"I wouldn't know how to be a mother."

"No one knows what to do until the time comes. We'll learn as we go."

"It won't work."

"Because your parents told you it wouldn't. Come on. I want to talk to them. Let's go."

Her heart raced. "They don't want to see you, Nick."

"That's too bad. I'm the father of our unborn baby and have an equal say in its future."

Ten minutes later they'd arrived at the house and he'd echoed those same sentiments to her parents, but her father remained intractable.

"I'm sorry, young man, but neither of you is in any position to be a parent. Can't you see that giving up the baby for adoption is the only sensible thing to do, not only for yourselves, but for the child?

"You're still three semesters away from getting your undergraduate degree. Samantha isn't even out of high school yet. Given the chance, she has a brilliant future ahead of her. But you can both kiss your planned careers goodbye if you have to sacrifice everything because of a mistake."

"My husband's right, Nick," Samantha's mother chimed in. "Why not turn this into a blessing and give the baby to a well-deserving married couple who've been preparing to become parents for a long time? They'll have the financial and emotional means to give it everything it needs and shower it with love."

Nick turned toward Samantha. "I already love our baby. I'm prepared to shower it with all the love I have in me. How about you, Sam?"

"I don't know, Nick. This wasn't something we planned. You might grow to resent me and the baby later."

"There's no 'might' about it," her father declared.

"You don't have the right to speak for me, Mr. Bretton." Emotion caused the cords in Nick's neck to stand out. "All I can see is that Sam and I will have a brilliant future with our child. I intend to take care of the two of them forever. The day she turns eighteen we'll get married."

Her dad shook his head. "You're deluding yourself if you think our daughter will be ready for such a step."

"Maybe neither of us is ready, but I'm going to at least try," Nick said, still staring at her. "I'll be the one taking care of our baby, Sam. I'm the father. God gave me that divine right, and no court will take it away from me."

His head swerved toward her parents once more. "If in the end your daughter is swayed by your arguments and opts to forgo marriage and motherhood, then let me give you fair warning. I'll hire the best attorney around and sue for full custody of our baby, because there's no way under heaven I'll let it be put up for adoption."

"Nick!" Samantha cried, running after him because he'd wheeled around and disappeared out the front door. "Wait!" she called into the wintry darkness. "I'll drive you back to the center!"

But he'd broken into a run and was gone.

"Let him be, honey. It's better this way," her father murmured as he shut the door. "He needs his space to think about everything. By the time you deliver the baby, the two of you will have spent six months apart. He'll have finished another semester. It'll give him the perspective to understand that your mother and I were right about this."

Samantha stood there with her wet face buried in her hands. "No, Daddy. He's not going to change. You don't know him the way I do. Nick's a man of deep convictions. That's why I love him."

"He's still a boy. Not even twenty-one. One day when you're both all grown up, you'll fall in love with other people and it'll be right."

Her mom put her arm around her shoulders. "Listen to your father, honey. Concentrate on giving the baby to a wonderful couple who want a child more than anything in the world and can't wait to have a family."

"Mom," Samantha blurted, "you heard Nick. He said he was going to keep it!"

"I agree he gave a very impassioned speech. I'm sure he meant it at the moment. But that was the impetuosity of youth talking."

"Your mother took the words right out of my mouth, honey. In a few months, another girl will catch Nick's eye. He'll be thankful for his freedom, and relieved that the baby will be going to a perfect home with loving parents waiting to dote on it." Sam's father put a protective arm around her.

"Come on. It's time for bed. Tomorrow I have a surprise for you. The old Tudor mansion you've always loved on Sixth Avenue in the country club area is for sale. A Denver Realtor is going to show us through it at eleven."

Once upon a time nothing could have excited Samantha more. Now nothing mattered. Not friends or school, or where she lived. Not even Nick, who'd said all the right things tonight. Did he really mean them?

If she hadn't gotten pregnant, would he have asked

her to marry him? Or was her mother right and he'd only said those things in the heat of the moment because he'd felt obliged and guilty? To marry him without knowing how he truly felt would be horrible.

They would be another one of the many couples in the world who'd made a mistake.

As Samantha's mother was quick to point out, Samantha's best friend, Brenda, had an older sister who'd gotten pregnant in high school and had married the boyfriend she thought she couldn't live without. But six months after the baby came, he took off and never returned.

With the inevitable divorce she turned bitter and started dating other guys, while her parents took over the responsibility of raising their grandchild along with their other children.

Brenda's sister never went to college and eventually left home. She rarely saw her child, leaving their whole family in upheaval. If she had done the sensible thing and given up her child for adoption, all their lives would have been different. Better.

"Nick has his dreams, too, Samantha," her father reasoned with her. "But if you marry, he'll have to put them on hold for years while you're in school at Harvard. Do you really think he'll stay the course? Don't you know he'll come to resent you?"

OVER THE NEXT few months her parents' arguments dominated her fears. Once her family had moved to Denver, Samantha went through the motions of living, of visiting the doctor, of being a part-time student. Yet because of her doubts she refused to see Nick, who called her every day without fail.

Each time she heard his voice, she grew more confused and heartsick. On her birthday he sent her an engagement ring by courier. In the letter that accompanied it, he asked her to marry him. Though it wrenched her heart, she sent everything back, convinced he felt trapped.

Nick still kept calling. When the day finally came and she started having contractions, she phoned him because she'd promised she would let him know the baby was on the way. Throughout her long labor she knew Nick was out in the hall waiting.

The doctor understood she was giving the baby up for adoption. As soon as it was delivered, he took it away before she could get a look at it.

Her parents were there to comfort her. They said it was for the best that she didn't see the baby. That way she wouldn't form an attachment.

Both sets of her grandparents came to the hospital. They sided with her parents. All agreed that giving up the baby was the right thing for her to do.

But Nick came to her room in the middle of the night. He kissed her lips gently and begged her to let him bring in their beautiful little daughter, who had red-gold hair like her mother. She could tell by the way he spoke that he was enamored of the baby, but that didn't mean he was enamored of Samantha.

She shut her eyes against him, too vulnerable and afraid to believe his avowal of love. They quarreled.

He gave her one last chance to tell him she would marry him. When she remained silent, he told her she wouldn't be seeing him again, and he left the room.

Contrary to what Samantha's parents had assumed would happen, Nick did sue for and obtain full and sole custodial rights of Jessica Kincaid, infant daughter of Nicholas Pratt Kincaid and Samantha Frost Bretton, born June 25 at Stapleton Regional Hospital, Denver, Colorado.

"DR. LOFSKY? Thank you for returning my call. As I told you in my message two days ago, my name is Samantha Bretton. I'm an attorney in Coeur D'Alene, Idaho, working for the Idaho National Wildlife Federation. At the moment I'm trying to reach a field biologist named Nicholas Kincaid.

"The placement office at Colorado State in Fort Collins indicated he went to work for the Rocky Mountain Biological Research Lab after graduating with his master's degree nine years ago. Is there any way you could tell me if he's still on the staff there?"

"The name's familiar. Just a minute while I transfer you to Dr. Crapo's office. He'll be able to help you."

"Thank you." *Could it be this easy to track him?* Samantha squeezed the pen in her hand while she waited.

"Ms. Bretton? This is Dr. Crapo. I understand you're asking about Nick Kincaid."

"Yes. Because of a case I'm working on, I'm very anxious to locate him." It wasn't a lie. She *was* working on a case. Her own.

"I remember him well. He did excellent work for us on the High Elk Conservation Corridor Project. That was before he turned traitor after a year and accepted a position at Grand Teton National Park." The doctor chuckled.

The Tetons! "Is he a ranger then?"

"That I don't know, but we sure hated losing him."

It was all she could do not to ask a lot of personal questions about Nick, but she didn't dare. "Thank you for the information, Dr. Crapo. I'm very grateful."

"You're welcome. Good luck finding him. When you do, tell him to give me a call."

"I will. Goodbye."

She glanced at her watch. Her Friday afternoon meeting with the conservation board wouldn't begin until two o'clock. That gave her twenty minutes to make the call.

Without hesitation she dialed the Wyoming operator to get a phone number for Teton Park. After listening to the recorded messages she finally made contact with a live female voice.

"You've reached Moose Headquarters Rangers Station. Mindy Carlson speaking."

"Hello. I'm sorry to bother you, but I've been trying to get in touch with a biologist who was hired by the park service about eight years ago. I have no idea if he's still working there or not."

"What's the name?"

"Nicholas Kincaid."

"You've found him. He's the resident chief ranger in charge of biological wildlife research for Teton Park."

Nick...

Tears welled in Sam's eyes. Despite the enormous responsibility of raising their daughter, he *had* realized his dream. Thank God for that.

"I—is he there?"

"He has an office here at headquarters, but he's rarely in it. I can take a message. When he checks with me later, I'll give him the information."

Think fast, Samantha. You don't want to tip your hand yet.

"Will you ask him to phone Lori Watts?"

"You bet. What's the number?"

After she gave it to the woman Samantha said, "Tell him to call collect."

"Will do."

"Thank you very much."

After she hung up the receiver, she rushed out of her office to talk to the receptionist in the other room. She was breathing hard, but knew it wasn't because of her physical health.

"Lori? Before the day is over, you might receive a collect call from a man named Nick Kincaid. If so, the operator will ask if you'll accept the charges. Say yes. When he identifies himself, tell him to wait a moment, then poke your head around my door so I'll know he's on the line."

"Okay."

Samantha didn't know what to expect. By now Nick was thirty-three years old and undoubtedly married with a family. Jessica would be the oldest child. But maybe not. He could have met a woman with one or more children and they'd combined their families.

Anything could have happened in the intervening years. Samantha was going to go crazy imagining the various scenarios while she waited for the call that might or might not ever come.

If Nick were happily married, then he had a lot of things to consider once he found out who was trying to reach him on the phone.

Besides his own violent reaction, there would be his wife's when he told her Jessica's birth mother was trying to make contact with the daughter she had given up.

As for Jessica herself, she might not want anything to do with the woman who'd refused to look at her after the delivery. The heartless woman who'd resisted Nick's pleadings to let him bring Jessica to her hospital room in the middle of the night for one tiny peek.

CHAPTER TWO

IT WAS HALLOWEEN. Knowing Jessica was waiting for him, Nick bypassed the park headquarters located in Moose, Wyoming, and drove the truck straight to the complex of ranch-style houses a couple of blocks away.

He'd just come from the tailwaters below Jackson Lake Dam. The investigation to find out why there were so many young, dead, fine-spot cutthroat showing up was going to take time. The ones he'd just examined had gaping jaws, misshapen heads, trunks and spinal curvature denoting *Myxosoma cerebralis.*

Tomorrow he would have to spend the day gathering samples from the soil and water to look for spores.

"Hi, Dad!" his daughter called to him as he entered the kitchen from the garage. Her hair was in tiny rollers all over her head. "You're only a half hour late! That's pretty good for you."

Nick chuckled. "I timed it so I could test out your cupcakes." He reached for a couple she'd iced with orange frosting and candy corn, and popped them in his mouth. "Umm, they're good. I could eat a ton of them."

"No more!" She put out a hand to restrain him, but he managed to snatch another one. "You're impossible!'' But he detected a smile as she said it. ''These are our contribution to the Halloween party.''

''How soon do we have to be there?'' The monthly get-together for the park employees at the teepee in Moose Village was something they always looked forward to.

''As soon as you shower and change into your costume. They're getting things going a lot earlier than usual so the little kids will have time to trick-or-treat.''

He'd already started down the hall for his bedroom, but paused midstride. ''What costume?''

''I told you about it yesterday.''

''You did?''

''Yes…! As usual, your mind was on salmonid whirling disease or some such thing.''

He burst into laughter. ''If I'm not mistaken, that's exactly what those cutthroats have. I'm going to make a biologist out of you yet.''

''Maybe! Anyway, I put the outfit on your bed. Don't touch anything until you've washed. You smell like dead trout. Yuck.''

Besides possessing a razor-sharp brain, she was turning into quite the little homemaker. Fussy, fussy, fussy.

A few minutes later he emerged from the shower and opened the garment bag from Brough's Costume Rentals in Jackson. She'd draped it over the end of the bed. Inside was a man's black suit with a black vest and white shirt. She'd gotten the sizes right.

At first he assumed he would be escorting his daughter to the party as Count Dracula. That was until he saw the outrageous brown-and-white polka-dotted bow tie.

"Are you dressed yet?" Jessica called.

"Almost! Who am I supposed to be?"

"Just a minute and you'll find out!"

As he was fastening the tie in place, a perfect facsimile of Little Orphan Annie appeared in the doorway. She'd taken out the rollers and had backcombed her red curls in a style that looked so much like the famous cartoon character, he was stunned.

She wore a little red top and a skirt with white trim. To complete the outfit she'd donned knee-high white stockings and oxford shoes.

"Figured it out yet?" Her heart-shaped mouth broke into an artless smile. For a moment it reminded him of another heart-shaped mouth. He'd loved everything about Jessica's mother, especially that mouth he could never get enough of. No kiss was long enough, deep enough.

The memory coming from out of the blue filled him with intense longing. If he'd received an actual physical wound, it couldn't have been more painful.

"There's no doubt who *you* are," he managed to murmur.

"Here." From behind her back she produced a full head mask. "Put it on."

He did her bidding. When he looked in the mirror he discovered bald-headed Daddy Warbucks staring back at him.

"Don't forget your cigar."

She handed it to him. His daughter had thought of everything.

Too full of emotions—some that didn't bear close scrutiny—he grabbed Jessica and swung her around. "We're going to knock 'em dead tonight!"

Her face broke out in a happy smile. "I think so, too. After Leslie drove me to the rental shop, she showed me how to do my hair."

"It's perfect, honey."

His daughter was crazy about Leslie Gallagher, the new wife of Nick's best friend, Pierce, the chief ranger of the park. Nick was pretty crazy about Leslie, too. Talk about the perfect woman.

Six-year-old Cory Gallagher already called her Mom. As for Pierce, being deeply in love again after having lost his first wife in a plane crash had made a new man of him.

Some men were lucky. Pierce was twice lucky to have married the two women he'd fallen in love with.

"Dad?"

Nick blinked. "Yes?"

"Are you all right?"

"Of course. Why?"

"Because I've been talking to you and you're miles away."

Already the mask had made him claustrophobic. He pulled it off. "Sorry. I guess I couldn't hear very well with this thing on."

"Do you mind wearing it?"

"No," he lied. "Do you know what? The only thing missing is Annie's big yellow dog named Sandy."

"Cory offered to let us take Lucy on her leash."

Nick laughed. "Cute as she is, I'm afraid a basset hound would spoil the effect." He remembered the day he and Pierce had brought the puppy home to Cory. What a happy moment that had been for Pierce's boy.

"I thought the same thing," she said as they left the bedroom and started down the hall for the kitchen. "Leslie told him it wouldn't have worked, anyway, because Lucy would have been too frightened by all the costumes."

"She's right. Animals should be kept home and safe on a night like this. What's Cory going to be?"

"Sponge Bob."

"I should have known."

"Leslie glued a whole bunch of sponges to a box he's wearing over his head. She's so clever I can't believe it!"

Pierce's wife had made a huge impact on his little teenager. Her advent into their world underlined Nick's daughter's need for a woman in her life. He had been able to provide Jessica everything but that.

"Dare I ask if I'll recognize her and Pierce?"

"Nope. You'll have to die of curiosity while you wait." She rolled her big blue eyes, and he immediately thought of a similar pair of dancing blue eyes.

Nick took a moment to ponder the reason for tonight's painful recollection of past memories, then he realized it was because his daughter was growing up faster than he could imagine.

Soon he would turn around and discover she'd become a woman. That day wasn't far off. He suddenly felt old and wished to God he could stop the march of time.

After his daughter picked up the covered tin of cupcakes, they went out to the garage and he started the motor of their silver Xtera. En route to the teepee over by the visitors' center, he phoned headquarters to find out if he had any messages.

There were five of them, four names he recognized. There were no emergencies, and he could wait until Monday when he was back in his office to return the calls.

The message from a woman named Lori Watts was something else again. He'd never dated a Lori or had dealings with one on a professional basis. Her name rang no bells. He glanced at his watch. It was twenty to six, probably too late for anyone to answer. But the fact that he'd been asked to call collect gave him pause.

"Hold on a minute, Mindy."

He pulled into the parking lot, which was filling fast, and drew a notebook and pen from the glove compartment. "Okay. Go ahead and give me the Watts number."

More curious than ever because it was an Idaho area code, he wrote it down. Maybe some of the trout in Idaho waters had whirling disease, too. After thanking the receptionist, he clicked off, then punched in the digits.

His daughter's protesting sigh resounded in the vehicle's interior.

"Honey, give me thirty seconds to find out if this is urgent, then Daddy Warbucks is all yours for the rest of the night."

"Promise?"

He nodded.

She opened her door. "I'll take in the cupcakes and be right back so we can make our grand entrance."

"It's a deal."

Distracted by everyone in their costumes, Nick was ready to hang up on the fifth ring when a female voice said hello. Unless he had the wrong number, he found it odd she didn't say something to identify herself.

"This is Nick Kincaid returning Lori Watts' call."

After a silence she said, "You were supposed to phone collect."

Her voice sounded vaguely familiar but he couldn't place it. "Is this Ms. Watts?"

"No."

He frowned. "Is she there?"

"No. She's gone home, but it doesn't matter because I'm the one who wanted to talk to you."

Nick had reached the end of his patience. He could do without Halloween pranksters. "Who is this?" he demanded, ready to click off.

"If I tell you, you'll hang up on me, which is your right. But if I don't tell you, I'll never find the courage to do this again."

What in the hell?

"Forgive me, Nick. I—I'm not trying to be deliberately provocative."

The slight catch in her voice, the way she said his name, hurled him back through time. His heart slammed into his ribs so hard it hurt to breathe.

"*Sam…*" he whispered.

"Yes. I'll make this fast. I've been battling cancer for a year and a half. At first I thought the transplant and chemo hadn't done me any good, but two days ago some tests proved my cancer has gone into remission. For how long, only God knows.

"I'm doing everything possible to fight it so it won't come back. The other night my pastor asked me if my life was in order. Was there anything I needed to resolve that might help me keep the disease at bay?''

Lord.

''*Resolve* isn't the right word. He should have asked me, 'Is there anything I want?' Then I could have told him I want to go back thirteen years to that hospital room and beg you to bring our daughter to me so we could be a family.''

Soul-destroying pain and anger ripped through Nick's body. ''It's too late to ask to see her.''

''I know, but I had to take the risk. Nick? W-would it be possible for me to look at her from a distance?'' she stammered. ''Just so I had an idea of what she's like? She would never have to know. If you were at a mall or something, and I was hiding so she couldn't see me, I swear I wouldn't reveal myself.''

The desperation in her voice was killing him. ''I don't think it's a good idea, Sam.''

A palpable silence ensued, followed by such a tortured sob, he knew he couldn't handle this conversation much longer.

''You're right,'' she replied at last. ''Thank you for not cutting me off.'' He could hear her voice shaking. ''You always did have more nobility in one little finger than anyone else I've ever met had in their whole body. I'm sure the woman you ended up marrying considers it your greatest character trait.

''Tonight when you're kissing your children, give Jessica an extra squeeze. She won't know it's from me, but *I* will. Through you I'll be able to feel her in my arms, because I know what your arms feel like. I've forgotten nothing. Goodbye, Nick.''

His low groan coincided with a rap on the window. He jerked his head around to discover a tall man in a Herman Munster costume peering at him through the glass. In the next instant Pierce had flung off the mask and opened the door.

"Nick—you look like you're going to pass out!"

That was one way to describe his condition.

"How can I help?"

"Dear God, Pierce—I don't believe what just happened."

His friend's compassionate blue eyes studied him with alarm. "Jess said you were on the phone and asked me to come and get you. Who were you talking to? What the hell's going on?"

Another groan escaped Nick's throat.

"Can you still drive?"

He nodded.

Without saying a word, Pierce shut the door. He walked around the car and got in the passenger side. "Drive to the back of headquarters, where we can talk in private."

As Nick pulled out of the parking lot, Pierce called his wife. He told her a small emergency had arisen, and asked her to keep an eye on Jessica until they returned.

"Okay," he said, putting the cell phone in his pocket. "Everything's taken care of."

The skeletal night staff had parked in front of headquarters. Nick braked at the rear of the building and shut off the headlights.

Pierce turned toward him. "In all the years I've known you, I haven't ever seen you in this kind of pain. It must have something to do with your past."

"Your instincts are never wrong," Nick muttered. "When Mindy gave me my messages a little while ago, one of them was from a person named Lori Watts. I was asked to call her collect." He took a breath.

"The name meant nothing, but I sensed it might be important so I asked Jessica to give me a minute to call the woman back before I went inside the teepee."

"And this Lori turned out to be Jess's mother?"

"Yes." Nick's eyes closed tightly. "For the last year and a half she's been battling cancer. Evidently it has gone into remission. Now she wants to see our daughter."

"Good Lord."

"I told her it was too late."

"How did she handle that?" his friend asked in a quiet voice.

Tears prickled beneath Nick's lids. "With amazing grace before she bade me a final goodbye." He pounded the steering wheel with his fist. "What am I going to do, Pierce?"

"What do you *want* to do?"

Nick couldn't articulate his thoughts, not when Sam's words still filled his head, blotting out his ability to reason.

"You've known a call like this would come one day."

Pierce read him like a book. He nodded. "I expected her to get in touch with me years ago. You'll never know how I ached to hear her voice telling me she'd made a mistake and wanted to be with me and Jessica forever.

"But in those dreams she'd been young and eager.

I'm afraid the threat of death didn't play a part in any of the scenarios created by my imagination.''

"No. It's the one finality none of us is prepared for.''

Nick glanced at his friend. "If anyone understands, you do. When Linda was killed, I honestly don't know how you handled it.''

"As I look back, I'm convinced the only reason I did is because we didn't have any issues left unresolved. But Jessica's mother has been given a second chance at life. I have to presume the soul searching she has been through led her to make that phone call.''

A cry of grief escaped Nick's lips. "I can't believe I just told a woman who thought she'd be dead by now that she couldn't see the daughter she gave birth to, not even from a distance. What kind of a monster does that make me?''

"You were speaking as Jess's loving father, a great man who has done everything to make her life happy and shield her from pain.''

"But do I have the right to go on shielding her, knowing what I know now?'' he cried.

"Give it time and the answer will come, Nick.''

"Except that Sam doesn't know how much time she has been given.''

"Does anyone after they've gone into remission?''

Nick bowed his head. "No. Some people stay there for the rest of their lives. Some have recurring bouts....'' He let his voice trail off.

"Maybe she's one of the lucky ones. Is she well enough to travel?''

Nick stared blindly out the windshield. "I don't know. I shut her down too fast.''

"Then you didn't find out if she has a husband or family?"

"No. She assumes I'm married and have other children besides Jessica. The call ended before I could disabuse her of those facts."

"I'm sure the thought has occurred to you that a less honorable woman, one centered only on herself, might have shown up at your door without warning and caused real trouble."

This was agony. "Where was that honor when she wouldn't let me bring her own flesh and blood to her in that hospital bed?"

"Perhaps if you saw her again, she could explain so you would understand."

"I'll never understand, Pierce. But this situation isn't about me."

"Does Jess have a driving need to find her mother?"

"Not that I'm aware of. All I've told her is that Sam was underage when we found out she was pregnant, and that her parents prevailed on her to give up the baby. Jessica has never questioned that explanation. But since I haven't encouraged her to talk about her mother, for all I know my daughter has been harboring feelings she has been afraid to share for fear of hurting me."

"It would only be natural. If ever a daughter loved her dad…"

"How in heaven am I going to keep a secret like this from her?"

"Some people I know could manage it. You're not one of them, because you have too much integrity.

Whatever you choose to do, I have no doubt it will be the right thing for everyone."

"Then you have a lot more faith in me than I do." After expelling the breath he'd been holding, Nick pulled on his mask and started the car. "Tell Leslie I'm indebted to her for helping Jessica with my costume. Little did I know I was going to be thankful for this camouflage."

"Amen," Pierce muttered as he put on his own mask.

"THIS IS SUCH A GREAT condo, Samantha. I love it more every time I come over."

She eyed Marilyn May, who'd become more than a best friend and confidante. "You always say that."

The two women, still dressed in their sweats, sat curled up on opposite couches facing each other with mugs of herbal tea in hand. After their Saturday morning sessions of qigong, they looked forward to this time of sharing.

"The view of Coeur D'Alene Lake is beautiful, even if it's raining. When you've lived in the desert all your life, this is paradise."

"I like it, too, especially because the balcony overlooks McEuen Park and I can see the downtown area as well. When another condo in the building goes up for sale, I'll let you know right away."

Marilyn set her mug on the teakwood coaster. "I'm afraid I'll be going home to Phoenix before that, but thank you for thinking of me."

The revelation brought more pain to Samantha, who would never recover from last evening's experience of hearing Nick's voice. She'd taken the greatest risk of her life. As it turned out, her chances for licking cancer, at least for now, were greater than those for being allowed to see her daughter.

"So you've decided to let your parents take care of you when you go through your series of chemo next month?"

Marilyn nodded. "I've fought burdening them for so long that I think they're worse off than I am."

"I can't bear to see you go, but I know all about not wanting to be a burden. For the last thirteen years I've suffered the consequences because of that decision, and I can tell you now it's not worth it. You're much wiser than I ever was."

"Stop crucifying yourself. You didn't want Nick to feel he had to marry you."

"I should have believed in him, in us."

"You were afraid to trust in Nick's love. It's perfectly understandable, when you were so young and influenced by your parents and grandparents. They only wanted the best for you and your baby."

"I know. In the end, my baby got the best. Nick's the best there is. That's my consolation."

"Samantha? Now that you're in remission, would you be willing to visit me in Phoenix next month? There's plenty of room, a swimming pool in the backyard."

The invitation hadn't been extended lightly. Over the last year their friendship had come to mean everything to both of them due to their common enemy. They'd been through so much together.

Samantha had been an only child, and Marilyn represented the sister she'd never had. The friends she'd made at law school and at the wildlife federation were great. But she felt a spiritual closeness to Marilyn, who reciprocated those feelings although she had two other sisters.

"Tell you what. I'll talk to Reed about the possibility of my doing work for the federation long distance for a couple of weeks. He's been a very understanding boss so far."

"That would be wonderful."

"I agree." Samantha swallowed hard. "Though my parents have been saints and have done everything possible for me, I don't know how I would have made it this far without you."

"I feel the same. No one else understands the way you do. To be honest, I don't want to go through the chemo without you to talk to," Marilyn admitted.

Samantha stared at her dear friend and smiled. "Depending on what Reed says, you won't have to."

BY THREE IN THE AFTERNOON Nick had gutted the last dead trout from below the dam and had prepared some slides for examination. Jessica had spent the day helping him gather the rest of the water and soil samples, which she was now putting in his carrying case.

A recent snowstorm over the park had made the work more difficult, but she hadn't once complained. After they'd won first place in the costume contest last night, his daughter's mood was euphoric.

All day he'd tried to find the courage to talk to her about a subject that was going to change her life, but the moment never seemed to present itself.

So far she hadn't seemed to pick up on his private agony. Maybe that was because she was looking forward to their plans for the evening.

The organizers of the Halloween party had given them the grand prize—two free movie passes and two gift certificates for an Italian dinner in Jackson. As soon as they got back to Moose and showered, he planned to drive them into town to return their rental costumes and celebrate their winnings.

"Dad? How come you've been so quiet since last night?" she asked after they'd been driving for a few minutes.

Nick stifled a groan. He hadn't fooled his daughter, after all.

"I'm always concerned when I find unexplained problems in natural habitats."

"I noticed Pierce was really quiet."

"You know he always has a lot on his mind."

"I think you do, too. Do you want to talk about it?"

His daughter had turned the tables on him. When had she grown so wise?

The moment he'd been waiting for had come. He couldn't avoid it any longer.

"Yes. I do."

Her eyes rounded in surprise as he brought the truck to a halt on the slushy shoulder of the road. "What's wrong, Dad?" She looked and sounded anxious.

"Let me ask you a question first." Inside his chest, his heart was pounding like a sledgehammer. "If you had a chance to meet your mother, how would you feel about that?"

He'd already made up his mind he wouldn't tell her about Sam's battle with cancer or the fact that she was in remission. Any decision on his daughter's part needed to come from a gut reaction, not sympathy or pity.

"Was she the person who asked you to call her back last night?"

Nick could barely breathe. "Yes."

"Was it hard to talk to her?"

He jerked his head toward her. "Hard?"

She nodded. Her capacity to feel empathy endeared her to him in ways he couldn't explain.

"I have to admit it was."

"If you don't want me to meet her, I won't."

"Jessica…" He fought not to give way to the dichotomy of emotions exploding inside him. "This doesn't have anything to do with me. She gave you birth. Now she's asking to see you."

His daughter stared at him for the longest time. "Would you do it if you were my age and the same thing was happening to you?" Her purity and earnestness utterly defeated him.

Jessica might not know a lot about the past, but he'd never been dishonest with the things he'd been forced to tell her. If he lied to her now, it would be a betrayal of everything he believed in.

"I'm sure I would."

"Where does she live?"

"She phoned from Idaho, but that's all I know."

"Does she want me to call her?"

"Is that what you would like to do?"

It was a foolish question. He didn't need to hear the answer because he could already see her heart in those hopeful, thirteen-year-old eyes.

The deed had been done. Heaven help them all.

CHAPTER THREE

"SAMANTHA? Line two for you."

She glanced at her watch. Four-thirty already. Monday was almost over. "Do you know who it is? Unless it's important, I'm finishing up a brief for court in the morning."

"Her name is Jessica Kincaid. She said she was returning your call. Sounds like a teenager to me."

The room started to spin. Samantha clung to the edge of her oak desk.

Nick had changed his mind!

Perspiration soaked her body. She stood up, then felt so weak she had to sit down again. For thirteen years she'd been waiting for this moment. Now that it was here, she didn't know what to say, let alone how to say it.

"I—I'll take the call, Lori. Thank you."

As if it had a will of its own, her hand crept to the receiver. She lifted it to her ear, then pressed line two to connect them.

"Hello, Jessica?"

"Hi." The female voice sounded young and tentative.

"Hi, yourself." Emotion had practically closed off Samantha's windpipe. "After all these years, I can't believe I'm talking to my own daughter."

"I can't believe it, either."

Samantha's body started to shake and couldn't stop. "When you were born, your father told me you had red hair."

"Yup. And blue eyes. A long time ago Dad gave me a picture of you. We look a lot alike."

My darling girl. Tears rolled down her cheeks. "I would give anything in the world to meet you in person."

"Me, too."

"Honestly?"

"Yes."

Maybe she'd given birth to Jessica, but there was no doubt the girl was Nick's child. Samantha could hear it in the mature, forthright manner she had of expressing herself.

He had probably told Jessica about the cancer. It was possible her daughter had only made this phone call out of a mixture of obligation and pity. If that was true, so be it—Samantha was through second-guessing feelings or motives. His unselfish goodness had brought about this miraculous exchange. She would consider whatever happened from here on out a blessing she didn't deserve.

"I understand you live in Grand Teton National Park. I could come there if you'd like."

"How soon?"

The rapid-fire question thrilled her. "As soon as your parents say it's all right."

After a slight pause Jessica said, "There's only Dad and me."

"Oh." Once again Samantha's world reeled.

"Do I have any half brothers or sisters?" her daughter asked in a quiet voice.

"No. Only you. I never married."

After a silence, she asked. "Are my grandparents still alive?"

Tears stung Samantha's eyes. "Yes. And a great-grandma and great-grandpa who are both in their early nineties."

"Dad's parents died when he was a little boy." With that comment her daughter had just discreetly steered the conversation back to her life and Nick's.

"I know." Samantha had to clear her throat. "How is your great-uncle Willard?" The older brother of Nick's father had been a widower by the time Samantha met him. He'd raised Nick along with his own children after Nick's parents had been killed in a fatal car accident.

"He died of cancer when I was eight."

Samantha's body shuddered at the news. The fact that her daughter hadn't hesitated to give her that information led Samantha to believe Nick hadn't told his daughter about her illness. But she couldn't be positive about that.

"I'm so sorry. He was a terrific man." No doubt he'd helped Nick to hire an attorney to make certain he retained full custody of Jessica.

"I loved him! Dad and I go to Gillette on the holidays to visit his cousins and their kids." Another silence ensued before she asked, "Have you ever been to the Tetons?"

"No, but I've always wanted to see them. I bet you think you live in the greatest place on earth."

"We do!" Her enthusiasm fairly leaped through the phone line. "Where do you live?"

"In Coeur D'Alene. That's in northern Idaho. It's French for Alene's heart."

"That's pretty. Do you have a house?"

"No. A condo."

"What kind of job do you do?"

"I'm an attorney."

"Whoa." Her daughter made a sound of surprise, provoking a chuckle from Samantha.

"Are you in eighth or ninth grade?"

"Ninth."

"Do they have a high school in the park?"

"No, we're bused to Jackson. It's about a half hour from Moose."

"I see. Do you like school?" Samantha wanted to know anything and everything about this fabulous child of hers. She couldn't get the questions out fast enough.

"I love it."

"I did, too. What's your favorite subject?"

"Science and math. What was yours?"

"Science and math."

They laughed at the same time before Samantha said, "Your father was brilliant in both."

"I know. He's so smart he makes me sick."

There was a wealth of personal information she could tell her daughter about Nick, but she didn't dare. Not yet. Depending on a variety of factors, maybe not ever.

"Your dad's views on the preservation of nature in the wilds had such a great influence on me, it's the reason I work for the Idaho National Wildlife Federation today.''

''That's so cool!''

It killed Samantha to think of bringing this conversation to a close, but she had an idea Nick was close by, waiting for her to get off the phone. He wouldn't appreciate it if she took advantage of the situation.

''Jessica? Why don't you have a talk with your father and decide when would be the best time for me to visit.''

''Okay,'' she said in a wistful tone, as if she didn't want the call to end, either.

The problem was, Samantha was flying blind here. This was the first contact she'd had with her daughter, and she didn't want to push too hard at this precarious stage.

''I could come to Jackson and stay overnight at one of the lodges. Maybe you would meet me for dinner. How does that sound?''

''I'll check with Dad, then call you later. Oh—you probably won't be at work then. Do you have a cell phone?''

''Yes. If you've got a pen, I'll give you the number.''

''Just a sec and I'll get one.'' By the time her daughter came back on the line, Samantha's face was bathed in moisture. ''Okay. What is it?''

Once she'd given her the information Sam said, ''I'll be waiting to hear from you.''

''Don't turn off your phone.''

No, darling, I won't. ''I'll leave it on.''

''Good. Sometimes Dad forgets. Bye for now.''

''Bye.''

Before Samantha broke down completely, she punched in Marilyn's cell phone number. To her chagrin she got her voice mail.

"Marilyn? It's Samantha. I spoke to my daughter for the first time a few minutes ago! She's so wonderful I don't know where to begin. Call me back as soon as you can. I'm going to die if I can't talk to you."

WHEN NICK DROVE IN the garage at six, Jessica was waiting for him in the doorway leading to the kitchen. The fact that she came running around to the driver's side of the truck meant she had made contact with Sam. The excitement in her eyes blinded him.

She opened his door before he could. "I just got off the phone with my mother."

Nick drew in a sharp breath. He'd hoped she would have waited until he arrived home, but it was too much to expect.

Sam had only left a work phone number with Mindy. Nick's daughter had been forced to suffer through the whole weekend, then put in a full school day before making the most important phone call of her life.

"That must have been an amazing experience."

Her nod caused the red-gold curls to bounce. "At first I was really nervous."

"And now?"

"She was easy to talk to, like Leslie."

His body quaked. Putting Sam on a par with Leslie Gallagher was high praise for someone his daughter hadn't even met yet.

"When I told her I wanted to meet her, she said she

would fly to Jackson and stay at one of the lodges so we could have dinner together. Would that be okay with you?''

Nick felt relief Sam had suggested a meeting on neutral ground. ''I think that's a good idea.''

''When should she come?''

''Not on a school night.'' Though he was aware both mother and daughter were anxious, Jessica had to be his first priority. The emotions already building would drain her in ways she couldn't possibly anticipate.

''How about this Friday? I'm supposed to baby-sit Logan, but I'll call his mom and tell her I can't come.''

Friday—that was only four days away. He broke out in a cold sweat. ''If she can come that soon, it's fine with me.'' Better to get this over with right away.

''She's never been here before. Which lodge should she stay at?''

Trust his little nurturer to be worried about her mother's accommodations.

''I'm sure she'll be coming with her husband. Let's let them take care of those details.''

''She doesn't have a husband, Dad. She said she never got married.''

Not married?

''Dad?''

He took a steadying breath. ''In that case the Elk Inn is comfortable and has a good restaurant,'' he muttered.

It sat on the outskirts of town, where they'd be less likely to run into people Nick knew. For thirteen years he'd kept his past private. That was the way he intended things to stay. Two redheads at one table would be a dead giveaway.

The uncomfortable thought that Sam might have lost her glorious flame-colored locks tugged at him. He had no idea what physical shape she was in, after her fight with cancer.

Obviously she wasn't too weak from the chemo or she wouldn't be able to fly here. Nevertheless, that didn't preclude the possibility of her arriving in a wheelchair, wearing a hat or a wig.

Though she'd told him the cancer was in remission, the fact that her voluptuous body had come close to death at the age of thirty-one was still anathema to him. His thoughts flicked to her parents.

Though he'd never had any reason to like them, there was no question they adored their daughter. Being a parent himself, he realized they had to have been grief-stricken when they'd first learned about her illness. The joy they must be feeling now to learn it was in remission would be indescribable.

"Dad?"

Once again his daughter's voice brought him back from his torturous thoughts. "Yes, honey?"

"I was asking if we could pay for her room. I'll give you my baby-sitting money."

Bewildered by her question, he said, "Why would you be concerned about that?"

"Since she's never been married, I thought it would be a nice thing to do. She lives alone in a condo."

To hide the shocks his daughter kept giving him, Nick levered himself from the truck.

While he was reaching for his carrying case in the back he said, "Since she's the one who phoned you and made plans to come, I think it best to let her handle her own arrangements.'' His daughter's protective instincts were working overtime, the very thing he'd hoped to prevent.

''Okay.''

Jessica followed him through the modest ranch-style house to the third bedroom, which he'd turned into a lab a long time ago. He set his case on the floor.

''Guess what? Math and science were her favorite subjects in high school, too.''

''Your mother had a brilliant mind. So brilliant, in fact, she took college classes while she was still in high school.''

''She said you were brilliant, too.''

Nick grimaced, not wanting to hear any more. Talking about Sam made it feel like yesterday, but in reality thirteen years had gone by. She still wasn't married?

''Will it be all right if I phone her now and tell her to come on Friday? Dad?'' she prodded.

He jerked his head around and nodded. ''Go ahead while I shower, then we'll fix dinner.''

His daughter remained in place. She gazed at him with soulful eyes. ''Do you really feel okay about my seeing her?''

''Of course.''

''Even if you didn't, you wouldn't tell me. Leslie was right. You and Pierce always act tough no matter what.''

He reached for her and wrapped her in his arms. ''It's not an act, honey. You have every right in the world to see your mother now that she has decided she wants to meet you.

"I lost my parents when I was very young, but I have memories of them. Now you'll have a memory, too. It's important, so stop worrying about my feelings."

She raised up on tiptoe and kissed his cheek. "Thanks, Dad. I love you."

"I love you."

"Oh…" She paused in the doorway. "Guess what? I found out she's an attorney."

"That doesn't surprise me," Nick acknowledged. "Her father's a very well-known, wealthy corporate lawyer in Denver. After she graduated from Harvard, I'm sure she went to work in his firm."

After his daughter's eyes widened at that unexpected piece of information, she said, "No, she didn't. She works for the Idaho National Wildlife Federation in Coeur D'Alene. And guess what else? She says *you're* the reason why."

SAMANTHA TIPPED THE LIMO driver, who'd carried her suitcase to the front desk of the lodge.

"Hi!" said the friendly female receptionist. "Welcome to the Elk Inn."

"Thank you. I made a reservation for Samantha Bretton."

"Let me look it up on the computer. Have you ever been to Jackson Hole before?"

"No, but I've heard about it all my life. The area is more breathtaking than I had imagined."

"I know what you mean. We've had bad weather all week, but today it cleared. You flew in at the right time. There's no sight like the snow-capped Tetons from the air just before the sun goes down."

"The mountains are incredible."

More than ever she could understand her daughter's excited outburst about living in the greatest place on earth. Nick had been working here eight years. They'd already experienced so much of life in this beautiful part of the world without Samantha being a part of it. Pain pierced her heart.

"Found it. If you'll sign the register, I'll get your key."

Samantha filled it out and gave her a credit card. The receptionist handed her some brochures, then directed her to the hall on the right. "Enjoy your stay."

If only the receptionist knew what this visit was all about.

Since Samantha only intended to be here for one night, she'd packed everything she would need in a small, easy-to-carry suitcase. Halfway down the corridor she found her room and let herself inside.

Once she'd hung up the clothes she planned to wear to dinner, she lay down on the queen-size bed, which had called to her the minute she'd locked the door behind her.

Physically, her stamina was pretty good. She owed it to the strict routine of exercises and meditation she followed when she was away from her qigong class. Obviously the fatigue she was experiencing right now had everything to do with her emotional state.

She was scared. In fact, terrified was more like it.

Though a person's voice might not change over the years, Samantha was certain there'd been plenty of changes in Nick's life—and in her own. Like the fact that she was no longer the barely eighteen-year-old mother Nick remembered from his visit to her hospital room.

That girl was gone.

What he would think of her now, she couldn't imagine. When Samantha looked at herself in the mirror, all objectivity left her.

Marilyn insisted Nick would see a beautiful redhead who looked to be in her late twenties. If he were really observant, he would detect her suffering in the fine lines around her eyes and her weight loss in the faint hollows of her cheeks. Ah, the lies of a good friend...Samantha loved Marilyn for it.

Her gaze drifted to the black suit she'd bought. From junior high to the advent of cancer, she'd stayed five feet four and had always worn a size ten. Though still the same height, she now fit into a size four and could buy the styles she liked at Ann Taylor.

The blouse she'd purchased to go with the suit was an oyster-pink with white trim on the lapels and wrist cuffs. She hadn't thought the color would go well with her hair until she'd tried it on. Even before all three salesgirls raved that the outfit was made for her, she'd felt it suited her.

Never in her life had she cared so much about the way she looked. Not just for Nick, but for her daughter. If this was the only night they would have together, she was desperate to appear at her best despite the illness that had ravaged her body for more than a year.

Samantha had told Jessica she would meet them in the lobby of the inn at six-thirty. That gave her an hour to rest before she had to shower and get ready.

Succumbing to a sudden lack of energy, she closed her eyes with two prayers on her lips.

Let Jessica like me a little bit.

Don't let Nick completely despise me for what I've done.

NICK LEFT HIS OFFICE to find Pierce. He didn't have to go far. His friend was walking down the hall toward him at a fast clip.

It was after five and the receptionist had already gone home. On Friday nights headquarters emptied fast before the skeletal night crew arrived.

"How about a beer before you and Jessica have to leave for Jackson?"

"Do I look like I need one?"

Pierce flashed him a penetrating gaze. "The truth?"

"Always."

"I'd say you're a candidate for a bottle of Jack Daniels."

"Don't think I haven't thought about it."

"No matter how late it is when you get back, Leslie and I will be up if you want to talk. Don't bother to phone. Just pull in the driveway and I'll hear you. Jess can sleep on the other twin bed in Cory's room."

"Thanks, Pierce. I just might take you up on your offer."

His friend nodded. "What's the verdict on the cutthroat?"

"Swirling disease. The good news is there's no outbreak above the dam. If the men at the spillway will do a series of flushing flows, that ought to wash out the spores. They could have been lurking there for thirty years. It's anyone's guess why the mud brought them back to life. I'll have a full report on your desk Monday morning.''

"Great work as usual. I'll call Ralph at the dam and get things moving.'' They both walked out to the parking lot.

Pierce clapped him on the shoulder. "Agonizing as this is, you're doing the right thing for your daughter, Nick.''

"I realize that. Just knowing her mother wants to see her has done something for her I could never do.''

"That's true. All you can do is go on being the terrific father you already are.''

"I hope it'll be enough, Pierce, because Jessica's riding for a fall.''

"Unfortunately, our children aren't exempt from pain.''

Their eyes locked. "In Cory's case, he overcame his pain when he gained a new mother. My little girl's pain is going to start as soon as she meets her mother for the first time and Sam does something to disappoint her. Then there won't be a thing in hell I can do about it,'' Nick said in a quiet voice.

"You already have done something by making tonight possible. Meeting her mother is going to answer many questions for Jess. No matter what the future holds, she'll be a stronger, more confident woman for it.''

Nick grimaced. "I'll try to keep that in mind when everything hits the fan. Thanks for being there.''

"You mean the way you were there for me when I was shattered?''

They didn't come any better than Pierce.

"I'll talk to you tomorrow, if not before.'' With

that, Nick climbed in his truck and took off. Already he was anticipating a lecture from Jessica about getting home later than he'd promised.

She didn't disappoint him. The second he walked into the kitchen from the garage she said, "We're going to be late, Dad! You'll have to take a quick shower. I put out the charcoal suit and blue shirt you wore to Pierce's wedding."

"I appreciate your thoughtfulness, honey, but I'm not getting dressed up."

She followed him down the hall to his bedroom. "How come? We're going out to dinner!"

Up to this point he'd tried to fall in with her wishes, but this was one time where he had to draw the line.

"Your mother invited *you* for dinner. Once we've all said hello, I'm not going to stay."

Her face fell. "Why?"

He started unbuttoning the shirt of his uniform. "I've had you to myself for thirteen years. She's only asking for one evening. With me there, you won't be able to talk freely."

She didn't have an immediate comeback, which meant she couldn't refute his reasoning. Finally she said, "Where will you be?"

"I'll grab a steak at the Cowboy Grub."

He'd been thinking of asking out the new manager of the restaurant, an attractive brunette named Amber Sharp. The last few times he'd been in, she'd done everything except stand on her head to get him to make a date with her. Now would be a good time to follow up on her interest.

"When you're ready for me to pick you up, call me

on my cell phone.'' He chucked her chin. ''I like that sweater and skirt you're wearing. You look beautiful.''

''Thanks,'' she whispered in a tremulous voice. ''Leslie took me shopping.''

''Pierce's wife has good dress sense.''

He disappeared into the bathroom, making further conversation impossible. His daughter might feel as if he was abandoning her, but he couldn't see another way of dealing with the situation. The fact that Sam was a recovering cancer patient only exacerbated the violent emotions churning inside him. The less contact between them, the better.

A half hour later he backed the car out of the garage and they were on their way to Jackson.

''Dad?''

He heard a lot of angst in that one word. His hands tightened on the steering wheel. ''Yes?''

''The ninth grade girls' association has planned a mother-and-daughter party for next Friday night. We're going to have a talent show and a sleepover in the gym.''

Here it comes.

''I was going to ask Leslie if she would go with me, but now that my moth—''

''Hold on, honey.'' Nick broke in before she could say another word. They hadn't even left the park boundary so she could meet her mother for the first time, yet already his daughter was anticipating a future that included the woman who'd given her up at birth.

Only now did Nick realize how long he'd been deluding himself that his daughter hadn't missed having a mother. All these years he'd tried to be both mother and father to her, but that wasn't possible. He understood that now.

A woman was required for the mother's role. And if that woman was Jessica's biological mother?

Through some mystical bond that defied logic, his daughter had already accepted and embraced Sam into her life, sight unseen.

For thirteen years it had been just he and Jessica. His daughter hadn't wanted anyone else.

Only recently had she reached out to Leslie, who was safe. Because she was another man's wife, she couldn't come between Nick and Jessica to ruin their father-daughter relationship.

Yet all Jessica had to do was hear that the woman who'd signed away all rights to her child, the woman who hadn't once held her baby or looked at her in that hospital, the woman who hadn't come near her in all these years, suddenly wanted to see her. In an instant, this stranger had full access to his daughter's mind and heart. No password needed.

Nick's lips twisted in bitter pain at the irony.

His daughter had even been willing to give up her baby-sitting money to get her mother a room because she lived alone and didn't have anyone to look after her.

His poor, innocent Jessica. If Sam hadn't married, it wasn't because she'd lacked opportunity. She'd been a raving beauty. That, combined with a great mind, assured that any man would have been attracted to her. She wouldn't have gone without a lover all these years. Probably a fellow attorney on her same wavelength.

"Dad? I'm sorry if I said something that made you mad."

He swallowed hard. "I'm not mad, honey. I just want you to slow down. It's taken thirteen years for her to even attempt to make contact with you. She may not be married or have other children, but that doesn't mean she isn't involved with a man who has other claims on her time."

"*You're* not. Involved with another woman, I mean. Maybe it's the same with her. Maybe she's a workaholic like you."

He darted her a stunned glance. "Is that what you think I am?"

"Yes," she answered with gut-wrenching honesty. "Whenever I go over to Logan's to baby-sit, his dad always says 'doesn't that workaholic father of yours ever knock off early?'"

Nick had to stop the rebuttal he could have made in defense of his actions. Like the fact that in the last five years, every relationship he'd had with a woman had been sabotaged.

No one could do it better than his pint-size daughter, who managed to get stomachaches and hysterical crying spells the moment she sensed her daddy's interest strayed from her, however temporarily.

It was another strange irony that for the first time in their lives his daughter was showing an interest in someone besides him. Now Nick seemed to be the one who suddenly had a stomachache and was feeling hysterical.

"Dad?"

He knew what was coming. No force on earth could stop it.

"If my mother wanted to go to the party with me and could find the time, would it be all right with you?"

CHAPTER FOUR

AT SIX-TWENTY, Samantha left her room and walked down the corridor to the lobby. She planted herself on a bench at the side of the entry so she'd be able to see Nick and their daughter before they spotted her.

She could hear the music of a live country-and-western band coming from the bar. Judging by the number of people filing into the lodge, bringing the cold air with them, the restaurant located down the hallway near the bar was a popular place to dine.

Her heart fluttered faster than it had the first time she was given her prechemo medication to control anxiety and nausea. That was a black period, when she didn't know if she would survive her disease.

At twenty-five to seven she stood up unable to sit still any longer. That's when she spied a tall, powerfully built male with dark-brown hair appear at the entrance. While he held the door open for their red-headed daughter, Samantha's hungry eyes fastened on him first.

The promise of the man in the boy had come to fruition.

Like the rugged Tetons thrusting majestically in the rarified air, the father of Samantha's baby was every bit as spectacular. Beneath a sheepskin jacket similar to the one he used to wear, she glimpsed a black turtleneck. Faded denims molded his rock-hard thighs.

Lines of experience added character to his strong, handsome features—the same attractive features bequeathed to their daughter. No amount of imagining what Jessica might look like would ever measure up to the reality of her vital, living presence.

In a word, she was adorable.

The closest description that came to Samantha's mind was the shining star on top of a Christmas tree. The wonder of the moment left her breathless.

An instant later she became aware that she was the target of a pair of dark-fringed eyes the color of gunmetal. Like someone battling a riptide, she tried to stay upright and survive their merciless scrutiny.

"Hello, Nick," she murmured.

"Sam." He gave an almost imperceptible nod of his head.

She'd asked the impossible of him. She knew that now.

The only thing that saved her was another pair of eyes, blue like her own, staring at her in total fascination.

"Jessica—"

"Hi," she said, just the way she had done over the phone.

"Do you feel as strange as I do?"

A nervous smile broke out on her precious face. "Yes."

Nick's hands were gripping their daughter's shoulders. "I told Jessica you two should spend this time together by yourselves." He tousled her curls in such an affectionate gesture, Samantha could have wept.

"Call me when you're ready and I'll come for you, honey."

"Okay, Dad."

"Enjoy your meal." His eyes studied Samantha's upturned features for a heart-stopping moment. Was he remembering the way it used to be with them? Did he still find her attractive after all this time?

"Thank you, Nick," she whispered. But he moved away with such lightning speed, she ended up saying it to his retreating back.

Her gaze returned to Jessica. It was hard to keep from staring at her. Samantha had missed out on examining her from head to toe when she was a baby. She'd missed the first thirteen years of her life. The realization crucified her all over again.

This lovely girl was her baby, her daughter, her flesh and blood.

"Jessica? I'd planned for us to eat dinner in the dining room, but I was wondering if you'd like to go to my room instead. We could have dinner delivered."

"I'd like that a lot better."

"I hope you're not saying that to please me. It's just that there's so much I have to say to you, and so much I want to learn about you, I don't want to be around a lot of other people. But if you don't think your father would approve, or if you're uncomfortable with the idea, we—"

"I'd rather be alone, too," the teen declared with the maturity of someone twice her age.

"Then let's go. My room's down this hall."

It was an incredible experience to be walking alongside her daughter. Jessica was probably an inch shorter than Samantha and about the same weight. She radiated an energy and vibrancy that was almost tangible.

"I love your suit. You look beautiful."

"So do you. I'm crazy about that sheepskin jacket. I wish I had one just like it."

"Dad and I went to Western Outfitters to get ours. I could show you where it is tomorrow."

Much as Samantha wanted to take her up on her offer, she couldn't. Nick had made it clear she'd only been given this one night.

"If I had more time, that would be wonderful."

"You mean you have to go back to Idaho tomorrow?"

The disappointment in her daughter's voice was a balm to Samantha's soul. She knew the answer she should give so she wouldn't undermine Nick's wishes.

"Tomorrow evening I have plans with a friend I can't break, but we've got all of tonight to get acquainted. Come on in."

She used the card key to let them into the room. After turning on the lights she said, "Make yourself comfortable while I find the menu."

Jessica removed her coat. "I just want a hamburger and fries."

"Me, too. What about a drink?"

"Root beer."

"I think I'll have the same."

Samantha called room service and placed their order. Once that was accomplished, she reached in the dresser drawer and pulled out one of the scrapbooks she'd brought in her suitcase.

"Jessica? If you'll come over to the table, I have something to show you. I would have come back to the room after dinner to get it for you, but since we're already here, now seems the appropriate time.''

Her daughter did as she asked, eyeing her with avid curiosity as she sat down opposite her. ''What is it?''

''Hopefully the answers to questions only I can give you. Go ahead and look through it to your heart's content.''

Maybe it was a trick of the light, but she thought her daughter's fingers were trembling as she opened the cover.

''Oh my gosh! It's Dad! He looks so young I can't believe it!''

''You look just like him. You're his daughter, all right.''

''No one ever says that, because of my red hair.''

''All they have to do is picture you with brown hair and you're the exact replica of your handsome father.''

''My girlfriends think he's gorgeous.''

Samantha winked. ''He is. Take it from me. We met the week he turned twenty. I'd seen him several times in the campus student center studying at one of the tables.

''Nick Kincaid was so attractive, I never looked at another guy after that. You could say I fell in love with him on the spot. The kind of love that hurt, it went so deep.

''Onc night in desperation I dropped all my books next to his chair to get his attention.''

Jessica's face lit up in a huge smile. ''Did he pick them up?''

''Yes. But it was the most horrible moment of my life. When I thanked him, he didn't say one word. He just gave me one of those scary silvery looks only he can give, and went back to his studies.''

Jessica laughed. ''He still does that when he's really mad about something.''

''Well, I was so hurt, I left the building and ran to my mom's car in tears. Before I could unlock the door, he caught hold of me.''

''Then what happened?'' Jessica cried, totally caught up in the story.

''He said he thought I was really cute, but he didn't date cute little freshman girls. I told him he was crazy if he thought I wanted a date with him. He said he didn't believe me and could prove it. The next thing I knew, he kissed me.''

''Oh my gosh!''

''You can say that again. It lasted kind of a long time.''

Her daughter giggled in pure delight.

''When we had to stop because everyone was honking at us, he asked me if I wanted to celebrate his birthday with him that weekend. The cake in this first picture is the one I made for him. I used my grandmother's recipe. It was a real hit with your father.''

Jessica lifted her head. Her blue eyes were blazing. ''Is it chocolate mint cake?''

Samantha's heart turned over. ''Yes. How did you know?''

'''Cause Dad always tells me to put peppermint extract in the chocolate icing when I make us a cake. I've always wondered why.''

Even a simple thing like finding out Nick still enjoyed the type of cake she had first baked for him was almost more than she could stand.

"Will you give me the recipe?"

"Yes. Of course."

Her daughter turned to the next page, then squealed. "That's you and Dad on a motorcycle! Every time a motorcycle gang comes roaring into the park, he tells me motorbikes should be abolished."

Sam smiled at her. "You know how parents are. Do as I say, not as I do."

A grin broke out on Jessica's young, enchanting face. "I can't wait to show this to him!"

"It'll bring back memories, that's for sure. He had a close friend, a roommate named Joey, who let us ride around Fort Collins on it. In fact, we couldn't have gone on all the dates we did without it.

"You could go a long way on a tank of gas, and it was cheap. Back in those days your dad didn't have a lot of money. He had to work hard just to pay for his tuition and housing."

"He put himself through school, huh?"

"Absolutely. Unlike some students, he took a full load of classes and held a job, yet he still got straight As. I lived in awe of him."

"I still do," Jessica admitted.

So do I, darling. So do I.

"Joey took this snap of us on his cycle with my camera. Your dad hated having his picture taken, but I forced him to endure it."

Jessica chuckled. "He still hates it."

Every photo had a story. Picnics, football games. Samantha had recorded every precious moment of their lives together. At seventeen, she had imagined this scrapbook would be the first of many she would fill throughout the rest of their lives.

As it turned out, they'd only had ten months, the last six being long distance.

Dinner arrived. Samantha and Jessica ate their hamburgers between anecdotes. Her daughter begged to hear every detail. Samantha was so excited to share with her, they completely lost track of time. After dinner, they returned to the scrapbooks.

"That's you on water skis!" the girl cried.

"Yes. In this picture you can see your dad in the back of the boat, spotting me."

"You're fabulous!"

"Hardly."

"Dad's still a good water-skier. That is, when he quits working long enough in the summer to go for a couple of runs on Jackson Lake."

"Your dad was good at everything. Turn the page and you'll see some more photos of him. One of his friends took these pictures from another boat."

"Oh my gosh! Dad's on a slalom ski! I can't believe it. My girlfriends have got to see these pictures! Would you let me borrow this scrapbook sometime?"

"It's yours. That's why I brought it. I want you to take it home so you'll have it forever."

Her daughter's blue eyes filled with tears. "Thank you," she said in a tremulous whisper.

"You're so welcome. No one else in the world could ever appreciate this scrapbook the way you do. Someday when you're married and have children, they'll love to pore over these pictures. You can say, 'See? There's your grandpa and grandma when they were young.'"

Jessica's eyes held a faraway look before she finally

lowered her head to finish reading the explanations below the snaps. "Horsetooth Dam. Where is that?"

"Right by my old house in Fort Collins. You could always water-ski there until Halloween. Then the weather turned cold."

When her cell phone rang, they both looked at each other in consternation.

"I'm sure that's your father."

"I am, too."

Samantha let out a quiet gasp when she checked her watch and saw that it was close to midnight. Where had the time gone? Five and a half hours had passed in a blink. "I'll get it."

If Nick was angry, let it be at her, not Jessica.

"Hello?"

"I'm in the foyer," said the deep, familiar voice. "Will you please tell Jessica I'm waiting?"

"Of course. Thank you for this, Nick. You'll never know how grateful I am. She'll be right out."

He clicked off before she could say anything more.

Hardly able to breathe, she turned to Jessica. "As you heard, that was your father. He's in the lobby."

Forcing her legs to move, she walked over to the bed and picked up Jessica's jacket. After helping her on with it, she handed her the scrapbook lying on the table.

Her daughter's eyes never left Samantha's face. "When does your plane leave tomorrow?"

"At noon."

"Do you want to have breakfast together?"

"I'd love it, but that's up to your father."

Jessica nodded. "Can I call you in the morning?"

Only if Nick lets you....

"Of course. I'm always up early. Before you leave, I have one more gift for you."

She hurried over to the dresser and pulled another scrapbook from the drawer. With trembling hands, she handed it to her daughter. "This is the baby book I started when I found out I was pregnant with you.

"I'm sure your father told you why I gave you up, but I'm equally certain you've still never understood how I could have done what I did. I wouldn't be able to understand it if I were in your shoes."

At this point Samantha was shaking so hard, she couldn't stop. "Though we can't go back and do it over again, I'm hoping this book will help you realize I loved you with all my heart from the second you were conceived.

"My parents didn't know I kept a baby book. No one did. It was something I made for myself and for you, hoping the day would come when I would have the opportunity to give it to you. That day is here.

"Just know that there's never been a moment when you haven't been a part of me, Jessica. You'll always be a part of me. I love you."

She opened the door for her, then clung to it so she wouldn't reach out and crush her daughter in her arms. If she ever did that, she wouldn't be able to let her go.

"Now you'd better hurry. Your dad's anxious to take you home."

"Okay," she replied in a quiet little voice. "I'll talk to you in the morning. Good night."

"Good night."

Your father isn't going to let you have breakfast with me in the morning. Goodbye, my darling, darling girl.

NICK WAS ABOUT TO PHONE Sam once more when he saw his daughter come running around the corner of the lobby with her head down. She was carrying what looked like a couple of albums.

Without saying anything, she rushed past him and hurried through the double doors to the parking lot. By the time he'd helped her into the car, she was sobbing her heart out. He'd never felt so helpless in his life.

Right now she was too upset to talk. The scrapbooks seemed welded to her body. All he could do was start driving and wait until this first paroxysm of tears had passed.

To his chagrin she was still broken up by the time they drove into the garage twenty-five minutes later. The second he shut off the motor, she slid out of the car and ran into the house.

After he locked everything up and turned off lights, he entered her bedroom and found her under the covers poring over the smaller of the two albums.

He sat down next to her. "Do you mind if I look at this?"

She shook her head.

He reached for the larger one propped against her knees and opened the cover. For the next ten minutes he was treated to a painful trip down memory lane. It was all there.

Sam had preserved every conceivable memory of their love affair. She'd saved literally everything....

The effort she'd put into its photographic presentation, not to mention the tiny mementos she'd placed under clear plastic, astounded him. Nick remembered she'd like to take pictures, but he'd had no idea she had this sentimental side.

His incredulous gaze took in the halves of a pair of Denver Broncos football game tickets, his old student ID picture, a postcard they'd bought in Gillette, a program from a concert they'd attended, a napkin from a friend's wedding reception, every card or note he'd ever written her.

Each item had a history, one that worked his heart over until he had to close the scrapbook because he couldn't take any more.

"Jessica?" he whispered.

She lifted tear-drenched eyes to his. "My mother loves me, Dad. This is the baby book she made for me."

Baby book?

"Look—"

Now *he* was the one who had trouble functioning as she put the photo album in his hands.

When he opened the cover he saw the title Sam had printed there: "The Family Tree of Jessica Bretton Kincaid."

He blinked to see photographs of Sam, her parents and grandparents glued to one side of the tree. Photos of Nick, his parents and grandparents, his uncle Willard, had been glued to the other. She must have gotten the pictures of his family from his uncle when they'd gone to Gillette.

Nick had had no idea....

At the bottom of the page she'd put in a lock of her red-gold hair with the following note: "When you look at the pictures on your family tree, you'll see you inherited your red hair from your great-grandmother O'Roark on my mother's side.''

There were photos of Sam posing sideways in front of her house in Fort Collins. One had a caption: ''Today the doctor told me I was pregnant. I'm eleven weeks along.'' Everything had been given a date and a time.

The next pictures showed her at each stage of her pregnancy, with notations about what the doctor said at each medical checkup.

Another picture showed a side view of her standing in front of the Bretton's Tudor mansion in Denver. ''Today I'm six months along.'' Her flat stomach was now a tiny mound. More pictures showed her at seven and eight months. She'd even managed to get in a photo of herself two days before the delivery, when she'd blossomed.

Stunned, he turned to the next page and saw a photograph of the hospital where Jessica had been born. Sam had even put in a picture of the doctor, which she must have taken at one of her office visits.

She included a chart of her weight and blood pressure, the first time the doctor detected the baby's heartbeat. Everything to do with the baby and its progress had been noted, including her feelings.

On the inside back cover she'd put in a one-page letter under clear plastic. It had been signed and dated one day before she'd gone into labor.

To my beloved baby—
I don't know if you're a boy or a girl yet, but I've lived with you for nine months and you're a

part of me and your father forever. When the doctor told me I was going to have you, I couldn't believe such a fantastic miracle had happened to me.

I've barely graduated from high school, and my parents believe you'll have a better life if you go to a home where there's a loving couple waiting to adopt you.

Your daddy has said he won't let you go to anyone else, that he'll take care of you by himself.

I believe him and know he will honor that commitment because he loves you and he's a wonderful man. I can promise you he's going to make you the best father in the world.

If the time should ever come when you read this letter, then know that I made this baby book just for you. All you have to do is put a picture of yourself in the center of the family tree and it will finally be complete.

Since I can't be there to put my arms around you and hold you close, I've asked God to help your daddy raise you. I'll pray for both of you every night for the rest of my life.

I love you, my dear innocent angel child.

Your loving mother.

Nick's eyes swam until everything went blurry.

He closed the baby book and got to his feet, too torn apart by conflicting feelings and emotions to articulate his thoughts.

Sam had given their daughter two priceless gifts, gifts he hadn't known existed. The baby book was the one thing he would never have credited her with making.

Over the years he'd gradually come to accept the fact that Sam really had been too young psychologically and emotionally to be a mother, that her parents had understood their daughter's immaturity better than he had.

At the time, the knowledge that she hadn't known what she was doing had helped him to forgive her for giving up their baby. But it had taken him many years to forgive her for not marrying him, for smashing all his dreams.

The baby book, which she must have hidden from her parents, changed his perception of the situation, of Sam. Her moving, heart-wrenching letter to their unborn child contained the words and emotions of a woman, not a girl. The letter confused him in new ways he didn't want to analyze, and filled him with fresh pain.

"Dad? I asked her if I could have breakfast with her in the morning before she flies back to Coeur D'Alene. She said yes, but only if it was all right with you."

No.

It wasn't all right with him.

Nothing was ever going to be all right with him again. But he couldn't say that to his daughter, who'd been starving thirteen years for a moment such as this.

Now that she'd feasted on every jot and tittle of these memory books—guaranteed to fill her hungry heart with joy—Nick would no longer be the wonderful, honorable father if he thwarted her wishes.

"Wake me in the morning when you want me to

drive you,'' he muttered. His legs felt leaden as he headed for the door.

"You're upset, aren't you."

He turned slowly toward her. "This situation isn't about me, honey. I only want what's best for you."

"Do you know what?"

His eyes closed tightly. "What?"

"I was afraid I wouldn't like her."

Nick had been afraid she *would*. Now his worst fear had come true. Sam had become a breathtaking woman, exhibiting a depth of character he'd only this moment discovered. What daughter wouldn't be thrilled, overjoyed to know this beautiful, intelligent woman was her mother? A mother, furthermore, who'd always loved and wanted her.

"Dad?"

"Yes?"

"Besides you, I like her better than anyone I ever met."

Jessica, Jessica. My poor, transparent daughter.

"I can see why you loved her, Dad."

Don't say any more. "That was a long time ago. We were kids."

"She *really* loved you." Jessica spoke as if he hadn't responded to her comment.

Apparently not enough.

Yet there was no doubt in his mind that giving up their daughter had affected Sam's life as profoundly as it had affected his own.

That was news he hadn't suspected or expected, in spite of the role her cancer had played in the scheme of things. In spite of everything else she'd told Jessica.

''Let's drop the subject and say good-night. Morning will be here before we know it.''

''I'm not going to sleep yet.'' Jessica had survived her baptism of fire. The tears were gone. In their place a new light shone in her eyes, a tangible radiance only Jessica's mother could have put there.

''I've got to find a picture of me to put on the family tree in my baby book. If you want to talk, you can come back in after you get on your pj's.''

Reverse psychology from his thirteen-year-old? He watched her sort through the pictures in her wallet, trying to choose the right one, and was unable to process the fact that they were actually having this conversation.

In truth, he couldn't comprehend that the woman he'd consigned to the far reaches of the universe was back. Tonight Nick had learned a lot more about Sam than he wanted to know.

Lord—she was staying in a hotel room only twenty-five minutes away from the house. All he had to do was drive over there and show up at her door.

And then what, Kincaid? Take up where you left off before she told you she was pregnant?

''Dad?'' Jessica had found her scissors in her top dresser drawer. Now she was cutting the picture she'd chosen into an oval. ''Before you go to bed, I need to talk to you about that school party next week.''

He knew what was on her mind. No force on earth could stop it.

''Tomorrow morning I'm going to ask my mother if she'd like to go with me. I know she might be too busy, but maybe she'll say yes. The thing is, she told me she had a date tomorrow night and that's why she has to get back to Coeur D'Alene. So you're probably right that she has a boyfriend."

Nick felt the impact of that word like a blow to his gut.

"I thought Leslie was beautiful, and she is, but my mother is even more beautiful. No wonder you kissed her after she dropped all her books to get your attention."

Good grief. Sam had told Jessica all that?

"She said you were so handsome she fell in love with you on the spot, that it was the kind of love that went so deep it hurt. You must have felt the same way because I can't picture you running out of the library after her and then kissing her in front of all those people. Whoa, Dad!

"Wait till I tell Pierce and show him these pictures of you and Mom on your friend Joey's motorcycle! He won't believe it!"

She taped the picture of herself to the root of the family tree. "How come you've never mentioned Joey to me?"

"A week before our college graduation he died going around a mountain curve on his motorcycle."

Jessica lifted soulful eyes to him. "That's awful."

"It was."

"So that's why you hate motorcycles so much."

"Yes."

"I bet my mother doesn't know he died."

"No. She was in Boston by then."

"She had to be superintelligent to go to Harvard, huh."

Nick nodded.

"Is my grandfather Bretton superintelligent, too?"

"Both your grandparents have fine minds. They met at Stanford, where he received his law degree. Your great-grandfather Bretton was a brilliant federal circuit court judge before his death. As for your grandmother Bretton, she has a masters in nineteenth-century English literature."

"They're sure different from your side of the family."

Before the phone call from Sam on Halloween night, Jessica would have said, "They're sure different from *our* side of the family."

"That they are, honey."

The Kincaids were ranchers from Gillette, Wyoming. None of them had gone to college except Nick. But that didn't count to the Brettons, who were much more ambitious for their daughter.

What a devastating blow to have found out Sam had been diagnosed with cancer, the one thing in life no amount of schooling could prepare her for.

Her parents, along with Sam herself, had to be thanking God she was in remission. *For how long would she be given this miraculous stay of execution?*

That was the question worrying Nick. His daughter's newfound happiness could be destroyed if Sam's immune system suddenly shut down again.

CHAPTER FIVE

SAMANTHA CHOSE THE TABLE next to the window of
the Elk Inn's restaurant so she could look at the magnificent snow-swept Tetons while she waited for Jessica.

Her daughter had phoned at seven-thirty and said
she'd be there by eight-thirty. Again there'd been no
mention of Nick. Samantha knew he had to be impatiently counting the seconds until she boarded the
plane and flew out of their lives.

That gave her two more hours to cram in a whole
lifetime with her precious daughter before she had to
bid her farewell.

The scrapbooks had been delivered. Since it was out
of the question to live with Jessica and help finish
raising her, the albums were the only tangible proof
of love Samantha could offer.

When she'd signed those custody papers giving up
all her rights to Jessica thirteen years ago, they'd been
final. She had no legal recourse to her daughter. None.

Only out of the goodness of Nick's heart had she
been given this sliver of time to let Jessica know she'd
always been, and always would be, loved and cherished.

Most of last night Samantha had kept Marilyn on
the phone talking about her darling offspring. Tonight

there would be more talk with her friend once Sam returned to Coeur D'Alene.

More talk, more tears. Oh yes. There were going to be more tears. Days, weeks, months and years of them flowing over the what-ifs.

Marilyn would tell her it was a torturous gesture in futility. Samantha would agree with her friend before she again wallowed in fresh layers of remorse over what might have been, what could have been.

Seeing Nick—the man he'd become—had fueled her desire for him all over again, with a burning new intensity.

"Hi!"

"Hi yourself!" Samantha's hungry eyes took in the vision of her delightful daughter wearing jeans and a kelly-green sweater beneath her sheepskin jacket. Her coloring might be Samantha's, but her classic bone structure and demeanor shouted Nick.

She didn't dare ask where he was or she would give herself away. There had to be a woman in his life. Samantha would find out soon enough, and dreaded the moment.

"Are you hungry?"

"Kind of."

"What do you say we order some juice and rolls, then call for a taxi and go shopping?"

Jessica's eyes sparkled at the idea.

A half hour later they climbed out of a taxi onto sidewalks store owners had shoveled since the blizzard a few days earlier. Samantha glanced at the sky. No new snowstorms threatened, although it was cold and overcast.

Western Outfitters carried everything. Jessica led

the way to the department where, after some consideration, Samantha bought a jacket similar to hers. Then they walked around the store eyeing the latest sportswear.

Both of them stopped to admire some new brushed-suede cotton suits in a rich chocolate. Paired with silk blouses in a café au lait color, they made a striking outfit.

"With your red hair, you two would look terrific in those," the female clerk commented from a nearby counter.

Samantha glanced at Jessica. "Shall we?"

"Yes!"

Because the clothes had just been put out, they both found a size four before hurrying into the same fitting room. Jessica beamed when the two of them faced the mirror. "This is so cool. Mom and daughter look-alikes."

It *was* cool. In fact, it was the kind of experience Samantha had dreamed about having with her daughter. Growing up with her own mom doting on her, her younger self had taken for granted that she would share this kind of experience with her child. She took nothing for granted now.

She stared at Jessica in the glass. "We need the right shoes to go with our outfits. What do you think?"

The second Jessica nodded, they left the changing room and walked across the store to the footwear department. Soon they'd both been fitted with brown leather flats.

Conscious of the time, Samantha paid for everything, then they left in the outfits they'd just bought.

The clerk put the clothes they'd worn before into shopping bags for them.

After a stop at a photography studio, where you could get passport photos on the spot, Samantha asked the taxi driver to take them to a local jewelry store.

"We'd like to see some lockets, please."

Her daughter bubbled with excitement as they picked out matching round gold ones hanging from gold chains. With the clerk's help, they were able to insert the new pictures. Samantha took turns with her daughter fastening them around each other's necks.

With her hands still on Jessica's shoulders she said, "There. Now we've preserved a memory we can both share."

Jessica's eyes glistened with unshed tears. "Could I ask you something important?"

Samantha's heart swelled with emotion. "Anything."

"Do you think you could come to the mother-and-daughter's ninth grade party at school next Friday night? There's going to be a sleepover in the gym."

Her breath caught in her throat. *Nick let you have this time with her, Samantha. He didn't have to do it. He's expecting you to play fair, so you have to prove to him you can be as noble as he is, even if it kills you.*

"Thank you for asking me, darling. I can't think of anything I'd rather do, but I'm going to be out of town on federation business for the next while," she lied.

"Oh." That was all her daughter said before turning away.

As they left the store and got in the taxi to head

back to the Elk Inn, the pain and disappointment in Jessica's expression almost incapacitated Samantha.

This was the downside of a once-in-a-lifetime reunion. It was what Nick had dreaded, she was sure.

Samantha had been afraid of it, too, but she'd believed her daughter would grow up to be a happier, healthier woman if she knew how much her mother loved her.

Now Samantha knew better.

You didn't sweep into your long-lost daughter's life one night, then disappear into the blue the next day without creating chaos.

Nick had every reason to view Samantha as the most selfish creature who ever existed. No one had a greater right to despise her.

Yet *he* had allowed this visit.

Because he's the personification of unselfishness. Dear God, what have I done to my daughter? To Nick?

In the next little while Samantha would be leaving, and once again he'd be left to pick up the pieces. It was utterly cruel to Jessica, and totally unfair to him.

If the ride back to the Elk Inn had lasted longer than a couple of minutes, Jessica's silence would have been excruciating.

''There's Dad.''

Samantha could see his distinctive profile at the wheel of an Xtera parked in front of the lobby entrance. The taxi pulled up behind him. She found the sack containing Jessica's clothes and handed it to her.

''I'm sure he's impatient to get you home. What are your plans for today?''

''He usually works on Saturdays so I go with him.''

"You lucky girl. My father didn't have the kind of job that allowed me to tag along. You'll probably end up being a biologist, too. A brainy one, just like your dad."

"Maybe." She opened the door. "Thank you for the clothes and the locket. Every time I wear them, I'll think of you."

"I'll do the same," Samantha whispered with her heart in her throat. "Now you'd better go."

"Okay." She climbed out her side of the taxi. "T-thank you for everything," she stammered in a tear-filled voice before closing the door.

Goodbye, Jessica.

Samantha purposely took her time getting money from her wallet to pay the driver. She didn't want Nick to see she was wearing the same outfit as Jessica. It would have been like plunging in the knife that much deeper. Enough blood had already been spilled.

NICK HAD NEVER THOUGHT of his daughter as stunning. She was too young. But the shopping spree with her mother caused him to reassess his thinking. Seeing her in such a grown-up outfit, he could imagine Jessica the way she would look three years from now. The way Sam had looked....

Smothering a groan, he drove away without glancing in the rearview mirror.

"Do you want to see my new locket?"

No. He knew what would be inside. Sam had thought of everything. No stone had been left unturned. The takeover was complete.

Jessica removed it from her neck and opened it for him.

There they were. Mother and daughter, both wearing the same blouse and suit, from what he could see.

"She bought me new shoes, too."

"I noticed." He handed the locket back to her before accelerating. "Your mother always did have great taste in clothes. I hardly recognize you, looking this sophisticated. You're very lovely."

"Thanks. So's Mom."

Nick had noticed that, as well. If Sam hadn't told him about her battle with cancer, he would never have been able to tell. Her glistening, chin-length red hair, worn shorter than he remembered, flattered her features. In that black suit and pink blouse she'd worn last night, she'd stolen his breath.

Sam had always been a knockout. She always would be. He'd be lying to himself if he insisted that his reaction to her was based solely on the fact that she'd surprised him by not looking ill.

If anything, her slight weight loss enhanced the beauty of her bone structure. More than ever her eyes reminded him of the brilliant blue alpine forget-me-nots growing at the highest elevations.

The old Sam was unforgettable. The new one had an allure that had caught him off guard. She brought his senses alive just being near.

"Is she coming to your school party next week?"

"No. She's busy with a court case she's working on."

Nick's hands tightened on the steering wheel. He had a gut feeling Sam was rushing back to a man. How long had they been lovers? Had he seen her through the stages of her illness? Had he held her and comforted her, done the things that should have been Nick's privilege?

Forcing down the gall rising in his throat, he said, "Did she suggest coming another time?"

"No. She doesn't want to see me again, Dad."

His head jerked around in anger. "She *told* you that?"

Jessica blinked in surprise. "No. She didn't say anything at all. That's how I know." She bit her lip exactly the way Sam used to do. The unsolicited memory devastated him.

"I should never have asked to eat breakfast with her. I—I'm sure she didn't want to," Jessica's voice faltered. "She only took me shopping for something to do until it was time to catch her plane. That's what divorced parents do."

He couldn't bear the resignation and pain in her tone. "What do you mean, honey?"

"I've told you about Marsha Gardiner's parents." He nodded, wondering what was coming next. "Her dad only sees her once a year. As soon as he arrives, he takes her shopping."

"That's probably because he wants to do something nice for her." Nick defended the other man when there was no defense for a father who'd virtually abandoned his children.

"Marsha wishes he wouldn't come at all if that's the only thing he can think of to do."

"What would she like him to do?"

"Anything! Invite her to visit him in California. See where he lives. Go to his work. Stuff like that."

And you wish your mother had asked you to come to Coeur D'Alene and stay with her, Nick thought.

Damn you to hell, Sam. You set up our daughter with those scrapbooks, then fly out of her life as easily as you flew in. But then you're the pro at dangling the carrot before snatching it away.

"How would you like to drive to Gillette and wow your cousins with your new outfit?"

"You mean today?"

He'd never heard less enthusiasm. "Why not? I can afford to take the time off."

"No you can't. I heard you talking to Pierce about needing to meet with the men at the dam this afternoon."

"That can wait until next week." Trying to help his daughter recover from this nightmare was the real emergency here.

"I don't want to go anywhere."

"Then why don't we invite the Gallaghers for an early dinner and a video." Leslie was good for his daughter. So was Cory. Nick would tell him to bring his little basset hound along. Jessica was crazy about Lucy.

"Can't we just be by ourselves? I'd rather go to work with you, anyway. Do you mind?"

"What do you think?"

Nick wrapped his arm around her shoulders and gave her a squeeze. Inside he could feel his rage building. He hadn't experienced that destructive emotion for thirteen years. But it was back, it was alive and it was doing well.

"Let's get you home first so we can both change clothes."

She nodded. "Mom asked me what I was going to do today."

Don't, honey.

"I told her I'd probably go to work with you. She said I was lucky because when she was young, she couldn't hang around with my grandpa."

"Robert Bretton was too high-powered and driven to give his daughter the time she craved."

It was probably the reason she'd sought a serious relationship with Nick so early in her life. But he could never forget she had a lot of her father in her to opt for a law career instead of early motherhood.

"I'm so glad you're not like that, Dad."

"I thought you called me a workaholic," he teased to cover his emotions, which were spilling all over the place.

"But you always let me be with you. That's the difference. Mom said I'd probably turn out to be a brilliant biologist like you."

Mom this, Mom that.

Nick wondered how often that emotive three-letter word would come up in their conversations from now on.

"I've decided I'm going to be a biologist. Then I can live in the park and work with you until you're old. You'll never have to worry about anything because I'll always take care of you."

Oh Jessica.

He shook his head. "A lot of water's got to shoot through the spillway before you're all grown up. Life will be very different by then."

"No it won't. Mom said there was no mistaking me for your daughter. I'm going to get straight As like she said you did. And then I'll graduate with a degree in biology, too."

They'd already entered Moose. A couple of rangers on patrol honked in greeting, but Nick was so immersed in what Sam had told his daughter, he forgot to honk back.

"Even so, honey, there'll come a day when you'll meet a man and want to get married."

"I'm not going to get married. I plan to be like you. We don't need anybody else."

Oh hell.

He roared into the driveway, afraid he was going to lose it right there. Fortunately, Jessica shot out of the car ahead of him with her shopping bag.

By the time he'd changed into work clothes and went to collect his daughter from her room, he'd pulled himself together enough to realize it had been her pain talking.

Time would heal her wounds. He had to believe that.

As for their conversation, it had jarred Nick out of the deep sleep he'd been in. He was going to act on the advice Pierce had given him at the wedding two weeks ago.

Pierce had been right about him letting Jessica's insecurities manipulate him for too long. But after seeing Sam again, Nick realized there was an underlying reason why he'd never been able to commit to another woman and settle down.

There was only one Samantha Bretton. No other woman in his past had ever compared to his memory of her. After seeing her again, he feared no other woman would ever come close. But for the sake of his future happiness, he had to try to make it work with someone else. ASAP!

On Monday Nick had business over in Yellowstone Park. While he was there, he would stop by the Mammoth ranger station to see Gilly King.

He'd always toyed with the idea of asking her out, but had held back because she was a ranger and colleague who until three months ago had worked in Teton Park. Nick hadn't acted on his inclination because of the gossip it would create.

But her transfer to Yellowstone Park due to harassment by another ranger, now out of the picture, had changed the dynamics of the situation. If Gilly was still interested in going out with him—and she'd given out certain signals that said she was—the distance between the two parks was far enough to squelch a lot of the usual talk.

Better still, Jessica wouldn't be intimidated by seeing Gilly around all the time. Depending on how things progressed—*if* they progressed to a stage where Gilly came to mean something important to him—then his daughter would have to deal with it.

The brunette ranger from Billings, Montana, was smart, cute and nice. All the traits that would threaten his daughter. But after what Jessica had said about taking care of him in his old age, Nick needed to dispel that myth in a hurry.

He was about to knock on Jessica's door to let her know he was ready to go, but stopped when he heard her sobs. The kind that poured from her soul.

His head reared back in agony. He knew in his heart of hearts that time wasn't going to heal this wound.

Filled with fresh alarm, he entered her bedroom and sat down on the bed next to her prostrate body. She was still dressed in the suit Sam had bought her.

"Honey...." He put a hand on her back in an attempt to calm her.

She rolled over, presenting a tear-ravaged face. "I thought she loved me, Dad. She said she did, so why couldn't she come to one little party with me next week?"

Nick bowed his head. He needed all the strength he could muster right about now. "If she's caught up in a legal dispute with set court dates, then it might not be possible for her to get away."

"At night? On a weekend?"

Sam wasn't the only one with a razor-sharp brain. Their daughter had inherited more than her fair share. Sam's excuse didn't ring true with him, either.

Yet he couldn't reconcile Sam's rejection with the agony he'd heard in her voice when he'd told her outright it was too late to see Jessica.

He supposed there could be another explanation. Though her cancer was in remission, maybe she still didn't feel well yet. Perhaps the effort of coming last night had drained her. If that was the case, then she wouldn't be able to make future travel plans knowing she might have to cancel them.

No matter what, he didn't think Sam would intentionally hurt their daughter. If she thought she couldn't follow through with arrangements, then it was possible she'd decided it was better not to make any.

But he said something quite different to Jessica. "Maybe she's involved with a man who's possessive of her time. Naturally she wouldn't want to tell you that, so she used her work as the excuse why she couldn't say yes."

"I don't think she's in love with another man, Dad."

He struggled for breath. "You don't have to be in love to enjoy a relationship with someone, honey."

"My mom's not like that."

He blinked. "Like what?"

"You know." She sniffed. "She said she lives alone. I believe her."

"Jessica—she could be seeing someone on a regular basis and still live by herself."

"I don't think so. You once told me that before Mom went to the hospital, the two of you agreed that if you'd waited to get married first, and then had sex, you would still be together. Was that a lie?"

Good grief. "No, honey."

"Well then, I don't think Mom would do the same thing again *now*. Unless you're just making everything up like a lot of parents do."

"I've always told you the truth," he declared. "It's important you understand what happened so you won't repeat our mistake."

Tears gushed from her eyes. "That's what I was, huh."

"Jessica…" He raised her up and cradled her in his arms. "No, No. That's not what I meant."

"I know you love me, Dad, but I *was* a mistake. So was Amanda."

Amanda Tanner was Jessica's best friend, yet this was the first time he'd heard that surprising bit of news.

It was true what they said about parents being the last to learn what their children were up to. Nick had thought himself privy to Jessica's secrets. With that small revelation, he realized it was probably the tip of the iceberg of the things he *didn't* know.

With all animation wiped from his daughter's face, she looked older to him. Before he knew it, she'd eased out of his arms and stood up.

"Why do you think Mom bothered to get in touch with me after all these years? What was the point? If she wanted me to have these scrapbooks so badly, why didn't she tell someone to mail them to me after she was dead?"

Jessica, Jessica.

His daughter needed help. He got to his feet. "Why don't you call her and ask her those questions yourself?"

"I think I will," she said without hesitation. She glanced at her watch. "There's still forty-five minutes before she boards her plane."

He hadn't meant right this minute, but it was too late to recall his words.

With his heart knocking against his ribs, he watched his frantic daughter look for Sam's number in her purse and reach for the phone next to her bed.

She punched in the digits and waited. Her body was shaking. He wanted to go over and hold her, kiss her forehead. Tell her it was going to be all better. But he couldn't do that. She was no longer a little girl he could heal with a hug and a cookie.

After two more attempts to reach her mother, she hung up. "She must have turned off her phone. I'll call her later."

"That might be better," he murmured. "Honey? Why don't you change? We'll grab some lunch on the way to the dam."

"I've decided I don't want to go. Will you drive me to Amanda's instead? She wanted me to come over."

Nick didn't know if that was a good idea or not, but his daughter was in too much pain to hear any arguments from him right now. "Sure. I'll be out in the truck."

"Sam?"

No one had ever called her by that name except one man. With her heart thudding out of rhythm, she turned in the plastic seat of the lounge where she'd been waiting for her flight to be called.

Nick came striding toward her in work boots, well-worn jeans and a white T-shirt she could see beneath his jacket. She couldn't imagine what he was doing here, but judging by the dark expression hardening his masculine features, whatever he had to tell her wasn't good.

She rose to her feet, brushing madly at her wet cheeks with the back of her hand. It was too late to hide her face, which had to be glistening from tears she hadn't been able to stave off. "What's wrong?"

He cupped her elbow and ushered her away from the half-dozen passengers seated in the waiting area. She felt his touch charge her body like a current of electricity. His eyes were the stormy slate color of the clouds obscuring the peaks of the Tetons.

"That's what I'm here to ask you. I left my daughter in tears, and discover her mother's in the same condition."

"I didn't mean to cause her pain, Nick."

He must have realized he'd been holding on to her

because all of a sudden he let go of her arm as if it scalded him.

"Why did you turn your cell phone off? She's been trying to reach you."

She shook her head in confusion. "I didn't know. I don't remember turning it off."

"Come on, Sam. What's the real reason you can't come to the mother-and-daughter party next Friday night? I don't buy the excuse that you can't get out of a prior work commitment to spend one night with Jessica. She doesn't buy it, either."

Samantha's thoughts reeled. He was upset because she *hadn't* said yes?

"Are you still too weak from the chemo to try and make plans with her? Are you afraid you'll have to break them at the last minute?"

"No!" No, no, no.

"Then why didn't you give her an answer she can live with? Is there another man who doesn't want you to have anything to do with your daughter?" His mouth had gone white around the edges.

"No, Nick. No. It's nothing like that." *There's never been anyone but you!*

"Then what prevented you from granting her one little wish that would mean heaven and earth to her? By telling her you couldn't come because your law practice keeps you too damn busy, you might just as well have driven a stake through her heart."

His pain was tangible. She shook her head. "You don't understand. I'd give everything I possess to go to that party with her, but I know I don't have the right!"

Her answer caught him off guard. His whole demeanor changed. "Explain that to me," he said in an oddly shaken whisper.

"Nick—I signed away my parental rights to her thirteen years ago. You're her father. I never dreamed you would let me see her, but you did. After your incredible kindness to me, I didn't dare take advantage of that. It would have defied all the laws of decency."

He rubbed the side of his jaw. She'd seen him do it many times in the past when he was pondering something serious. Apparently it was a habit he hadn't lost.

"Didn't you realize I gave you the right when you received the first phone call from Jessica? Don't you know I expected a call from you years before now?"

No—she hadn't known. What was he saying? Had he *hoped* she would call him? Was it possible?

Her eyes filled again. "I realized you'd given me permission for *one* night. I knew I had to fit a whole lifetime into it," she cried. "Being able to have breakfast and go shopping with her this morning was a bonus I never expected. We had such a wonderful time, the last thing I wanted was for it to end. But I thought it *had* to."

His breathing sounded ragged. "She's going to be calling you later today to ask you why you really turned her down."

Joy surged through her body until she could hardly contain it. "Then I'll tell her the truth. That I wanted to come, but because I hadn't cleared it with you first, I wasn't sure if it would be all right to say yes."

A bleakness entered his eyes. "Once you admit that, then it won't be her last request. What will you tell her when she asks you to do something else?"

If he was saying what she thought he was saying, then another miracle had happened, much greater than the news that her cancer had gone into remission.

"Nick, my answer will always be yes unless—"

"Unless what?" he cut in. "Don't make promises you can't keep!" he warned before she could finish.

She nervously moistened her lips. "I can't promise my cancer won't come back. If I got too sick, that would be the one and only thing to prevent me from honoring a commitment to her."

Like a live wire, the possibility of her illness recurring hovered in the air between them. In truth, Samantha still had trouble believing she was no longer on the verge of death. She'd lived with the inevitability of it for too long. Nick's grim countenance reflected her own tortured thoughts.

"Does she know I've been ill?"

He studied her for a long, intense moment. "No. Not if you haven't told her."

A smile broke out on her face. "Then she really wanted to see me?" The news that Jessica hadn't responded out of sympathy or pity thrilled her in ways Nick could never comprehend.

"What do you think?" he ground out like a person who'd reached the limit of human endurance. "She's your flesh and blood."

Samantha averted her eyes. "I may have given birth to her, but that doesn't make me a mother. It would be understandable if she hated me."

"She called you Mom today."

Her head lifted. "She did?"

"Yes." He admitted it with such reluctance, she

knew this situation wasn't of his liking and never would be.

But there was one thing about Nick she could always count on. He possessed an innate honesty that compelled him to be truthful, even if it almost destroyed him in the process.

"Do you want me to tell her? About the cancer, I mean? I'll do whatever you say."

He stood there with his hands on his hips. His eyes searched hers—for what exactly, she didn't know. "It would probably be best if it came from you. Knowing Jessica, she'll be full of questions only you can answer."

She nodded. "I'll tell her when the moment's right. She's an exceptional girl, Nick. You've done the mos—"

"Don't!" He cut her off with brutal finality.

"I'm sorry," she whispered. "I only mea—"

"I know what you meant." He flashed her a wintry smile. "Let's agree Jessica's a gift and let it go at that."

Nick wasn't about to take any credit from her. He wanted nothing from her. She understood that and would stay out of his way.

But he was demanding she be there for Jessica. That's what he'd meant when he'd made the remark about expecting a call from her long before now. As he would come to understand in the years ahead, where their daughter was concerned, Samantha would never fail him.

An announcement came over the loudspeaker. Passengers started getting out of their seats. "My flight's been called. I should be back at my condo in about three hours.''

''Don't misunderstand.'' His silvery eyes flashed a warning that sent chills racing across her skin. ''As far as Jessica's concerned, you and I never had this conversation,'' he informed her. ''She was so distraught a little while ago, I have no idea what shape she's going to be in when I get home. She's gotten it in her head she was a mistake.''

A mistake!

''I'm not sure if you'll ever hear from her again.''

In the next instant his long strides ate up the expanse until he'd disappeared from sight.

Thirteen years ago he'd stormed out of her hospital room declaring that she wouldn't be seeing him again.

Just now he'd said virtually the same thing about Jessica.

Samantha could hear the flight being called one final time, but she couldn't bring herself to walk through the doors.

Without considering the consequences, she reached for her overnight bag and started running out of the terminal.

''Nick?'' she cried when she saw his tall physique in the distance. He'd almost made it to his truck. ''Wait!''

He wheeled around in disbelief that she hadn't boarded the plane. By the time she'd caught up to him, she was a little out of breath from the exertion.

''Why aren't you on the plane?'' Obviously her actions had shocked him.

''How could I leave knowing Jessica believes she's a mistake?''

She heard him curse under his breath.

"Nothing could be further from the truth, Nick, and you of all people know it." Her voice trembled. "I begged you to make love to me. I planned to spend my whole life with you and have lots of babies with you.

"My parents may have seen me as a foolish teen-ager who'd experimented without knowing what I was doing, and shouldn't be held accountable for my actions, but I *did* have a heart, which I gave to *you.*

"I'd hoped the albums would prove it, but a few pictures and mementos don't tell the whole story. Jessica needs to hear from me how I felt back then, otherwise she'll grow up warped! I couldn't be—"

"Sam—"

"Please, Nick," she interrupted. "Every day for the last thirteen years I've wanted to explain to her what happened. If you'll drive me back to the Elk Inn, I'll get another room. Then I'll call Jessica and tell her I decided not to leave until tomorrow, so we could have more time together. She'll never know you and I talked. I swear it."

He rubbed his jaw again. "That's not going to work."

"Why not?"

"At this point, if there's any hope of convincing our daughter of anything, we need to present a united front to her."

Sam swallowed hard. "Meaning what?"

"Meaning…" His chest heaved. "Her heart might be willing to listen if she discovers you in the truck when I pick her up at Amanda's. The knowledge that she's dealing with two mature people who've put bitterness aside to do what's best for her should go a long way to help her construct a truer picture of our lives.''

Samantha fought her tears of gratitude and won. Nick didn't want to see them any more than he wanted to hear her observations about what a terrific father he'd been. He would only tell her you didn't congratulate a father for doing the job he was born to do. In Nick's mind, being a good dad was a given.

Every human being should have him for their role model.

''What about tonight?'' she asked quietly.

''Jessica will figure out the sleeping arrangements. Our daughter is nothing if not the busy little homemaker.''

He took the suitcase from her and placed it in the truck bed. Forever the gentleman, he walked her around to the passenger side to help her in.

Riding in a truck with Nick was a new experience. Gone were the college days when he did favors for his friends in order to use their cars or motorcycles to take her on dates. He could buy what he wanted now.

As chief ranger of biological research, he held a vitally important job dealing with wildlife problems affecting all of the major national parks across North America. It was a surreal moment for Samantha to be here with him like this.

When she saw the sign that said they were entering Grand Teton National Park, she experienced such a thrill of excitement, she purposely kept her face turned toward the passenger window for fear of giving herself away.

CHAPTER SIX

RIDING THROUGH MOOSE with Samantha Bretton meant Nick had broken every rule in his own unwritten book of rules. But if she was going to show up at the mother-and-daughter party with Jessica next Friday night, he couldn't very well pretend she didn't exist.

Fact one: From here on out, he knew in his gut Sam was going to be part of Jessica's future. An integral part.

Fact two: From here on out, Sam would be an occasional visitor seen coming and going from Moose.

Fact three: From here on out, every ranger would speculate on what was happening between him and Jessica's mother.

More than ever it was imperative he visit Gilly King on Monday. And if that didn't work because the feelings weren't there, then he'd tell Rex Hollister, Pierce's assistant, to go ahead and line him up with his wife's younger sister.

Melanie had recently graduated from medical school and was now practicing pediatrics in Evanston, Wyoming. From the pictures Rex had shown Nick, she was an attractive blonde who loved to get out in nature.

Up until twenty minutes ago, the idea of a blind

date had been horrifying to Nick, but no longer. Not since Sam had caught up to him in the airport parking lot, sounding out of breath and looking a little pale. A part of him had been alarmed because the exertion might have been too much for her.

Another part of him was shaken because he cared so much, he'd wanted to sweep her into his arms and kiss away her tears.

Lord—it was happening all over again. That certain feeling that had gotten him into trouble the first time.

Waves of desire were washing over him. He didn't know how in the hell to fight them, not with her sitting there within touching distance, unknowingly tempting him. He had to do something to fight his yearnings.

While Jessica bonded with her mother, now would be the time to work on the one element of his life that had been missing for too many years. Pierce had been dead right about that.

Nick pulled to a stop in the Tanners' driveway. "I won't be long." Without casting Sam a backward glance, he levered himself from the cab and walked up to their door.

Amanda's brother told him she and Jessica had left with their girlfriends. Nick thanked him and headed for the truck.

Under the circumstances, he decided it might be better if he took Sam to the house first, then went hunting for his daughter. She might have gone to the general store. Then again, she could be at one of the other girls' houses.

He would like to be able to talk to her right now, to tell her something important had happened. In the past he'd fought against letting Jessica have her own cell phone. But Sam's unexpected advent in their lives had already changed things so drastically, he was beginning to think it might be a good idea.

Ever since Leslie had bought a phone for six-year-old Cory, Jessica had wanted one. Nick had been forced to explain that Cory's case was special because he had an irrational fear of losing his father and needed to stay in close touch with him.

Now the joke was on Nick. Though it might not be irrational, he *did* fear for his daughter's happiness. When he'd dropped her off at Amanda's, she'd been deeply upset. They needed to talk.

He climbed back in the truck. "She wasn't there," he said. "I'll take you to the house, then call around to some of her friends."

During the sixty-second drive home, the woman at his side didn't say anything. When he pulled into the garage, she got out of the truck before he could help her. Once he opened the door to the house, she followed him through the kitchen to the living room.

How strange to think of the thousands of times he'd entered his house never dreaming Sam would walk over the threshold one day. Yet it felt so natural for them to be together again, he was stunned by the rightness of it.

At a glance, he spotted several parkas on the couch. Relief swept over him to see Jessica had brought her friends home. He could hear pop music coming from her bedroom.

His gaze swerved to Sam, who must have removed her new sheepskin jacket on the way in. There'd been a time when relieving her of her coat provided an excuse to pull her into his arms and kiss her senseless.

Was that why she'd been so quick to do it herself? Because she remembered? No. *Don't think about that, Kincaid.*

"Just a minute. I'll tell her you're here."

Might as well get the introductions over with now. Hopefully Sam's arrival would only cause a brief wonder, then everything could settle down to…normal.

What was that, anyway? Normal as he knew it was gone forever. As soon as he got a jump-start on a relationship with Gilly or whoever, he would create a different kind of normal. One that was good for him and his daughter.

One that would help him combat the emotions ripping him to pieces right now.

He walked down the hall and poked his head inside the room. Jessica and three of her friends were making posters for what looked like next week's school party. Nick didn't see the photo albums anywhere.

She'd been so distraught earlier, he had a hunch she'd decided not to show them to her friends yet. Jessica wasn't about to share precious information like that if she couldn't be sure of seeing her mother again.

"Hi, honey."

She lifted a despondent face to him. No sign of tears, but her eyes were still red-rimmed. "Hi, Dad."

"Hi, Mr. Kincaid," the girls said in unison.

"Hi, girls. You guys look busy."

Jessica got up from the floor and walked over to him. "How come you're home from work this early?"

"I didn't make it to the dam. Your mother has decided to stay over for another night. She's out in the living room."

His announcement was met with instant stillness.

There was no such thing as magic, but his daughter underwent a profound change, as if all the atoms in her body had suddenly lined up at attention.

"Come and introduce your friends to her before I take them home."

Like a star whose light had finally reached earth, her face gave off a new radiance. She turned to the others. "Do you guys want to meet my mom?"

Surprise dominated their expressions. Eager and curious, they left their markers and posters on the floor and followed Jessica to the living room. Nick watched from a distance.

"Mom? This is Amanda Tanner. Her dad's a ranger. And this is Jenny Hughes, whose dad owns the gas station in Moose. And this is Sandy Grayson. Her dad owns the guest cabins down the road.

"Guys? This is my mother, Samantha Bretton. She's an attorney for the Idaho National Wildlife Federation in Coeur D'Alene, Idaho."

The pride in Jessica's eyes as she showed off her mother told Nick this had to be one of the supreme moments of her life.

Her friends took their own mothers for granted. It was only natural. In Jessica's particular circle, everyone had two parents who were still married to each other and lived together.

Nick's daughter had grown up with good friends, but there'd been a few people in her past who'd labeled her the product of a broken home. The stereotype carried a certain sting.

There was a point in her childhood when she'd mentioned feeling inadequate because she didn't have a mom in the house. Nick understood Jessica's feelings, but was powerless to do anything about them. It seemed to her that the golden kids, the ones with two parents, sailed through life with feelings of superiority and confidence.

So Jessica feared there were those who thought a person with only half a family couldn't possibly reach maturity and expect to be a whole person.

Certain shows on television discussed the pros and cons of being raised in a one-parent home. It was argued that some children might not make the best marriage prospects if they grew up without having had both role models to learn from.

Nick knew some people thought of her as his love child. No marriage, no divorce, only abandonment by her birth mother.

Jessica's journey had definitely been harder than Nick's. Growing up, he'd been viewed by some as that poor boy who'd lost his parents—how tragic it was that he didn't have a father to teach him how to be a man. How tragic to be left with a daughter to raise all alone. That Kincaid boy must have been born under an unlucky star.

Nick had heard it all. So had his daughter, who'd poured out her heart to him in her dark moments. But it didn't matter. So far they'd made it through the growing years just fine. In spite of everything, he and Jessica were happy. That's what counted.

Given the chance to do things over again, he would have made the same choice to keep his daughter with him. If he'd listened to the Brettons, she would undoubtedly have been adopted by a loving couple.

But no one could ever have loved her the way he did. Thank heaven for his uncle Willard, who'd understood his deepest feelings. The man who'd taken over the responsibility of raising him had been a thousand percent behind him when he'd made certain he got custody of Jessica.

Maybe he was looking over Nick's shoulder right now. Nick could imagine him smiling at his little redheaded poppet, a replica of the woman who'd endowed her with those blue eyes and that porcelain skin.

As he watched his daughter interact, he realized this was Jessica's moment in the sun, to brag and preen over her mother's four-year academic scholarship to Harvard, her prestigious law degree.

Do it, honey. Knock 'em dead listing all the accomplishments of the Bretton side of your family. Make them sit up and stare.

Nick knew he shouldn't be enjoying this so much, but he couldn't help it. With every revelation about Jessica's remarkable mother, her friends' eyes grew bigger and rounder.

"Did you know there's going to be a mother-and-daughter party at our school next Friday night?" Sandy informed her. "My mom and I are in charge of it."

"Jessica told me," Nick heard Sam say. "I'll be coming with her. Can we bring food? My daughter makes a fabulous chocolate mint cake from an old Bretton family recipe."

Sandy blinked. "I didn't know that. Sure! The party's potluck. Mom's going to make chili dogs."

"How about if Jessica and I contribute some barbecued baby back ribs, too? They're another family favorite."

"That would be great." Sandy sounded totally shocked.

Nick had problems holding back his laughter.

"Did you know there's going to be a talent show too?" Jenny asked.

Sam nodded. "What are you and your mom going to do?"

"Probably sing a medley from *Fiddler On The Roof*."

"Don't you love Tevye?"

"Tevye?"

"Umm. The father. You know. 'If I were a rich man…'" Sam's eyebrows lifted expressively. "'Yabba yabba yabba yabba doo.'"

"Oh," Jenny murmured. "I don't know that one."

"There were a lot of songs from that musical. Tevye's was a man's song, anyway." Sam smoothed over the moment. "What about you and your mom, Amanda?"

"We're going to do a gymnastics routine. She did gymnastics in college."

"How exciting!" Sam exclaimed with genuine pleasure. "I can't wait to watch." She turned to Sandy. "Are you and your mom going to perform, too?"

"Yeah. I play the violin. Mom's going to accompany me."

Sam smiled at all of them. "With everyone so talented, it sounds like a wonderful evening's in store. I can hardly wait."

Nick decided it was time to step in. "If you girls want to get your posters out of the bedroom, I'll drive you home."

They hurried to gather up their things. He helped them on with their parkas. Everyone walked out to the Xtera, even Sam. "It was wonderful meeting you girls. See you next Friday!"

As Nick backed out of the garage, the sight of her standing in the doorway leading into the kitchen haunted him. He looked away to discover two pairs of eyes staring at him from the back seat.

Jessica's friends were definitely viewing him in a different light. He was no longer the man of mystery he'd once been. His past had caught up to him.

Nick could hear them having to reconstruct their thinking. It was serious business trying to figure out who Jessica Kincaid really was.... No doubt about it. Sam's unexpected entry into Jessica's life had given them a lot to think about.

Unfortunately, Sam had given him a lot to think about, too.

ONCE THEY WERE BACK in the house, Samantha turned to her daughter. "Is that upright piano in the living room a decoration only?"

A tiny smile bent the corner of her mouth. "Dad's family gave it to us when his uncle Willard died. They said he wanted me to have it because I always liked to make noise on it when we went to his house."

"What a fabulous gift. He must have loved you a lot."

She nodded. "Dad told me I'd better learn to really play it so it wouldn't go to waste."

"And do you?"

"Kind of. In seventh grade I started taking piano lessons from a lady in Jackson. Now the high school orchestra teacher gives me a half-hour lesson every Tuesday and Thursday after my last class. But I'm not very good.''

''Do me a huge favor and let me hear you?''

''Okay. But promise you won't laugh.''

''I would never do that.''

She followed Jessica into the living room and watched her pull some music from the piano bench. After a false start, her daughter played a familiar Beethoven prelude with surprisingly good technique.

''That was terrific! Don't stop. Play something else.''

Soon Jessica had executed an excellent rendition of the ''Shepherd's Song'' from Debussy's *Children's Corner.*

''You have a fine touch,'' Sam declared when she'd finished. ''Let's see what else you've learned.''

With a smile on her face, Jessica moved off the bench so Samantha could look through the rest of her music. Her eye fell on a book of Schubert duets. She drew it out and closed the piano bench.

''Have you learned any pieces from this yet?''

Jessica nodded. ''The 'Marche Caracteristique.' My teacher plays it with me.''

''I bet you had to learn the top part.''

''Yup. How do you know that?''

''Because I took piano lessons from the time I was seven until I was sixteen. My teacher made me learn this piece, too. Come on. Let's see how we sound together.''

For the next little while Samantha had the time of her life playing the lower part of the duet with her daughter. They did several run-throughs to work out the kinks, then pulled off a fairly polished performance.

When they'd finished, their cry of triumph was drowned out by someone clapping. Samantha turned around on the bench. Nick had come into the living room without them being aware of it.

Earlier, at the airport, his eyes had resembled twin thunderheads. Now they gleamed silver. "I know a gymful of mothers and daughters who'll be green with envy when the Kincaid-Bretton duo takes all the honors."

Jessica ran over and hugged her father. "Can you believe Mom plays the piano, too?"

"I knew she'd taken lessons."

"But your father never heard me play. I'm afraid I gave it up before we met," Samantha confessed. "As of now, however, I repent of every minute I ever cursed my parents and piano teacher for making me practice. I'm in awe of your talent, darling. In fact I'm so proud of you, I can hardly stand it!"

Her daughter's face glowed. "Thanks, but you're the expert."

"No. I haven't touched the piano in years."

"It didn't sound that way to me," Nick said.

"You know what they say. It's like riding a bike. You never forget. Except that there's all the difference in the world between getting around the block in one piece, and winning the Tour de France."

Nick burst into laughter.

Samantha hadn't heard that beautiful sound since before the night she'd told him she was pregnant. Right now a smiling, laughing Nick from the past was too much for her to handle.

Jessica gave her a speculative glance. "How come you decided to stay another night? I thought you had a…date."

A date.

If her daughter meant with a man, Samantha needed to disabuse her of that notion. Jessica was so busy internalizing every bit of information, the last thing Samantha wanted was for her to get the wrong impression.

Nick was the only special man in or out of Samantha's life. To tell her daughter anything else would be a lie, and it would worry her unnecessarily.

"I have a friend named Marilyn May. She might as well be a sister to me. We're that close. She still thinks I'm coming back tonight. I need to call her and let her know I won't be home until tomorrow."

"Oh." Jessica's face brightened. "Are you staying at the Elk Inn again?"

"I haven't made any plans yet."

Nick moved closer to them. "I went to the airport to see if I could catch your mother before she left. Luckily, she hadn't boarded the plane, so we were able to talk. I told her how upset you were."

Their daughter's features froze. "I wish you hadn't done that, Dad."

"I'm glad he did," Samantha interjected, "otherwise I wouldn't have known how he really felt about my going to the mother-and-daughter party with you."

"What do you mean?"

The truth, Samantha. She would always tell the truth from here on out. Once upon a time she'd lied to Nick by not telling him she was underage. That sin of omission had changed the course of history. *Never again.*

"When you were born, I'd made the promise to my parents that I would give you up, so the doctor didn't allow me to see you or hold you after the delivery." In the retelling, she found her nails digging into the palms of her hands.

"Soon after your father took you home from the hospital, I had to sign papers giving him sole custody of you. That meant I had no moral or legal rights to see you or be with you ever again. It was the law." Sam took a breath.

"But I broke that law by calling him last week and asking him if I could visit you, anyway. He was noble enough to tell you I'd phoned, and to let me come. I didn't know if it was a one-time concession he'd made for me out of the goodness of his heart or not. To be honest, I was terrified to ask for more time with you in case he felt I was trying to take advantage of that goodness.

"It's the only reason I told you I couldn't go to the party with you. Do you understand what I'm saying now?"

"Honey…" Nick put a hand on Jessica's shoulder because she wasn't talking. "I couldn't figure out why Sam had turned you down for the party. I must confess it angered me because, like you said, it seemed pointless for her to bring the albums if she had no intention of seeing you again.

"I wanted an explanation from her so I could put a stop to your pain one way or the other. When I learned the truth, it cleared up the misunderstanding. She wants to go to the party with you. *I* want her to go with you.''

Their daughter studied them for a full minute. Samantha could almost hear her brain working. ''If it was against the law to try and see me, but you broke it anyway, how come it took you so long before you did it?''

So much pain and longing echoed in that one question....

''I never wanted to sign the papers, Jessica, but a promise is a promise. Don't forget I lied to your father by not telling him I was only seventeen. When he told me he didn't date cute little freshmen girls, I knew I couldn't reveal the truth. Otherwise he really *wouldn't* have dated me. It was a sin of omission, and it was wrong.

''Your father deserved better. In fact, he deserved the best I could give. I felt that if I honored that promise, then it would be the best I could give. So life went on. He went his way with you. I went mine. I excelled in school and was able to pick the job I wanted after receiving my law degree. But I would be telling a lie if I said that I never looked back.

''A few weeks ago the pastor of my church came to visit me. He asked if there was anything in my life I hadn't resolved. His question set off an explosion inside me like the one that blew the top off Mount Saint Helens. I thought, I hoped, I prayed maybe your father would forgive me if I tried to see you this one time so I could tell you how much I've always loved you.''

Jessica's eyes welled with tears. ''I'm so glad you called.''

"So am I, darling."

Whether it was right or wrong, Samantha opened up her arms. Her daughter came running into them.

Through the red-gold curls she could see the concern in Nick's eyes. During the next heart-to-heart with her daughter, and there were going to be more in the future, thanks to his generosity, Samantha would tell her about her medical history.

"Dad?" Jessica said after finally letting her go. "Can Mom stay here tonight? I'll put her in my bedroom, and I'll sleep on the hide-a-bed in here."

"You two make any arrangements you want. I'm going to run to the dam, and should be back for dinner by six-thirty."

Jessica turned a euphoric face to Samantha. "That means seven-fifteen to seven-thirty."

Samantha chuckled.

"What do you want for dinner, Dad?"

"Tacos will be fine," Nick called over his shoulder. Within seconds Samantha could hear the sound of the truck as he backed out of the garage.

"Mom? What was one of dad's favorite foods when you two were dating?"

"Pizza."

"Besides that? We have it all the time, and spaghetti and tacos."

"Well, he didn't have much money to pay for anything more expensive. Sometimes I provided the picnic if we went boating. Most of the time he and his buddies ate macaroni and cheese in the dorm, and we went out for ice cream. He put up peanut butter sandwiches to take to work."

''Dad still does that.'' Her brows met together. ''Can't you think of anything else?''

''Hmm. Sunday dinner was sacrosanct at my home. Because I knew my parents would be upset if they found out how much time I spent with your father, I never asked if he could come to dinner.

''As soon as it was over and I'd helped with the dishes, I'd drive one of our cars to his work and stay with him until he got off at nine. Sometimes if I could get away with it, I'd take some leftover roast in foil so he could make sandwiches. He often talked about the great roast dinners he ate at his uncle Willard's.''

''What kind of roast?''

''Probably beef, since your relatives ran cattle on their property.''

Jessica glanced at her watch. ''It's three-twenty. If we bought a roast, how long do you think it would take to cook?''

''You don't have one in your freezer?''

''Dad never buys roast. Besides, he uses the freezer to store all his experiments and stuff.''

It was Samantha's turn to chuckle. ''A beef tenderloin roast cooks up pretty fast.''

''If you drove me to the store we could be back in ten minutes.''

She bit her lip. ''Your father might not like me taking his car.''

''I promise he won't care. There's an extra set of keys in the drawer.'' Jessica dashed into the kitchen for them. ''This is so cool. I finally have someone who can drive me besides Dad!''

They both put on their jackets before leaving. Samantha was happy to do her part, but she drew the line at going in the store. She was afraid it might create too much attention. Nick wouldn't like it.

"Tell you what," she said once they'd pulled into the parking area. "While you get the meat and a nice cauliflower, I'll fill the car with gas. It's running on empty as we speak."

"Okay. Charge it to Dad. He has an account there."

"Fine," Samantha said, though she had every intention of paying for the gas herself. "I'll be back in five minutes."

She made a U-turn and started down the road. Buying gas for Nick's car was the least she could do for him. He'd made a miracle happen by allowing her to have a relationship with Jessica. There wasn't enough she could do for him in return.

When she pulled in next to a pump, she closed her eyes for a minute. *If this is a dream, don't let me wake up.*

Someone tapped on the window. She jerked her head around, then pressed the button to lower the glass.

"Hi there." A fortyish-looking man smiled at her with male admiration.

"Hello. Would you fill it with unleaded please?"

"You bet." After he'd put the nozzle in the tank he came back to her. "For a minute I thought Jessica had taken her dad's car on a joy ride."

Uh-oh. "No. I'm her mother."

He grinned. "You look too young."

The man had to be kidding!

"I'm Bill Hughes, a friend of Nick's."

"Oh yes. I met your daughter Jenny a little while ago. She's a lovely girl."

"Thank you. So's Jessica. Are you here on a vacation?"

What to say? "I came to visit my daughter." Before he could ask another question she said, "I'll be back in a week to go to the mother-and-daughter party with her at the school."

"That'll make Jessica's day."

"It has already made mine. How much do I owe you?"

"That's okay. This tank's on me."

Samantha could have argued about it but decided not to. "Thank you very much, Mr. Hughes. It's nice to have met you."

He nodded. "You're welcome. Next time call me Bill."

"I will," she said, doubting very much she'd be seeing him again.

After putting up the window, she swung the car around and drove back to the store. Jessica still hadn't come out yet. While Sam waited, she decided now would be a good time to call Marilyn.

To her dismay she got her friend's voice mail instead of a live person. Samantha left a brief message about her plans and told her she'd see her tomorrow after she arrived at the condo.

As she was putting her phone back in her purse, there was another tap on the window. She turned her head in time to see two rangers in hats standing there studying her. They looked to be in their early twenties. Cute.

"Yes?" she said after lowering the window again.

"Sorry, ma'am. We thought Jessica was driving

Ranger Kincaid's car and came over to give her a lecture before her dad caught her.''

This was probably going to be a regular occurrence until Samantha met everyone in Moose! But she couldn't help wondering if Jessica had a bit of a problem. Most teenagers wanted to drive a car before they were old enough. Did Nick know about it?

"I'm her mother."

"Sorry for the mistake, Mrs. Kincaid." They both tipped their hats and stepped away from the car to their patrol truck.

"Wait—" she called out, intending to correct them, but they took off too fast. Samantha sat back in the seat.

Mrs. Kincaid...

That's what she could have been if—*No, don't even dare think about it.*

"Hi, Mom." Jessica shut the passenger door. "I got everything we needed. What did the rangers want?"

She turned her head toward her daughter and told her about both incidents.

Jessica's mouth broke into a smile. "That's so cool. Everyone thinks we look alike."

Samantha had her answer. Jessica hadn't been doing anything illegal behind Nick's back. They started for the house. "There's only one problem. They called me Mrs. Kincaid."

"That'll frost Dad." But she said it with a grin.

"I'm sure it will," Samantha muttered.

"Don't worry about it, Mom. They're new recruits who don't know anything yet. Dad says they're wet behind the ears."

Her dad was bigger than life to her.

When they carried the groceries into the kitchen a few minutes later, the phone was ringing. Jessica reached for it. "Kincaid residence."

Samantha removed her jacket, then washed her hands and took the paper off the roast. Jessica anticipated her actions and found a pan so it could go in the oven.

"I'd love to baby-sit Cory, but my mom stayed over and won't be going back to Idaho until tomorrow. I'm sorry—"

"Jessica? Tell her just a minute."

Her daughter blinked. "Leslie? Hold on for a sec." She put a hand over the mouthpiece. "What is it?"

"I don't mind if Cory comes over. He's the son of your dad's best friend. I'd like to meet him. I want to be a part of your life, get to know your friends." *I want to be a part of Nick's. I want things I have no right to ask for.*

"Cory's a lot of fun. I'll tell him to bring some of his games."

"Good. I love games."

Her daughter flashed her a smile that reminded her of Nick at his most competitive. "So do I."

She turned back to the phone. "Leslie? Mom says it's fine with her. She wants to meet Cory. Bring him and Lucy over anytime. What? Okay. Just a minute." Jessica handed her the phone. "She wants to talk to you."

Samantha nodded. "Hello, Leslie? This is Samantha Bretton. I've heard a lot about you. All of it absolutely wonderful."

CHAPTER SEVEN

NICK HAD JUST PUT the last soil sample into his carrying case when his phone went off. He glanced at the caller ID and answered. "Hi, Rex. What's going on?"

"My wife's sister drove up from Evanston for the weekend. We thought we'd invite a few friends for dinner. How would you like to come? This is totally impromptu."

"What time do you want me to be there?" He fired back the question without having to think about it.

There was a pause. "Am I talking to the right Nick Kincaid?" Rex asked, sounding as if he didn't quite believe his ears.

"Do you know another one?" he teased.

"Yeah. I know a Nick who wouldn't accept a blind date if you bribed him with a million bucks."

"Oh. *That* Nick. He used to have a problem with his daughter who suffered from separation anxiety. But the problem appears to have been fixed. At least for this weekend. So I'm your man."

"You sound different, you know that?" Rex said in a more serious tone. "For a lot of reasons I'm glad to hear it."

"What time do you want me for dinner?" Nick redirected the conversation. Right now he didn't want to think, let alone talk, about Sam.

"Seven-thirty. Don't worry about my sister-in-law. She's as gun-shy as you are in the being-set-up-for-a-date department. If there's chemistry between the two of you, it's anyone's guess which of you will be the more surprised."

"Message received. Thanks for the invite, Rex. Tell your wife I'm looking forward to it."

He rang off and climbed in the cab of the truck. His watch said twenty to seven. It would take him a half hour to get home. If he hurried, he'd make it to the Hollisters' by seven-thirty or thereabouts. Jessica had probably fixed tacos for her mother. He would enjoy the leftovers tomorrow.

He knew he was dead wrong the second he walked into the kitchen. The smell of roast and everything that went with it assailed him. The kitchen table had been set with a cloth and matching napkins for four people.

On the way to his bedroom he glanced into the living room and discovered towheaded Cory at the piano with Jessica. They were playing chopsticks. Lucy followed Nick down the hall. She sniffed at his pants, which smelled of dam water, sending her into ecstasy.

When Sam unexpectedly came out of Jessica's bedroom dressed in a pair of navy sweats, the kind he liked to wear around the house, his heart missed several beats.

She let out a soft gasp. "You're home! Jessica will be thrilled. She has worked so hard on this dinner for you. The only thing she let me do was set the table according to her exact specifications."

Nick stifled a groan. How could he have been so stupid? Of course his daughter had wanted to impress her mother with this first meal. She wanted to show that she'd grown up to be the perfect little hostess who'd been taking good care of her father all these years. This was something she needed to prove in front of both her parents.

Unfortunately, he'd already committed to Rex and couldn't back out now. He had to think fast to come up with a solution that wouldn't disappoint his daughter or his friend.

"I'll be ready in five minutes. I have other plans for this evening so I'll have to eat quickly."

She didn't flick an eyelash. "Then I'll help her put everything on the table right now."

"Thanks."

His eyes followed her retreating figure before he realized he didn't have time to dwell on the curves she'd retained in spite of her weight loss. While Lucy raced after her, he dashed into his bedroom and took a two-minute shower.

Once he'd shaved and dressed in a pullover and trousers, he phoned Rex and told him not to hold dinner for him, that he'd be there by eight-fifteen at the latest. Being the good man he was, Rex didn't ask questions, only thanked him for the call.

The vegetables and gravy along with the roast were so good, Nick asked for a third helping. Jessica may have done the cooking, but Sam had provided the impetus and the know-how.

Cory's blue eyes looked huge behind the glasses he wore to correct his amblyopia. "How can you eat that much?"

"Like Popeye and his spinach, rangers have to eat lots of meat and potatoes to keep up their strength," Sam explained.

"But I like pizza," Cory said, sounding a little worried before he took another bite from the slice Jessica had warmed up for him.

Sam smiled. "Everyone loves pizza, Cory. Nick ate it almost every day at college. All that protein and calcium in the cheese gave him big muscles and beautiful white teeth."

"Really?" Cory stared at Nick with new appreciation.

Nick was afraid to look at Sam, who'd just given Cory a lot to think about. In the process of making him feel good about his limited food preference, she'd brought up a whole host of intimate memories better left in the deep freeze.

He pushed himself away from the table and walked around to hug his daughter. "That was the best meal I ever tasted. Thanks, honey."

"You're welcome."

"It was out of this world, darling."

"Thanks, Mom."

Jessica looked happy.

Obviously Sam had told his daughter he was going out. To his amazement she seemed all right with it, otherwise his departure would have robbed her of the joy of the moment.

"Where are you going?" Cory asked.

"To the Hollisters'. They're having a party."

"Mom and Dad already left for their house."

That news didn't surprise Nick. Rex and his wife must have figured the more friends around, the easier this blind date would go. "Are you going to sleep over at our house tonight, sport?"

"Yup. I brought my sleeping bag. Lucy'll be good."

"Terrific. See all you guys in the morning."

"We'll be quiet in case you want to stay unconscious till ten, Dad."

"I appreciate that. Good night."

Because the Xtera needed gas and Nick couldn't fill it up until tomorrow when he took Sam to the airport, he drove the truck to the Hollisters', who lived a couple of blocks away.

Pierce had parked his Grand Cherokee in front of the house behind an unfamiliar Chevy Tahoe. It probably belonged to Evanston's newest doctor.

Rex's wife showed him inside and introduced him to her sister, Melanie, a tall blonde who was attractive in an athletic kind of way. It looked as if everyone was at the dessert stage of dinner. Though Nick was stuffed, he didn't dare refuse the apple pie à la mode.

Except for Pierce and Leslie, no one knew Sam was in Moose. Though Nick could depend on the Gallaghers' discretion not to say anything about it, the coincidence of Melanie visiting her sister at the same time was amazing to say the least.

The evening turned out to be a pleasant one. Melanie was laid-back, yet interesting to talk to. Nick found the Hollisters' latest home movies of a family trip to Cancun with their eight- and nine-year-olds entertaining.

But before they'd finished viewing everything, Pierce received an emergency call from headquarters at the same moment a couple of the younger park rangers appeared at Rex's front door. Everyone assembled in the foyer to find out what was wrong.

It seemed a semi had plowed into one end of the Moose visitors' center following a high-speed police chase. The rangers had gotten involved when the truck didn't stop at the entrance to the park.

"That's a new one for the books," Pierce muttered. "We're on our way."

Nick eyed Pierce. "We'll go in my truck."

"Do you want us to run your wives home?" one of the rangers asked.

"I thought you guys knew I'm not married," Nick told them.

"Whoops. Today we saw your Xtera in front of the store and thought Jessica was in the driver's seat. That is until we went over to talk to her and met her beautiful mother." *What?* "I called her Mrs. Kincaid by accident. Sorry."

Oh hell. Did the idiot have to blurt it out for Melanie to hear? Nick turned to her. "I'll call you tomorrow before you leave for Evanston."

"That's okay, Nick. I'll be leaving early, but it was nice to have met you."

AT EIGHT IN THE MORNING, everyone tiptoed down the hall to the front door as prearranged. Cory hurried out to Leslie's Grand Cherokee with Lucy and got in front. Samantha stood on the front porch and breathed in the cold air while she waited for Jessica to put the note she'd written to her father under the fridge magnet.

This morning like yesterday was overcast. Mist shrouded the peaks of the Tetons. She didn't think the temperature had dipped to freezing, but it had to be close to it. Not the greatest weather for flying, but no new storms had been forecast.

"Dad came in at five, so I shut off his alarm," Jessica informed her.

If Nick hadn't come home from a party until this morning, then he had to be involved with a woman who mattered to him. The knowledge shouldn't have hurt Samantha, but it did. In fact, she felt shattered, but she couldn't let her daughter know it.

Jessica pulled the door shut before they both walked to the car, where Leslie Gallagher stood waiting. With her stylish, light-brown hair and hazel eyes, Cory's new mom was a stunning woman, Samantha thought. She imagined they were about the same age.

The other woman had been so easy to talk to on the phone that Samantha was already prepared to like her. When Leslie gave her a spontaneous hug instead of a handshake, Samantha felt as if she'd gained a new friend.

Leslie took her suitcase and put it in the rear of the car while Samantha and Jessica climbed in the back. The heater was going strong. It felt good.

Once they were off, Leslie said, "Guess what, Cory? In just a minute you're going to see a sight you've never seen before."

Hugging his dog, he peered at her from behind his glasses. "How come?"

"Because I don't think an eighteen-wheeler truck has ever driven straight into the wall of the Moose Visitors' Center before."

"You're kidding!" Jessica cried.

"Nope. That's why Pierce and your father didn't get home until five this morning. There was so much cleanup to do, the poor things will probably sleep till late this afternoon."

"Oh my gosh!" Jessica blurted the moment the center came into view. It did look like a war zone to Samantha, with all the yellow police tape and cars and rangers milling around keeping tourists away.

Sheets of plastic protected the gaping hole in the end of the building. The damaged semi had been moved to the side parking lot. There was already a construction crew on the site.

"What a mess!"

"You can say that again, honey." Leslie patted Cory's arm.

"How come the driver rammed into the building?"

"Your dad said he was a bank robber from Jackson who killed the real driver to get away from the police. By the time he reached Moose, the police and rangers had him blocked so he couldn't go forward or backward, so he drove into the center."

"Is he dead?"

"No. He's at the hospital being treated for cuts before they take him to jail."

Samantha leaned forward. "Was anyone in the center hurt?"

"No. None of the skeletal crew were in the reception area at the time of the accident."

"That was a blessing." The thought of anything happening to Nick made Samantha ill. On the other hand, the fact that he hadn't been out with a woman all night made her so euphoric she wanted to shout for joy.

"You're right," Leslie murmured, sounding shaken by the threat to her husband's safety. Who could blame her?

Jessica bit her lip. "Thank goodness Dad's and Pierce's offices are down on the other end."

"Can we go look inside?"

"We don't have time, Cory honey, but your father will show us around later. Right now we need to take Samantha to Grayson's so she can book a cabin for next weekend. Then we're going to have breakfast in Jackson before we take her to the plane."

Cory looked over his shoulder at Samantha. "I wish you didn't have to go home today. Will you play Dragon Ball Z with me again when you come next weekend?"

"I'd love to," she exclaimed before Leslie could say anything. "Maybe we could all go to a movie in Jackson on Saturday after the school party. And later, you could come to my cabin with Lucy. We'll play games, eat pizza and have another sleepover."

"Goody! Can I, Mom?" he begged.

"Are you sure?" Leslie asked Samantha, eyeing her through the rearview mirror. "After being up all night with the girls, you may be too exhausted."

Samantha appreciated the other woman's concern. Undoubtedly Nick had told Pierce and his wife about her medical history.

"We're positive, aren't we, Jessica!" she declared in an attempt to reassure Leslie she was fine. Getting involved in her daughter's life was the greatest thing that had happened to her in thirteen years.

Jessica looked starry-eyed. "It'll be perfect."

"How come you have to go home today?" Cory demanded.

"Because I've got a court case in the morning to prepare for."

"Did somebody do something bad?"

"They *want* to. I'm asking the judge for an injunction to stop loggers from building a road."

"What's an injunkshun?"

"It means I want him to tell those people 'No, you can't build a road there.'"

"Where do they want to put it?"

"In the Kelly Creek area."

"Where's that?"

"In the Wild Clearwater country in north-central Idaho. They call it the Yellowstone of Idaho. Every time a new road is built, it ruins the habitats of the animals, and brings people who pollute the clean air and water. More roads mean more mining, all of which destroys the rivers and streams."

"Dad says that's really bad."

"Your father's right, Cory. We all have to fight to preserve the environment."

Jessica eyed her mother. "Dad could use you to fight for the Endangered Species Act."

"Why hasn't he hired an attorney before now?"

"The funding has been cut off except for necessities. Pierce has asked the governor to do something about getting extra money for one. I'm a reporter on the school newspaper staff covering issues that Teton Park has to deal with," Jessica told her.

"Good for you! My daughter the nature activist!"

Leslie chuckled. "Living in the park is turning me into one, too."

"Isn't it unfortunate that everything always comes down to money," Samantha mused aloud. Nick had to be frustrated out of his mind.

"Look, Mom. There's Grayson's! I'll get Sandy to

ask her dad to give you the corner cabin. It's the biggest one, and has a picnic table along the window where we can play games.''

Samantha's gaze swerved to the grouping of white-trimmed guest cabins, very rustic and cozy-looking with curls of smoke rising from some of the chimneys. The Tetons formed a breathtaking winter backdrop. She couldn't wait to stay here.

She never wanted to leave....

NICK CAME AWAKE all of a sudden, which was strange because the house seemed quiet as a tomb. He glanced at his watch. One-thirty?

Sam. She was supposed to be on the noon plane!

His adrenaline surging, he jackknifed into a sitting position and checked his alarm. It was pushed in. He distinctly remembered setting it for eight o'clock before collapsing into bed after the all-nighter at the visitors' center.

Had he heard it go off and then gone back to sleep?

Pulling on the bottoms of a pair of gray sweats, he hurried out of the room. The bed in Jessica's room was made up, with no sign of Sam or her suitcase. Further investigation proved no one was in the house.

His daughter had left him a message in the usual place.

Dear Dad, Leslie came and got all of us in her car. We've gone to Jackson to have brunch at the Moran Grill, then we'll take Mom to the airport. Cory wants to go ice-skating later, so we might do that. When you get up, there's plenty of roast to make sandwiches, and there's chocolate mint

cake in the fridge, too. Enjoy your day. Love,
Jessica.

Nick reread the note. *Enjoy my day?*
What daughter was this?
Certainly not his little guardian of hearth, home and
family. Not the little worrywart who until yesterday
needed to know his every move ahead of time if it was
at all possible.
He couldn't ever remember having this kind of luxury to be alone in his own house, knowing Jessica was
feeling totally secure away from him.
Security.
That's what Sam had given their daughter by entering her life. But if she didn't stay in remission, the
thought of what it could do to Jessica was too terrible
to contemplate.
Nick bowed his head. Right now he'd be ungrateful
to entertain negative thoughts. He'd done too much of
that since the moment Sam had signed over their
daughter to him. That kind of thinking got you nowhere.
Seize the day, Kincaid. He was a free agent for a
few hours. He intended to make the most of them.
Before another minute passed he needed to call
Melanie. But when he reached for the receiver in the
kitchen, he couldn't bring himself to punch in the Hollisters' number. What would he say to her if she hadn't
left yet?
*You're a very nice, attractive woman who will make
some lucky man a wonderful wife?*
Maybe it was a blessing she'd overheard the ranger
talk about Jessica's mother being in Moose. Melanie

wasn't looking for a man with baggage. At least this way she wouldn't view last night's experience as a personal rejection.

Better to leave it alone and wait to thank Rex and his wife tomorrow when things were back to normal.

There was that word again. He shook his head. There was nothing normal about anything. Who was he kidding?

What he ought to do was call Gilly King. If she were free for lunch tomorrow, then he would avoid wasting time driving out of his way to see her, only to discover she wasn't there.

He headed for his bedroom where he kept a master list of phone numbers. After sinking down on the side of the bed, he picked up his cell phone and dialed the Mammoth ranger station.

The ranger who answered said she was off duty, but she'd be back on first thing in the morning. If Nick wanted to leave a message, the other man would make sure she got it.

Nick gave him his name and number asking her to call, then he hung up.

Normally he'd be starving by now, but for some reason he couldn't understand, he wasn't that hungry. He went to the living room for the Sunday paper, but the headlines with their usual attacks against the president bored him.

He threw it down on the coffee table, deciding to take a shower. Once he'd dressed, he would drive the car over to the gas station and fill it up so he could take off early in the morning.

Twenty minutes later he pulled up to one of the self-serve pumps. When Bill Hughes saw him from the doorway, he walked over. "How are you doing, Nick?"

"I'm good. How about you?"

"Can't complain."

"When Jessica's mother asked me to fill the tank with gas yesterday, for a moment I thought it was Jessica at the wheel. You could have knocked me over. Now I know why your daughter is such a little beauty."

Bill was the second person to tell him Sam had been driving around in his car yesterday. With her red hair and blue eyes, she was impossible to miss. Certainly Nick hadn't been immune to her charms the first time he'd seen her in the Lory Student Center. She'd stood out like a heavenly scented candle glowing in a dark room.

"Excuse me a minute, Bill," Nick muttered. He removed his hand from the gas hose and got back in the car to turn on the ignition. One glance and he could see the gas tank no longer registered empty. He hadn't even noticed on the drive over!

Jessica knew where he kept an extra set of car keys. She must have prevailed on Sam to drive them to the store, and Sam had realized it was almost out of gas. Nick had assumed they'd walked to the grocery store.

He turned to Bill. "Did she charge it to my account?"

"No. She tried to pay me cash, but I told her to forget it."

"That was very nice of you, but I'll take care of it now." He pulled a twenty dollar bill out of his wallet and tucked it in the chest pocket of Bill's uniform.

Nick could tell Jenny's father was dying to ask

questions, but he managed to refrain. It was just as well, since Nick was in no mood to answer them. In twenty-four hours, Sam had made a shambles of the ordered world he'd taken years to build.

"Thanks, Bill. See you later." He shut the door and drove off. Without knowing what he was doing, he ended up in Pierce's driveway.

To his surprise his friend's garage door suddenly opened and he saw the taillights of his truck flash red.

Nick honked so they wouldn't collide.

Pierce stood on his brakes. In the next instant he jumped down from the cab and walked out to the car. He shot Nick an ironic grin.

"We'd really make history if one of our young rangers happened to drive by and see the latest in a series of car-truck accidents within park boundaries. It would get back to Lewis Fry from the cable network, who has already sensationalized last night's story to the limit of his ability."

A sound of exasperation escaped Nick's throat. "I should have phoned first, but I didn't know I was coming over here until I pulled in your driveway. Now that I think about it, I left my cell phone on the nightstand."

"That explains why I couldn't reach you."

Sensing something was wrong, Nick sat up straighter. "What's up?"

Pierce's blue eyes studied him for a moment. "Jess admitted to Leslie that she turned off your alarm so you could sleep."

"That little monkey." She'd never done anything like that before. But then Sam had never been in Jessica's life before. Her presence had turned his daughter's life inside out just as thoroughly as his. "Leslie shouldn't have had to worry about getting Sam to the airport."

"My wife wanted to do it. It gave them a chance to get acquainted. When I couldn't reach you on the phone a few minutes ago, I thought either you were still dead to the world or…you were at the Hollisters'."

Nick stared back at him as they communicated without words. "Now you know."

"Yup. In that case, how would you like to go to Jackson? The kids should be through ice-skating by the time we get there. Cory wants to get hamburgers at Shiver's. I thought we'd join them."

"I'll drive," Nick said without having to think about it.

"Give me one second." Pierce moved his truck back into the garage, then joined Nick. "Let's get out of here."

"I owe Leslie for this."

"No you don't. Samantha booked a cabin at Grayson's for next Saturday night following the school party." Nick's body quaked. Sam was coming for the whole weekend? "She has already asked to let Cory sleep over with her and Jess. He was ecstatic when he told me about it on the phone.

"My son has always been crazy about your daughter. Now it seems Samantha has made a real hit with him, too, which is no small feat as we both know. Since he's all excited about it, Leslie and I have decided we're going to enjoy a mini honeymoon at the house."

Nick cleared his throat. "That's good. You two need it and deserve it."

"With Jess taken care of for the weekend, it looks like you'll be free to do whatever you want for a change."

Whatever I want. I wish I knew what that was.

You'd better figure it out fast, Kincaid. Otherwise you're facing the weekend from hell.

CHAPTER EIGHT

As Jessica entered the kitchen from the garage ahead of Nick, they both heard his cell phone ringing.

"That's probably Mom! She promised to call and let me know she got back to Coeur D'Alene safely. I'll get it!" Jessica was off like a shot.

He glanced at the clock on the wall. Seven-thirty. While they were eating hamburgers, Cory had informed Nick that Sam's plane had taken off at one. She would have been home quite a while by now. Did her friend pick her up, or had she left her own car in the airport parking lot?

According to Cory, he and Jessica had prevailed on Leslie to stay and watch the plane leave. Pierce's son was full of admiration for Jessica's mother. She'd taught him a new version of chopsticks on the piano and could beat everyone at his Space Raiders game. *And* she'd said pizza was good for growing boys who wanted to be rangers.

The disturbing realization that every thought in Nick's head had to do with Sam drove him to his lab to check out the latest soil samples for spores. Hopefully the first series of dam flushings had eradicated the problem.

He'd just opened his carrying case when Jessica said, "The phone's for you, Dad. I left it in your bedroom. It's Gilly King returning your call. Is it okay with you if I call Mom on *our* phone?''

What? No third degree to find out why he'd called Gilly in the first place?

''Go ahead.'' Jessica was so consumed by thoughts of her mother, nothing else seemed to register right now. Like daughter, like father?

The question haunted him all the way to his bedroom. He reached for his phone. ''Hi, Gilly. How are you?''

''Hi!'' She had a little-girl voice that was cute and deceiving because she was one tough ranger. ''I'm great! The question is, how are you? The news about the semi crashing into the visitors' center is all anyone can talk about around here.''

It took him a second to remember there'd been a disaster last night. Other things had been on his mind. Another woman had filled his thoughts.

''You'd be amazed what a mess it made. Too bad there has to be a funeral for the driver of that rig. He was just trying to do a day's work when he was attacked.''

''Isn't it always the culprits who seem to walk away without a scratch?''

''You've got that right.''

''Obviously you were trying to reach me about something. What's going on?''

''How would you like to have lunch with me tomorrow? I'm going to be in the general vicinity on business.''

''Lunch? I haven't had an invitation to lunch in so long I can't remember. I'd love it!''

''What time would be good for you?''

"Twelve-thirty?"

"All right. I'll pick you up at the ranger station and we'll drive to the Park Street Grill in Gardiner."

"Sounds terrific, Nick. Thanks for calling."

"My pleasure. See you tomorrow."

He hung up. That was easy enough. Too easy?

What in the hell is wrong with you, Kincaid? Did you want her to give you a hard time? Were you hoping she would tell you she was involved with someone else, but thanks anyway?

In a vile mood, he headed back to his lab. As he passed Jessica's room, he could see her on the bed, lying on her stomach with her legs up, ankles crossed. She moved them back and forth while she chatted happily with her mother.

He'd raised his daughter not to eavesdrop on other people's conversations, so took his own advice. But it almost required an act of nature for him to keep moving to the other bedroom. He could picture Sam on a bed in much the same position, her red-gold curls a lick of flame in the lamplight.

No sooner had he prepared some new slides than Jessica breezed into the room. "Dad? There's something important I have to ask you, but I don't want you to think it's because I don't love you."

His mouth grew taut. "I know you love me, honey. Just tell me what it is you're trying to say."

"How would you feel about me spending Thanksgiving with Mom and my grandparents in Denver?"

One of the slides fell to the floor and broke.

"Mom told them about seeing me, and they want to meet me."

He rubbed a hand over his face.

Like the big volcano that was building beneath Yellowstone Park—one that would make Mount Saint Helens look like a firecracker when it blew—the world he'd known with Jessica was starting to crack with a burst of steam here, a new geyser there, a hot lava bed suddenly visible where no lava bed had ever been before.

"If I go to their house, then I'll be able to meet my two great-grandparents from my grandfather's side, who are still living. They're too old to travel, but they'll be at my grandparents' for dinner.

"Dad, if you don't want me to go, I won't. But since the family has already invited us to Gillette for Thanksgiving, I thought maybe you wouldn't mind going alone this once. What do you think?" His little girl was so excited she had to catch her breath before continuing.

"Mom understands completely if you say no. She said the way her parents treated you was so unforgivable, she's not assuming anything. It's just that she wanted me to know she'd rather be with me than anything else this coming holiday."

Nick stifled a groan. He had to admit there'd been a time when he'd considered the Brettons' actions inhuman.

Nevertheless, having been a parent himself for thirteen years, and especially now that Jessica was a teenager, he understood to a greater extent where they'd been coming from when they'd learned their seventeen-year-old, not even out of high school yet, was pregnant.

These days Nick didn't see life in black-and-white, the way he once had. The fact that Sam had chosen to seek out her daughter whether her parents cared or not proved how independent she'd become.

It also indicated that her brush with death had softened their hearts to the extent they would welcome Jessica into their home, if only for their daughter's sake. The love of a child made you do a lot of things you never thought you would.

"Is your mother still on the phone?"

"No. She had to get off. Tomorrow she's got a big case to present in court, and she needs to work on it. Because she stayed over to be with me an extra night, she'll be up late preparing."

"What kind of case?" he asked before he could stop himself.

Jessica told him what she'd learned from Sam. "Next week Mom's going to bring me some copies of decisions she has won for the federation. I can use them to help document next month's school article on the ESA. She knows a ton of stuff, Dad. It's fantastic!"

It was fantastic all right. Fantastic that until ten days ago his cousins and their kids had made up the sum total of Jessica's family. With Sam's phone call, that world had expanded to include grandparents and great-grandparents.

Nick would have given anything if his own parents could have raised him and had the opportunity to know Jessica. So how could he deny her the experience of meeting her flesh and blood from Sam's side of the family?

"If you want to plan to spend Thanksgiving with her, it's fine with me, honey."

"You're the best, Dad." She gave him a hug. "Mom will pay for my flight to Denver and back."

He stiffened. "I think I can afford to send my daughter on a trip."

"Mom said she knew you would say that. She hopes you'll let her do it because it would make her feel more like a parent and she loves the feeling."

Sam had the knack of getting to him and breaking down his defenses the way no one else could except his own daughter.

When he'd first seen Sam in the student center on campus, she'd had *freshman* written all over her. For several days he'd fought his instant attraction to her, yet that hadn't put her off. She'd seen it as a challenge. Who else would have used such a forceful approach and simply drop all her books next to his chair?

Her phone call on Halloween had had the effect of those heavy texts, exploding like a hundred-ton bomb when they reached the floor of the quiet library. *Boom!* There she was in his face again, up close and personal.

He remembered her words—"I've battled with cancer and have won this round, Nick. Will you let me see my daughter?" It had been a fait accompli before he could think of an exit strategy.

If she handled herself in court the same way, the opposition didn't stand a chance. No one did, least of all their vulnerable daughter, who was more like her mother than either of them knew.

Only now was Nick beginning to realize just how similar.

AN ODD NOVEMBER warm spell prompted Samantha's rowing instructor to get everyone out on Coeur

D'Alene lake for one more session before class resumed in the spring. The sun at high noon kept the chill out of the air, but the denuded trees let them know autumn was fast fading into winter.

Samantha hadn't thought she would live to see another one. At this time last year she'd had no hope of meeting her daughter in the flesh. She'd assumed that opportunity would have to wait until the next life.

Now, unbelievably, she was flying to Jackson Hole tomorrow afternoon to be with her adorable Jessica. Nick would be there!

The following weekend she would be taking her daughter to Denver to meet the family. While they were in Colorado, Samantha intended to show her all around the college town of Fort Collins, an hour's drive from Denver.

While she was counting her blessings, she heard the instructor say, "We're coming in to shore. Secure your oars."

In a few minutes everyone had climbed out of the boat and said their goodbyes until next year. Samantha drove Marilyn back to the hospital, where she worked in the pharmacy.

Before her friend got out of the car she turned to Samantha. "I'll be in front of your condo tomorrow at one to take you to the airport."

"Thanks a million, Marilyn."

"You don't need to thank me. I'm so grateful Reed is giving you the time off to come to Phoenix after Thanksgiving, you'll never know. If you're there for the first week, I feel like I can make it through."

"Of course you're going to make it through! You're

a survivor like me!'' She'd decided to take the pastor's words to heart. *Think of this as permanent remission.*

They stared at each other. ''Those are beautiful words, Samantha Bretton. Wouldn't it be amazing if it were true? I'd love to get to know that daughter of yours.''

Samantha brushed tears from her eyes. ''You will. I promise.''

''I'll hold that thought.''

Once her friend got out of the car, Samantha headed to work without stopping at the condo to change clothes. Since she didn't have to see a client until tomorrow morning, she could hibernate in her office for the rest of the day. There was a lot of paperwork to finish up. More importantly, she'd promised Jessica some material for her next school newspaper article.

Ever since she'd learned that Nick had given his permission for their daughter to go to Denver, Samantha's feet hadn't touched the ground.

Before her transplant, she'd bared her soul to her parents where Jessica was concerned. They'd wept tears to realize she'd suffered for so long in silence.

Then the truth came out that they too had grieved, because she was never the same Samantha after that. Their fear grew when none of her relationships with men worked out.

That conversation had acted as a catharsis for her pain. Samantha had learned that her parents had done a lot of soul searching in private. They'd worried about causing irreconcilable damage by forcing her to give up her baby.

Though she'd assured them it had been her decision

when all was said and done, they'd still blamed themselves.

Now that they knew she'd had contact with Jessica, and could see the joy it brought her, they not only accepted this new state of affairs, they were excited and eager to meet their only grandchild. They'd even gone so far as to suggest Samantha invite Nick, too.

Much as she would love to do that, Samantha felt she couldn't. She'd already asked too much of him. Besides everything else, the history between her parents and Nick had all been negative.

Though she already considered him the man she most admired on this earth, her regard for him knew no bounds because he was unselfish enough to let Jessica spend the holiday away from him. Just contemplating his first Thanksgiving without her had to be a wrenching experience.

That's how she knew what a fabulous parent he was. He put Jessica's happiness and welfare above his own. Samantha could only hope she would always do the same, consciously or otherwise.

TWENTY-FOUR HOURS LATER she drove her rental car into Nick's driveway. She'd bought the best baby back ribs she could get from the butcher in Jackson. Now she and Jessica could cook up a storm before they had to be at the high school at seven.

While she was opening the trunk, Nick came out the front door dressed in jeans and a dark-green polo shirt defining his broad shoulders. She was so surprised to see him, she found herself staring and had to look away.

"Hello, Nick." The words sounded breathless, even to her ears.

"Hi. How was your flight?"

"Less bumpy than last time. The weather seems as clear here as in Coeur D'Alene."

"It's been beautiful the last two days. Perfect for tonight's party. Jessica will be relieved to know you made it on time. Her bus hasn't pulled up yet. Let me help you with those groceries."

"Thank you," she whispered. He carried the sacks in the house. With her heart thudding, she followed him into the kitchen. After removing her jacket, she put it over one of the chairs. "Do you mind if I get started cooking? The ribs will take a couple of hours."

"I'll help you. What do you need?"

"A big roasting pan and a large bowl to mix the barbecue sauce."

He pulled the items from the cupboard. "How high do you want the oven?"

"Three hundred fifty degrees."

"Done. What else can I do?"

Go away, Nick.

He wasn't supposed to be here. She couldn't handle it when he was this close to her. It brought back too many memories. From the first moment she'd seen him, she'd wanted him in all the ways a woman could want a man. That hadn't changed.

He smelled good, just the way he used to. He looked good. In fact he looked so much better than good, either he needed to leave right now or she did. This house, this village, this state wasn't big enough to hold both of them. Not the way she was feeling.

"Mom?" Jessica came bursting into the kitchen

from the front door. Sam had been laying out the ribs in the pan. She turned to hug her daughter without using her hands. They both laughed.

"Dad! What are you doing home this early?" Jessica left her mother's arms to give her father a kiss on the cheek. He'd been lounging against the counter with his arms folded, watching Samantha.

"Today I made a concerted effort to be here in case your bus was late."

"It took forever. As soon as I wash my hands, I'll be in to start the cake."

The minute Jessica left the kitchen Nick said, "What time does your plane leave on Sunday?"

Sam's hand shook as she poured the vinegar into the cup. With that one question, she knew he wanted to know her plans because he'd made some of his own. Big ones, depending on Samantha's cooperation. The lucky, lucky woman, whoever she was.

Don't worry, Nick. I'm going to help you out.

"I have to be at the airport at noon, so I'll bring Jessica back here at eleven-thirty. Between now and then I'll try to take perfect care of her, so please feel free to do whatever you want."

For some reason her comment seemed to annoy him, because she could feel a certain tension coming from him. "Jessica can always reach me on my cell phone."

"Of course." Sam opened a couple cans of tomatoes. Why didn't he say this to their daughter? What was he hanging around the kitchen for?

"When are you going to tell her you're recovering from cancer?"

She slowly lifted her head to look at him. So *that's*

why he lingered. He was worried about Jessica's reaction. Naturally he was. Sam had been worrying about it, too.

"I'd planned to have a talk with her after we dropped Cory off at his parents on Sunday morning, but if you don't think it's a good time, please tell me."

He pursed his lips. "There's no good time to have a serious conversation like that."

Jessica had to be told at some point, and he obviously wanted to be there for her because it's the way he was made.

"I tell you what. Sunday morning I'll casually suggest Jessica phone to let you know what time to expect her. That way I'll find out whether some emergency cropped up that prevented you from being available. If that's the case, I won't say anything to her until I'm sure you'll be there to talk to after I've gone, even if it means I have to stay at Grayson's until Monday before flying back to Coeur D'Alene."

He rubbed the back of his neck. "I don't anticipate anything preventing me from being at the house when you bring her home, but—"

"But we both know the unexpected can happen," she interjected. "Last week that semi tried to tunnel through the visitors' center, and you had to be gone all night helping with the cleanup. I understand. So if anything else unforeseen should arise, be assured I'll take care of her."

Nick started to say something, but Jessica chose that moment to come back to the kitchen, ready to get busy cooking. His pewter eyes sent Samantha a private thank-you.

You don't need to thank me for anything, Nick. She

knew how much love and concern he had for their daughter.

More than ever Samantha realized the sacrifice he'd made to let her into Jessica's life. It had been a huge risk that opened all of them up to more hurt and pain, depending on how everything was handled. Yet he'd been willing to do this for Jessica's sake. Samantha's heart ached with love for him.

Their daughter walked him to the door leading to the garage. While he gave her a big hug goodbye she said, "Have fun with Gilly, Dad. Don't worry about Mom and me."

Gilly. What a cute name. No doubt the other woman lived up to it, otherwise Nick wouldn't be interested.

Stop it, Samantha. What Nick did or didn't do had nothing to do with her. She'd lived without him for thirteen years. She could live without him for thirteen more, and thirteen more after that.

"I'd love to be a fly on the wall when you play your duet."

His comment produced a broad smile on Jessica's face. "Nobody knows we're going to do it. We'll perform last. I can't wait!"

"You can tell me all about it on Sunday."

"I promise!"

Samantha refused to watch him leave. It was bad enough he was taking her heart with him. When she heard the garage door open she turned to Jessica. "I forgot that I parked the car in the driveway."

"Don't worry, Mom. It's on the side behind the truck. He takes the Xtera when he goes on a date."

"Do you like this Gilly?" Samantha could have bitten her tongue off for asking the question, but it came out of her mouth before she could prevent it.

"Yes. She's really cute."

Nick didn't date cute little freshman girls. Sure he didn't.

It was a good thing Samantha had chosen that moment to pour the contents of the bowl over the ribs because it slipped from her hands. No harm done, thank goodness.

"H-has he been dating her for a while?" she stammered before putting the pan in the oven.

"No." Jessica got the eggs out of the fridge. "He took her out for the first time on Monday when he went over to Yellowstone on business."

Samantha's pulse rocketed. Monday was his first time with the other woman?

"She's a ranger who transferred there from Teton Park after a maniac ranger named Dave Cracroft started harassing her."

"Ooh. That doesn't sound good."

"He's in jail right now waiting to stand trial."

"You're kidding!"

"Nope. He tried to kill Pierce and could have killed Dad at the same time because they were both together when Pierce got shot. It was right after a tornado swept through part of the park."

A shudder rocked Samantha's body.

"You can't believe all the terrible things that happened. Dave tried to get Leslie to go out with him. Then Pierce fired him and everything went wrong."

For the next little while Samantha listened in fascination and horror as her daughter recounted the events surrounding their lives. That horror intensified when she heard about the manhunt for Cracroft, who needed psychiatric help, and how Pierce had captured him.

There was an incident with a grizzly bear in the Teton high country that almost took Dave's leg off. Nick had fired the shot to bring the bear down. Leslie, a former photojournalist, had caught the whole thing on film. The thought of the danger they'd all been in made Samantha shiver again.

"Dave was jealous of Pierce. He accused him of being interested in Gilly and getting her transferred from the park. But Pierce loved his first wife, who'd died in a plane crash, and he never liked any other woman until Leslie came to work as Cory's nanny."

Samantha had already learned how Leslie had ended up in the Tetons. While in hiding from her stalker ex-fiancé, who was a psychopath, she'd fallen in love with Pierce.

Attempting to digest everything Jessica had just told her, Samantha couldn't understand why Nick had waited until last week to start dating the female ranger. If she was so cute, what had taken him so long to ask her out?

For that matter, why wasn't he married? It should have happened a long time ago.

Then she gave a self-deprecating laugh. People had asked her the same question, not only to her face but behind her back. "Why haven't you found a wonderful husband by now? Why is a lovely, intelligent woman like you still alone?"

Samantha knew exactly why she hadn't settled down and never would. She was doomed to love one man who wasn't available to her. That wasn't the case with Nick.

The more Samantha thought about it, the more she decided Nick had stayed single because the love he and their daughter shared was enough. When he wanted a woman like this Gilly, he didn't have to marry her to satisfy his needs.

Nick Kincaid was the kind of man who would always have his pick of women, if that was his desire. But it was obvious he had never let an outside relationship, no matter how intense or involved, infringe on the life he'd built with Jessica.

Maybe he was waiting until their daughter got married before he decided to take a wife. That made the most sense. Nick had a scientific mind. He was a methodical man, the kind who planned and met his goals, never deviating from a course once it was set.

Samantha had never known anyone so resolute in his thinking. Because of that single-mindedness, he'd raised Jessica to be the most wonderful girl in the world.

"Darling? I brought us a present to wear to the sleepover."

Jessica was ready to put the cake in the oven, but they had to wait for the ribs to brown. Her eyes sparkled when she looked at Samantha. "You mean pajamas?"

"You're close. There's a woman who sews for your grandmother from time to time. I asked her to make us old-fashioned matching nightgowns and bed caps like the Ingalls women used to wear in *Little House on the Prairie*."

Jessica let out a shriek of delight. "Where are they?"

"In the sack with handles in the back seat of the car."

"I'll get it!" On her way out of the kitchen she paused long enough to throw her arms around Samantha. "I love you so much, Mom."

"That's only a hundredth part of how much I love you."

"PIERCE?"

The chief was on the phone with another ranger. He took one look at Nick and motioned him inside his office while he finished up the call.

Nick complied and sat down in one of the chairs facing the desk. He'd been out in the field all week and hadn't come into headquarters at all. The place looked pretty much back to normal now that the remodeling was complete, following the accident.

Being a Friday evening, most of the staff had left the building. Pierce was staying on as part of the skeletal crew so he could take all day Saturday as well as Saturday night off to be with his wife.

Thank heaven for Pierce. Nick needed to talk to him or he wasn't going to make it through the next ten minutes, let alone the weekend.

Once Pierce had hung up, he stared at Nick. "You look almost as bad as you did on Halloween. I thought you were on your way to West Yellowstone."

Nick grimaced. "That was the plan. Yesterday afternoon I changed my mind and called off the date with Gilly."

Pierce sat forward in his swivel chair. "How did she take it?"

"Like a trooper. There's something wrong with me, Pierce."

His friend studied him for a long time. "You can't force feelings if they aren't there."

"It's not even about feelings. At this point nothing excites me."

"Since when?"

"I don't know."

"Yes you do. Let's face it. You've never had to share Jessica before. Your whole world has revolved around her. Suddenly you've been given a little time off. Though it was something you've always wanted and needed, you wouldn't be human if you weren't a little hurt that Jessica's so happy with Sam."

"That makes me some kind of a monster, doesn't it."

"No. It makes you human like the rest of us. For thirteen years you've had the sole responsibility for your daughter. Now her mother has entered the picture, giving you a little space. But you don't have anything to fill the void yet."

"*Void* is the right word," Nick muttered. "Here I am floundering, wondering what foot to put in front of the other, while my daughter is off to a party with her mother, having the time of her life. You know what's the irony of all this?" he cried. "I couldn't have gone to that party even if Sam *weren't* in Jessica's life!"

"That's true. Leslie would have taken her, and you would have been content until Jessica came home to give you a debriefing. The difference is, your daughter is making memories with her mother, memories that until now she only made with you. That has to hurt.''

"It does," he admitted. "She's a new person, Pierce. Happier. No matter how hard I tried, I couldn't do that for her."

"No. Because you're not her mother."

"My daughter has been transformed by the knowledge that Sam loves her and wants her in her life. How do I get over my anger and jealousy?"

Pierce sat back. "The same way you got over your pain years ago. The same way I got over mine after Linda died. Time is the great healer. Time plus the knowledge deep down in your soul that Jessica's life is better for having Sam in it."

"Somewhere inside of me I know you're right, but every time I think about Sam and what she did to us…" Nick couldn't finish the thought.

After a pause Pierce said, "So you still haven't forgiven her."

Nick put his head down. "I sound like a bastard, don't I."

"No. You sound like a man who never fell out of love. But before you go on torturing yourself over the fact that she couldn't have loved you and do what she did, just remember one thing.

"Sam was a vulnerable seventeen-year-old girl, not much older than Jessica is right now. She was an only child with an intelligent mind, a daughter doted on and loved by her parents and grandparents. It was asking a lot, maybe the impossible, for her to have gone against their combined advice and wishes."

Maybe it *was* asking the impossible. Nick buried

his face in his hands, not knowing what to believe anymore.

"Nick?" His head came up. "Do you think your anger goes deeper than Sam?"

"What do you mean?"

"Perhaps you never forgave your parents for dying, and took it out on Sam for refusing to marry you."

That was exactly what it was like. He'd needed her so badly, and she'd shut him out forever, too. "You're in the wrong field of work, Pierce. You should have been a psychiatrist."

His friend's grin was lopsided. "You know what they say about psychiatrists. They can help other people, but when it comes to themselves, they're as clueless as the next person."

"Well, you've given me a hell of a lot to think about. In repayment, I'm sending you home to your wife. I'll stay on duty till morning. There's a pile of paperwork on my desk I need to start plowing through. No time like the present to get it done."

"I can't let you do that." Pierce was trying to pretend the offer didn't excite him, but he failed miserably in the attempt.

"Go on. Get out of here," Nick ordered. "You'll be doing me a big favor and you know it."

"I *do* know it," his friend said. "That's the only reason I'm leaving."

"It's not the only reason," Nick teased him. "But I'm glad you're going willingly, otherwise I might be forced to take drastic steps."

Pierce chuckled before he got up from the chair. "Let's touch base Sunday night."

Sunday night.

Nick looked forward to it and dreaded it at the same time. It was anyone's guess how life at the Kincaid house would be once Jessica heard about her mother's recent illness. No matter what, their daughter was headed for a new emotional crisis.

CHAPTER NINE

AT TEN AFTER ELEVEN Sunday morning, Samantha pulled the rental car into the Gallaghers' driveway. "It's been so much fun, Cory. We'll have to do it again soon."

"Yeah! Thanks!" He got out of the car.

"Bye, Cory!"

"Bye, Jess."

He opened and closed his hand, his manner of waving. Samantha thought he had to be the cutest boy in the world.

When he darted to the front door of the house with his sleeping bag and the games he'd brought with him, Pierce and Leslie were there to open it for him. Lucy bounded out on the porch and jumped all over Cory, licking him. It was a precious sight.

"Thank you!" the Gallaghers called to Samantha.

"You're welcome!" she answered before raising the window.

A final wave and they were off to Nick's house a couple of blocks away. The nice weather had held. It was cold, but beautiful. The Tetons were so gorgeous, she couldn't believe they were real.

"I wish you didn't have to go back to Coeur D'Alene," Jessica mumbled.

If she meant *ever,* then her darling girl wasn't alone.

Samantha's heart constricted with emotion. She loved her daughter so much it hurt. "I know how you feel. But only five days from now we'll be in Denver together. Your grandparents can't wait to meet you, and that's the truth."

"I can't wait to see them, either."

Jessica was such a mature, honest, open, loving girl. She accepted explanations without condemning people. Her positive outlook on life and her ability to forgive were revelations.

Samantha had to hope all those wonderful qualities would help her daughter deal with some news that was going to upset her.

It would be impossible to know how Samantha's confession would affect Jessica. Only time would tell. Unfortunately, Nick would have to bear the brunt of the initial fallout after she left for the airport.

Rather than drive around, Samantha decided to take Jessica home and talk to her in the car. Her daughter's phone call to Nick earlier in the morning indicated he would be there waiting for her.

Once they reached the driveway Samantha set the brake, but she didn't turn off the motor. They needed heat.

"Darling? Before you go in, I want to tell you something about myself." Her daughter's expressive blue eyes flew to hers, alert to some nuance in Samantha's voice. "Almost two years ago I was diagnosed with multiple myeloma, a cancer of the body's plasma."

"You've got *cancer?*" In that moment her daughter seemed to fall apart.

Samantha reached out and took hold of her hand. "It's in remission now."

The tears gushed from her eyes. "What does that mean?"

"It means that my transplant and chemotherapy worked. The cancer has been halted."

"You promise?" she cried, her voice throbbing.

"I wouldn't lie to you."

"Is it gone forever?"

The zero hour had come. "I can't promise that. For some people, it never comes back. I'm hoping I'm one of those people, but no one knows for sure."

Jessica was trembling. "But you don't have it now?"

"No, darling."

Her daughter looked at her as if she didn't believe her. Samantha reached out and pulled her into her arms. "I swear I'm not sick right now," she whispered into her red curls.

Jessica was sobbing. Samantha continued to hold her. "You need to know I'm doing everything possible to keep it from coming back. I have too much to live for. I have a daughter to get to know. We were the hit at talent night, weren't we?"

Jessica wasn't listening. Samantha let her cry it out. News like this, especially when it was your mother, took time to process. That's what Jessica needed. Time, and possibly some professional help if she suffered too long.

Finally she raised her head and sat back on her own side of the car. Her eyes seemed to take up her whole tear-ravaged face. "How did you know you had cancer?"

"I got a pain in my ribs and had it checked out."

"When did it happen?"

"A year ago last February."

"Was it awful?" she whispered in a shaky voice.

"Yes."

"Were you supposed to die?"

"Yes."

"But then you didn't?"

"No."

"How come?" She sounded like Cory just then.

Samantha took a deep breath. "No one knows the answer to that. It could be because of a lot of reasons. I'd like to believe my body is good at fighting disease. I inject myself with medicine to keep the protein down, and I've been doing things to help me stay mentally and physically strong."

"Like what?"

For the next few minutes Samantha told her about her martial arts and rowing classes, her meditation sessions, the qigong therapy.

"You've done all that?"

"All that." Samantha nodded. "I have good friends who are also recovering. We do things together to stay positive."

"Is your friend Marilyn one of them?"

The whole truth, Samantha. "She's my best friend, and she's still fighting her cancer."

Jessica looked sick. Her face went whiter. "When did you get better?"

"About a month ago my blood test showed my protein level was back to normal."

Samantha watched as her daughter continued to digest everything in her mind. Suddenly she cried, "Oh my gosh! You're going to be late for your plane! Pop the trunk so I can get my things!''

Before Samantha could tell her not to worry about the time, Jessica scrambled from the car. "Thanks for everything, Mom!" she said before hurrying around to the rear end.

Nick must have been watching from the window because he came out of the front door with a solemn expression that gave his rugged features a slightly chiseled look.

Just as Samantha slid from the driver's seat to help, Jessica darted toward the house juggling two pans, her suitcase and her sleeping bag. She whipped past her father as if he weren't standing there, and disappeared into the house.

Their eyes met. Nick looked ill. Samantha's heart almost failed her as he stepped over to the car. "What do you want me to do? Shall I stay or go?"

He closed the trunk. "Go."

Samantha had never felt so helpless in her life.

"I HATE MY MOTHER, Dad! I never want to see her again!''

While Nick had waited for the endless weekend to be over, he'd imagined every reaction from his daughter but this one.

He'd honestly thought she would say that she wanted to live with Sam from here on out because no one knew how much longer her mother had before the cancer might come back.

For the last thirty-six hours he'd been searching his soul to see if he had what it took to let his daughter go if that was her deepest desire. The thought of shared custody greatly pained him, but Jessica had to come first here.

He'd assumed there would be the inevitable side effect of Jessica fearing she might get cancer, too, since she was Sam's daughter. So many worries had bombarded him.

Yet this strange reaction was something he hadn't considered when he'd made up his list of possible traumatic scenarios. Naturally her emotions were violent at the moment. He'd expected that. But he hadn't imagined that his daughter could say she hated Sam and didn't want to see her again.

That didn't make any sense to him, unless she was more his child than he'd realized. He thought of last Friday night, when Pierce had asked him if anger over his parents' death had compounded his pain when Sam wouldn't marry him.

Perhaps Jessica couldn't forgive Sam for not marrying him, thereby denying her the chance to live with a mother and father like all her friends. Perhaps that was where her anger was coming from.

Nick was a scientist and he tried to look at this situation objectively. Some ingredient was missing in this experiment. Some essential element that would change the whole equation. He would have to be patient and work it again and again until he discovered what it was.

He rubbed Jessica's back while she sobbed her heart out on the bed. They'd been here many times before in their lives, each one seeming the darkest to his daughter. But this time was different.

"She doesn't love me, Dad."

Jessica sounded so heartbroken he was at a loss

what to say. Since he patently knew that statement wasn't true, all he could do was continue to watch and wait for the elusive piece of information to manifest itself.

"I'm not going to Denver," she declared. "I don't want to meet my grandparents. Will you call her tonight and tell her for me?" Her question came out half muffled by the pillow.

"Why didn't you tell her that yourself while you were in the car?" Nick prodded.

"There wasn't time."

He didn't buy that. "She would have stayed over another night."

"I didn't want her to. I wanted her to leave."

After a long silence he said, "I'll do whatever you want, honey."

"Thanks, Dad. I love you so much!" She sat up and hugged him hard enough to squeeze the air out of his lungs. "I'm glad she's gone. We'll go back to being just the two of us. We never needed anybody else."

My adorable little liar. If Jessica could see her own glittering smile, the pain in her eyes.

"Let's drive to West Yellowstone and have an early dinner at the Lariat Hotel!" She rolled away from him and got off the bed. "I'll pay with my baby-sitting money." The same money she'd been going to use to pay for Sam's hotel room two weeks ago?

Nick made a path through his hair with his fingers while he watched her pull some bills from the top drawer of her dresser. She slid them in the pocket of her jeans.

He knew agony drove his daughter's abrupt movements. He had to do something to alleviate the worst of it. Maybe a drive *was* a good idea.

"I'm ready to go whenever you are."

"Great! Give me a sec."

While she headed for the bathroom, he grabbed his cell phone and jacket, then locked up the house.

She joined him in the kitchen wearing her jacket. Together they walked out to the car and took off.

He knew better than to ask about the party. All the joy his daughter had experienced with her mother over the weekend had been canceled out in the last hour by the news that Sam was a cancer survivor.

Cancer…the terrible word. One many people in the twentieth century didn't even dare say aloud. Some people thought if you had it, it meant you were bad in some way. The disease was shrouded in mystery. Nick's own great-aunt hadn't been able to talk about it; she'd referred to it as "*that* disease."

Jessica was a product of the twenty-first century, yet cancer still struck such fear in her heart, she couldn't deal with it.

At some point they would have to talk about it, but right now his daughter was like a trout in the Snake River. One minute the innocent thing had come up to the surface for a meal. In the next instant a hook had grabbed her by the throat. Going into survival mode, she was taking the line out as far it would go.

Nick would have to reel her in, but with great care and skill, to make sure he could remove the hook without damaging her more than she already was.

She broke the silence some time later on the outskirts of West Yellowstone. "How was your date with Gilly?"

"I called it off."

"I thought you might."

He lifted one brow in surprise. "How come?"

"If you'd wanted to take her out, you would have done it a long time ago. The only reason you went to lunch with her was to stop me from hoping you and Mom might get back together."

Good grief.

"Admit that's what you thought I would want, Dad. You were single. She hadn't married. It was perfect."

The blood pounded in Nick's ears.

"But you don't need to worry—I don't have any big dream like that. Mom didn't love you enough to marry you the first time, and she didn't love me enough to bring me those albums before she got cancer.

"She had to be dying to do that. Even then, it took her pastor to open up her conscience while she was lying in that hospital bed. It was his job not to let her die until he could tell her how to make things right with the baby she'd abandoned. He probably told my grandparents they'd better shape up, too, since they're getting real close to dying.

"Now I know what my Sunday school teacher meant about deathbed repentance. It doesn't work because it's too late. Mom is thirteen years too late to tell me she's sorry," his daughter declared, dry-eyed.

The essential element had just surfaced. Nick's patience had won out.

He pulled off to the side of the road beneath some pines, where a couple of squirrels were playing, and turned to his daughter. Her profile could have been carved out of granite.

"Jessica? Look at me."

When she complied, he barely recognized the hard veneer.

"You've got everything right except for two things."

"What?" she retorted abruptly.

"Her pastor didn't visit her in the hospital. When he happened to stop by her condo, your mother was already in remission."

Jessica gave a little gasp and her chin started to quiver. The first sign of a crack.

"When she told him she'd won her bout with cancer, he advised her that if she had anything left in her life to resolve, to do so. That it might make her so happy, her spirit would fight to keep her cancer from coming back. That's when she called me. Would you like to hear what she wanted to say to the pastor?"

His daughter slowly nodded.

"'I want to go back thirteen years to that hospital room and beg you to bring our daughter to me so we can be a family, Nick.'"

Jessica bit her lip. "What did you tell her?"

"That it was too late."

"What did she say then?"

Nick would never forget. "Your mom said, 'I know, but I had to take the risk. Thank you for not cutting me off. Tonight when you're kissing your children, give Jessica an extra squeeze. She won't know it's from me, but *I* will."

Sam had said some other things too. Private things meant only for his ears.

"For thirteen years your mother honored her promise to me to stay away, even though you and I both know it was the last thing she wanted to do.

"When she realized she was going to die, she could have asked her parents to find me. She could have begged me to bring you to the hospital so she could look at you one time before she died. But she didn't do that because she knew it would be utterly cruel and unfair to you.

"It wasn't until a miracle happened and she'd been given a second chance at life that the pastor's words gave her the courage to approach me. Even though she knew it would be breaking the law, so to speak, that's how strong her drive was—the drive of a mother wanting to be with her child."

Tears glistened in Jessica's eyes, removing the last trace of the veneer that had made her look so foreign to him.

"She didn't seek you out simply to tell you she was sorry for giving you up, Jessica. She wants to be your mother in every sense of the word, but she can't promise you she'll live forever. Her greatest concern was that you know the truth about her medical history in case the disease comes back."

"Do you think it will?"

Nick had asked himself that question too many times in the last few weeks. "No one knows the answer. We have to live by faith."

After a troubling silence, Jessica murmured, "Dad? I'm sorry if I hurt you when I said she didn't love you enough to marry you. I didn't mean it."

He reached out to tousle her curls. "I know you didn't, honey. But it's the one thing you said that *is* the truth. And I'm convinced the only reason she hasn't married before now is because she has been grieving over you."

"Are you still in love with her?"

He'd been waiting for that question. "No," he said without hesitation. "I *can't* be. Love has to be fed. The question is, do you want your mother as a permanent fixture in your life? She told you the truth about herself today so you could make up your mind once and for all. But Sam's a big girl now. If you decide you only want to see her when *you* feel like it, she'll understand. If you determine it would be too painful to continue the relationship with her, then she's prepared to leave you alone. It's up to you where things go from here."

"Honestly?"

Nick thought he understood what she was really asking. Though it would kill him, it was up to him to help her out. "Honestly. Even if it means you would like to live with her for a while to make up for lost time."

"You would let me do that?" she cried.

His gaze had returned to the road. "Whatever brings you the most happiness."

"Dad? Could we just get a hamburger and then head home? I want to call Mom. She should be at her condo by the time we get back to Moose."

Though Nick realized she would always harbor fear in terms of her mom's ability to fight off cancer, it seemed Jessica's fundamental concerns had been about a mother's love. With everything straight in his daughter's mind at last, there would be no stopping her.

How was he going to handle it when she decided

to move to Coeur D'Alene for a while? Nick's chest felt as if a giant boulder was inside it, the kind that came crashing down the mountain when the earth suddenly shifted beneath the Grand Teton.

IT WAS DARK by the time they reached the house. While Jessica rushed to her room to phone Sam, Nick closed the door to his bedroom to call Pierce on his cell phone. His friend picked up on the second ring.

"Nick?"

"Thank heaven you answered."

"I was expecting a call from you before now."

"Jessica and I have been to West Yellowstone and back."

"Then she's in worse shape than I feared."

"For once you're wrong. I'm afraid *I'm* the one falling apart here. Can you talk?"

"As long as you want."

Without preamble Nick told him everything. "I wouldn't be surprised if Jessica asks to move to her mom's after Thanksgiving to finish out the school year there."

"Did Sam say anything about that?"

"No. I'm reading between lines. But I know my daughter, Pierce. All the signs are there. She's got big plans. That's why I'm calling you. How would you feel if I took a leave of absence from the park until June?"

He could almost hear his friend mulling everything over. "Are you thinking of transferring to another park on a temporary basis?"

"You're reading my mind. Great Smoky Mountains National Park is having a problem with the inroad of rainbows and browns on the brook trout. That's one of my areas of expertise. I could work out a trade with another ranger who would live in my house, I'd live in his.''

"You know I'd fix anything for you, Nick, but I think you're jumping the gun here.''

"Maybe. But if I'm right, I need to have a backup plan in place or I'm not going to make it.''

"I hear you. I had my own backup plan when Cory was being so difficult. If he hadn't learned to love Leslie, I would have been forced to move us to my parents' house in Ashton.'' A deep sigh escaped his throat. "I tell you what. Tomorrow I'll put out a feeler and see what happens.''

"I knew I could count on you.''

"For what it's worth, I'm hoping you're wrong about everything. Temporary or not, our whole family will be devastated if you and Jessica leave. To lose my best friend, even for a season…''

"Now you know how I felt when you told me you might have no choice but to leave the park.''

"Dad?''

Nick got up from the bed. "I've got to go. Thanks for being there for me, Pierce. Talk to you tomorrow.'' He hung up.

"Come on in, honey.''

The door opened. Jessica's face was as alive as a bubbling Christmas tree light. "Mom's on the phone. She wants to talk to you.''

Steeling himself for what was coming, he reached for the receiver by the side of his bed. "Hello, Sam.''

"Nick—'' Every time she said his name in that breathless voice, it took him back thirteen years and nailed him to the spot. "Is Jessica on the phone with you?"

His daughter was standing right next to him. "No."

"Then I'll make this quick. Jessica seems to have taken the news better than I thought she would. Tell me the truth. Is it an act?"

"No."

"Thank heaven," she whispered. "Are you still all right about her coming to Denver for Thanksgiving?"

"Yes."

"I'll prepay her ticket and let you know the details of her flight in a few days."

"That'll be fine."

"Nick?"

"Yes?"

"I understand you'll be in Gillette with your cousins for the weekend, but Jessica is hoping you'll meet us in Fort Collins on Saturday so we can show her around."

Sam's suggestion that he join them in Colorado was such a far cry from his assumption that she wanted to discuss Jessica living with her, the shock of it staggered him.

"She's afraid to broach the subject for fear you'll say no, so I told her I would ask you. From her viewpoint it's understandable she would like to be with both of us when she sees where we once lived and dated. I realize it's unorthodox, but since our relationship was unique, anyway, does it really matter? In order to satisfy our daughter's curiosity, would you be interested in doing this for her sake? I've never been back. Have you?"

He swallowed hard. "No."

"We could stay overnight at a hotel and drive to Denver on Sunday to catch our flights. Will you think about it and let me know?"

Jessica was watching his face, studying his expression. If she'd put her mother up to this as some kind of test, and he said no, his daughter might think he hadn't meant it when he'd told her he wasn't in love with Sam.

As for Sam, she would have seen through Jessica's manipulations, but was in the unenviable position of not wanting to thwart their daughter in any way yet. Especially when Jessica had handled the news about her medical condition as well as she had.

Nick understood that the reality of Sam being united with their daughter was still too new, too sweet and heady to start setting limits.

But when the trip was over, the two of them would have to establish ground rules so Jessica wouldn't be able to get away with this again.

"I don't have to think about it, Sam. The answer is yes. I'll let you and Jessica make the arrangements. Here she is." He handed his daughter the phone.

He couldn't tell if the smile Jessica flashed him was one of relief or of secret satisfaction. Maybe it was a combination of both. She was starting to remind him of the Sam who'd once beguiled him.

He headed for the kitchen. Though he was craving a beer, he opted for cola. The last thing he wanted was for Jessica to see him drinking something stronger than soda and jump to the conclusion that he wasn't as in control of his emotions as he pretended to be.

But the minute he pulled it from the fridge and popped the lid, he realized he was allowing what his daughter might or might not think to manipulate him again. Hell—if he felt like a beer, he was going to have one.

He set the can down with a jolt, spilling cola on the countertop.

"What's wrong, Dad?"

Muttering under his breath, Nick wheeled around to discover his daughter in the entry dressed in a white gown and nightcap, like something from the pioneer days.

"Do you like it?" She came all the way into the kitchen and modeled it for him. She looked charming, adorable.

"I love it, honey."

"Mom had these made for us."

A vision of Sam in the same outfit ran through his mind, setting his pulse pounding without his permission. "I bet nobody's sleepwear at the party was as original."

"Nope."

"How did the duet go over?"

"Mom said we were sensational."

Nick could imagine. "Is that what you thought, too?"

She nodded. "All the mothers wanted the recipe for the barbecued ribs and the cake. Mom wrote them out without needing to look anything up."

"Does that surprise you?"

She grinned. "No. Mom's amazing. She knows more stuff about environmental issues than anyone else. When everyone found out what she did for a living, they wouldn't leave her alone.

"She and Pam Royter's mom got talking about the

snowmobile problem in the parks. Mrs. Royter asked her to come and speak to the Wyoming Sierra Club meeting in Sheridan the weekend after Thanksgiving.''

He took a swig of cola. ''Your mother's a busy attorney. I doubt she'd be able to get away for something like that unless it was planned months ahead of time.''

''Mom said she would have come, but she has to be in Phoenix that weekend.''

''Phoenix?''

Jessica's expression sobered. ''Her best friend, Marilyn May, is recovering from breast cancer and is going in for another chemo treatment. She wants Mom to be there.''

This time when he set the can down, cola burst out of it like an eruption from Old Faithful geyser.

CHAPTER TEN

SAMANTHA'S SENSE OF having done this before was so strong, her body felt weak as she, Jessica and Nick got out of the rental car and started walking around the corner to the Lory Student Center in Fort Collins.

It was eight-thirty, not ten o'clock on a cold winter night. It was the Thanksgiving recess, not the end of exam week before Christmas vacation. But in all other ways, tonight was like the night when the word *happiness* had been erased from Samantha's vocabulary.

This was the painful part.

Up until now the three of them had enjoyed driving around Fort Collins. They'd visited favorite old haunts—the schools Samantha had attended growing up, the building where her father had had his law firm, the Hilan Apartments, where Nick had lived. The campus building where he'd worked as a security guard, Samantha's former home, her friends' houses, the reservoir where they'd picnicked and water-skied. *And made love.*

But her father had sold their family's thirty-five-foot luxury cruiser when they'd moved to Denver. No evidence remained at the marina to remind her or Nick of those stolen hours of rapture in the bedroom of the cruiser her parents had never used. Only Jessica herself, the fruit of their union.

"Where were you sitting when Mom dropped her books, Dad?"

Samantha turned toward the spot where Nick was looking. A few students were studying, but the basement wasn't as full as usual.

He walked over to the table in question and put his hand on the empty chair. It probably wasn't the same one, but it could have been.

The only difference between then and now was the fact that Nick was thirteen years older, more attractive than ever in his sheepskin jacket, and Samantha was more in love with him than she'd thought possible. The pain of loving him and not being able to do anything about it was almost unbearable.

Nick flicked his gaze to hers. His eyes weren't as dark as a thunderhead or as silvery as a cloud's lining. Their color was somewhere in between, which told her little about what he was really thinking. "I would say we've done it all."

"Except for our favorite dessert, I agree."

A smile twisted his mouth, making Samantha's insides flutter as if a hummingbird were trying to escape. "Let's go."

He drove them to the Cache-Poudre strip mall, where the name of the shop was different, but the ice cream was still the same—rich and velvety. The three of them ordered double fudge with marshmallow.

Thanks to Jessica, the day had been spun out to its maximum length. Now it was time for everyone to go to bed. Samantha's spirit rebelled, but there wasn't anything she could do about it.

Outside the hotel room mother and daughter shared,

Jessica kissed her father good-night before running inside, claiming she was anxious to take a shower.

Nick's room was across the hall. To Samantha's surprise, he lingered at the door. "She's as transparent as glass."

Samantha chuckled softly. "You know what they say about a child's dreams."

His eyes played over her features. He seemed to be looking for something that was eluding him. "It didn't take much to make our world go round back then, did it?"

A flood of emotions swamped her. "No. Those months were the happiest of my life."

"And mine." His voice sounded husky. "What do you say we complete the picture for her? For old time's sake," he added. "Come here, Sam."

Suddenly her legs felt like mush. "I don't think—"

But that was as far as she got before he pulled her into his strong arms. "If you've forgotten how, don't worry about it. You didn't seem to have a problem the night I kissed you outside the center. I'm sure it'll come back to you with a little practice."

"Nick—" she cried before his mouth closed over hers. At the first touch of his lips, a voluptuous warmth stole through her. She'd dreamed about this so many times, it seemed like an extension of her desires.

Her mind had never forgotten anything about him. Neither had her mouth or body, which molded to his in the old, remembered way.

It was a revelation to Samantha that a decade and more had gone by without any contact, yet here they were, embracing like young lovers who'd never been apart. But there was one difference. Nick was kissing her with more primitive force than she remembered, a kind of refined savagery that reminded her they weren't kids anymore.

She felt anger in his kiss, too. That was a new element.

Only one person could have put it there. Pain and guilt over what she'd done to destroy their perfect love drove her to tear her lips from his.

She lowered her head, afraid to look into his eyes and read the accusation there. "Thank you for a wonderful day, Nick. Good night."

Relieved to go inside the room and shut the door, she lay against it while she attempted to catch her breath. She had an idea Jessica had been a spectator, but her daughter knew how to be discreet and was giving her the space she needed.

On Thanksgiving night Samantha's mother hadn't been as subtle. "You're still in love with Nick, aren't you," she'd said.

"Yes."

"Is there any chance…?"

"No, Mom. No chance at all. You don't do what I did to Nick and expect him to go on loving me."

Today's visit to Fort Collins had been the result of Jessica's manipulations. They may have taken a walk through the past for their daughter's sake, but that kiss at the door had been for Samantha's sake. Nick's way of letting her know she'd ruined something so precious they could never get it back.

"But after all this time he's still single, honey. Doesn't that tell you anything?"

"Yes. That he has devoted his life to Jessica and his career. And obviously he has forgiven me enough to let me have a relationship with our daughter. Her happiness is the most important thing to him. But Nick's still young, Mom. Only thirty-three. Some men don't marry until their thirties or forties. One of these days, when the time is right, he'll fall hard for a woman, maybe even start another family. But he'll make sure his daughter is happy and secure first."

There was a long silence before her mother said, "Did you speak to Nick about some sort of arrangement so Jessica can spend part of the year with you in Coeur D'Alene?"

The minute she raised the subject, Samantha disabused her of the notion. "No, Mom. They're too close. Jessica would never be happy away from her father except for a short holiday visit like the one we're having now. No matter how much she loves me, Nick will always come first with her."

Nick was their daughter's raison d'être. Her hero. Samantha could never be envious of that fact or resent it. Little did Jessica know he was Samantha's raison d'être, too. He always would be.

"One thing I've learned about Nick in the short time we've been together is that it would kill something inside him if he had to let her go for any length of time."

Her mother's eyes grew dim. "Your father and I should have given our permission for you to marry him. We should have helped give you and Nick the best start possible, especially with Jessica on the way."

Samantha hugged her tightly. "Don't do this to yourself. It's not your fault. I would have married him if he'd ever talked about marriage before I told him we were going to have a baby. I didn't want to end up like Brenda's sister.''

''We know now that you wouldn't have,'' her mother said with tears in her eyes. ''Nick has been a superb father. Jessica's such a marvelous girl. Your dad adores her.''

''As I told you on the phone, Jessica's a gift. I want to be worthy of her love and Nick's trust. That's why I'll never take advantage of the situation.''

''You're as noble as Nick.''

''No, Mom.''

''Yes, and so courageous in ways that still astound me. I'm proud to be your mother. I love you, darling.''

''I love you, too. Did you know Jessica's already crazy about you? She's convinced your genes are the reason she decided to join the newspaper staff.

''I happen to know she's going to read all those novels you're sending home with her. She wants to be able to connect with you on your level. At the mother-and-daughter party, she bragged about her grand-mother Bretton's post-graduate degree in English literature. You would have loved it, Mom.''

Their weekend had been glorious. On Friday Jessica had gone to the country club with her grandfather for lunch. Then he'd taken her downtown to his law firm to show her around—just the two of them.

Friday night the whole family had visited with the great-grandparents, who'd come to Thanksgiving dinner the day before. The weekend had been a voyage of discovery for Jessica and a time of great happiness for the Bretton household.

But Samantha's happiness was marred by the day in Fort Collins spent with Jessica and Nick, which had turned bittersweet with one kiss. It had been the fitting end of a visit to where their great love affair had begun and flourished until Samantha had ruined everything.

After today's experience, she felt it was possible for them to be friends for Jessica's sake.

It was more than Sam could have ever hoped for. Therefore she had no right to be upset that tomorrow Jessica and her father would go back to the Tetons, and she wouldn't be seeing them for another couple of weeks.

Marilyn needed her in ways no one could understand unless they'd been fighting cancer, too. Samantha wanted, needed to be there for her friend, but already she felt the ache of separation from the two people she loved most in this world.

A FRESH BLANKET OF SNOW had turned Jackson and the whole Teton range into a fairyland. Before Nick did anything else, he had to clean a ton of white stuff off the Xtera sitting in the airport's short-term parking area.

Once they drove out to the connecting road, he noticed few cars were moving. The plows had yet to clear the highway.

Halfway to Moose his cell phone went off.

"I bet that's Mom."

Nick's heart raced at the mention of Sam. With the taste of her lips still fresh on his, he couldn't think, couldn't concentrate. "It's Pierce," he said after checking his ID. His friend had amazing timing. Disappointment swept through him that it wasn't Sam.

"Oh." Jessica sounded just as upset.

"Her flight left Denver after ours, honey. She'll call when she can."

He had no idea if Coeur D'Alene had been hit by the same storm. No doubt his daughter was picturing her mother knee-deep in snow with no one to help her. The hell of it was, since their plane had landed, that same picture had been emblazoned in Nick's mind.

For so many years he hadn't known where Sam lived, and he'd long ago convinced himself he didn't care. Now that he *did* know where to find her, he still shouldn't care and it still shouldn't matter. Not after the way she'd abruptly broken off that kiss—a kiss he'd needed so badly, he'd risked everything for it.

He was damn sure she hadn't given him a second thought after waving them off at the airport with a cheery goodbye!

For Jessica's sake she'd walked through that doorway to the past with him yesterday. During the long, excruciatingly painful ordeal, she'd exhibited a sangfroid he would have given anything to possess.

Such composure, feigned or real, had to be dynamite in the courtroom. The opposition wouldn't know what was going on in her head.

Nick clicked on after the fourth ring and said hello.

"Uh-oh. The trip to Fort Collins should never have happened."

Nick gritted his teeth "You've got that right."

"Where are you?"

"Eight minutes from home."

"Why don't you and Jess stop by our house first? Because of the storm, Leslie's sister and her family decided to fly back east tomorrow. The kids would love it if Jess came over. While they're playing in the snow, you and I can talk. Much as the selfish part of me doesn't want to tell you this, the feeler I put out has produced results if you're still interested.''

"More than ever."

"That's what I was afraid of," his friend muttered. "See you in five. Thanks." He hung up.

Jessica regarded him with curious eyes. "What's going on?"

"Pierce wants us to drop by on our way home. Leslie's family won't be going back to New Jersey for another day. Cory needs you to help him and his cousins build a snowman."

She studied him closely. "You and Pierce were talking about something else."

Her radar was lethal. "It's just ranger business, honey."

"What kind?" she persisted.

Might as well lay the groundwork now. "Remember a few years ago when I recommended keeping minimum flows instream for cutthroat trout habitat? To make sure they didn't get on the endangered species list?"

"Sort of."

"Well, there's a ranger like myself working in Great Smoky Mountains National Park who's having problems because there's an inroad of non-native trout endangering the brook trout. Since the plan I instigated seems to be working, maybe I can help *him* out."

"Clear back in Tennessee?"

Yup. Clear back and far away from your mother. New scenery. New people. New women.

Nick expelled the breath he'd been holding. After kissing Sam, after feeling her warm, curvy body in his arms again, the idea that any other woman could fulfill him wasn't in the realm of possibility.

"Would you have to go there?"

Jessica displayed curiosity, not anxiety. Since Sam's appearance, a monumental change had come over his daughter.

"I couldn't do much good from here. Assessing the impact and extent of a species invasion requires hands-on experience before coming up with a solution. I'd have to determine how many of what species are present in the water, what habitats they occupy and what they eat, their rate of propagation and so forth."

"How long do you think it would take?"

"That's hard to say. Six months maybe?" At this point he was swimming in deep waters.

"When would you have to go?"

Nick paused. "That all depends on you."

Her eyes widened. "I'm ready whenever you are. It would be cool to go to school in Tennessee. I've never been there."

Nick almost lost control of the car. "What about your mother?"

"She'll fly out to see me on weekends and holidays, so it doesn't matter where I am."

Until she wants you with her for longer than a few days at a time.

They'd just pulled into the Gallaghers' driveway. Pierce had already cleared it with the snow blower and was now working on a path to the front door.

Cory left the big ball of snow he was rolling with his cousins, and came running over to the car, with Lucy in pursuit.

Maybe Pierce was right and Nick had jumped the

gun on this one, but these were early days yet. Who knew how things would change once Sam got back from Phoenix?

"Honey? Don't mention this to anyone yet. I'm only toying with the idea."

"I won't. Does that mean you don't want Mom to know, either?"

Naturally, a mother was different.

"I would never presume to tell you what to discuss with her."

Jessica leaned over to kiss his cheek, then opened the door and jumped out. Whatever was on her mind, she didn't intend to share it with him. Nick watched the other children drag her through the snow. Their shrieks of excitement resounded in his aching heart.

"TEN DAYS SINCE THE CHEMO and you're sitting around the pool eating watermelon. I think you're a fraud, Marilyn May."

Samantha's friend smiled from her chair beneath the umbrella. "The nausea's gone."

"What about the weakness?"

"I'm feeling stronger today. Maybe not quite enough for rowing."

"Come spring and you will be."

Marilyn stared hard at her. "I've decided to stay in Phoenix and work at a pharmacy here, but you're the first person I'm telling."

Samantha had seen it coming. "Your family's going to be overjoyed."

She nodded. "Knowing you've united with your daughter makes me realize we have to take advantage of these second chances we've been given. I've lived away from home long enough."

"I'm going to miss you," Samantha whispered.

"I'll miss you, too, but there's always the phone and weekend visits." Her friend studied her closely for a moment. "Something's going on with you, Samantha. I've sensed it for a couple of days. Don't hold back on me because you think I'm too sick. I'm not, and even if I were, it wouldn't matter. We've been through too much together to keep secrets."

The tears Samantha had been suppressing ran down her cheeks. "Oh, Marilyn. I'm so afraid."

"Of what?"

In a burst of emotion, she told her about the trip to Fort Collins and Nick's fiery kiss at the door. "Now he's thinking of transferring to Great Smoky Mountains National Park in Tennessee."

Marilyn blinked. "When?"

She wiped the moisture off her face. "Soon, I think."

"How long have you known about this?"

"Since the night I called Jessica to make sure she got home from Denver safe and sound."

"This has been on your mind for almost two weeks and you never said anything about it until now? Shame on you," Marilyn chastised her, but she said it with all the affection in the world.

"I couldn't do that to you."

"Well, I'm well enough now, so tell me—did Jessica say he'd been thinking about it for a long time, or did it come out after kissing you?"

"I don't honestly know. But I'm sure the idea of leaving the Tetons never entered his head until I came along and destroyed the beautiful world he'd created for him and Jessica.''

"You know better than that, Samantha Bretton. As you've told me so many times, he's a scientist who never acts impulsively. He considers all the possibilities first before carefully making a move. There's no way he would have told his daughter you wanted to meet her if he hadn't thought it all through first and decided it was for the best. He knew the risk he was facing, and he took it.

"Sounds like he decided to take another risk and kiss you to see if the old fire was still there.'' She cocked her head. ''Was it?''

"You know it was! I couldn't believe I was back in his arms again, but the longer the kiss went on, the more I could feel an edge to it.''

"Hunger, you mean? Longing for what you took away from him?''

"No, Marilyn. It was anger.''

Her friend's eyes trapped hers. ''Are you sure? Or are you just assuming everything, like you've always done?''

"I don't think so. Otherwise why would he be ready to pull up roots and move to the other side of the continent?''

"What did Jessica tell you, exactly?''

"That another ranger hasn't been able to solve a problem with the native fish being eradicated. They need someone with Nick's expertise to go there and help. It could take six months.''

"Then it's just a temporary thing.''

Samantha shook her head. ''No, it isn't. Nick might

have told Jessica that to pacify her, but I know what it means. For once his nobility has backfired on him."

"What do you mean?"

"Isn't it obvious? He isn't as ready to share Jessica with me as he thought he was," she cried in pain. "I never meant to cause all this trouble, Marilyn. Now I don't know what to do.

"Jessica assumes I'll fly out to Tennessee to be with her every weekend. You should hear the plans she's made. Yet that's exactly what Nick is hoping to avoid by moving so far away. I'm sure he's thinking along the lines of a once-a-month visit.

"So far he's been civil to me, but if I try to satisfy my daughter's wishes, he'll end up despising me, and could stop the visits altogether. The trouble is, if I don't fly out there every Friday night, Jessica's going to think I didn't mean it when I told her she was my life."

"You're jumping to conclusions. In the first place, he hasn't gone anywhere yet. And if he does, it could be a case of him really being needed for a temporary period. It's possible the decision has nothing at all to do with you. He might even welcome your help if he has to work long hours on the weekends, too, and doesn't know people he can trust to be with Jessica."

"Possible, but not probable, Marilyn. This was no coincidence. Nick loves the Tetons. He and Pierce Gallagher are close, like you and me. It's where he has made his home with Jessica. Nothing in the world except a threat to his happiness could make him leave paradise, because that's what it is."

She buried her face in her hands. "I've posed an

enormous threat, and now I don't know what to do about it.''

''Don't do anything. Haven't you and I both learned that after we've done all we can do, the rest is up to providence? Leave it alone for now. You act as if you're guilty of something.''

At that remark Samantha's head came up. ''What do you mean?''

''Jessica came into this world because two people loved each other. You behave as if you're the one wholly responsible for everything that happened.''

''I am, Marilyn.'' Her voice hardened. ''I'm the one who lied to Nick. I'm the one who begged him to make love to me.''

''I *knew* it!'' Marilyn sat forward. ''You're still stuck in that old groove. Listen to yourself! You talk as if Nick didn't have a say in the matter. What is it going to take to convince you he could have told you *no?* This paragon you've put on a pedestal had a weakness. It was *you!* As far as I'm concerned it's still you. Why else would he have put his heart on the line once again to kiss you outside your hotel room door? So help me, Samantha, if you tell me you're to blame for *that,* then I'm going to pick you up and throw you in the pool!''

The idea that Marilyn would try it in her condition was so ludicrous, Samantha started to laugh.

Her friend grinned. ''What do you know. I think we've achieved a breakthrough.''

''Of sorts,'' Samantha conceded. ''I'll admit I didn't put a gun to his head.''

''All right—we're making progress. Now let's take that thought a little further. No gun was pointed at his head when he told Jessica you were trying to make contact with her.''

She sucked in her breath. "Agreed."

"In other words, he acted as a free agent where the most important decisions of his life were concerned."

"You've got me there, counselor."

"*So...* it makes no sense that he suddenly wants to zap himself and Jessica to the other end of the universe unless he's falling in love with you all over again. Be honest with me. You're the one who stopped kissing him before he was ready to let you go, right?"

Samantha bit her lip. "Yes."

"Which means you were exhibiting perfect Bretton form."

"What do you mean?"

"You know exactly what I mean. The same Bretton form he remembered in that hospital room. A woman without an Achilles' heel."

Samantha averted her eyes.

"I realize that sounded cruel," Marilyn murmured. "I only said it because I love you like a sister. Don't you know I want you to see the situation for what it might be? But you can't do that without taking off the blinders. I thought it was time I helped you do that."

"And I thought I was here to help *you.*"

ON FRIDAY AFTERNOON Nick trained his binoculars on two skiers he'd sighted above the Gros Ventre Campground area. The only way they could be on that slope was if they'd been airlifted in by helicopter earlier in the day. He'd climbed from his truck and walked to the spot where it would land to pick them up.

Last winter a law had been passed limiting forest

service commercial helicopter permits so there'd be no overflights of the Teton range. The wolverine and lynx populations used this portion of the high mountain territory for denning.

Somebody had deliberately broken the rules. He would wait until the helicopter landed to pick them up, then issue a citation before informing the forest service the pilot in question needed to be fired.

While he was reporting the incident to headquarters, another call came in on his cell phone. It was Jessica. The bus must have just dropped her off from school. No doubt Sam had arrived from Phoenix and his daughter was calling to tell him their plans.

This was the weekend he'd been worried about. By the end of it, he would probably hear that she'd decided to live with her mom for a while. Nick had had no appetite for several days now.

He rang off with Sally, who would leave the information on Pierce's desk, then he phoned Jessica. "Hi, honey."

"Hi."

Such a dull, lifeless voice when he was expecting exuberance warned him something had gone wrong. "What's the matter?"

"There was a bomb threat at the Phoenix airport. It could be a terrorist thing. No planes can fly in or out. Mom went back to Marilyn's house to wait."

His eyes closed tightly. "Is your mother all right?"

"Yes, but she doesn't think she can fly out until tomorrow, and she said she really has to get back to Coeur D'Alene after being gone from work this long. S-so it looks like I'm not going to get to see her until next weekend."

He could tell Jessica was fighting not to break into tears. Unfortunately, he could hear the helicopter in the distance.

"I'm sorry, honey. Why don't you go over to Cory's and wait for me? I'll be home as soon as I can."

"How long?"

"Six o'clock?"

"That's too long. Hurry, Dad."

"I promise, honey."

After he hung up, he phoned Leslie. To his relief she was home. When he explained the situation, she said she would take care of everything. No sooner had they quit talking than the helicopter touched down.

Nick made his approach. He told the pilot to shut off the motor and climb out.

"Cut me some slack, will ya? My buddies are just having a little fun away from work for a couple of hours."

"That little fun may have cost the lives of several animals this park is supposed to protect. If enough guys like you have their way, there won't be a park one day. Let's see your ID."

"You're really going to write us up?"

"That's right."

By this time the other two men, probably in their late twenties, had approached on their skis.

Nick shook his head. "You guys know better. You've violated the National Environmental Policy and Forestry Management Acts. I need to see your ID."

Unlike the pilot, they didn't say anything as he issued their citations. He gave each of them a copy, then tipped his hat. "See you in court." He waited until the copter was airborne before heading back down the mountain to his truck.

There'd been quite a few incidents with heli-skiers and snowmobilers already this winter. Because the park didn't have the funds to hire an attorney who could prosecute these cases to the full extent of the law, guys like this probably wouldn't lose their jobs. Worse, they'd be back again, knowing the law lacked the teeth to do any lasting damage to them.

At quarter to six Jessica phoned him again. She'd been at Leslie's, and now was home waiting for him. Five minutes later he pulled into the garage expecting she would come running. Instead he found her dry-eyed in the kitchen making dinner. Something had changed since Sam had phoned her earlier.

"Those tacos smell delicious. I'll join you in a minute." After freshening up, he hurried back to the kitchen and helped her put everything on the table.

"Is the airport still closed?"

"No. Just before you drove in, Mom phoned to tell me she's going to get a flight to Coeur D'Alene tonight."

"I'm sorry, honey. I know how much you were counting on seeing her."

She nodded. "Dad?"

He knew what was coming next. She was going to ask if she could fly to Coeur D'Alene in the morning to be with her.

"Yes?"

"When Cory asked me why I was crying and I told him, he said, 'Why don't you ask her to be your nanny?'"

What? "Honey—"

"I knew you'd say that, but I bet Mom would do it. Then it wouldn't matter if we had to go to Tennessee."

He didn't know whether to laugh or cry. "Did you mention this to your mother on the phone?"

"No. I was waiting for you to get home so we could talk about it first."

"Jessica—aside from the fact that it just wouldn't work, your mother has a career she can't walk away from."

"She could be an attorney here or in Tennessee."

Good grief. He should never have mentioned transferring. It seemed to have given her ideas. "It isn't that simple, honey."

"But what if she said yes? I think Cory had a great idea."

Nick pushed himself away from the table and got to his feet. "Cory's a six-year-old boy who needed someone to look after him while Pierce was at work. Leslie answered the ad in response to that need. Our situation isn't the same thing at all."

"Yes it is. You always tell me I need someone to look after me while *you're* at work. And Mom's my mom!"

Nick eyed his daughter. "You're grown up enough to understand why your mother couldn't live in the same house with us."

After the way Sam had torn her mouth from his the other night, she wouldn't put herself in the position of letting it happen again. As for Nick, he couldn't promise that he wouldn't reach for her whenever she was around. That's what was killing him. She was his sickness. An addiction.

"I didn't mean in the same house, Dad. If she stayed at Grayson's the way Leslie did before she married Pierce, wouldn't that be all right?"

"No, honey."

"Why?"

"Because this is our world, not hers. She has her own life, her own friends. I'm sure she has a fabulous condo. You saw your grandparents' home and know the kind of background she comes from. To live here would be giving all of that up. It isn't realistic to even consider the possibility, honey."

"She said *I* was her life. What if she were willing to move here for my sake?"

"No matter how much she loves you, I can promise you she wouldn't do it. Trust me on this."

Her cheeks splotched with color, Jessica jumped up from the table. "You hate her, don't you. I bet you wish she had died."

In all these years Jessica had never talked to him this way. "You know better than that."

"If I could live with her, I would!"

He quaked inside. "Has she asked you?"

"No. She said she never would because I belonged with you and it would hurt both of us too much to be apart from each other."

Nick stood there planted to the floor long after Jessica ran to her room, sobbing.

CHAPTER ELEVEN

DUE TO HER EXERCISE and meditation class after work, Samantha didn't get back to her apartment until nine Monday night. She'd needed that time to get herself centered again.

Not only had it been difficult to tell Jessica she couldn't see her until the weekend, Samantha had a doctor's appointment at eight-thirty in the morning. He would draw blood for her first test since she'd gone into remission.

She wouldn't be human if there wasn't a part of her that feared her protein level had gone up again. But the mental and physical discipline she worked on to keep herself in positive mode had taken hold.

After her shower she climbed into bed with a new brief to study. Three pages into it the phone rang. It was her parents calling to wish her good luck at the doctor's in the morning. They'd offered to fly to Coeur D'Alene and go with her, but she'd assured them this was routine and she was fine.

Deep down inside, she admitted that the idea of their coming would somehow place more importance on the appointment than was warranted. Marilyn had agreed that Samantha would be better off to treat this like she would a trip to the dentist.

After she'd studied another fifteen minutes, the

phone rang again. She checked the caller ID. It was Nick's call. Suddenly, her chest felt tight.

"H-hello?" she stammered. How incredible that just knowing he was on the other end made her as nervous and excited as a schoolgirl.

"Hi, Sam. Forgive me for phoning so late, but there's something important I need to discuss with you. If this isn't a good time, let me know what time we can talk tomorrow."

"Anytime is a good time if you need to get in touch with me. Go ahead."

"When did you last speak to Jessica?"

"Last night about seven. She called me from her friend's house." Samantha slid out of bed, unable to lie still. "What's wrong?"

"Jessica didn't go to school today. She woke up with a stomachache, so I stayed home with her. To-night she told me she knows she's too sick to go to school tomorrow."

Samantha pressed a hand over her heart. "It's be-cause I couldn't come last weekend, isn't it. I could hear her disappointment, but by the time the planes were flying again, I had to get back for a case I've been working on."

"You had no control over that bomb alert," he stated tensely. "Jessica knows that."

"It still doesn't make the news any easier to bear. I promised her I would come this Friday and spend the weekend. Do you want me to call her tonight and reassure her? I would have done that, but I barely got back from my exercise class and was afraid you might not want me disturbing you."

"Aren't we past the point where you need to worry about my reaction to your dealings with her?" he said.

"No, Nick. I want to operate by your rules. You're Jessica's father."

"You're her mother," he retorted. "That gives you rights, even if it means phoning her in the middle of the night if you deem it necessary."

When Nick sounded this upset, she had difficulty reading between the lines. "Tell me, what's wrong?"

He gave a muffled exclamation—whether of pain or exasperation, she couldn't tell. Probably both. "Over the weekend Cory put it in her head you could be her new nanny."

An incredulous laugh escaped Samantha's throat and tears welled in her eyes. Dear, darling, adorable Cory.

"My reaction exactly. The idea is ludicrous! But she doesn't really get that, so I've tried to explain in terms she'll understand. I'm forewarning you now so you'll be forearmed when you get here on Friday."

"Nick—"

"I credited our daughter with being more mature," he stated, "but she's still a child with a child's propensity for seeing only what she wants."

"Nick." She cut him off before he could say anything else. "You've misunderstood my reaction."

Marilyn's observation had been all Samantha had been able to think about since she'd left Phoenix.

If Samantha had let nature take its course that evening at the hotel, would there have been a different outcome? Would Nick have admitted that he was still in love with her, too? By halting that kiss, she might have sabotaged a second chance at happiness because of another false assumption.

Maybe it still wasn't too late to correct the damage. She had nothing to lose.

Taking another huge risk, she said, "I think Cory's suggestion is absolutely brilliant."

Nick's gasp of shocked surprise was everything she could have hoped for, and more.

"I knew I loved that little boy. Now I know why." She wiped her eyes. "Since the moment my secretary told me Jessica was on the phone and I realized you'd told her I wanted to meet her, I've dreamed of living and practicing law in Jackson Hole so I could be near her.

"Because I deal with wildlife issues, I've taken the bar exam to practice in four Western states, one of them being Wyoming. My boss at the federation is aware of my situation and is already prepared that I might leave Idaho if it means being in closer proximity to our daughter.

"Cory might just as well have pulled the idea right out of my heart. But if you're planning to transfer to Tennessee and live there, then there's no point in this discussion, so—"

"I'm not going to Tennessee," he interrupted her. Now it was her turn to let out a quiet gasp. "I was only considering the possibility because I believed you were intending to ask Jessica to live with you for the rest of the school year. It...seemed a good idea at the time."

Samantha's instincts had proved correct. Nick couldn't handle the thought of being without his daughter. Their bond was too great. In his pain, he'd thought a change of scene would help him to deal with their separation, if it came to that.

"I'm sorry if I caused you any worry. Let me make it clear once and for all that I have no desire to disrupt the life you've made with Jessica. She would never want to live with me if it meant being away from you. She worships the ground you walk on, Nick." *So do I.*

"Sam—"

"Don't say it!" she cried as her fears took over once again. "I know what I want is asking the impossible. You said it on the phone the first time—it's too late. You've made your own wonderful life with Jessica. I may be her mother, but I don't have the right to come along and rip apart everything you've created.

"Please be assured I would never have made the suggestion to you or Jessica about moving to Jackson. It's only because you told me what Cory said that we're having this particular conversation. It'll remain our secret.

"Please Nick—be honest with me. I need to know what you really want in terms of my seeing Jessica. I'll accept and be grateful for whatever you decide."

While she waited for his answer, perspiration broke out on her body.

"What I want is for our daughter to be happy," he said at last. "She has let me know in the most graphic of ways that she wants you around all the time. Anything short of that won't satisfy her.

"Since you want to be with her every bit as badly, and it would be asking too much of you to commute back and forth, I have no problem with you moving to Jackson."

Samantha had to hold the phone away for a moment so he wouldn't hear her cry of joy. He *had* forgiven her. And maybe Marilyn was right. Maybe he wanted her in his life again.

When she'd gathered her composure she said, "After you get off the phone, will you tell Jessica that when I come on Friday we'll look through the real estate listings together? On Saturday she can help me go house hunting. I—if you could join us, we'd love your input."

She could almost hear his mind mulling over the suggestion. "Provided there are no emergencies, I'll be there." She hugged her free arm to her waist for joy.

After another pause, he added, "I must say you've come up with a novel cure for Jessica's stomachache. There's no doubt in my mind it will do the trick. Good night, Sam."

"Good night," she whispered.

On Friday morning she called the doctor from her office to find out the results of her test. The nurse put her on hold for a minute, then came back. "Everything's normal."

"Thank you."

It seemed the pastor's words were prophetic. *Matters of the heart have a strange and powerful effect on the body's ability to fight disease.*

ON SATURDAY AFTERNOON the Jackson Realtor walked Samantha and Leslie back to the living room of a charming two-story log home.

"One of the features I find most attractive about this house is the glassed-in deck," the man said.

"Even if it's twenty degrees below zero outside, you can sit in the hot tub and look at the Tetons in total comfort. In summer, you can remove the windows and enjoy an open deck."

There were many wonderful aspects to the house, not the least of which was the loft, where an enchanted Cory leaned over the balcony and waved to them. He and Jessica had gone upstairs to explore, and had never come down.

"I'll be outside if you need me," the Realtor added.

"What do you think?" Samantha asked Leslie when they were alone.

She smiled. "With that large office and its own private entrance, it's perfect for your law practice. I don't believe anything else we've seen today compares."

"I agree. I'm still pinching myself to believe a house like this is available right here in Jackson. In good weather Jessica could walk from the high school if she had to."

"Pierce will be coming any minute to take us to dinner and a movie. He knows a lot about construction and can tell you if the house is in good shape."

"His opinion will be worth everything. I wouldn't put down earnest money otherwise."

Nick had told her on the phone he would try to make it, but an emergency had cropped up at the last minute. He'd phoned Jessica to tell them he'd be late. The news had come as a blow. Samantha had to fight hard not to show her disappointment.

"I don't think you'll have to worry about anything being faulty," Leslie said. "It's too new."

Samantha didn't think so, either. She wanted the house. The vaulted ceilings gave a feeling of space she craved. Her contemporary furniture would fit right in.

With three bedrooms and three baths, her parents and Marilyn would be able to stay in comfort when they came for visits. Every window looked out on a breathtaking view of the Tetons.

"Please can we get this house, Mom?" Jessica called out. "The loft is perfect for sleepovers!"

"Please buy it!" Cory echoed. "Lucy will love the stairs!"

Both Samantha and Leslie chuckled.

"When we have parties we'll soak in the hot tub, and then make popcorn and bring it up here." Jessica chatted away. "The bedroom has a window seat. It's big enough to sit in while you read and look out at the trees."

That was another plus. The property bordered the national forest.

"Dad!" Cory cried out all of a sudden.

"Hi, sport!"

He'd seen his father coming through the door before the rest of them. Like a shot he rushed down the stairs to hug Pierce.

"You've got to see Jessica's house!" He started pulling him toward the staircase. "We're going to sleep upstairs and have parties. Jessica says I can bring Cameron and Logan."

After the ranch-style houses they'd lived in, Samantha realized a two-story house was a genuine novelty.

"You've already bought it then?" another deep male voice inquired.

Samantha spun around to discover Nick on the

threshold. She went weak just looking at him. It had been so long. Weeks.

He'd changed out of his uniform and wore a brown cashmere sweater with darker brown trousers. He was so handsome she couldn't catch her breath.

"Not yet," she said in a voice that sounded way too shaky. "Leslie suggested you and Pierce take a look around first. Maybe you'll see a problem I don't. I've never bought a house before. It's quite different than a condo."

"Guess what, Dad?" At this point Jessica had joined them. "There's an office for Mom, and a barn out in back. We could bring some horses from Gillette next spring."

"I think you're getting a little ahead of yourself, honey." His gaze swerved from his daughter to Samantha. She glimpsed a vaguely anxious expression in his eyes that surprised her. "Are you ready to take all this on?" he asked her.

"Yes. Jessica said she would teach me to ride. But it's a moot point if you think I should keep looking."

"Come on!" Their daughter grabbed his hand. "You've got to see everything. Did you know there's a shop in the garage? It would make the coolest lab for you."

"Is that right?" At this point the lines were blurred in Jessica's eyes. *What's mine is yours.* It was very sweet, very touching, really. Nick wasn't unaffected by the situation, but Samantha would give anything to know what he was really thinking.

For one breathless moment, she found herself visualizing the three of them living here as a family.

"Much as I'd like the grand tour, honey, we don't

have time right now. Did you forget Marsha Gardiner's birthday party?''

''Oh my gosh!'' She put a hand to her mouth.

''I thought it had slipped your mind. I'd forgotten about it, too. Amanda called the house to see if you wanted a ride. I told her I'd bring you. I've got your present.''

Jessica eyed both of them with a pained expression. ''I don't want to go.''

''Sure you do, darling. It'll be fun,'' Samantha declared. ''Call me when you're through and we'll pick you up.'' She'd spoken for Nick, too, hoping he didn't mind.

''Where you will be?''

''At Grayson's.''

''But you flew all the way from Coeur D'Alene to be with me.''

''Jessica—it's only for a few hours. Pretty soon I'm going to be living in Jackson. So go on, and have a blast!''

''Okay.'' She gave her a hug.

Nick glanced at Samantha, an unreadable expression in his eyes. ''I'll see you back here in a little while.''

''The Realtor has another appointment right away. Why don't you meet me at Grayson's instead? I'll show you the brochure.''

''Sounds like a plan.''

Samantha followed them to the front door and waved as they drove off. Just then Pierce and his family stepped out of the garage. The Realtor stood a little distance apart from them.

She waited till the Gallaghers came up to her. Pierce had his arm around his wife.

"Well?" Samantha asked in a quiet voice. "What do you think?"

"You already know my opinion," Leslie said.

Pierce's blue eyes lit up with his smile. "I think it's a great house. Go for it." Cory gave a little jump in the snow, he was so excited.

"I'm excited too, Cory." The little boy had no idea just how much.

"Come and have dinner with us," Leslie urged. "We'll call Nick to join us."

"Thank you, but I want to drop by a hardware store and find some paint and wallpaper samples to take to the cabin. I would like Jessica to be able to decorate her own bedroom."

"Your daughter will be in heaven."

"She won't be the only one."

"For eight years I've watched Jess grow up," Pierce commented. "There's a new glow about her since you came into her life. I'm happy about your plans to move here."

Her eyes glazed over with tears. "Coming from you, that means a lot." Pierce's opinion carried a great deal of weight with Nick.

They all hugged before Pierce helped his family into the car. Once they drove away, Samantha approached the Realtor. "I'd like to make an offer."

AFTER DROPPING JESSICA off at the party, Nick headed back to Moose. Since his phone call with Sam the other night, his world had changed. She'd asked for his help and she was going to get it, because he'd decided to face the truth about himself.

For thirteen years he'd been stuck in a time warp. No woman since Sam had ever made him want a permanent relationship. Her image had always been before his eyes.

Raising Jessica had made it impossible for him to forget her mother. Now, incredibly, Sam was back in his life, saying and doing all the right things, hooking her womanly tentacles into him deeper and deeper.

She was going to be living here for good. Translated, that meant as long as her cancer stayed in remission.

What am I going to do about you, Sam? I can't go on like this any longer.

If the memory of their love had prevented her from finding someone else, then he intended to wring that admission from her. Otherwise why was she willing to move to his world?

Their conversation on Halloween would forever be burned in his memory. She'd told her pastor she wanted to go back in time so the three of them could be a family.

If she'd meant it, then that explained why she hadn't stopped him from kissing her outside her hotel room. She could have turned away in time, using Jessica as an excuse. Instead, she'd launched herself into his arms and had kissed him with the kind of hunger he'd never felt from her before.

So why, in the middle of such intensity and rapture, had she unexpectedly wheeled away from him, leaving him bereft?

It was time he found out, but he needed to be smart

about it. One thing was certain. He couldn't handle another rejection.

As one of his favorite college professors had taught him, don't try to fight or alter nature. It doesn't work. You have to let it take its course if you want to see the true pattern of things emerge and develop. Then learn from it.

That's what Nick intended to do with Sam. He wouldn't fight his feelings. Instead he would let things take their natural course and see what happened.

If nothing did, then he would have learned from the experience and could finally move on.

The drive to Grayson's seemed to take forever. They kept the place well-lit for their guests. Out of the corner of his eye he saw Sam at the door of her cabin. She was juggling a pile of things as high as her head.

Without hesitation he pulled off the road and levered himself from the car to help her. "Sam?"

He must have startled her, for everything she was carrying fell to the porch with a loud thud and she spun around. If his eyes weren't mistaken, she'd lost color.

"Nick! I didn't realize you were there." She seemed to have difficulty swallowing.

"I'm sorry to have frightened you. I thought you heard me coming on the path." He hunkered down to gather the wallpaper books. When he stood up, she was struggling with the lock.

"Let me." He took over and jostled the key into the opening until it gave. A little oil would fix the problem.

Once they were inside the warm, rustic room she

cried, "I swear I didn't drop those samples on purpose!"

Her response stunned him. He put the books on the pine picnic table arranged beneath a picture window framed with red-and-green-plaid curtains. "Did I accuse you?"

"After what I did to get your attention years ago, you would have every reason to think so," she said in a trembling voice. "Here you've been going along all these years minding your own business, and now I've turned up again like a bad penny."

His brown brows formed a bar. "Is that how you see yourself? A bad penny?"

"Yes. That's what I was. A willful teenager who threw herself at you. I was always the one who made you do things you didn't want to do. Lying to you about my age was unforgivable, but I was afraid of losing you."

Nick had heard all this before, but he had the advantage of being older now.

Hopefully maturity and fatherhood had helped him put emotion aside long enough to read between the lines and hear what she was really saying. If he bided his time, he might find the answer to the one question that had eaten him alive.

She stood behind an easy chair, clutching the corner. "To call you out of the blue after all these years and ask to see our daughter... I shouldn't have told you about the cancer."

He rubbed the back of his neck, trying to understand. "Did you feel you needed the excuse?"

"No! After the first lie I told you, I vowed I would never lie again. If I hadn't made that promise to myself, I wouldn't have said anything to you about my illness. I would have just phoned to tell you I wanted to see my daughter, and hoped you might let me.''

''If that's true, why didn't you call years ago?''

Sam averted her eyes. ''Because I was afraid you would see me as the same needy girl who kept putting you in a position of having to deal with me, one way or the other. It wouldn't have been fair to you. I was never fair to you.''

''So what you're saying is it took the prospect of escaping death to override your fear of approaching me again?''

She shook her head. ''No. It was the pastor's unexpected visit at the condo. When he asked me if there was anything I needed to resolve, I thought that, because I'd suffered remorse over my sins for so long, maybe it was a sign that I'd finally been forgiven.''

Nick's throat constricted as he heard her anguish. ''I had no idea you felt such tremendous guilt.''

''I didn't know, either. Not in the beginning. It took months after Jessica was born before the numbness went away enough for me to feel anything again. Then the pain and guilt descended in full force.

''When I talked to my old pastor in Fort Collins, all these feelings came out. I admitted lying to you about my age. I'd lied to my parents about the amount of time I spent with you. I'd had a sexual relationship outside of marriage. I'd given up my baby.'' Tears gushed down her cheeks.

''The pastor told me I was forgiven. That it was my job to forgive myself and make the best future I could from there on out. He promised me that in time the pain would lessen, and he could think of no better outlet to assuage it than to pursue my studies.

"So I left for Boston with the determination to be the top student in my class. I studied day and night. It's all I did. Throughout undergraduate school I couldn't think of dating. I didn't feel worthy yet.

"Later on things got better. The guilt subsided. I went out with several guys in law school. I tried to like them, but after a few dates the idea of a relationship turned me off. It was such a relief to finally get my degree and move to Coeur D'Alene, where there wasn't the pressure from friends to go on a blind date, or meet somebody's brother."

Nick could relate to that.

"Life was good, but there was a void."

He could relate to that, too. But he still had to hear why she'd refused to marry him.

"Sam—if you loved me enough to lie to keep me, to lie to your parents so you could continue in the relationship with me, then what held you back from saying yes to my proposal?

"The baby book you made is proof you had the instincts to be a wonderful mother. Your parents wouldn't have disowned you if you'd decided to marry me the day you turned eighteen. So what was really going on in your head when I couldn't change your mind in that hospital room?"

Her face took on a tragic cast. "Haven't you been listening to me?"

"Every word," he declared through gritted teeth. "You've suffered a lot, that's clear, but I'm still waiting for an answer."

He could see a shudder run through her beautiful body. "It wasn't because I didn't love you, Nick."

He stiffened. "You could have fooled me."

"It was just the opposite!" she cried. "I realized I loved you too much. I'd lied to get you and keep you. Brenda's older sister did the same thing to hold on to her boyfriend. He left her after they'd been married only six months! Her life was a mess after that, and her parents ended up raising her baby. I couldn't bear to be like her and trap the man I loved into marriage if he didn't really want me. I'd already lied to you about my age and felt sick with shame."

Nick's heart was racing. "You never told me about your friend's sister. I thought those ideas came from your parents!" He could barely remember the girl, whom he'd been introduced to on only one occasion. After finding out Sam was still in high school, Nick had realized she'd kept her friends from meeting him so he wouldn't learn the truth.

"They did, but I wouldn't have listened to them if I hadn't already seen what happened in Brenda's family. They would have financed her college, but the divorce devastated her. She lost interest in school and old friends. Eventually she left home and got into drugs. Her rare visits to see her child had to be supervised, increasing her parents' emotional burden.

"There was resentment and tension from the other siblings. The father of the baby never came around because he'd never loved Brenda's sister in the first place. I was convinced you would end up despising me and would leave me after we were married. I couldn't bear that."

"Sam, you would never have turned out like that, and I would never have left you."

"Maybe not. But I could understand my parents' fear that my dreams to become a good attorney with a successful career would be jeopardized by getting married so young. You have to understand that because they're socially prominent, I was afraid to be an embarrassment to them.

"But more than that, I was terrified you felt like you had to marry me, and that one day you would leave me. It would have been the punishment I deserved for not telling you the truth about my age."

She wrung her hands. "In the end I wanted to do the noble thing, so I set you free, but my heart died that day."

"So did mine," he whispered.

You have your answer, Kincaid.

"Perhaps now you understand why I don't want you to think I'm trying to manipulate you or the situation with Jessica. I'll never lie to you again. I've found out life's too short to be anything but honest."

He took a fortifying breath. "In that case, I want to know what your plans are for the future."

A wistful smile curved her mouth. "Since I found out I have a future to look forward to, you have no idea how just hearing the word makes me feel."

"I'm sure I can't imagine," he murmured. She'd been to hell and back. It tore him apart thinking about that. It tore him apart to know she'd loved him so much she'd sacrificed everything to let him be free.

"My plan is to live near our daughter so we end the commuting. Taking airplanes is a disruption we can all live without."

Amen to that.

"My parents will come often to visit. I'm hoping to get my friend Marilyn here, too. As for Jessica, she can't spend every weekend with me, and she won't want to once things settle down. I don't expect to see her every spare moment, and I'm not going to encourage it. Frankly, I'd like to be here as a backup for you."

Backup? "I appreciate that."

"Thirteen years is a long time to shoulder all the responsibility, Nick. No matter how much you adore Jessica, there are times when you're sick, when you need to travel, when you want a…a breather."

"You mean a date?" he demanded.

A blush crept up her neck into her face. "Yes. From now on I'll be here to help out. Because you're a ranger, I can't imagine any kind of a visitation schedule we could come up with that would work."

He folded his arms. "You're right. Too many emergencies arise, over which I have no control, like the one this afternoon. Besides, our daughter's old enough to decide these things for herself."

"I agree. You've been such a wonderful father, Nick. I know you don't want to hear it from me. But please let me say it just this once. She's a remarkable girl, and all of the credit goes to you."

His heart gave a fierce kick. "Jessica inherited her mother's protoplasm. It gave her a head start."

Sam laughed softly. "Spoken like the scientist you are. You love it here, don't you."

"Yes."

"I love it here, too. The Tetons have a majesty that speaks to your soul. Today I put money down on the log house. You know what sold me? The view of the Grand Teton from the office window. This is God's country.''

It was a fact. Another fact was that one of His most beautiful creations was standing in front of Nick right now. "Do you think you're going to want to set up your own law practice, or work in an established firm?''

Her eyes ignited, making them an even more intense blue. "I'm glad you asked that question. I—I have a proposition for you.'' Her voice faltered.

"What's that?'' Any attempt to tamp down his excitement over being here with her like this failed.

"Since you have a lot of influence with Pierce, do you think the park might hire me to be their legal representative?''

Just when he thought she couldn't do or say anything else to surprise him... "He'd welcome you with open arms, but there's no funding to pay you a salary.''

"I know. The thing is, I don't need one.''

"Sam—''

"Hear me out, please? My maternal grandparents left me an inheritance of five million dollars. I've already given half away to cancer research. Since I found out I have a second chance at life, I know where I want the other half to go. A fund could be created that would last for many, many years. It would be anonymous, of course. I'd be paid the normal salary for a park employee.''

With a surge of emotion he grasped her shoulders, drawing her close. "You would give away that much money to work for the park just so you could be with our daughter?'' He could hear his own voice shaking with emotion.

Her eyes filled with tears. "Yes. I don't want to be anywhere else ever again.''

Nick had difficulty swallowing. "Sam..." In the next instant they were in each other's arms. He needed her kiss more than he needed air to breathe. This time she gave him the response he craved without pulling away. Her beautiful mouth and body were his for the taking.

"Dad? Mom?''

Jessica's timing couldn't have been worse.

"Hurry and unlock the door! I'm shivering out here!''

For once it was Nick who was forced to relinquish the luscious mouth clinging to his. Samantha's protesting moan made his heart leap.

CHAPTER TWELVE

Nick unlocked the door before Samantha could even begin to think about moving her limbs. Jessica rushed in, bringing the freezing air with her.

"How was the party, honey?" he asked.

"It was fun. What have you guys been doing?"

He shut the door. "Your mother and I have had things to discuss."

The way he moved in slow motion as he removed their daughter's coat and draped it over the end of the couch, Samantha knew he too was having difficulty pulling himself together after their explosion of passion.

There was no question she'd shocked him with her proposal. If she did become the park's attorney, she would make up part of Nick's inner circle.

Outside of marriage, that was about as up close and personal as you could get to the man you adored. When Marilyn heard about this, she could never again accuse Samantha of being inscrutable.

She gave Jessica a hug. "I thought you were going to phone us to come and get you."

"Sandy's mom offered to bring a bunch of us home."

"That was nice of her."

Jessica nodded before tucking her hands in the back

pockets of her jeans. She eyed both of them expectantly. "What happened at the house after I left this afternoon?"

Nick flashed their daughter a mysterious smile reminiscent of the old Nick who used to love to surprise Samantha with little treats. When he looked like that, her bones melted. "The answer is sitting over on the table."

"Oh my gosh!" she cried the minute she recognized the wallpaper samples. "You bought the house!"

Samantha smiled at Nick. She couldn't help it. Their daughter was in heaven. "I made an offer, but I think we can safely assume it's ours—mine," she amended. "One of those books has some Waverly prints like the ones you admired in the upstairs bedrooms at your grandparents' home."

To Samantha's joy, Nick walked to the table with her. They sat down on either side of Jessica, who'd already started poring over them. For the next hour all three of them became amateur decorators, expressing their preferences like any normal family.

"I like this one best!" Jessica had her eye on a small print of tiny blue flowers against a white background. She'd gone back to it again and again.

"It'll be perfect in that upstairs bedroom with the window seat. We'll have to buy you a big four-poster bed and an armoire."

"I can't wait!"

"We'll shop for them online and have them shipped."

"I wish we could do it tonight."

Moments such as this were so precious, Samantha

held her breath for fear it was a dream that would disappear the longer she tried to hold on to it.

"Look at that, Dad!" Jessica had turned to the last page in one of the books. It displayed a tiny all-over print with a border done in a charming horse motif.

"It's cute."

Samantha thought it was very cute. "I can see it in the guest bathroom between the office and the door leading out to the barn."

"That'll be perfect!" Jessica's sparkling blue eyes dazzled her.

When Nick's cell phone rang, there was a collective moan of protest. Samantha held her breath while he answered it. *Please don't let it be an emergency.*

She saw him grimace before he said, "I'm on my way."

"What's wrong, Dad?" Jessica had just taken the words out of Samantha's mouth.

"A tourist hit a moose on the Teton Park Road. Sometimes the animals use it as a corridor to migrate at night, but the ranger summoned to the accident says this moose looks sick. It could be disoriented and that's why it wandered onto the highway. I have to investigate. See you tomorrow, honey."

After giving Jessica a kiss, he shrugged into his jacket. His glance flicked to Samantha. "I'm glad you're here."

"I am, too," she said in a whisper.

Their daughter let him out of the rental cabin. That was good, because Samantha wasn't capable of moving one foot in front of the other. Just then Nick had sounded as if he really meant it. She'd felt a lingering warmth in his regard. She longed to bask in it forever.

Her thoughts darted back to that first precarious moment when they'd seen each other in the foyer of the Elk Inn. One arctic look from him had shriveled her. She couldn't believe how different the situation was tonight.

"It sounds like your father has just given you more information to put in one of your newspaper articles. How's your latest one coming, by the way?"

"Thanks to something you said in one of your cases about the foresight of enlarging the Wild Clearwater country, I've almost finished it. The headline will read Yellowstone and Grand Teton, One park? Extravagant Concept or Visionary Thinking?"

"That's an attention grabber if I ever heard one! Bravo!"

Jessica sounded so savvy, Samantha couldn't wait to tell Nick. Being around Leslie Gallagher had rubbed off on her. Maybe Samantha and Nick were wrong and their daughter was going to grow up to be like Pierce's wife, a former staff journalist for the *New York Chronicler*.

On the other hand, Jessica showed signs of being a dedicated conservationist who'd been absorbing her father's philosophy. Whatever she ended up doing, it was going to be exciting to watch, because her analytical thinking exhibited real brilliance.

Overwhelmed by emotion, since at this time last year Samantha hadn't expected to survive the winter, she hurried to the couch to turn it into a bed for Jessica.

"After you've slipped on a nightgown, I want to hear about the party."

"We watched the old version of *Freaky Friday* and had pizza."

"That was a fun movie. After the way I've been twice mistaken for you, we would probably be able to pull off a mother-daughter switch and no one would notice."

"Except Dad. Did he like the house?"

Amused that the child was vetting the parent, Samantha decided honesty was still the best policy. "I'm sure he did, but mostly we discussed how things would work once I'm living here practicing law."

"Dad has to plan everything out, even though he rarely sticks to it."

"But he gets points for trying, right?"

"Right! Marsha always says she wishes she had a dad like him."

"Your father's one in ten billion."

Jessica studied her for a long moment before she removed the locket around her neck. "Want to see what I put in this?"

Samantha's heart raced as she opened it. Her daughter had added a picture of Nick. The very serious look brought his handsome features into sharp relief. Yet it underlined his male beauty, which reached out to her like a living thing.

"Cory took it at the wedding last month and gave it to me."

Sam had to clear her throat before a sound could escape. "It appears Leslie is turning him into quite the amazing little photographer."

Her daughter nodded. "I think Dad looks sad. Don't you?"

"Yes. It's not every day your best friend gets married."

Jessica flashed her a perplexed glance. "He and Pierce didn't lose each other."

"Of course not. But when two people marry, they cling to each other. It's so special, everyone around them feels it."

"Do you wish you'd married Dad?"

Oh Jessica…

The truth, Samantha.

"Yes."

SODIUM CYANIDE POISONING. All the signs were there. Slobbering, bleeding from the nose. As soon as Nick studied the stomach contents and ran tests on the blood and liver of the moose, he'd have viable proof.

How in the hell had it been poisoned? Moose were plant eaters. He surmised the poor cow had probably found some tender willows in the snow, and had accidentally caused the spring of the hidden 'coyote getter,' or M-44 as they called it, to discharge the poison capsule.

Using the flashlight, Nick followed the animal's split hoofprints through the snow into the forest. Every so often he discovered scat, the long round pellets, and traces of the animal's vomit.

Toxic fumes created when the moisture in its mouth activated the dry poison had killed it before the Jeep had crashed into it. Nick shuddered to imagine the animal's terrible agony before it died.

Almost every day he encountered evidence of man's destruction. Though there were laws on the books, the park had little money to enforce them. Nick couldn't help but consider Sam's proposition.

He shut his eyes for a moment. Her generosity and legal expertise would be a godsend.

"Nick?"

At the sound of Pierce's voice he stood up and turned. "How come you're not home in bed?"

"On the way home from Jackson, I checked in with dispatch and heard you suspected we have a poisoned moose on our hands. I thought I'd drive over and see what you found."

"Sodium cyanide."

"Damn."

Their breath curled in the freezing night air.

Like Nick, Pierce grieved over every treacherous human act against the wildlife they put their lives on the line to protect.

"If I had the money, I'd track down the person who did this and make certain he or she was sent away for the duration. It's times like this I wish I believed in the lottery and could use the winnings for something truly meaningful."

A half moon had come up over the Grand Teton, bathing them in enough light for Nick to see the lines of tension in his friend's face.

"What if I told you I know someone who holds the winning ticket for two and a half million dollars, and is ready to give it to us, no questions asked?"

Pierce let out a bark of laughter. "Then I would say you've been going heavy on the Jack Daniels to-night."

"Do you smell alcohol?"

His friend sobered. It was starting to dawn on him Nick was being serious. "Run that by me again."

"You heard me the first time. However, there is one small catch." Pierce stared at him as if he'd never seen him before. "It all has to stay in the family, so to speak."

"What are you talking about?"

"Sam."

"I don't understand. Speak English."

"She wants a job only you can create for her. The job we've needed doing around here since day one."

"You're joking…" His head reared back. "Lord, you're *not* joking. Her family has that kind of money?"

Nick nodded. "Her grandparents. No one can ever know. Once the funding's in place and the superintendent informs you, then you would have to open up the job to all who want it. The board will have to vote on the best candidate."

"Which Sam would win hands down."

"When she comes in for the interview, you'll see she's a force of nature."

They studied each other for a full minute before Pierce said, "I take it Cory's going to be sleeping in that loft in a few weeks."

"And riding his own pony next spring. Jessica has it all planned out."

Pierce cocked his head. "When's the wedding?"

"I don't know. Right now I'm letting nature take its course and I'll see what happens."

A silence ensued, followed by a whoop that filled the forest. Before Nick could react, Pierce gave him a bear hug that would have knocked the wind out of him if he'd been a smaller man.

"Chief?" One of the younger rangers came running through the trees, kicking up snow. "Is something wrong?"

"Nope." Pierce tried to hide the ecstatic grin on his face. "A private joke, but I appreciate the concern."

"Sure."

As soon as the other man was out of earshot again he said, "Let's go to headquarters and work out the details right now."

"I'll drop by my lab first, then meet you there."

"Good. In the morning we'll all have breakfast together at my house. I'll take Sam aside and have a chat with her before she leaves for Coeur D'Alene."

Nick felt dazed. "You realize what this means if everything comes together...."

"*I* do," Pierce muttered, "but I know for a fact it hasn't hit *you* yet."

"THE MOVING VAN'S HERE, Mom!"

It wasn't too soon for Samantha, who'd had to forgo spending Christmas with her daughter, and had flown into Jackson only this morning, her last commuting flight.

Until now there'd been too much to do in Coeur D'Alene. Besides getting ready for the move, she'd had to go over important cases with the lawyer hired to replace her at the federation. She had yet to be interviewed though by the U.S. Attorney General's office in Cheyenne for her job with the park. That would happen on Monday.

With only two days before New Year's, she still had

a house to put together before her parents arrived tomorrow afternoon. She was determined to see the New Year in with her daughter and Nick, having put down her roots here for good.

Jessica and Nick had spent Christmas in Gillette with relatives. School was out for the break, and Jessica was dying to help. Samantha had never seen anyone so excited, except herself, of course.

The painting and wallpapering had been done. She'd bought some new furniture, all of which was now in place, including the pieces for her office, her daughter's bedroom and the guest bedroom.

Samantha greeted the driver at the door and gave him a quick tour of the house so he and his partner would know where to put things.

First off the truck came the endless string of boxes containing the law books belonging in her office library. A euphoric Jessica called Cory on the new cell phone Nick had bought her for Christmas. She told him to hurry over as soon as his mom could drive him.

The two of them were like brother and sister. Samantha couldn't have loved him more if he were her own flesh and blood. She loved the people who made up her daughter's world. She loved Nick, whom she hadn't seen for two weeks! If he didn't show up soon, she didn't know how she was going to stand it.

For the next fifteen minutes the movers brought in more boxes marked for the various rooms. Then came the furniture. Samantha turned up the heat to compensate for the freezing air entering through the open doorway.

''Oh my gosh!'' Jessica cried out when the black Steinway baby grand was wheeled in on a dolly. She turned a glowing face to Samantha. "You didn't tell me you had a piano like this!"

Samantha just smiled and told the men to set it up in the corner of the living room next to the stone fireplace and inner wall, away from any windows. While they were attaching the legs, she heard voices outside, among them Nick's. She thought she would faint from the thrill.

"Dad!" Jessica pulled him inside the living room. "Look!"

"I'm looking," he said, but when Samantha chanced a glance in his direction, their gazes collided, sending a shock wave through her system. "Welcome home, Sam."

"Nick—" It was the only word that would come out with any coherence.

In the background Sam noticed Cory and realized he and his parents had also arrived. Everyone was dressed in casual clothes, ready to go to work. No one looked better in a T-shirt and jeans than Nick. Being a ranger kept his body fit and well-defined. It was a body she'd once known intimately.

Waves of heat suffused her face at the memory. She quickly turned her head away, but feared Nick had read her mind.

"Oh my gosh!" their daughter exclaimed again.

"Oh my gosh" pretty well described Samantha's emotions right this minute, but Jessica was referring to the large, heavy hutch, which came in two pieces. Samantha told the movers to set it up in the dining room. The bottom half was a bombé style with drawers. The top had been styled in an eighteenth century Flemish motif with glass doors and shelves. The painted exterior was an off white with tiny blue flowers.

"It looks just like my wallpaper!"

"Genes don't lie," Nick whispered from somewhere behind Samantha.

"No," she said, slipping a trembling arm around Jessica's shoulders. "Blue and white has always been my favorite color combination. When I saw this in a furniture shop in Amsterdam years ago, I had to have one just like it. Wait till you see the blue-and-white Delft plates that go inside it."

Jessica literally squealed in delight.

Next came the hand-carved, oval oak table and matching dining room chairs, then the living room furniture—two matching love seats, a coffee table, two easy chairs, end tables and lamps, all of light wood and white fabric in a contemporary design.

The driver approached her. "We're all through except for this last box, which isn't marked."

"Those are some personal things that belong in my bedroom."

"I'll take it." Nick reached for it and disappeared, leaving Samantha with nothing more to do than sign the form.

"Thank you for everything."

"You're welcome, ma'am. It's a beautiful house. What I'd give to live at the foot of these mountains."

She smiled. "That's why I'm here," she said before closing the door.

Cory came running. "Mom said for you to come in the kitchen. She's made a picnic."

"You've got the greatest mother in the world. Come

on, Jessica. I don't know about you, but I'm starving!''

THE MASTER BEDROOM on the main floor featured a superb view of the Tetons. Nick's gaze took in the Italian provincial decor. For a moment he focused on the queen-size bed Samantha had brought from Idaho, the bed she'd slept in alone all these years.

His heart hammered in his throat. As if it were yesterday, memories of nights they'd spent in the bedroom of her father's cruiser flooded through his mind.

When he heard Leslie calling him to lunch, he turned his eyes away and pulled the last item from the box. Out came a black, leather-bound book. Curiosity took hold of him and he opened the cover.

Sam had kept a journal. He knew he shouldn't be looking at it, but he couldn't help it. Sinking down on the bed, he opened it to the first page.

Coeur D'Alene, Idaho
February 7
Today I found out I have cancer.

Nick felt the statement slice through him like a knife.

My doctor advised me to keep a journal to record my feelings. He said the process of writing them down would help to keep me sane.

Sane? What's that? I went to him for a pain in my ribs and was tested for a kidney infection. But some lab work revealed that my protein level was elevated. The doctor told me it could be related to a cancer called multiple myeloma, a disease I've never heard of.

But he didn't believe I had it because I'm only twenty-nine. The patients he has seen with this disease are normally in their fifties or older. I have to see an oncologist tomorrow for more tests.

Like a person at the scene of a fire, horrified yet mesmerized, Nick turned to the next page.

February 9
I learned the horrible truth today. I have MM, a cancer of the body's plasma cells. After reading about it, I looked at myself in the mirror a few minutes ago and can't believe what's going on inside of me.

Plasma cells are present in the bone marrow and make up five percent of it. They are responsible for the production of antibodies when the body is dealing with infection.

Cancerous plasma cells build up in the marrow, interfering with normal immune response. They invade and damage the bone, causing tumors to form. Myeloma cells travel to other parts of the body, causing further tumors.

My mind keeps flashing back to a movie Nick and I once saw on video called *Fantastic Voyage*. A team of scientists in a miniature submarine were injected into the bloodstream of a human body through a hypodermic needle.

I remember the frightening moment when the body's alarm system summoned the antibodies.

Nick was remembering that moment, too, but at the time he'd laughed.

> They began attacking the sub, sending it flying through the aorta away from the heart with the speed of an F-5 tornado.
>
> Right now I can visualize the insides of my own body turning traitor, releasing those dreaded myeloma cells. They're going to fill me with tumors. It's hideous, but the doctor says I'm not ready for therapy because they haven't invaded my bones yet.
>
> He says I have to have a transplant sometime within the next six months to a year. For now I have to watch and wait for the disease to progress.
>
> All I want to do is cry. I can't believe this is happening to me. I want normal back. I want everything back I've ever taken for granted. I want Nick. I want our baby.

Dear God. Nick's eyes closed tightly for a moment before he could bring himself to read on.

> *February 11*
> Today I'm trying to learn everything I can do to fight it. I've been reading about other victims who've pursued a number of alternative remedies—the most important being training in meditation and the martial arts. Imagine me learning martial arts!
>
> *June 15*
> The training has stopped me from going insane.

For the first time in five months I'm feeling much stronger mentally and physically than I did before my diagnosis. I believe it's keeping me from needing active therapy. The doctor thought I would need a transplant by now.

Nick shook his head, marveling over her indomitable will. Riveted to every word of pain pouring from her soul, he digested the next few entries.

August 20
Today I learned my IGG protein is on the rise. I've been taking a conservative approach to the disease, deciding I would smolder as long as possible. But the time has come to start the treatment. I have no other option.

Sam's pain and fear drove Nick to his feet while he continued to read.

August 23
I've begun treatment using VAD and Decadron with Aredia.

September 29
I've had five ports installed into my superior vena cava. But they have no blood return and are infected. I feel like I've got the flu. I get a raging fever every time they give me another dose of Aredia.

October 30
The Decadron made me go into a dive after the last dose of the cycle. My hair is falling out. I'm

so horribly fatigued and nauseated by the chemo. Thank God Nick can't see me now. Thank God he was spared this.

Great heaving sobs came out of Nick.

December 3
The doctor says I have a staph infection. He removed the Hickman port and put in a femoral line to collect my stem cells.

January 10
I'm so physically sick. But it doesn't compare to the pain I suffered when I lost Nick and the baby in a matter of seconds. Those papers from Judge Sarkins stating that I'd given up all rights to Jessica brought me such exquisite pain, I'm surprised I've lived long enough to undergo this ordeal.

Sam, sweetheart...

February 4
I've had my transplant. My doctor won't tell me if the torture I've gone through has been for nothing because my protein level is still high and my IGG level is at 2750.

April 21
Because of possible exposure to infected people and germs, I'm still being forced to take a leave of absence from my job. I've been staying at Mom and Dad's house while I get over this emotionally and physically draining experience.

They are saints.

July 10
My goal is to continue injections of Interferon and increase my physical therapy so I'll feel stronger again. As soon as I can manage it, I'm going back to Coeur D'Alene.

August 16
I'm back at work. Marilyn May, a recovering breast cancer patient who's been attending qi-gong with me, has talked me into joining the rowing club with her, through Northern Idaho College. It will provide me another outlet requiring a mental and physical discipline that I hope will help me think with more clarity on the job.

September 18
Everyone in the rowing class is great and tells me I look wonderful, but I see myself in the mirror. This thirty-one-year-old face and body have been through hell. Marilyn says I'm beautiful. She's another saint. I love her better than a sister.

My hair has grown back, a little thinner than before. I'm keeping it shorter to hide the white hairs creeping in among the red. At some point I'll need to start using a rinse.

October 16
I've been back on the job for two months, working a law case for the Idaho Conservation League to ensure that the state and the Environmental Protection Agency enforce the Clean

> Water Act. There's a specific drive to recover
> salmon and steelhead to the rivers polluted by
> the mines and other factors.
>
> This case reminds me of the many long talks
> Nick and I used to have about saving and pre-
> serving the wilds. His ideas have always had a
> great influence on me.

Moisture bathed Nick's cheeks. He came to the entry
marked October 29. The date held particular significance for him, since it had been written two days before her phone call to him.

> By some miracle I'm still here. It appears my
> cancer has gone into remission. I just learned
> the news this afternoon.
> Maybe it's a coincidence, maybe it isn't, but
> tonight the pastor of my church came to see
> me....

His eyes could barely read the rest for the blur.

> Nick will either tear up my letter or hang up on
> me. No matter. I have to try, otherwise this life
> has made no sense at all....

He wiped away the tears with the back of his arm. His
biggest problem now was to face Sam and pretend he
hadn't trespassed on the secret part of her soul.

Hurriedly he placed the journal in the bottom of the
box before putting back the jewelry case and bedside
radio she'd packed on top of it. After leaving it on the

floor by the other boxes the movers had brought in, he left the bedroom.

Before he joined the others, he needed to get his emotions under control. Using the entrance to the office down the hall, he let himself outside and breathed in the frigid air.

Before, whenever he'd looked up at the Tetons, he'd always felt an accompanying loneliness that was at once awesome and inexplicable. It took Sam's heart-wrenching outpourings for him to understand why.

The realization that he hadn't been the only traveller along the seemingly endless, solitary path of suffering brought healing to his wounds. Now his whole soul yearned to heal hers.

He would wait until the next time they were alone. That wouldn't be until her job interview was over, and her parents had gone back to Denver.

Only a few more days, Kincaid.

CHAPTER THIRTEEN

A RECEPTIONIST CAME OUT of the attorney general's office. "They're ready for you now, Ms. Bretton."

"See you in a little while, Dad." Samantha's father had flown to Cheyenne with her to keep her company. She kissed his cheek before entering the conference room full of men.

The attorney general invited her to sit down before he introduced himself and his two assistants, then the governor of Wyoming who was sitting in on the board in an advisory capacity, and the superintendent of Yellowstone and Teton Parks.

"I understand you already know Pierce Gallagher, the chief ranger of Teton Park."

"Yes. It's a pleasure to meet all of you."

"Everyone here has looked over your impressive résumé, Ms. Bretton. Before you came in, it was the consensus of the group that we find out why you would want to fill the new position being created as a special assistant to the U.S. Attorney General's office in Teton Park. With your sterling credentials, you could go into private practice and name your price.

"As you're probably well aware, we've stipulated this is a lifetime career position. You're thirty-one years old, which means you could give thirty-four years to this office. That's a definite plus, since many of the programs in the park are ongoing and need continuity under one guiding hand.

"On the other side of the coin, you're young, attractive, single. Naturally we're concerned that your plans could change. Can you give us any reason to help us not be concerned that unexpected circumstances might cause you to leave prematurely?"

Samantha nodded. "That's a very fair, understandable question. In the first place, I have a thirteen-year-old daughter who lives with her father, Nick Kincaid, the chief ranger for biological wildlife in Teton Park. I've bought a home in Jackson Hole to be near her, and plan to live there and work out of my office for the duration of my life. The only thing that would change my ability to keep working would be if my cancer comes back. I'm in remission and pray that I remain healthy.

"As for my reason for wanting to serve the park, it was Jessica's father who taught me about the sacredness of wildlife. His ideas influenced me to study the kind of law that would help to protect it.

"Nick used to talk about the impact of machines in nature—aircraft overflights, for example—and how they endanger so many species of animals. Working for the Idaho Wildlife Federation, I've come to appreciate what he meant.

"When you're out in the woods, it's the sound of silence that makes the forest such a desirable, even spiritual, place to be. Lovers of the outdoors expect to find that silence in our national parks. It's my opinion the animals and the plants are God's gift to man. It's man's obligation to take care of them. That means we protect them by removing any menace to them in the air, in the water, in the land.

"Gentlemen, I would deem it an honor and a privilege to fight for their right to exist as creation intended, whether it be in Teton Park or elsewhere."

After she'd finished, there was such a long silence she worried that her admission about being a cancer survivor must have spooked them. But it didn't matter. If she didn't get the job, she was glad the money would be there for someone else to fight for the park.

She would always be able to run her own law practice and continue the struggle for the preservation of the environment by representing private citizens and groups.

To her surprise, the superintendent started clapping. Soon everyone joined in. The attorney general got to his feet. He looked around, then smiled at her. "It appears the vote is unanimous. Welcome aboard, Ms. Bretton."

Thank you, her heart cried. She was one step closer to Nick.

"Thank you. I'm thrilled."

Samantha stood up and shook hands with each of them. When she came to Pierce, he squeezed her palm extra hard. "I'll hug you later," he whispered.

"MARILYN? How are you feeling today?"

"Better and better. At this rate I'll be looking for a job in another few weeks."

Samantha moved the receiver to her other ear. "That's wonderful! When you're well enough for that, you'll come stay with me to celebrate."

"I'm counting the hours!"

''Do you think you can stand a little more good news?''

''I already know you got the job.''

''How could you have heard that? I just returned from Cheyenne with Dad a few minutes ago and haven't told anybody but Mom.''

''Hey—it's *me* you're talking to. Of course you got it, you silly goose! It was a foregone conclusion. What I'm waiting for is the *big* news.''

''The kind you're talking about may never come.'' Samantha's voice trembled.

''Want to bet? If Nick didn't want you around all the time, you'd be commuting to Tennessee on a limited basis instead of living in Jackson.''

''That still doesn't mean he—''

''Oh, for heaven sake,'' Marilyn interrupted. ''You didn't survive for nothing. Right?''

There was no one in the world like Marilyn. ''Right. Thank you for being the greatest friend on earth.''

''I was just going to say the same thing to you. Call me tomorrow and give me the latest chapter and verse.''

''I will. I promise.''

The second Samantha hung up the phone she heard, ''Honey?'' When she turned, she saw both her parents standing in the doorway of her bedroom.

She could sense a certain tension coming from them she hadn't felt when she'd first walked into the house. Her adrenaline surged. ''What's wrong?'' she cried in alarm. ''Has something happened to Jessica or Nick?''

''They're fine,'' her mother assured her. ''While you were on the phone, your cell phone went off. We thought it was probably Jessica calling from school to see if you were back from Cheyenne yet, but it was Dr. Blake.''

Dr. Blake?

A cold sweat broke out over her body.

"Apparently he was on vacation when you phoned to get the results of your last blood test. Whoever gave you the information was reading from the first results."

Samantha's stomach lurched.

"While he was reviewing your chart today, he noticed the latest results weren't in, so he called the lab. For some reason, those results never reached his office. He says these things happen, but it's very rare.

"Anyway, he's calling the lab at the hospital here in Jackson to arrange for the blood work. If possible, he's going to see if they'll fit you in before closing today. He said to give it fifteen minutes, then phone over there to find out."

Oh no.

Her father smiled. "You're going to be fine, honey."

Her mother walked over and put her arms around her. "You've felt marvelous for several months and have never looked more beautiful. Don't worry about another routine blood test, darling. Too many miraculous things have happened for your happiness to be taken away now."

Samantha loved her parents. They'd always been positive about her illness. Her fight had been their fight. But this time things were different. The stakes were too high—she had everything to live for.

She eased away from her mother. "I don't know about that, Mom. All I asked was to see my daughter again so I could tell her how much I love her. That wish has been granted and much more.

"The mistake at the lab is probably a sign that I went too far when I wanted Nick, too. Maybe—" Her voice broke.

"Samantha Bretton!" Her father spoke to her as he had when she was a little girl who didn't want to get back on her bike after she'd fallen. "Over two months ago you were given a clean bill of health. That hasn't changed, and it isn't going to.

"Call the lab. If they're ready for you, we'll drive you over and wait for you. The number is on the pad in your office. Let's go."

Her limbs felt like lead as she followed them down the hall. Each time in the past she'd been able to call on the reserve of faith deep inside to get her through the blackest periods.

But that was before she'd accomplished what needed to be done. Now that she'd had the reunion with her daughter, did it mean she'd run out of blessings?

When she reached for the phone, the answer came with full force. She could almost hear the pastor telling her to look upon her remission as permanent, and treat it as a rebirth.

That was what she was going to do. What she *had* to do.

"JESSICA? Over here!"

Nick's daughter had been walking toward the school bus with her friends. The second she heard her dad's voice she came running to the car and got in.

"Did Mom get the job?"

"There was never any question about that, but now it's official."

Pierce had called to tell him about the reverent ovation after Sam's eloquent speech. Between her conviction that it was a sacred duty to protect wildlife, plus her statement that she was a recovering cancer patient, there hadn't been a dry eye in the room. It had brought the members of the board to their feet.

The news that she'd given Nick the credit for guiding her along her chosen path was a little present Pierce tacked on at the end of the conversation for him to savor. Though Jessica had already told Nick the same thing weeks ago, and he'd read the words for himself in Sam's journal, hearing his best friend repeat them stirred his emotions more than ever.

"Do you think she's home yet?"

"I'm sure of it. I thought we'd drive over and congratulate her." Surprise her would be more like it. Nick didn't care if her parents were still at the house. The desire to see Sam had turned into a burning need.

Jessica didn't know about the money her mother had anonymously donated to enable the park to always have an attorney in residence. One day when his daughter was older, he would let her know what a truly rare and remarkable woman Sam was.

"There's Grandpa's car. They're home!"

He pulled in the driveway and they both got out. The blood pounded in his ears while he waited for Sam to answer the door.

"Maybe they can't hear the bell. Mom gave me a key so I could always let myself in." Jessica got it out of her purse. After she'd unlocked it, they went inside. "Mom? Grandma?"

Nick frowned. "Maybe they decided to grab a bite to eat in town. Let's check the garage."

To his disappointment, the new green Pathfinder Sam had bought over the holidays was missing.

"Heck. I'll call Mom on my cell phone and we'll drive wherever they are." In a minute Jessica said, "I got her voice mail."

"She probably turned the phone off for her interview and forgot to turn it back on."

"I guess."

Nick heard a dejected Jessica leave a message for her mother to call back as soon as she could. After she hung up she said, "Dad? Can we go look for them? Maybe they're at Shiver's."

She was reading his mind. "Good idea. We'll get a hamburger at the same time."

He purposely drove them on a circuitous route through the downtown area of Jackson in the hope of spotting Sam's car, but there was no sign of it.

"Grandpa said he wanted to get a sheepskin jacket like Mom's before they flew back to Denver. Maybe she drove them over to Western Outfitters."

"That's possible. We'll see if we can spot them."

When that failed to produce results, he drove them to Shiver's on East Broadway for a meal.

"Let's order takeout. Then we can eat on the way back to the house," Jessica suggested.

Nick agreed. He was as anxious as she was to find Sam.

Ten minutes later they started down Broadway. Near Willow Street a couple of cars pulled out into the evening traffic from the parking area of St. John's

Medical Center. One of them was the latest model green Pathfinder.

Nick's blood turned to ice water.

Jessica was busy eating her hamburger and hadn't noticed. It was just as well, since he didn't want to alarm her.

To play it safe he stayed several car lengths behind, but there was no doubt it was Sam at the wheel. He'd caught the glint of red-gold in the dying rays of the winter sun before it had dipped below the horizon.

Why had Sam gone to the hospital with her parents? Why hadn't she told him that she had an appointment scheduled?

Oh, no.

Why now? Why today on the heels of her trip to Cheyenne? She'd accepted the job offer. It was official. She wouldn't have followed through if there'd been any question she couldn't do it because of failing health.

Had the flight been too much for her? Had she been working too hard, trying to get settled, and reached the verge of exhaustion?

He would never forget the entries in her journal, the descriptions of what her physical suffering had been like, not to mention her mental and emotional agony.

"Dad? Don't you want your hamburger?"

"I'll eat when we get to the house."

"What's the matter? You look kind of sick."

Nothing escaped his daughter's eagle eye. "Today I verified that the moose had been poisoned."

"That's awful. When you find out who did it, Mom'll be able to prosecute them."

"I'm counting on it, honey." *I'm counting on living the rest of my life with her. I'm planning on us both living a long, long time.*

Nick followed Sam to her home. If she knew he'd been driving behind her, she showed no evidence of it. The garage door went up and the Pathfinder disappeared inside.

Once again he and Jessica went up to the front door, but this time his daughter unlocked it and they entered the house without ringing the bell. "I'll wait for you in the living room," he said before she ran off to find her mother.

He glanced around. Sam had Mrs. Bretton's flair for decorating. The house reflected elegant taste without being ostentatious. He'd never guess she'd barely moved in. Paintings had been hung. She'd placed art books on shelves and tables next to pots of azaleas and poinsettias.

Nick realized that Sam had never done anything in her life that he didn't love except reject him in order not to trap him.

What was the old saying? Set something free. If it doesn't come back, it was never yours to lose.

I was always yours, Sam. He'd never wanted to be set free. *Now you're back in my life, I'm going to keep what's always been mine.*

"Hi, Nick. You remember my mom and dad, of course."

Sam's steady voice sounded too in control for whatever she was hiding. He turned in her direction. She'd come into the room with her parents and Jessica. She made a sensational picture in a tailored green suit with a green-on-white print scarf. Professional, yet feminine.

He shook their hands. "It's good to see both of you again. You don't seem any older." It was the truth. "I find it hard to believe thirteen years have passed."

Nick saw pleading in their eyes, particularly in Mr. Bretton's. They wanted and needed forgiveness for their role in keeping him and Sam apart.

"Let's agree to forgive the past," Nick said.

"You've grown into a wonderful man who has raised a beautiful daughter." His voice shook. Not from age, but emotion. Something was wrong. Nick could feel it in every atom of his body. It was tearing him apart.

He smiled at his daughter. "Jessica's always been a joy."

"Of course she has," Mrs. Bretton cried softly, hugging her granddaughter around her neck.

He turned back to gaze at Sam, studying her features for any sign of distress. There was none. She was a master at hiding her feelings when she needed to. He wasn't about to let her get away with it this time.

"After the board concluded their meeting, Pierce called me. I hear congratulations are in order."

She nodded. "For better or worse, I'm the new park attorney."

What was she telling him? Was she talking about the job being more than she could handle? Was she talking about her health?

"This calls for a celebration." Nick stared at Jessica. "You won't mind if I steal your mother for a little while, will you? Pierce and Leslie have planned a small surprise. I've been ordered by the chief to deliver her to their house, then I'll bring her back." He turned to Sam's parents. "Is that all right with everyone?"

"Of course," Mrs. Bretton replied. "We'll have loads of fun here, won't we, Jessica?"

As she nodded, her grandfather said, "You two go on. This is a red letter day for the park. We'll watch out for our Jessie."

Our Jessie...

Who would have ever dreamed up a scenario like this? One look in Sam's eyes and Nick knew she was remembering another night long ago when her parents had dismissed any possibility of him marrying their daughter.

"If you'll get your coat, we'll go."

Sam kissed her daughter's cheek before leaving the room. Jessica walked him to the front door. "Have a good time, Dad."

"You can't *not* have a good time at the Gallaghers." He tousled her curls. In a moment Sam joined them, wearing a fitted black cashmere coat. She was so breathtaking, words failed him.

"Let's go."

They stepped outside. Though it was only a few minutes after six, it felt like midnight. He helped her into the car before going around to the driver's side.

Once they reached the main road leading to the park he said, "You didn't sign on with the park anytime too soon. I've got a case you can dig your teeth into right now."

The conversation he intended to have with her

couldn't take place until after they'd reached their destination, so he'd decided to talk shop instead.

"Tell me about it."

"A moose was accidentally exposed to poison meant for a coyote and it died. I traced the animal's prints back to the source and delivered a citation to the ranch owner. He said I couldn't prove anything, and even if I could, nobody would do anything about it because everybody knows coyotes are a nuisance."

"What kind of evidence do you have?"

Nick spent the next few minutes giving her the gruesome details.

"I'd say that man's in bad trouble. From what you've told me, I'll be able to prosecute his case as a felony under the Lacey Act. It carries heavy penalties including imprisonment and fines. When word of that gets out to the other ranchers in the area, it should make them wary."

"That case was just for starters. I've got more I need to tell you. One involves some guys I caught heli-skiing where the wolverines are denning. The other is a real problem. We're still searching for the person who killed two large adult mule deer east of the Kelly Road.

"I discovered them the other morning. They'd been killed for their trophy size antlers. One buck had been shot and his antlers removed. The other deer was dead, but its antlers were intact, probably because someone came by, causing the poachers to run away."

"That's horrible."

He nodded. "Pierce has put out a bulletin through the Park Watch and Jackson Hole Crimestoppers. A five thousand dollar reward has been posted for information leading to an arrest.''

Sam let out a heavy sigh. ''Killing beautiful, gentle animals in cold blood for a wall trophy is one of the most appalling crimes I can think of.''

Nick grimaced. ''I agree. What's worse, every time it happens, the gene pool for the mule deer population is diminished. As I said earlier, the park has needed someone like you in the worst way.''

I need you in the worst way.

''Fortunately, the funding is in place so there can be an advocate for wildlife for many years to come, no matter who it is,'' she said in a quiet aside.

Shut up, Sam. You're terrifying me.

''Didn't we just pass the Gallaghers'?''

''We're not going to Pierce's house.''

Her head jerked toward him. ''I thought you said they were having a little party.''

''I lied.''

CHAPTER FOURTEEN

SAMANTHA *had* been right!

There was a new aggressiveness, a kind of steely determination about him that reminded her of the old, confident Nick. After all the years of wishing she could be with him again, after all these weeks of suppressing her longings in front of him, was it possible he was finally going to let down his guard and tell her how he felt about her? She didn't know how much longer she could stand the suspense.

They'd driven to Nick's house, straight into the garage. She heard the door close behind the car, isolating them from the world.

"Why were you at the hospital earlier?"

"How did you know I was there?"

He shut off the motor. "I saw your car."

She was trying to read between the lines. Was it possible he was more frightened about her cancer coming back than he'd let on? Had he been putting on a brave front for Jessica, when all this time he was worried sick?

Before she made too many assumptions that could be wrong, she got out of the car before he could come around and walked through the kitchen to the living room.

While she waited for him to say more, she took off

her coat and placed it over a chair. In the shadowy light of one of the lamps he'd turned on, his features looked gaunt, his eyes bleak and pain-filled. He stood in the center of the room with his strong legs slightly apart, as if bracing himself.

"I'm waiting for an answer."

Tell him the way it is, Samantha. The way it's always going to be until the end.

"A recovering cancer patient has to be checked and rechecked on a constant basis. You know that."

He folded his arms. "Not on the day she pulled off a coup that will benefit the park for a score of years to come. What changed after your plane landed at the airport in Jackson? Don't insult my intelligence by telling me you had a standing appointment at St. John's for five o'clock in the afternoon on today of all days."

She averted her eyes. "I'd just walked in the door when I received a call from my doctor in Coeur D'Alene. It seems the results of my last blood test never arrived at his office from the lab. The nurse who told me everything was normal had mistakenly read the first set of results. So he set things up here for me to have another test."

"But the first one indicated you were well, right?"

Her heart came into her throat. "Yes."

"So the results of this test will reveal the same thing."

"Yes. I'm positive they will," she said, wanting to assure him because the lines in his rugged face had grown more pronounced.

"You wouldn't lie to me. You haven't been sick and didn't tell anyone?"

She shook her head. "I've never felt better."

There was a whiteness around his lips.

Oh, Nick—

"When will you know the results?" His words were terse, anxious.

"They said it would take a few hours, then they'd inform the doctor. Because it's so late in the day, I won't hear before tomorrow."

His gray eyes glistened with tears. She moved toward him. Her whole body was trembling. "Don't be afraid for me."

"How can I not be?"

With one question, he'd bared his heart and soul to her.

"Because this is going to be the state of my life from here on out. Blood tests and the wait for results. I'm convinced I was given a stay of execution long enough to get to know my daughter and assure her she had a mother who loved her and never wanted to give her up. I expect to live a long time."

"But some of the entries in your journal don't—" His hands had formed fists.

"What do you know about my journal?"

His eyes studied her features. "I know everything. The day the movers came, I emptied the last box they brought in. Your journal was on the bottom. I read it from cover to cover. Every word."

She gasped and looked away. No wonder he was frightened. She'd held nothing back in those entries.

"Don't be angry with me. You took thirteen years of my life from me, Sam. I had every right to find out why. At least that's what I told myself until I started reading about your pain. That's when I began the journey through mine…''

Her head swung back toward him. "What do you mean?" she asked in shock.

"Do you have any idea of my self-loathing for not coming after you years ago? For not understanding your grief? Your guilt? For not lifting a finger to help you because my damnable pride got in the way?

"In my rage I thought about finding you. For years I dreamed about walking into the library at Harvard where you were studying and dragging you out of there without giving a damn if I made a scene. I wanted you to pay for what you'd done to me.

"I'm not the saint you've made me out to be, Sam." He paced the floor, then stopped and threw his head back as if he were in the throes of agony.

"I've committed the greatest crime a father could commit against his daughter. From the beginning I shut out all the questions Jessica wanted to ask about you before she could dare put voice to them. I was going to show you I didn't need you, that Jessica didn't need you.

"It was easy. My anger over your rejection sustained me for the years I spent hiring one nanny after another. I must have gone through dozens of them.

"Several of the eligible nannies would have made great wives and mothers. They were vocal and willing. But I wasn't having any of that. Neither was Jessica, who was so jealous of every woman who came near, she made the perfect buffer.

"There were lots of women along the way, women I met at work or through friends. Naturally, they hoped we would end up planning a wedding. I scoffed at the idea. Your refusal to fight for Jessica and me because you couldn't trust me enough to love and care for you, had killed the desire for marriage on my part.''

Samantha hugged her arms to her waist while she listened to the pain that had been bottled up inside him all these years. Pain *she'd* caused.

''This summer when Jessica knew she'd be starting high school, she protested against me hiring another woman. The change in her had a lot to do with Leslie, the one female my daughter took to because she was Cory's nanny and posed no threat.

''Without making it official, Pierce's wife more or less filled the breach when there was an emergency and I couldn't be home on time, or not at all. We were limping along. Then I heard your voice on the phone....''

His emotions were so palpable, she bowed her head.

''The morning after Halloween, Jessica went to work with me. It took all day for me to find that place in my soul where I had started to forgive you for what you'd done to me.

''Jessica sensed something was wrong and asked me if I needed to talk. My little girl, the parent. She'd reversed the roles.

''I said, 'If you had a chance to meet your mother, how would you feel about that?'''

A hushed quiet followed while Samantha waited to hear the rest.

''You should have seen her eyes.... That's when pain and guilt scorched my soul like a red-hot poker. It was clear she wanted her mother. She'd always wanted her mother.''

His expression grew black. ''Later on, when you

told her you couldn't come for the mother-daughter party because of some work commitment, I swear I could have strangled you with my bare hands.''

''I'm so sorry.''

''Stop apologizing, Sam. Listen to what I'm saying.'' The cords stood out in his neck. ''It was my fault. All of it. I was so brutal to you on the phone and at the Elk Inn that you were terrified of my reaction, with good reason.''

She shook her head. ''Not terrified, never that. Only conscious of a blessing I'd been granted, and didn't dare ask for more. Don't do this to yourself, Nick,'' she begged. ''I've been down that path. Between the two of us, I think we've crucified ourselves long enough. We have to think of Jessica now.''

She heard his sharp intake of breath. ''You mean the Jessica who became an instant grown-up when she thought you'd rejected her? The one determined to take care of her good old dad?''

Samantha let out an incredulous cry. ''Old?''

He slowly nodded. ''Oh yes. She let me know she'd be there to watch over me in my old age. We didn't need anyone else. It had always been the two of us, and that was the way things were going to stay.''

''Oh Nick…'' Tears rolled down her cheeks.

''That's the kind of great father I turned out to be,'' he said in self-recrimination. ''My anger toward you has done psychological damage to our daughter.

''A parent is supposed to give his child the tools to grow up well-rounded and independent. You live in the hope that one day, at the right time, she'll find a great guy and go off happily into the sunset to start her own family.

"Not our Jessica. I'm the one responsible for stunting her growth. That became obvious when you told her you couldn't come to the party. She immediately informed me she was going to get straight As like you and become a biologist like me. Together we would live in the park doing the work we love side by side, and I would never be alone.

"Give a psychiatrist a crack at Jessica and you would discover a father who has done it all wrong from day one."

"But you haven't!" Samantha disagreed. "She's loving and forgiving. I've noticed how open she is to everything."

A solemn expression stole over his handsome features. "That's because you're in her life. It has changed everything." He took a step toward her. "It has changed me. Now I want to talk about *us*. I want you for my wife as soon as possible."

"You mean it?" she cried. "You're willing to risk marrying me knowing my history? Knowing that every month I go in for a test, you'll be worried about the results?"

His body went rigid.

"I'm not saying this for me, Nick. I'm saying it for you. Now that you've put your anger behind you and we've made our peace, are you certain you wouldn't rather find another woman to love who doesn't have my past problem?"

"There's a risk to loving anyone. You're worth that risk."

"Oh Nick! I want us to be happy. You need to be very sure about this before we make any plans or tell Jessica. At least sleep on it tonight and we'll talk more in the morning. Please take me home now. To be honest, I'm very tired. It's been a big day for so many reasons.''

SAM WASN'T LYING. She looked utterly exhausted and spent. It brought out an ethereal beauty. He didn't want to see her like this. It reminded him of all she'd gone through. Her journal entries still haunted him.

She was right about one thing. If he couldn't get past his fear for her, then a new nightmare would begin. If she was sick again, then so be it. They would fight it together. Tomorrow her parents were leaving. After she'd heard from the doctor, Nick would force her to marry him, even if it meant kidnapping her to do it. She would have no choice in the matter. Pierce would help him.

Not trusting himself to get within five feet of her, Nick left her to freshen up while he waited for her in the car.

En route to Jackson his cell phone went off.

''That's probably Jessica.''

Nick checked the caller ID. ''It's business.'' He clicked on. ''Rex? What's up?''

''You know those guides camping in Garnet Canyon?''

''Yes?''

''From the stories filtering in, there was a sudden earth tremor. I'll be damned if they weren't caught in an avalanche. I need you on the mountain to help with the rescue. Are you home?''

''I'm on my way to Jackson.''

''Then I'll tell one of the rangers to bring some extra gear for you.''

"Fine. I'll be at the rendezvous point as soon as I can."

"What's wrong?" Sam asked the question the second he'd hung up.

"There's been an avalanche. It has trapped some guides and professional skiers doing winter maneuvers. They've been working toward their mountaineering certification with the American Avalanche Institute. If they come out of this alive, they'll have experienced one lesson that couldn't have been gained any other way."

The thought of being buried under a mountain of snow was too horrible to contemplate. What if more fell while Nick and the others were out there?

"Where are you meeting everyone?"

"The airport. I'll fly in with one of the rescue helicopters."

"I thought you were a biologist!"

"I am, but I also trained under Pierce to learn mountaineering skills for emergencies like this. He's probably there now. This park is his baby."

"You two are very close, aren't you."

"Yes. In some ways he reminds me of Joey."

"Jessica told me he was killed on his motorcycle right before graduation. I'm so sorry. He was a wonderful friend to us. If I'd known—"

"Don't go there, Sam."

She flashed him a brave smile. "I won't. Since the airport is on the way to town, I'll drop you off, then go on home. When you want me and Jessica to come for you, we will."

"It could be an all-night operation. We'll have to wait and see. If so, Pierce will give me a ride to the house after we get back. I'll phone you tomorrow to bring my car home.''

''No matter how long it takes, Jessica's going to be anxious until she hears from you.''

Too soon they reached the airport. It was hell having to be separated right now. While he was taking the house key off the ring, he could feel Sam's anxiety.

Without conscious thought he caught her face between his hands and kissed her long and hard.

''I'll see you in the morning.''

AS HE STRODE AWAY, Sam climbed into the driver's seat and started the car, but she was still trembling from his passion. Like the tremor that had caused the avalanche, Nick had unleashed such a powerful force inside of her, all she could do was ride it while it swept her along at heart-stopping speed.

When she finally landed in her driveway in Jackson, she rested her head against the steering wheel, willing her equilibrium to come back.

''Mom?''

At the sound of Jessica's voice, she recoiled and opened the door. Her daughter's face was a study in fright. ''Where's Dad? What's wrong?''

She needed a minute before answering any questions. Nick had disoriented her, and Sam was afraid it was permanent.

''Your father had to help rescue some people trapped by an avalanche. While I was pulling the keys out of the ignition, they slipped from my hand.''

''No they didn't, Mom,'' Jessica said with that

forthright honesty of hers. "Are you still feeling sick?"

Samantha got out of the car and shut the door. "What do you mean *still,* darling?"

"When Dad and I were driving home from Shiver's earlier, I saw your car pulling away from the hospital."

"Why didn't you ask Grandma and Grandpa? They would have told you I went in for a routine blood test."

"Promise?"

"Promise. I'll be getting periodic blood tests from now on. They take about five minutes and don't hurt."

"I bet you're scared, huh."

Always the truth, Samantha. "Yes."

"If your cancer comes back, will you have to get more chemo?"

"Yes."

"I hope you're okay."

She grabbed her daughter and hugged her tightly. "I hope so, too. But if I'm not, I'll do whatever I have to do to get better again."

"My history teacher's husband has cancer. I told her about you, that yours might come back. She said it's not really so terrible because everyone has to die sometime. And since she knows her husband doesn't have a long time to live, it has helped their family to enjoy every day they have with him. She said it could be a blessing."

"Oh darling." Samantha held her tighter.

She was going to have to meet this teacher of Jessica's and thank her for the priceless gift she'd given her.

"You don't have to worry about anything, Mom. I'll go to all your doctor's appointments with you. I'll take care of you. You'll never have to be alone."

My precious, precious girl.

The words reminded Samantha of the conversation she'd just had with Nick at his house.

Clearly, Jessica was able to deal with the cancer threat much better than Samantha or Nick had ever dreamed. It was the situation between her parents that was tearing her daughter apart. There was only one way to solve that problem.

Tonight Nick had bared his soul to her. He'd asked her to be his wife. He'd called on her heart, body and soul, all of which had always belonged to him.

Later, when she went to pick him up, she would tell him she wanted to get married no matter what. Nothing was more important than being together. But right this minute, it was time to help their daughter.

"Come on, darling. Let's go in the house. It's freezing out here."

Her parents met them at the door. *Two more people Samantha needed to help.* Two loving, marvelous human beings riddled with guilt and pain, who'd never been able to forgive themselves for what they imagined they'd done to ruin her life.

Tonight all the pain and the guilt and the self-flagellation were about to end.

They went into the living room. Her father relieved both of them of their coats. "Where's Nick?"

"Dad's out with the rangers helping some guys caught in an avalanche," Jessica explained in a matter-of-fact tone. She'd grown up with a father whose life was dedicated to the rescue of animals and humans.

Samantha had a lot to learn from their daughter, since right now part of her was terrified something could happen to Nick, either on the mountain or in the helicopter.

"Did you have a nice time at the Gallaghers'?" her mother asked.

With that question Samantha's heart picked up speed. "Why don't you all sit down and I'll tell you."

Something in her tone must have alerted them it was no casual directive. They did her bidding, but three pairs of anxious eyes remained fastened on her.

Filled with a restless energy, Samantha stood behind a chair and held on to it.

"There was no party. Nick only said that because he wanted to be alone with me. We went to the house and had a long talk about everything. It was one that should have taken place years ago, but that's irrelevant now. What's important is Nick and I are going to be married."

A collective cry of relief rang throughout the living room. Jessica's young, smooth face radiated joy. She jumped up to hug Samantha and almost knocked her over.

Through the profusion of red-gold curls, Samantha smiled at her parents and watched the lines of sorrow vanish from their faces. All that remained were the etchings of life experiences, both the good and the bad, that had formed their character over the years.

Their eyes sent her an implicit message. They rejoiced in her decision to grab her happiness with both hands and not let the amount of time she had left on this earth matter.

While she rocked her daughter in her arms, they heard her cell phone go off.

"Maybe they didn't need your father, after all, and he wants us to come and get him!"

She let go of Jessica long enough to pull it out of her purse. To her disappointment the caller ID said Out of Area. It could be Marilyn, or even Reed, her former boss.

"Hello?"

"Samantha Bretton?" She recognized that voice.

"Dr. Blake?" His call had the effect of knocking the wind out of her. Sudden tension filled the living room once more. "I didn't expect to hear from you until tomorrow."

"Good news deserves to be delivered as soon as possible."

She gripped the phone tighter. "I'm still normal?"

"You are. As I told your parents, the loss of a lab test result is something that rarely happens. I'm sorry you had to go through the ordeal of waiting and worrying unnecessarily."

She gave her family a thumbs-up, but could hardly see because of her tears. "I'm not. I'm convinced it happened to help me make the most important decision of my life. I've moved to Jackson, Wyoming, and I'm getting married."

"Now you've made *my* day. When you get a new doctor where you're living, I'll have the records sent. To be safe, you should plan on having another test in a month. Have you experienced more flulike symptoms associated with the Interferon?"

"Once in a while I get a chill, but nothing else to speak of."

"Terrific. Phone me anytime, Samantha."

"I will. You have no idea how much this call has meant to me."

"I think I do. Good night."

"Good night, Dr. Blake, and thank you."

As she hung up, the floor suddenly moved beneath her feet. She grabbed hold of the end of the couch to keep from falling. It was a heavy sofa, yet it seemed to be moving of its own accord.

Everyone looked at each other as a few books fell to the floor. The brass candlestick on the hearth toppled over. Jessica's eyes grew round while they waited to see if anything else would happen. When it didn't she cried, "We've just had an earthquake!"

"Will you look at that dining room chandelier?" Sam's father exclaimed.

Sure enough, it was swinging back and forth like a pendulum.

"Do you get these often?" Samantha's mother asked Jessica.

"No. Dad says there are tremors all the time throughout the Yellowstone-Teton corridor, but we don't usually feel them."

"I remember there was a major quake in the fifties near here. It broke the Hebgen Lake dam in Montana and created a lake."

"Quake Lake! We studied about it at school."

Samantha's thoughts flew to Nick and Pierce. "Jessica, honey? Call Cory on your cell and find out if he and Leslie are all right."

"Okay. Poor Lucy," her daughter moaned. "I bet it frightened her to death. Dad says earthquakes terrify animals."

"And people," Samantha's mother murmured.

"Mom? Are you okay?"

"Yes." She smiled. "Just startled."

"How about you, Dad?"

"I'm fine. Come on, my love. Let's walk around and see if there has been any structural damage to the house."

He helped his wife to her feet. They set the things up that had fallen, then disappeared into the other room.

Samantha kept an arm around Jessica while she talked to Cory. "Just a minute…" The girl lifted her head. "Mom? Cory told me they didn't feel anything, but Leslie wants to talk to you. I'm going to turn on the TV!"

"Thanks, honey." She took the phone from her before Jessica dashed off. "Leslie?"

"Hi. Are you all right?"

"We're fine."

"Cory said your chandelier was swaying."

"You should have seen it!"

"I don't know, Samantha. I'm kind of glad I didn't. Cameron's mother called me while Jessica was talking to Cory. She's the first person designated to relay information on our phone tree. Her husband just got word that the epicenter was in Idaho."

"I thought it came from Yellowstone."

"I assumed the same thing. From what I've gathered, no one in Moose was affected. Sometimes it happens that way."

Beads of perspiration dotted Sam's hairline. "Leslie—"

"I know what you're going to ask," her friend interrupted gently. "I haven't heard from Pierce. The minute I do, I'll call you. So far no park rangers have reported any problems to dispatch except for the avalanche."

"Thank heaven."

"Yes indeed," Leslie commiserated. "Cory says they're talking about it on the cable network."

"I'm going to go look right now. If I hear from Nick, I'll call you."

"Good."

After they hung up she rushed through the house to the family room, where Jessica had turned on the TV.

"...but the early reports indicate no fatalities yet. The epicenter of the 6.9 earthquake near Borah's Peak in central Idaho sent out tremors that have been felt in parts of Montana, Nevada, Oregon, Utah, Washington, Wyoming, and the provinces of Alberta, British Columbia and Saskatchewan, Canada."

By now Samantha's parents had joined them. "Nothing's broken, honey. No cracks in walls or ceilings that we could see. We were lucky."

"That's a relief. Thanks, Dad. Jessica, honey? Will you turn to another station and see if they've got any local information?"

"...tuning in, some Jackson residents got a surprise tonight when the Idaho quake knocked glasses and cans off shelves and caused some vending machines in a few local businesses to topple over. Fortunately, no injuries have been reported yet.

"The biggest story tonight focuses on a rescue attempt being carried out in Grand Teton National Park. Seismologists say an earlier tremor foreshadowing the major quake dislodged a wall of snow off the Grand

Teton, burying some avalanche experts who've been camped at the base for several days, carrying out a training session.

"Rangers and other rescue workers are doing everything possible to free the victims. The public is being asked to stay away. We'll keep the following Jackson number on the screen for those people inquiring about the victims through the sheriff's office. Please do not call unless you're a relative."

While the announcer was still talking, Jessica turned to Samantha. "Dad gets so mad when people show up to watch. They just get in the way."

"It's human nature, Jessie." Samantha's father turned off the TV. "I've got a great idea. While we're waiting to hear from your dad, let's get in the car and go out for a steak dinner. I'd like to celebrate your mother's new job." *And her good news from the doctor,* his expression said.

"It's a terrific idea, Dad." If Samantha had to stay here and think about all the things that could happen to Nick, she would go mad.

TWO HOURS LATER Samantha pulled into the driveway of her house. They'd been at dinner all that time. There was still no word from Nick.

Her parents looked tired. Once they entered the house, she urged them to go to bed. Jessica wanted to watch more cable news coverage of the earthquake, but by midnight her eyelids were drooping, and no wonder. It had been a long, emotional day.

Samantha turned off the TV. "Come on, honey. Time to go upstairs." Jessica didn't protest.

Tucking her daughter into bed was a joy that Samantha cherished. "Thank you for letting me treat you like a little girl sometimes."

Jessica was almost asleep. "I like it," she whispered.

"Honey? Since your grandparents are here, I'm going to drive to the house and wait for your father."

"That's good. It'll make him so happy to find you there, Mom."

"If by any chance he calls you, pretend I'm here asleep. I want to surprise him."

"Don't worry. I won't give you away."

"I can always count on you. Is your house key in your purse?"

"Yes. It's in the living room."

"I'll find it. Talk to you in the morning." She leaned over to kiss her forehead. A contented smile on her daughter's face was the last thing Samantha saw before she turned out the light.

Not the least bit tired herself, she hurried downstairs to wash her hair and shower. After donning jeans and a cable knit sweater, she left the bedroom with her journal. After retrieving her jacket and the key, she was ready to go.

Once she'd left the town behind, the grand image of the jagged Tetons shooting up from Jackson Hole in the middle of the winter night startled her. Tonight she understood why they were heralded as America's most famous mountain vista. To think this was Nick's backyard. Now it was hers, too....

All was quiet in the park. As she drove into Moose, she felt above the visor for the remote control device. Once the house came in sight, she raised the garage door. With the aid of Jessica's key, she let herself into the kitchen.

After removing her jacket, she sat down at the table to write in her journal. Until Nick walked in the front door, she would bring her entries up to date.

Jackson, Wyoming
January 3

It's quarter to three in the morning. I'm in Nick's kitchen, waiting for Pierce to drop him off. They've been out on a dangerous rescue operation.

As soon as Nick gets here, I'm going to tell him I want to get married as soon as possible.

Seven hours ago I made that decision. It seems fitting that as soon as I did, there was an earthquake. It shook the earth and a huge part of the continent.

Tonight at dinner my adorable daughter asked me and my parents why we thought the quake had happened when it did.

Dad said no one knew the answer. Pressure had been building under the earth's crust for years and for some reason it finally found release today. He gave her a perfectly sound, logical explanation, but I have my own theory.

I'm convinced there has been a special force at work in the cosmos. Today I got the job I wanted. Tonight I received another clean bill of health from the doctor.

All the stars and planets have lined up in a

particular way to open my eyes. I can see clearly now. I see what Nick saw so many years ago.

We belong together!

I've come to my senses at last.

Is it any wonder an earthquake followed?

I'm reminded of a game my friends and I used to play in elementary school. Red Light, Green Light. When it was red, you couldn't cross the line.

Today it's green, green, green.

CHAPTER FIFTEEN

THE MAN STRAPPED IN the toboggan drifted in and out of consciousness. He muttered something. Nick crouched down next to him. "What are you trying to say?" He put his ear to the man's bluish lips to listen.

"L—Leo…" His voice faded before he blacked out again.

Nick signaled the others to get the man to the snow machine, and from there to the chopper.

After putting his skis back on, Nick used his poles to push off toward the last group of rangers. They were huddled around one of the injured guides, who was suffering from a dislocated hip.

"Pierce?"

His friend turned around.

"Has everyone been accounted for from the master list?"

"Yes. This man's the last one."

"Was there a member of the group named Leo? The guy we just shipped out on the toboggan kept muttering that name."

Pierce frowned. "It doesn't sound familiar. I'll ask."

While Nick waited, he lifted his head to study the couloir where the avalanche had buried eight men in a sea of ice and snow. They'd survived because of their expertise and the quick response of the rescue teams. Still, it was a miracle their lives had been spared.

But the greatest miracle of all was Sam. She was a survivor. Nick couldn't wait to get back to her so their life could begin. They were going to have a life together. A long one.

"Leo's the guy's brother." Pierce said a minute later. "We told him we'd get word to him. We know eight men camped here, and eight have been shipped out to the hospital."

"That's good enough for me. Let's go home." Nick waited for him to put on his skis, then they shushed down the mountain to the snow machines waiting for them below.

When they arrived, one of the rangers approached. "Chief? Big news. There's been a whopper 6.9 earthquake in Idaho near Borah Peak. It was felt over most of the west and into Canada. The tremor that triggered this avalanche must have been a precursor. So far there's no report of injuries or damage in the park."

Pierce shot Nick a look before he said, "What about Jackson?"

"I heard of two fatalities, but most likely there won't be a detailed assessment before tomorrow."

With his heart banging in his chest. Nick whipped out his cell phone.

Pick up, Jessica. Wherever his daughter was, that's where he would find her mother.

"Hi, Dad. Where are you?"

She didn't sound alarmed, she sounded as if she'd been asleep.

"I'm on my way home."

"It's almost six in the morning. I bet you're tired."

Actually, he'd never felt more wide awake. "Honey—I just heard about the earthquake."

"It was amazing. Mom was standing up when it happened. If she hadn't grabbed hold of the end of the couch in time, she would have been thrown to the floor."

"Is she all right?"

"Yes. Everyone's fine and sound asleep."

His eyes closed tightly in relief. "That's good. Tell you what. I'll have Pierce run me home from the airport. When you and your mother wake up in the morning, she can bring you over. Okay?"

That's when he'd kidnap Sam and drive her to the church, where they were would get married. Pierce had already made the arrangements with the pastor.

"Okay. Dad? Did anyone…die tonight?"

"No."

"I'm glad. I love you."

"I love you, too."

The guys were waiting. After hanging up, Nick took off his skis and got on the snow machine. The trip to the chopper seemed to take forever, but once they'd climbed on board, it wasn't long before they reached the airport.

While in the air, the pilot told them about the fatalities in Jackson. They learned that the quake had caused a car with two teenagers to veer off the road. It overturned on the shoulder. They'd sustained head injuries, and wouldn't have died if they'd been wearing seat belts.

Tragic as it was, Nick couldn't help but be thankful it hadn't been Sam or Jessica.

Pierce had to be thinking the same thing about his own wife and son.

His wife.

Nick had always thought of Sam as his wife. He couldn't remember a time when he didn't feel married to her. It explained why he could never build a lasting relationship with another woman.

Our time has finally come, sweetheart.

Ten minutes later Pierce dropped him off in front of his house. Nick had discussed his strategy for the kidnapping with him. "I'll be waiting for your call," his friend said with a grin.

"Thanks, Pierce."

After waving him off, he hurried to the porch and let himself in the front door. Before hitting the sack, he needed a ton of food, a shower and shave, in that order.

On his way to the fridge, he froze. A woman with red-gold hair was sitting at his kitchen table. Actually, she was slumped over it with her head resting on her arms, sound asleep.

The sight of Sam gave his heart the workout of its life. He tiptoed toward her. She'd been writing in her journal. Unable to resist, he read a few words.

Talk about shaking the earth! There wouldn't have to be a kidnapping, after all.

She loves you, Kincaid. She wanted him in sickness and in health. They were, finally, going to be a family.

SAMANTHA STIRRED, thinking she could hear water running, but suddenly the noise stopped. She lifted her head from the table, shocked to realize she'd fallen asleep while she'd been writing in her journal.

Her watch said ten after seven. She couldn't believe that she'd been exhausted enough to sleep in the chair. But now that she was wide awake, she sensed she wasn't alone.

Had Nick come home?

She flew from the kitchen and through the house. Her feet barely touched the ground. As she turned down the hall toward his bedroom, she noticed him coming out the door dressed in a pair of sweats.

"Nick—"

"I know, darling—"

Samantha ran to him and Nick swung her around, both of them intoxicated by the knowledge they'd never be alone again.

He cried her name in a voice of intense yearning before his mouth covered hers. The world wheeled away. Only their love for each other remained as they tried to show each other the depth of their long suppressed feelings.

She quaked in response to the familiar feel of his lips, hands and body. Being back in his arms again, she could almost believe there had never been the painful thirteen-year separation.

Overwhelmed to find release like this, she smothered him with the love pouring out of her. When they eventually reached the bed and she looked into his eyes, she discovered his were wet, too.

He lifted trembling fingers to her face, tracing the bones and hollows the way he used to do. "I thought you were beautiful before…" He swallowed. "Sweetheart—"

His lips made a relentless sweep of her face and throat, finding the path they'd taken so many times in the past. He ended up burying them in her hair, crying out his need of her. "I love you, Sam. I've always loved you."

She crushed him closer. "I've always loved you, too," she said in a shaking voice. "I've missed you so terribly, Nick. I swear it was the memory of the love we shared that held me together during my darkest hours."

"We're back where we belong now. From here on out, we'll share everything, because this is forever," he vowed.

The realization that they were together at last, really together, that nothing would ever keep them apart again, still hadn't sunk in. Samantha couldn't get close enough. No kiss lasted long enough.

When the phone rang, they both let out a groan. She knew that because he was a ranger, he would always be on call. In case this was an emergency, he had to respond, but she could hardly bear to let him go long enough to answer it.

He pulled her with him as he reached for the phone on the bedside table.

"It's our daughter," he whispered against Samantha's lips, made swollen and tender by his.

She smiled. That was different. "You have to talk to her. Before I drove over here, I told her *and* Mom and Dad we were planning to get married."

At that revelation his eyes gleamed.

"Naturally, she's dying to know if you're home yet, let alone if we're together," Sam added.

"Nothing's sacred in our house," he teased, kissing her mouth long and hard.

"You mean the one in Jackson? I bought it for us."

"That's the one I intend on living in with you. I love it."

"I love you."

Their mouths clung feverishly. The phone was still ringing.

"Quick, darling. She won't be satisfied until one of us answers."

Nick clicked the phone on. "Good morning, honey."

"Dad?"

He grinned to hear the shock in her voice. "Yes?"

"You don't sound like yourself."

"I don't? What do I sound like?"

"Different, and younger, and *so* happy!"

You've got that right, daughter of mine. With my wife-to-be nestled in my arms, her gorgeous blue eyes trained on my face, life is almost perfect. "I'm going to be even happier in about four hours."

"How come?"

"Because there's going to be a wedding at the church."

"What?" Sam sat straight up, with an ecstatic expression. He put his hand around the back of her head and pulled her close so he could kiss her again.

"You're kidding!" Jessica's squeal of joy came over the phone line. "For real? Today?"

"I would never kid about the most important day of my life. If you guys think I'm going to wait a second longer than absolutely necessary before marrying this beautiful woman, then you have another thing coming.

"Pierce is arranging everything as we speak, so put

on that pretty dress you wore to his wedding, and tell your grandparents to get ready.''

''How soon are you coming home?''

''As soon as we pick up the license at the county clerk's office in Jackson. Your mom's making all kinds of noises that she needs more time to prepare, but since she couldn't be more beautiful than she is right now, I'm not going to worry about it. See you in a little while, honey.'' He hung up.

Sam had broken down, sobbing for joy.

He could relate. He, too, felt such relief that they would finally be joined. After kissing her again he said, ''Ever since you drove from the airport with me, I've had a dream of marrying you in the Tetons' rustic log Chapel of the Transfiguration.

''It's near the southern entrance of the park. There's a large window behind the altar framing the magnificent mountains. I can visualize us standing in front of it a few hours from now while we make our official vows to each other, before our daughter, our parents and our closest friends.''

''I can't believe this is happening.''

''Believe it, sweetheart. The time for the Kincaid family to rejoice is finally here.''

''But how can we get married so fast?''

''Very easily. There's no waiting period in Wyoming, no blood test. All we need is the license. Pierce has contacted the pastor and is arranging a private ceremony for us.''

''What about your work?''

''My work can wait. My love for you can't.'' He kissed the palms of her hands. ''I need you in my bed before the day is out, but I don't want you to suffer guilt because we once again anticipated our wedding vows.

"This time we're going to do it right, sweetheart. Today is a shiny new beginning for both of us. I won't allow anything to tarnish it. We'll drive to the church and claim each other in front of everyone before we enjoy our honeymoon."

He heard her breath catch. "That's going to be hard on Jessica. She's never been separated from both of us before."

He kissed the heart-shaped mouth he craved. "Our daughter can stay at the house with your parents for a few days while we hang out here. Knowing we're close by will help her."

"You're right. You're always right."

He could tell something else was bothering her. "What's wrong, sweetheart? Why does the mention of a honeymoon make you nervous?"

She averted her eyes. "If you must know, I'm frightened."

He put a hand under her chin and lifted it, forcing her to look at him. "Of what?"

Her eyes filled. "I—I'm not the seventeen-year-old you once made love to."

Nick smiled. "I'm not the twenty-year-old."

"You're more gorgeous than ever."

"So are you," he said in a husky voice.

"No." She shook her head. "My body has aged."

"So has mine."

"But mine has been sick. My hair's not the same. I'm thinner."

"You're more womanly."

"Don't try to make me feel better, Nick."

"Are we having our first fight?"

"Don't tease me, darling. I want to be the girl you remember, and I'm not!"

"No. You're not. You've grown up. I loved the girl you were, but I love the woman more. You're wonderful and remarkable, and I need to be your husband before the day is out. Do you hear what I'm saying?"

"Yes." Her voice trembled. "But what if I disappoint you?"

"In what way?"

Her face went red. "You know. I—it's been a long time."

"Did cancer rob your memory of the nights we made love in the dark on your father's boat so he wouldn't know we were out there?"

She hid her face in his neck. "You know it didn't!" she admitted in a shaky voice.

Nick laughed before pulling her closer. "Do you have any idea how happy it makes me to know you've never been intimate with another man?"

"But that's the problem." She lifted her head. "I know you've been with other women, and I'm scared that I won't compare."

"You've got that wrong, Sam. There were a few women in the past, but none of them could compare to you. Why do you think I stayed single all these years? As Pierce said, I never fell out of love with you."

Nick studied her lovely features. "I want to get you pregnant again so you can raise our next child. You were deprived of that joy with Jessica."

"I don't think it's possible now," she cried softly.

He smoothed some red-gold curls off her forehead. "Are you sterile?"

"I don't know. Now that we're about to be married, I have a lot of questions."

"Then let's call your doctor and get answers."

"You mean right now?"

"Why not? This ought to be the perfect time to reach him."

"My cell phone's in the kitchen. I have his number programmed."

"Then look it up and call on the house phone. If he's there, I'll pick up on this extension."

"All right."

"First I want something to help sustain me while you're gone."

"Oh, Nick."

They kissed hungrily before reluctantly he let her go.

Once she left the bedroom, he took advantage of the time to dress in his formal blue suit. While he was adjusting his tie, he heard Sam call out that the doctor was on the line. Relieved they'd caught him either at home or on rounds, Nick hurried over to the bedside table and picked up the receiver.

"I'm here, Sam. Good morning, Dr. Blake."

"Mr. Kincaid? I hear congratulations are in order."

"Yes. Now that we're going to be married in a few hours, we have some questions for you. In light of Sam's medical history, we need to know what to expect. I'll let Sam talk now, and I'll listen to the answers."

"Very good. Go ahead, Samantha."

"As you know, I never thought I'd be getting married, so the issues having to do with pregnancy never entered my head. Now everything has changed, and long before this morning our daughter let me know she has always wanted to have a little brother or sister."

That didn't surprise Nick. Jessica was crazy about Cory. She would go nuts over a baby in the house.

"Naturally, we'd love to be able to make that dream come true. I can't imagine how wonderful it would be to have another baby with the knowledge that Nick and I could nurture and love it together.

"But considering my recent illness, I'm wondering if I'm sterile, and if I'm not, would getting pregnant give our baby cancer?"

"I doubt very much you're sterile. Give it a year. If you haven't conceived by that time, then make an appointment with a fertility specialist to find out why.

"To answer your question, most women who've been treated for cancer in the past and are currently disease-free like you can plan on a pregnancy with the greatest of confidence."

"Honestly?"

The excitement in her voice brought more tears to Nick's eyes. He knew something would always be missing in her life if she weren't given the opportunity to mother a newborn. The doctor's words had just offered them hope.

"I'm very sure. You came through your treatment beautifully, with no long-term effects from the chemo or medication. Are you still having regular periods?"

"Yes."

"Then that's an excellent sign."

"It's the best," Nick interjected. The news was getting better and better. He felt euphoric.

"Let me reassure you that cancer only affects about one in a thousand pregnancies."

"I had no idea," Samantha murmured.

"It's too bad there are so many misconceptions out there. You may have heard that pregnancy can allow cancer to develop and grow more easily, but the statistics don't seem to support this.

"If you should get pregnant and your cancer does recur at the same time, your challenge will be to diagnose it early."

"We'll make sure Sam is tested regularly," Nick interjected.

"That's good," the doctor answered. "Once she's pregnant, it will be vital, because at some point you'll have a difficult decision to make about whether you want to start treatments that could place the fetus at risk.

"Then, of course, you may have to consider terminating your pregnancy in favor of pursuing the most aggressive therapies available. But that's a decision to be contemplated much further down the road between the two of you, should such an eventuality occur.

"My opinion, for what it's worth, is to 'go for it,' as my grandson says. We only get one stab at this life, so why not take all the risks you can to make your dreams come true?"

"My sentiments exactly," Nick replied. "That's why I'm making Sam my wife today. Thank you for talking to us."

Nick could hear Sam clearing her throat. "I want

to thank you too, Dr. Blake. We're going to take your advice. Bless you for being such a wonderful doctor.''

While she was still on the phone, Nick hung up the receiver and raced through the house to the kitchen. Sam took one look at him and flung herself into his arms. They clung to each other while she wept for happiness.

''MOM? Are you ready?''

''Almost.''

Samantha emerged from her closet. She'd just put on the top of her cream-colored suit and was fastening the buttons. It happened to be the only outfit in her wardrobe appropriate to wear to her own wedding. Jessica looked adorable as usual in a dressy two-piece knit.

''That shade of blue is heavenly on you.''

''Thanks. Leslie helped me pick it out before her wedding.'' Her eyes studied Samantha. ''You always look beautiful in everything!''

''How come I'm so lucky to have a wonderful daughter like you?'' She hugged her. ''This outfit wasn't my first choice, but I'm afraid your father didn't give me a chance to buy a wedding dress.''

''Do you care?'' she asked with the faintest tinge of concern in her voice.

''No, darling.'' Samantha smiled. ''I've dreamed about this moment for years. Nothing else matters.''

Relieved once more, Jessica said, ''Dad's so excited, he's been walking around the house whistling. I've never heard him do that before.''

''Sometimes he used to whistle while he was waiting to surprise me with something special. It was a dead giveaway.''

''I didn't know that. You and Dad really loved each other.''

Samantha nodded. ''We really did. My greatest regret is not marrying him when he first asked me. But that's all in the past now. I've closed the door on that chapter and am never going to think of it again. Today we're starting our new life together.''

''I have a gift for you. It's something borrowed.''

''What is it?''

''I'll lend you my locket because it has Dad's picture in it.'' She took it off her neck and put it around Samantha's.

Nothing could have touched Sam more. She felt its shiny smoothness with her fingers. ''Do you have any idea how much I love you, Jessica?'' She put her arms around her once more.

''I love you, too. Mom?''

''Yes?''

''Dad says you're going to honeymoon at our other house. How come you're not going away some place exciting?''

She eyed her daughter covertly. ''You wouldn't mind?''

''Of course not!''

Her dear little liar. ''To tell the truth, I think Grand Teton National Park is the most exciting place I can think of.''

''Well, it is, but since you're always going to live here, you should go some place fabulous like Hawaii!''

''I've been there with your grandparents and it *is*

fabulous. I've been thinking our family and Cory's ought to vacation on Maui over your spring vacation.''

Her eyes lit up. ''That would be so cool!''

''It would. As for a honeymoon, I'd rather be with your father in the home he made for the two of you. I just need to be with him in the place where he's most comfortable and familiar. We have a lot of catching up to do. I can't think of a better spot.''

Jessica looked totally relieved. ''It's kind of like when you and Dad took me around Fort Collins, huh.''

''Yes. It's exactly like that. I want him to show me around his life, let me see it through his eyes. We have years and years to take other trips and create new memories. Right now it's important to savor what we have right here.''

''Mom?'' Something serious was on her daughter's mind. ''Do you think you would ever want another baby?''

''Yes. It's something I've always longed for.''

''*Could* you have another one? I mean—'' She stopped midsentence. Samantha could tell she was uncomfortable, yet the hope in her eyes was blinding in its intensity.

''It's all right, darling. You can say whatever is on your mind about my illness, ask me anything you like. The answer to your question is yes.''

''Honest?''

''Yes. Your father and I talked to Dr. Blake this morning. If we're meant to have another child, he says it's fine.''

''Oh Mom!''

While they held on to each other, Samantha could hear Nick calling to them.

"Dad's in a hurry."

"So am I, but I have one more phone call to make before we leave for the church."

"I bet I know who it is."

"I'm sure you do."

"Okay. I'll tell Dad you'll be right out."

"Thanks, darling."

As soon as she was alone, she phoned Marilyn. "Guess what's happening to me in about forty-five minutes?" she said when her friend came on the line.

"Something tells me you're getting married."

"Yes! Our wedding will be at the church in the park. I'm so sorry you won't be here."

"It doesn't matter. What's important is that we're both going to live. Let me be the first to congratulate you, *Mrs. Kincaid.*"

"Can you believe it?"

"After our miraculous recoveries, I can believe anything!"

Tears sprang to her eyes. "Marilyn? How can I thank you for all you've done for me? If it weren't for you, I—" She couldn't talk. Too much emotion made it impossible.

"I know what you're trying to say. I feel the same way about you. How would you like a houseguest for a weekend next month?"

"Do you even have to ask?"

"Yes, I think I do. By then Nick might just be willing to share you."

"He and Jessica are going to love you as much as I do. I'll call you in a few days and we'll have one of our long talks."

"I guess you don't feel you can take a lengthy honeymoon knowing your daughter would miss you too much.''

''You understand everything.''

''Maybe not everything, but I *do* know your husband-to-be won't appreciate your staying on the phone any longer. Your future's waiting for you.''

Samantha could hear Nick calling to her from the hallway. ''You're right. I'll talk to you soon.'' She hung up, then rushed out of the bedroom, straight into his arms.

He flashed her that old heart-stopping smile before his head lowered and he drew a deep kiss from her.

''Hey, you two.'' Her dad had made an appearance at the end of the hall. ''We're ready to drive you to the church. Much more of that and you'll be late for your own wedding.''

''We're coming,'' Nick assured him after tearing his lips from hers. They were both out of breath. Samantha felt like a teenager who'd been caught on the front porch making out with her boyfriend.

Thank heaven she wasn't that teenager any longer. She was the woman Nick had always wanted to marry. He was the man she'd always worshipped. They'd found their way back to each other.

His thoughts echoed hers when half an hour later they stood before the pastor and Nick whispered, ''We've come full circle, my love.''

Samantha felt him slide a ring on the third finger of her left hand. When she looked down, she discovered it was the same ring with the etching he'd couriered to her in Denver on Valentine's Day over thirteen years earlier.

She lifted tremulous eyes to meet his adoring gaze.

The pastor cleared his throat. "By the authority invested in me, I now pronounce you, Samantha Frost Bretton, and you, Nicholas Pratt Kincaid, husband and wife from this day forth. You may kiss your bride."

EPILOGUE

Jackson, Wyoming
June 3

It's ten at night and I've decided to catch up on some writing. Nick is out taking care of a pair of black bears causing trouble at the Signal Mountain Campground. The house is quiet.

Our darling, brown-haired, two-year-old Tyler, named after his grandfather Kincaid, is finally asleep. Jessica, who graduated with top honors from Jackson High School three days ago, left today on a bus trip with all the seniors for a chaperoned vacation to Disneyland.

We're very proud of her. She's been offered a four-year academic scholarship to either UCLA, Stanford or the University of Utah. My parents are overjoyed to think she might attend their alma mater, but I have a hunch Jessica will stay closer to home and choose to attend college in Salt Lake. She's her daddy's girl and always will be.

I just got off the phone with Marilyn. She and her husband, Rich, will be coming to the Tetons for the Fourth of July. He's a pharmacist she met at her job in Phoenix. They fell in love right away and had a fabulous wedding Nick and I attended with the children. They're expecting their first baby in October.

Motherhood must be contagious, because Leslie is expecting baby number two any day now. Cory loves his little sister, Diana, but he's hoping for a brother this time. Pierce and Leslie decided they would wait to see what they had and be surprised.

Of course, Cory has announced to everyone they're going to call the new baby Max. According to Leslie, that's what Cory wanted to call his dog until he found out it was a girl, then he had to change the name to Lucy.

Now that summer's here, Nick's cousins will be coming down from Gillette next weekend with their horses. We're all going to take a two-day pack trip into the high country. Mom and Dad will stay here to baby-sit Tyler for us.

Since my grandparents have passed away, my parents visit us every three weeks. They're crazy about the children, but they're also crazy about Nick. I knew they would be if they ever got to know him.

I love my job, my friends, my family. I love my children. I love my husband. He's my lover, my friend, my rock, my idol. He's the reason I stay well.

The miracle is still in effect and life is glorious.

THE CATTLEMAN

Margaret Way

Margaret Way takes great pleasure in her work and works hard at her pleasure. She enjoys tearing off to the beach with her family at weekends, loves haunting galleries and auctions and is completely given over to French champagne 'for every possible joyous occasion'. She was born and educated in the river city of Brisbane, Australia, and now lives within sight and sound of beautiful Moreton Bay.

After more than 100 novels for Mills & Boon, Margaret is a prolific, bestselling writer and reader favourite.

Look for *The Cattle Baron's Bride* and *Her Outback Protector* in May and June, the next two novels in Margaret Way's exciting MEN OF THE OUTBACK series in Mills & Boon Tender Romance®.

Dear Reader,

It is with much pleasure I introduce to you the first in
my four-book series, MEN OF THE OUTBACK. The
setting moves from my usual stamping ground, my own
state of Queensland to the Northern Territory—not
yet a state, but under the direct control of the Federal
Government.

The Northern Territory is arguably the most colourful
and exciting part of the continent. Even today it is
frontier country. The Territory comprises what we call
the Top End and the Red Centre. The Top End has
as its capital, Darwin, the gateway to Australia and a
hop, step and a jump from South East Asia. The chief
town of the Red Centre is Alice Springs, which lies in
the middle of the fantastically coloured McDonnell
Ranges, the setting for one of the stories. The Top
End lies in the torrid zone well above the Tropic of
Capricorn. The Red Centre is the desert, the home of
our most revered desert monuments, Uluru and Kata
Tjuta. Thus we have in a vast area of one and a half
million square kilometres two extreme climatic and
geographical divisions. This is what makes the Territory
so fascinating.

The pervading theme of the series is family. It can be
a difficult and provocative subject because many highly
dysfunctional families are out there—fighting, loving,
hating, struggling, exploiting, betraying. Family offers
endless opportunities for its members to hurt and be
hurt, to love and support or bitterly condemn. What
sort of family we grew up in reverberates for the rest of
our lives. Were we blessed with a rock solid foundation
or left with memories that plague us? One thing is
certain at the end of the day, *blood* binds.

I invite you, dear reader, to explore the lives of my
families. Not all of it is invention. Such people as I
write about *do* inhabit families. *Now and then.*

My warmest best wishes to you all.

Margaret Way

PROLOGUE

Mokhani Station
Northern Territory, Australia
1947

ALL THE WHILE THEY WERE riding, Moira felt a stab of anxiety as sharp as a knife beneath her breastbone. She tried to tell herself not to be afraid, but it did no good. A sense of foreboding weighed on her so oppressively, she slumped in the saddle, her hands trembling on the reins. If her companion noticed, Moira saw no sign. It was another hot, humid, thundery day on the verge of the Wet, or the Gunummeleng, as the station Aborigines called it. There were only two seasons in the Territory, she'd learned. The Wet and the Dry. The Wet, the time of the monsoon, extended from late November to March, the Dry lasted from April through October. It was mid-November now. She had arrived on Mokhani in early February of that year to teach the Bannerman twins, a boy and a girl aged seven. Nearly ten months of sharing her life with extraordinary people; the ten most life-changing months of her life. Ultimately, they had turned her from just out of adolescence into a *woman*. Her great fear was she had chosen a tragic path.

Nearing eighteen and not long out of her excellent

convent school, she'd craved *adventure*. Mokhani had offcrcd it. After years of hard study and obeying strict rules, she'd been ready for a liberating experience. It was understood that at some time she had to continue her tertiary education, but if her parents hadn't exactly encouraged her to take a gap year, they'd put up no great objection when they'd seen how much she'd wanted it. As a much-loved only child, "the wonderful surprise" of her parents' middle years, their only wish was for her to be happy. The family solicitor, a good friend of her father's, had come up with the answer. His legal firm handled many Outback clients' affairs. It just so happened, the Bannerman family, pastoral pioneers with huge cattle interests in the Northern Territory and Queensland's Gulf country, wanted a governess for their children, someone of good family and proven academic ability, a *young* woman preferably, to better relate to the children.

She qualified on all counts. Her father was a well-respected family doctor. Her mother, an ex-nurse, helped out several days at his surgery. Moira had been a straight-A student, winning a scholarship to university. The Bannermans, for their part, were rich, powerful, influential. The present owner and heir to the Bannerman fortune was Steven Bannerman—ex-Squadron Leader Steven Bannerman, seconded to the Royal Air Force during the war, survivor of the Battle for Britain, who'd returned home a war hero. His wife, Cecily, was a niece of the South Australian governor. In short, the Bannermans were the sort of people to whom her parents felt no qualms about sending her.

The great irony was, they might have been signing her death warrant.

Moira lifted one hand, pressing it hard against her heart

to stop it from bursting through her rib cage. If her companion addressed a stray comment to her, she heard nothing of it. There were too many demons clamouring inside her head. She knew she wasn't very far away from a breakdown. In a sense, it was another version of the Aboriginal *kurdaitcha* man, the tribal sorcerer, pointing the bone. Yet nothing had been said to her. Her throbbing fears were virtually without proof, but like all victims, she had the inbuilt awareness there was threat ahead.

It was deliriously hot. That alone caused profound dislocation. Temperature nearing a hundred and rising. A thunderstorm was rolling in across the table-topped escarpment that from a distance always appeared a deep amethyst. The storm revealed itself as magnificent. Majestic in cloud volume, black and silver with jagged streaks of livid green and purple that intensified the colors of the vast empty landscape and made the great cushions of spinifex glow molten gold. Even *she* knew it was risky taking this long ride. If it poured rain, the track could become slippery and dangerous and they would have to walk the horses. But it wouldn't be the first time a thunderstorm had blown over, for all the fabulous pyrotechnics.

Nearly everyone on the station, even the Aborigines, the custodians of this ancient land, were feeling the peculiar tension the extremes of weather created. Heat and humidity. The humidity alone left one gutted. The monsoon couldn't come soon enough even if it brought in a cyclone. Not that she had ever lived through the destructive cyclones of the far north. Still she understood what the Territorians meant when they talked about going "troppo," a state of mental disturbance blamed on extreme weather conditions.

Was that it? For one blessed moment, she felt a lightening of her fears. Was she going troppo? Were her fears imaginary rather than real? No one meant her any harm. It was all in her mind. Her companion appeared almost serene, hardly the demeanour of an avenger. The heat did dreadful things to people, especially those not born and bred to the rigours of the inland.

We're white people living in the black man's land.

Steven Bannerman had said that to her when she'd first arrived, looking down at her with a strange intensity, his handsome mouth curved in a rare smile. Steven Bannerman was not an easygoing man. Many attributed that to his traumatic experiences during the war. Steven Bannerman was the symbol of power and authority on the station, as daunting in some moods as a blazing fire.

Steven!

She'd been destined to fall in love with him. Her heart leaped at the sound of his name. It resonated in her head and through the caverns of her heart. If she never saw him again, his image would remain etched on her mind, his touch imprinted on her skin. It was truly extraordinary the bearing *one* person could have on another's entire life.

She had felt it such an honor to work for a war hero. She had handled the high-spirited, mischievous little imps of twins who had seen off not one but two governesses remarkably well. Everyone said so. Particularly Mrs. Bannerman, Cecily, a benign goddess who, at the beginning, had sung her praises. Not that she had ever been invited to call the Missus, as the Aboriginal house girls called Mrs. Bannerman, by her Christian name. Steven, too, was only Steven when they were alone. At all other times, he was Mr. Bannerman.

A prince in his own kingdom; everything in the world to her. He had been since the first moment she'd looked up into his beautiful, far-seeing blue eyes—though it hadn't been revealed to her then. But each week, each month that passed, they'd grown closer and closer, learning so much about each other. Nothing had happened until a short time ago when their feelings for each other had broken out in madness.

Fate had delivered her like a sacrificial lamb right into his arms.

She had gone from innocence to womanhood all in one sublime destructive day. She was certain in her heart neither had deliberately chosen it. It had just happened, like an act of God; a flood, a drought, an earthquake, a deadly bolt of lightning from the sky. Acts of God were merciless.

The voice inside her head started up again. She let it talk. It was the next best thing to a conscience.

You know what you have to do, Moira. You have to get out of here. Leave before tragedy overtakes you. Worse, overtakes Steven. A scandal that would be talked about all over the Outback, affecting everyone, even the children.

She couldn't bear that. She had to make her decision. She had to put a thousand miles between herself and Steven. Steven had made his decision years ago before God and man. He had a wife and children. He would never leave them. Not that she'd dreamed for a single moment he would. His role had been drummed into him from childhood. He was the master of Mokhani Station. Outback royalty. She was nothing more serious than a passing affair.

Only, that wasn't true. Both of them knew it wasn't true. She had lain awake far into the night searching the corridors of her soul. There was a strong two-way connection between them, an instant bonding. Steven had told her she was his other half. His reward for what he had suffered during the war. They shared a dangerous kinship of body and spirit that opened the doors to heaven, but also to hell. Steven was passionately in love with her, as she was with him. Hadn't he told her he didn't know what love for a woman was until she'd come into his life? The admission hadn't been merely an attempt to break down her defenses; it had been wrenched from deep down inside him, causing him agony. A war hero, yet he had stood before her with tears in his eyes. Tears she understood. She too was on a seesaw.

Love and guilt. Their love was so good, so pure, yet she knew it could be equated with shameful, illicit sex. Women of other cultures had been murdered for less. When it came to dire punishment, the women were always the victims. Men were allowed to go on exactly as before. Except for the Aborigines, who meted out punishments equally.

Whether he loved her or not, Steven's marriage couldn't be counted for nothing. It was his *life*. He had married Cecily in a whirlwind ceremony before he'd gone off to war. He'd told Cecily he had wanted to wait. They'd been living through such tumultuous times and he could very easily lose his life. But Cecily had become hysterical at the thought of not becoming his wife there and then. She'd wanted his children, and what was more, she had conceived on their brief honeymoon. Cecily was a cousin of his lifelong friend, Hugh Balfour. Hugh had introduced them, and then been best man at their wedding. The tragedy was that after the horror and brutality of war, Steven had come home a different man. So had Hugh, once so full of promise, now well on the way to self-destruction. "A full-blown alcoholic" Cecily scathingly labeled him. "Hugh can't cut it as a civilian!" Cecily Bannerman, Moira had quickly learned, was extremely judgmental, like many who had lived only a life of ease and privilege.

But the tragedy hung over both families. She saw it clearly the first time Hugh had visited Mokhani after her arrival. Hugh idolized Steven. Steven in turn always welcomed his old friend, defending him even when Hugh's own family had written him off. Hugh had been so charming to her, offering friendship, asking her all sorts of questions about herself and her family. He'd made every attempt to get to know her, he had even painted her. Many times. Until, strangely, Steven had put a stop to it. She couldn't think about that now.

Moira plucked a long strand of her hair from her cheek. It glittered with drops of sweat. She had been so happy at first. Lost in the uniqueness of this exciting new world. This was real frontier country where nature in all its savage splendour dominated everything. A city girl, born and raised, she had grown to love this strange and violent place. It revealed itself to her every day, this paradise of the wilds. The space and the freedom! The absolute sense of grandeur. She loved the incredible landscape, saturated in Aboriginal myth and legend. The blood-red of the soil, the cobalt-blue of the sky. She looked up at it briefly. It started to spin above her.

They were heading up the escarpment, the track littered with rubble and orange rocks the size of a man's fist. The promontory overlooked the most beautiful lagoon on the station, lily-edged Falling Waters. No crocodiles were thought to swim this far inland, though they had done so in the past. Nowadays it was argued that from numerous rock slides the neck of the canyon had become too narrow. Besides, it was a known drinking place for the great rainbow snake, owner of all water holes in the vast arid inland.

She could hear the falling of water now. It grew louder,

sighing, hissing, splashing. From the track, the lagoon appeared likc giant shards of glittering mirror lost in the thick grove of trees. White-trunked paperbarks and graceful red river gums adorned the water hole, the sun turning their gray-green leaves metallic.

She remembered the first time Steven had brought her to this magical place. The two of them *alone*. Her heart contracted at the memory, one she would cherish until the day she died: how with a tortured oath he had pulled her body close…how her lips had opened spontaneously under his…how his hand on her naked breast had made an indelible brand. She would remember the way he'd picked her up and laid her on the warm golden sand. She had given herself to him willingly, overtaken by a great tide of passion, her blood sizzling, as he played her virgin body, his hands so knowing, so masterly, in turn demanding and tender. One could surrender the world for such lovemaking. Hadn't she? She had abandoned the tenets of her faith, honor, loyalty, cold reason. So many codes of conduct on the one hand. On the other?

Steven.

A world lost for love.

THEIR ARRIVAL ON THE PLATEAU, heralded by a miniature landslide of eroded earth and rocks, caused a huge congregation of waterfowl to rise from the glittering waters with a thunder of wings. They dismounted. Moira removed her wide-brimmed hat, shaking out her thick blond plait. Her body was soaked in sweat, not only from the heat and exertion. Dark forces were at play and she knew it. She had gone way beyond anxiety, moving toward acceptance. She followed her companion nearer the edge, acutely aware they were keeping their distance from one another as if a contagion were upon her.

The view from the top was sublime. There was nothing, *nothing*, like the vast burning landscape. The *sacred* land. It stretched away into infinity and beyond. She could see the length of the rocky, winding corridor of the gorge, the terraced walls glowing a rich, deep red with bands of black, rose-pink and ochre-yellow. The creek bed was little more than a chain of muddy water holes in the Dry, but the permanent lagoon, an extraordinary lime-green was very deep at the centre. There was an Aboriginal legend attached to it; the Aboriginals had a legend for everything. A beautiful young woman, called Narli, promised to a tribal elder, had drowned herself in the lagoon following the killing of her lover for having broken the tribal taboo. Narli's spirit was said to haunt Falling Waters, luring young men to their deaths. There was danger in being young, beautiful and seductive, Moira reminded herself. Beauty inspired obsession. Obsession inspired violence.

Half fainting, she drew breath into her parched lungs. Her tongue was dry. It tasted of dust, making it difficult for her to swallow. She wondered what lay ahead, in part, knowing she had already surrendered. The air still quivered with fierce vibrations. Not by nature timid, she'd allowed herself to be brought low by shame and guilt. She had a sudden image of Steven and her deliriously locked together, his mouth over her, cutting off her ecstatic cries. In her defense it could be said she was incapable of withstanding him.

The waterfall tumbled a hundred feet or more to the pool below, sending up a sparkling mist of spray, as intoxicating as champagne. In the rains, she'd been told, the flow that today ran like a bolt of silver silk down the blackened granite turned into a spectacle of raw power, with a roar that could be heard from a great distance. At those times, the breadth of the falls widened dramatically as it thundered down the cliff face, tiered like an ancient ziggurat to drop countless tons of water into the lake. So augmented, the lagoon broke its banks, engulfing the floodplains with enormous sheets of water—which become huge swamps that were soon crocodile rich. People and cattle had to be moved to higher ground. Afterward, the earth responded with phenomenal abundance—lush green growth and an incredible profusion of wildflowers, native fruits and vegetables. She'd been so eager to witness that sight. Now she felt she never would.

There was no redeeming breeze. Nothing swayed. No petals of the wild hibiscus scattered. All was quiet save for the tumbling waters and the heavy *thud, thud, thud* of her heart. Even the birds that fed on the paperbarks and the flowering melaleuca trees—the honeyeaters, the gorgeous lorikeets and parrots—normally so restless, were strangely silent. Moira dared to look across at her companion, who could at that very moment be settling her fate. Despite all outward appearances of calm, violence simmered just below the surface. Violence generated by perhaps the most dangerous and deadly of sins.

Jealousy.

GOD HELP ME! MOIRA WAS BEYOND all thought of trying to escape. Escape to where? This land was hostile to those on the run. She hadn't seen her parents in many months. The tears started to trickle down her cheeks as their dear, familiar faces swam into her mind. She loved them. Why had she never told them just how much? She should have stayed at home with them where she was safe. Instead, she had betrayed them. Betrayed herself. Betrayed Cecily, who had been kind to her in her fashion. She had inspired a devouring love that overwhelmed all else. In exchange, she had inherited consuming hate. She could feel that hate everywhere, even to the tips of her shaking fingers.

Moira lifted her unprotected face to the burning sun as if there were good reason to blind herself to what was coming. If she survived this, she would have to live with her sins for the rest of her life. It she didn't... *if she didn't...*

Hadn't Sister Bartholomew, in what seemed another lifetime, said to her whenever she landed herself in trouble, "Moira, you have no one to blame but yourself!"

Slowly her companion turned away from the lip of the precipice, jaw set, grimacing into the sun. The distance between them dramatically narrowed. "I've been waiting for this, Moira," came the chilling words.

What could she answer? Words died on her lips. There was no chance. None at all.

Moira's knees buckled under her. She was tired. So tired. The matter had to be decided. She was guilty. She deserved what was coming to her. She sank to the ground, for one extraordinary second so disoriented she thought there was someone else besides her and her companion on the escarpment. If only she could turn around...

CHAPTER ONE

The Present

RETURNING FROM LUNCH—no fun at all, she *loathed* hurting people—Jessica found a note from Brett De Vere, her uncle, summoning her to a meeting in his office. It was probably about the Siegal place, she thought, carefully hanging up her new Gucci handbag. It had cost an arm and a leg. She felt a tiny spasm of guilt, but she had decided she *must* have it.

And why not? She was single. She had a great job, a challenging, exciting life. Swiftly she took a hairbrush from the bottom drawer of her desk and ran it briskly through her long blond hair, which was naturally curly but straightened at the moment. The action freed her a little from thoughts of the upsetting lunch with Sean, who really was a thoroughly nice guy, as wholesome as rolled oats. Most girls would be over the moon having a guy like Sean love them. The sad fact was he hadn't found a way to her heart.

Jessica stowed her hairbrush away, then turned to stare out the huge picture window directly behind her desk. It offered a tranquil view of the quiet leafy street. It was the *bluest* day. A day to hold in the memory. She loved the location of their offices, the avenue of mature jacaranda trees that in November, six months away, broke out in blossom. At that time, the whole city of Brisbane became tinted with an exquisite lavender-blue no sooner spent than the great shade trees, the poincianas, turned the air rosy. She loved life in the subtropics. Not too hot. Perfect!

In the distance, the broad, deep river that wound through the city's heart glittered in the afternoon sunlight. Nature stirred her, gave her strength. Comforted, she tried to work out what she was going to say to Brett. Her uncle, trained as an architect from whence, becoming bored, had branched out into interior design, had given her the commission. She was desperate to show him she measured up, but despite her best efforts, things weren't going very well. She'd lavished a lot of time and effort on her designs for the Siegals' resplendent new river-front home. But the Siegals were proving to be rather difficult clients. At least the wife, Chic, a fixture at charity functions, was. Couldn't be her real name, Jessica suspected, though she stood by Mrs. Siegal's decision to make one up. She must have considered Chic had impact. After all, she was only five-two standing fully erect.

But it was hell trying to deal with her. The fact that her husband was a multimillionaire might have had something to do with her endless waffling. De Vere's Design Studio had a few millionaires on the books, but most of its clients staved off mini-heart attacks by having a firm budget in mind. Her uncle Brett was in his late forties and had reached the point in his career when he could handpick his clients. Such a shame, then, he'd let Chic Siegal through the door.

About ready to join her uncle, Jessica checked herself over in the long narrow wall mirror. The lime-green suit and the fuchsia-pink-and-lime camisole beneath it had cost a month's pay, but Brett was a stickler for looking good, considering it was part of the job. He, himself, was polished perfection. In her entire life, Jessica had never seen her uncle slide into sloppiness. She winked at her reflection then walked down the corridor to his office, waggling her fingers at Becky, a senior designer, and stopping at her door. Becky's desk was awash with swatches of gorgeous new fabrics she was tossing around with abandon. Turquoise, aquamarine, malachite. Jessica smiled. *Malachite* sounded much better than *olive*. As a schoolgirl hired for the holidays, Jessica had adored being in Becky's office. She still did. The space was a veritable Aladdin's cave.

Becky beamed back. "Love your suit, kid! Watcha pay for that?"

"Not telling."

"We're friends, aren't we?" Becky, fifty for a few years now, in her youth powerfully pretty and still hanging in there, peered over the top of the glasses she had finally made the decision to wear.

"Sure. I just can't get my tongue around the price tag."

"Well, you look like a million dollars." Becky gave her a thumbs-up.

"Thanks, Beck."

Jessica resumed walking, smiling left and right at staff, eight in all, clever, creative people very loyal to the firm. She had joined De Vere's Design Studio soon after completing her fine-arts degree with honors. As a result of her degree, she'd been offered a position at the Queensland art gallery, with good prospects for advancement, but she'd turned it down. A decision about which her eminent lawyer father, a pillar of society, a man who thought he had a perfect right to speak his mind at all times, had been most unhappy. "Working for your uncle is a very *frivolous* decision, Jessica. Your mother and I had high hopes for you, but our hopes don't seem to mean anything to you." Her father generally spoke with all the authority of the pope.

The fact that her stunningly handsome and gifted uncle was gay might have had something to do with it. Brett's sexual orientation made quite a few people in the family a tad uncomfortable, but she had dealt with the issue by moving out of the family home into a nice two-bedroom apartment in a trendy inner-city neighbourhood. She was able to do so thanks to the nest egg that Nan, her beloved maternal grandmother—Brett's mother, Alex—had left her. Jessica had been very close to Alex. In fact, her full name was Jessica Alexandra Tennant. Christening her *Jessica* had not been her mother's decision. She had wanted the name *Alexandra,* after her own mother, for her newborn, but such was her deference to her husband that she had given in to *Jessica* after her baby's strong-minded, paternal grandmother, a large imposing woman who wore so many layers of clothing that one never knew exactly what sort of body lay beneath. It was she who had descended on the young couple like a galleon in full sail, for frequent, unscheduled visits. Jessica's mother had once confided to her daughter that the early days of her marriage had been like living in a police state.

Jessica had been devastated when her beloved nan, with never a complaint, had died of cancer when Jessica was eighteen. She knew Brett greatly missed his mother. Nan had offered that rare thing—unconditional love. Jessica's formidable maternal grandfather, much like her own father, had great difficulty accepting Uncle Brett's homosexuality, seeing it as a blot on the family escutcheon and a major hurdle in life. The hurdle part Jessica was forced to concede had come into play; she had seen it in action.

But she loved and admired her uncle, and she got on famously with his partner of twenty years, both in business and in life, Tim Langford. Tim was a sweet man, exceptionally creative, with a prodigious, largely self-taught knowledge of antiques. Tim handled the antiques-and-decorative-objects side of the business.

Brett was working at his desk, smooth blond head bent over an architectural drawing, but when she tapped at his door, he looked up with his faintly twisted, rather heartbreaking smile. Very few people saw the full picture of Brett De Vere. "Hi! How did the lunch go?"

She took the seat opposite him. "Perfectly awful! Thanks for asking. At least it didn't amount to a *scene*. Sean's a really nice person, but I couldn't let him go on thinking sooner or later we were bound for the altar. That wouldn't have been fair to him. Besides, I like my independence."

"How could you fall in love with someone like that, anyway?" Brett, who had never hit it off with Sean, asked. "He could never make you happy. He's so damned *ordinary*."

"Maybe, but it took me a while to see it."

"At least you have," Brett said dryly.

"Next time I'll go for a Rhodes scholar," she joked. "I'm not ready to settle down yet. I'm enjoying my life just the way it is."

"Until the right guy comes along," Brett murmured, sitting back and making a steeple of his long, elegant fingers. "Then you'll change your mind. Have you managed to get that truly silly woman who never shuts up on side?"

"Ever so slowly," she sighed. "The trouble with having too much money is it opens up too many options. Mrs. Siegal spends her time trolling through design magazines to the point she simply can't decide whether she wants classical, traditional grandeur, lots of drama, ultramodern or a hybrid of the lot."

"Give her pure theatre," Brett advised. "The only trouble with that is De Vere's puts its name to it. Maybe *I* should make an attempt to help her decide?"

Jessica looked at him. Her uncle was an elegant, austerely handsome man with fine features and an air of detachment. Extremely intelligent, he was inclined to be sharp-tongued, even caustic at times. His eyes were green. Like hers. His hair ash blond, again like hers. They shared the family face. Alex's face. Alex's coloring.

"Well?" he prompted breaking into her brief reverie.

"Why not? She fancies herself in love with you." Indeed Brett's air of unattainability drove some women wild.

"A lot of good that will do her," he said with biting self-mockery.

"What I don't get is they know you're not interested, yet they fall in love with you all the same."

"A bitter pill no woman worth her salt can swallow," he returned. "It's the Liz Taylor–Montgomery Clift syndrome. Women always want the man they can't have."

"Is that what it is?" Jessica swiveled a quarter turn in her black leather chair. "Be that as it may, at this point I need help."

"Surely not the talented young woman short-listed for Best Contemporary Residential Project!" Brett raised a brow.

"It would be quite a coup to win it."

"A coup, yes, but not beyond you. You're *good,* Jass," he said, giving his professional, uncompromised opinion. "I haven't handed over a client who hasn't been delighted with your services. In fact, I could say with some confidence that my mantle, when I go to the angels, will fall on you. You're developing a following with your watercolor renderings of our clients' favourite rooms. They *love* them. Single-handedly you're reviving the old genre. Oh, and remember it was *my* idea."

"Don't I always give you credit?"

"Of course you do."

It was Brett who had encouraged Jessica to turn her hobby of painting interiors in watercolors, an art project carried on from her student days, into a lucrative sideline. For the past year, she'd worked very successfully on half a dozen commissions, along with the major commission of designing the stage sets for the Bijou Theatre's *A Midsummer Night's Dream*. Maybe one day she would follow her uncle into designing stage and movie sets.

"Is that what you wanted to speak to me about, the Siegals?" she asked.

"That was the second thing. First—" Brett ruffled through his papers again, this time finding a long fax "—what do you know about Broderick Bannerman?"

"Bannerman…Bannerman…rings a bell." Jessica sorted through her memory bank. "Hang on. Don't tell me." She held up a hand. "He's the cattle baron, right? Flagship station, one of a chain, by name of something starting with an *M*…*M*…*M*…Mokhani, that's it. Bannerman always figures in the *Bulletin*'s Rich List."

"The very one." Brett looked at her with approval. He leaned forward to hand over the fax, murmuring something complimentary about her powers of recall. "And he remembers *you!* He saw that interview on TV with the ubiquitous Bruce Hilton when he so easily could have missed it. That was just after you'd been short-listed for your award. Apparently he was so impressed he wants you to handle the interior design for his new temple in the wilds—'temple' is how some magazine described it. Lord knows what's wrong with the original homestead. I'm sure I read somewhere it was magnificent, or at the very worst, eminently livable."

Jessica, busy concentrating on the contents of the fax, lifted her head in amazement. "I don't get this. With all the established interior designers in the country, let alone *you,* purely on the basis of the proverbial fifteen minutes of fame on a talk show, he's singled out little ol' *me* with scant history in the business and only twenty-four?"

"It would appear so," Brett replied blandly. "Obviously he's a man who can sum up someone on the spot. Remember, you're a sophisticated twenty-four with natural gifts."

"How could he want *me* when he could have *you?*" Jessica asked in some wonderment.

"How sweet you are, Jass." Brett smiled. "In addition, you're respectful. Look, just believe in yourself. Take risks. I've taught you everything you know. Between you and me and the paper bin, I'm the best in the business. If I tell you you're ready, you're ready. I'm thrilled he wants De Vere's. I'm thrilled he wants *you.* For one thing, I love you, for another, there's no way I'm heading off for the Northern Territory. The great Outback isn't my scene, splendid though it is. Parts of it are downright eerie. Tim and I were quite spooked on our trip to the Red Centre. Wandering around the Olgas was a thoroughly unnerving experience. I could have sworn we were being watched by guardian spirits none too happy we were invading their territory. It was an extraordinary feeling and I'm told it's not that unusual."

"Well, it *is* sacred ground," Jessica commented, having heard numerous tales about the Outback's mystical ability to raise the hairs on the back of one's neck. "'There are more things in heaven and earth, Horatio, than are dreamt of in your philosophy,'" she quoted. "Getting back to the cattle baron, or should I say, king? Did you know Nicole Kidman is a descendant of Sir Sydney Kidman, the original Cattle King?"

"Few of us have your mastery of trivia, Jass. No, I didn't. Neither of them short of a bob."

"Unlike us, Nicole has a wonderfully supportive family," Jessica said. "Do you really think I'm ready for a project of this size?" she asked very seriously. The word had got around she was good, but she never thought an immensely rich Territorian would seek her services. Not for years and years.

Brett interlocked his hands behind his head, stretching his long, lean torso. "Are you doubting yourself?"

"I'm doing my best not to, but as I recall, Mr. Bannerman has a reputation for being ruthless. Who knows? Some of my designs mightn't suit him. He could turn nasty. I read an article about him a year or two ago. A lot of people interviewed weren't very fond of him, though most wisely insisted on having their names withheld. Word was, he did terrible things to them in business. His cattle stations represent only a fraction of Bannerman holdings. He's into everything."

"Don't let that worry you. As long as he's not into drugs. Then we'd have a problem." Brett straightened, shoving a file across the table. "On the plus side, he makes large donations to charity. Might help with his tax, but apparently he *wants* to, so he can't be all bad. He owns Lowanna Resort Island on the Great Barrier Reef. High-rise apartment blocks on the Gold Coast and the tourist strip in North Queensland, mining and exploration developments, foreign investments. He's loaded."

"Excessively rich clients are a pain in the neck," Jessica said from very recent experience. "We must consider he might be even more impossible to work with than Chic Siegal."

"Surely you're not going to turn the commission down." Brett shifted position, apparently trying, ineffectually, to make himself comfortable in his antique captain's chair.

"I have no intention of turning it down. I want lots and lots of commissions. Still, before I sign up, there's the small matter of crocodiles. They insist on getting their long snouts into the news." In a recent event on a remote beach in far North Queensland, one had waddled up from the water, crossed the sand and entered a camper's tent, dragging him out. All that had saved the hapless man was the incredibly brave action of a fellow camper, a grandmother in her sixties, who without hesitation had jumped on the crocodile's back, then another camper had shot it.

Brett grimaced. "It *was* a remote beach. One must treat crocodiles with respect like the Territorians do. We talk about their crocs. They talk about our traffic accidents. I don't imagine Bannerman has given crocs an open invitation to waddle around the station, anyway. Just think what could happen."

"You don't have to look so ghoulish. Speaking of which there was a big mystery on Mokhani many years ago." Jessica frowned, dredging her memory for more information. "Surely it's been the subject of articles over the years?"

"'The Mokhani Mystery,' as it came to be called," Brett said, having read a few of the articles.

"Didn't a governess disappear?"

"So she did," Brett said briskly, apparently not really

wanting to talk about the old story. "It made front-page news at the time. But for years now everything about it's been quiet, though I'm surprised someone hasn't written a book about it. Horrible business, but not *recent*. It must be all of fifty years ago. Which reminds me my big five-oh is coming. Aging is not fun."

"Don't take it to heart. You've never looked better." Jessica was sincere. "Anyway, you can always do what Becky does. Birthday every three years like the elections."

"Women can get away with these things. What's the old saying? 'If a woman tells you her age, she'll tell you anything.' I look after myself and I don't smoke. At least not for years now. Couldn't do without my wine cellar, but wine in moderation is good for you. I'll be very angry if the medical profession suddenly disputes it. But back to Bannerman. You can be sure he's put up plenty of signs warning visitors about nomadic crocodiles."

"You think a crocodile may have taken the governess?" Jessica asked with some horror.

"How can one not *hate* them?" Brett shuddered. "Poor little soul. I can just see her picnicking without a care in the world beside a lagoon and up pops a prehistoric monster. There have been a few cases of that in North Queensland in recent times."

"More likely in one particular case the husband pushed her into the lagoon," Jessica offered darkly, having come to that conclusion along with a lot of other people, including the investigating police officer, who just couldn't prove it. "I can't believe you're sending me up there."

"Sweetie, you're at no risk." Brett took her seriously when she was only teasing. "I'll be very surprised if you even lay *eyes* on a crocodile. I understand the station is a good way inland."

"I hope so, but I'm sure I've read it's within striking distance of Kakadu National Park, World Heritage area, reputed to be fabulous and home of the crocodile."

"I'm quite sure you'll be safe. The very last thing in the world I want is to have my favourite niece vanish into the wilderness. I love you dearly."

"I love you, too," Jessica answered. She resumed reading the fax. "He'd like me to be in Darwin by Monday, the twenty-second where I'll be picked up at Darwin airport and taken to the station. The twenty-second! That's two weeks away." Her green eyes widened.

"I know. Doesn't leave you much time." Brett gazed past her linen-clad shoulder, a smile transforming the severity of his handsome features. "Not *more* junk, Tim?" he drawled. "You're hooked on it."

Jessica swiveled around, a big, welcoming smile on her face. "Hi, Timmy. How did it go in Sydney?" Her eyes settled with considerable curiosity on a large canvas he was carrying beneath his arm. "What have you got there?"

"My dears, you'll *never* believe!" Tim, thick black hair, deep dark eyes, extraordinarily youthful-looking and dressed casually in T-shirt and jeans, staggered through the open doorway.

"We don't *need* any more paintings, Tim dear," Brett warned.

"You're going to love this one," Tim promised, his voice reflecting his excitement. "I had one hell of a battle to get it. Some crazy old bat I swear was in costume was after it. No manners whatsoever. We nearly had a fistfight right there on the floor of Christie's."

"If you've bought some bloody *flower* painting, I'll kill you," Brett said. Tim had excellent taste but he did overly favor flower paintings.

"Voilà!" Tim rested the painting against the wall of built-in cabinets, gesturing as if at a masterpiece.

There was total silence.

Then a stunned. "My God!" blurted out from Brett.

"Where in the world did you get this?" Jessica was equally transfixed.

"I told you. Christie's auction." Tim whipped a satisfied grin over both their stunned faces.

"That's one of the most haunting paintings I've ever seen," Brett murmured, standing up the better to examine it. "The girl could be Jass."

"Now you know why I wanted it." Tim suddenly slumped into a chair as though his legs were giving out. "It made my hair stand on end."

"So everyone has a double, after all," Brett muttered. "What can you tell us about this? What's the provenance?"

"I took a chance on this one," Tim admitted, addressing his partner, the dominant of the two. Both men were devoted to each other, though Brett had strayed a few times over the years, causing much suffering. Tim brimmed over with charm and good humor, far more comfortable in his own skin than the at-war-with-himself Brett.

"No one knows anything about the artist. It's signed in a fashion in the lower right-hand corner—H.B. It came in on consignment with a batch of paintings by established artists. There was comment about its beauty, but the serious collectors only buy *names*. The old girl I'm talking about was after it, I can tell you that. She even offered me far more than I paid for it."

"It's beautifully painted," Jessica observed, making her own close inspection. "Perhaps the artist was in love with her. It has a decidedly erotic quality, don't you think? I wonder who she was?"

"No date on it?" Brett asked.

"Nothing. From how she's dressed I'd say late fourties, early fifties." Jessica, who had studied fashion through the ages, remarked. "She's very young. Seventeen, eighteen?"

"It's a particularly fine example of color and light," Brett said. He had excellent critical judgment. For some inexplicable reason he wasn't comfortable with the sudden appearance of this remarkable painting. The work struck him as decidedly odd.

"Notice the background," Jessica was saying. "It's fairly loose. No clear outlines, but I'd say it's definitely the great outdoors. Not a suburban garden. The long, curly blond hair is marvelous. So are the green eyes staring right at you. It's quite powerful, actually. Sort of mesmeric. Don't you feel that?" She looked back at the two men.

Brett nodded, turning to Tim. "How much did this set us back?"

"Twenty thousand," Tim said, looking like he was about to get up and run.

"Wh-a-t?" Brett snapped. "An *unknown* artist?"

"But plenty of panache! That old girl knew him. Or of him," Tim said defensively. "I'm sure of it. Besides I couldn't let it go anywhere else. It belongs here." His dark eyes appealed to Jessica. "*She,* the girl in the portrait, wanted me to buy it. She *moved* me to do it. You understand that, Jass. You're so sensitive. For all we know, she could be a relation."

"Don't be ridiculous. We know all the relations, more's the pity," Brett said acidly, giving his partner a sharp look.

"Well, we all agree Jessica is extraordinarily like her."

"Proving as I said, we all have a doppelgänger, nothing else. Next time you go off to these auctions I'm coming with you."

"I'd love that." Tim grinned.

"Actually, we could put it up in a prominent place in the showroom." Brett was starting to come round. "It'll certainly generate discussion."

"I thought that, too," Tim was suddenly all smiles. "Besides, what's twenty thousand? You've got plenty."

"That's because I spend little time at auctions," Brett said dryly, returning to his desk. "By the way, I can't come to terms with this chair. It looks good, but it's not kind to my tailbone. Find me something else, will you, Tim?"

"Sure. I'd remind you that I did say it wouldn't be all that comfortable, except you don't like being reminded."

"Thank you for that." Brett lowered his long, lean length into the mahogany chair. "Now, you've shown us your big surprise. Hopeless to top that, nevertheless we'll try. We've got a surprise for you."

"Do tell." Tim slipped Jessica something he'd taken out of his pocket.

"What is it?"

"Just a little prezzie." Tim smiled at her.

"If you'd be so good." Brett raised a supercilious eyebrow, then continued. "Broderick Bannerman, the cattle baron. Hails from the Northern Territory—"

"How absolutely thrilling!" Tim broke in enthusiastically. "I know the name."

"It gets better. He's offered De Vere's a huge commission. Specifically he wants Jass to handle the entire interior design for his new Outback temple."

Tim's expression turned to one of amazement. He stared from one to the other. "You're making this up, aren't you?"

"No, Tim, we're not," Brett replied, somewhat testily this time. "Hand him the fax, would you, Jass. Bannerman saw her interview with Bruce Hilton and was so impressed he shot off that little lot."

Tim scanned the fax quickly, then looked up. "Good grief, I'm blown away. So is she going? It's a *big* job."

"One never knows what one is capable of until one tries," said Brett. "Of course she's going. There's plenty we can do to help and advise. It's a huge commission. There's bound to be good coverage and flow-ons for us."

Tim's brow furrowed. "Are you comfortable about sending Jessica by herself? She's our baby. Now I think about it, wasn't there some murder up there? Passed into Outback folklore? Remember, we found the Outback one scary place."

"Hell, Tim, don't say that to anyone else," Brett begged. "What would people think?"

"Who cares what people think?" Tim said. "On the other hand people might agree if they'd been there. Those Olgas, they were fantastic, if kinda forbidding."

"Look—" Brett tried to be patient "—forget the Olgas, okay? Incidentally, they've been renamed Kata Tjuta. A governess disappeared. A tragedy certainly, but no murder. An accident befell her some fifty years ago, but alas there was no body. Bannerman is perfectly respectable. He's one of the richest, most influential men in the country. He's not a drug lord. I'm certain Jass will be safe. I'd never let her go if I thought otherwise. She's young for such a big commission, but that shouldn't be a deterrent. She's genuinely gifted and she'll have plenty of backup. If for some reason Bannerman turns out to be straight out of a Stephen King novel, she can come home."

"You want to do this, Jessica?" Tim still looked unsettled.

"Hey, of course I do." She shook his arm. "I'll be able

to brag about it for the rest of my days. Don't worry, Timmy. It should be quite an adventure." She started to unwrap his little present. "Ooh, earrings. Aren't they lovely?" She leaned over and kissed him. "Victorian."

He nodded. "I knew you'd like them. I picked them up at Maggie Reeves. She has some really nice stuff."

"You spoil her," Brett said, sitting forward to look.

"*You* should talk!" Tim shot back.

"I'm her uncle."

"And I'm her honorary uncle."

"Stop, you two. These are lovely, Timmy. Thank you." Jessica was delighted with the gift—drop earrings, peridots set in gold. She had a jewelery box filled with the little gifts Tim had given her since she was a child. Bracelets, gold chains, pretty pendants, a crystal-encrusted sea horse that she still loved and wore as a pin. "They'll go beautifully with that vintage dress of mine. The green chiffon." Sometimes she felt very sad that neither her uncle nor Tim would have children. They were loving, caring people. They had been wonderful to her.

"My pleasure, love." Tim smiled, picking up Bannerman's fax again. "They reckon there's a dark side to this Bannerman?"

"Tim, dear, there's a dark side to us all," Brett responded. "Not even *you* are nice all the time. If you're concerned, maybe you can fly up with Jass."

"Both of us? I would go, but I'm sure they don't want me."

"Not to mention how having a babysitter would make *me* look," Jessica protested. "What else do we know about this man?"

"Well—" Brett drew another piece of paper, hitherto unseen, from the pile on his desk "—he has a son, Cyrus.

His mother was the heiress, Deborah Masters. Masters Electronics."

"You said *was?* She's dead?" Jessica inserted one of the earrings in her right earlobe, remembering Tim had gone along with her for support when she'd had her ears pierced a few years back and had been a little fearful of needles.

"A riding accident," Brett informed them. "That was in the early 1990s. Bannerman remarried. A woman with a child of her own. A daughter, Robyn. Neither wife was particularly lucky. The second suffered from some rare syndrome—I don't know exactly what. She died two years ago."

"How very bizarre," muttered Tim, trying to grapple with all this. "It's right up there with the Olgas."

"Don't be silly, Tim." Sternly, Brett held his partner's gaze. "Tragedies happen."

"Indeed they do. But Bannerman could be looking for a new wife. He could fall in love with Jessica on sight."

Jessica laughed, but Brett blustered testily, "God almighty, Tim! I think you're losing it. Bannerman has to be nearing sixty."

"That's not a good answer." Tim resolutely dug in. "He could live for years and years. Aging men often turn to young women. Especially *rich* old men."

"He's hardly an *old* man," Brett said caustically. "You're nearly fifty."

"Forty-eight, thank you. Same as you. Keep it up and you'll really hurt my feelings."

"Stop it, you two," Jessica intervened again. "I'm not in the running for Wife Number Three." She took Tim's hand in hers. "Broderick Bannerman is old enough to be my father. Grandfather, if he were exceptionally precocious."

"For all we know, temptation could be overwhelming in the Outback," Tim said. "There's a real shortage of women. Besides, men never get falling in love with the young and beautiful out of their system," he warned. "I know I sound overanxious, but there's something a little odd here, Jass. You know how intuitive I am. No matter how gifted you are, you're young and inexperienced. I know you've won that nomination and you deserve to carry off the prize, but why not Brett, for instance? He's a colossus in the industry. Well, *he* thinks so."

"I *know* so." Brett was pleased to see Jessica elbow Tim hard. "For God's sake, Tim, what are you on about?" Brett was irritated that some of Tim's concern was starting to rub off on him.

"I'm not sure." Tim shook his head. "I live by my intuitions."

"And your intuitions tell you Bannerman has an ulterior motive in choosing Jessica?"

"Amazing, but true. I should join a training class for psychics. Seriously, I just had to get it off my chest. I don't actually *know* why."

"Then why are you trying to put us off?"

"I'm not," Tim protested. "I'm only trying to say Bannerman mightn't be quite the man he seems. Sounds to me like he's been struck by lightning."

"Lightning!" Brett said irritably. "How you give yourself over to the sensational!"

"Sensational?" Tim protested. "Men have been making complete asses of themselves over young women since forever. Besides, what man ever thinks he's too old?"

"Look, Timmy, I've dreamed about doing something like this." Jessica sought to calm Tim down. "You know you tend to worry about me too much."

"True." Tim's face broke out in his easy smile again. "I wouldn't mind if you were working within shouting distance, or even Sydney. But the Northern Territory! Hell, you might as well be rocketing off to Mars."

"Tim, dear, stop talking," Brett advised. "It's all fevered nonsense, anyway. Jass wants the job. I want her to have it. It'll be a considerable step up the ladder. If the slightest thing happens to cause her concern, she's to drop everything and come home."

"Hear that, sweetheart? You get on the phone right away. I'll be there like a shot. I wonder what the son's like?" Tim asked speculatively, then answered his own question. "Probably a dead ringer for his godawful father."

"Okay, enough's enough!" Brett lunged to his feet. "Where are we going to hang this painting?"

"Maybe above the console in the entrance," Jessica suggested, giving the painting a tender, welcoming look for its own sake and not because the subject bore an uncanny resemblance to her. "She'll be right at home there."

CHAPTER TWO

FROM THE TOP OF THE ESCARPMENT, Cy had a near aerial view of the valley floor, semidesert in the Dry except for the ubiquitous spinifex and the amazing array of drought-resistant shrubs, grasses and succulents that provided fodder for Mokhani's great herd, one of the biggest in the nation and thus the world. Today, four of his men were working flat out to round up of some forty marauding brumbies that were fast eating out the vegetation they desperately needed for the cattle until the blessing of rain. The wild horses had to be moved on. Not only that, two of the station mares were running with the mob, seduced by the leader, a powerful white stallion the men had christened Snowy. Snowy was too nice a name for a rogue, Cy figured. More like Lucifer before the fall. The stallion was so clever, it had long evaded capture, though Cy doubted the wild horse could ever be broken. He'd been close up to Snowy when they'd both been boxed into the canyon, so he knew he was dealing with a potential killer. There were few station pursuits as dangerous as trying to cut off a wild horse from its precious freedom. Ted Leeuwin, the station overseer, had lived to tell the tale of his encounter with Snowy. Just as Ted had been attempting to rope the stallion, it had closed in, terrifying Ted's gelding before biting Ted on the shoulder. Not once but several times.

Vicious hard bites that forced Ted, as tough as old boots, to give up.

Cy was aware of his own excitement as whoops like war cries resounded across the valley. He knew the thrill of the chase. The men were right on target to herd the wild horses into the gorge. Two of the station hands were on motor-bikes; jumping rocks and gullies with abandon, another two were on horseback. He'd put one of the station heli-copters in the air to flush the brumbies out and guide the men.

He'd have to leave them to it. His father, known as B.B. wanted him to fly to Darwin to pick up the interior designer, Ms. Jessica Tennant if you please, he was hell-bent on hiring. As usual, they'd argued about it. Any sug-gestion that amounted to a differing opinion caused his father rage. B.B. wasn't a man to listen. Not to his only son, anyway. Often after such arguments, his father hadn't spoken to him for long periods, by way of punishment. But punishment for what? There could be a hundred things, and Cy had narrowed it down to two: for daring to cross a living legend and for being alive when his mother wasn't. He understood his father loved him at some subterranean level, but the very last thing B.B. would do was show it. Needless to say, they weren't close, but they were *blood*. That counted.

As far as this latest development went, his father had taken them all by surprise. What would a young woman of twenty-four be expected to know about furnishing from scratch what was virtually a palace? For that matter, what was wrong with the old homestead even if Livvy, his great-aunt, claimed it was haunted? He was sick to death of it all. The old story distressed him. He'd grown up with it, had been taunted about it in his schooldays. Poor tragic

Moira, the governess, had most probably been taken by a croc or she had fallen, her body wedged into some rocky crevice in a deeply wooded canyon, never to be found. God knows it happened. People going missing wasn't exactly a rare occurrence in the Outback. So why had journalists over the years continued to rake up the old story, when all the family wanted was to bury it? No one had ever been able to unearth any proof as to what had happened to her that fatal day.

His mind returned to Jessica Tennant. She might work for a top design studio, but surely there were many people more experienced and more qualified in that firm to do the job? He couldn't figure it out. B.B., who only dealt with the top people, never underlings, a man renowned for always making smart moves, had done something totally un-smart. He had hired a mere beginner to take charge of a huge project.

"She's coming here, Cyrus. I'm still making the decisions around here. As for you, Robyn—" B.B. had turned to his stepdaughter "—I don't want to hear one unpleasant word pass your lips when she's here. Is that understood?"

In that case, Robyn had better take a crash course on manners, Cyrus thought. For a moment he almost felt sorry for Ms. Tennant. She would be living in the same house as a very dysfunctional family. Perhaps not for long, though. Cy could still hope Ms. Tennant might decide the project was beyond her. There was no way, however, to avoid meeting her. He'd agreed to pick her up because he had business in Darwin, anyway. Otherwise, he'd have said he was far too busy, which not even B.B. could dispute. These days he ran Mokhani while regularly overseeing the other stations in the Bannerman chain. Unlike everyone else directly under B.B.'s control, he didn't toe the line unless there was substantial reason to. He had to accept his father was different. Never relaxed, never friendly, as though in doing so he would diminish his aura. The older he got, the more controlling B.B. became. Cy couldn't remember a time when he and his father had been in accord. Not even in childhood. The precious days when his mother, Deborah, had been alive. A few years back, after a particularly bad clash, he had stormed off, thinking his absence would solve the problem of their angst-laden relationship. In the process, he'd realized he could be throwing away his chance of inheritance. But what the hell! He had to be his own man, not the yes-man his father wanted. The sad fact was that B.B. liked grinding people into the ground. He had treated Robyn's mother, Sharon, like the village idiot. His own mother, who had won the love and admiration of everyone around her, had apparently been highly successful at standing up to her autocratic husband—a man given to unpredictable bouts of black moods—but a riding accident had claimed her when Cy was ten and away at boarding school. A *riding* accident, when she'd been a wonderful horsewoman. Cy was constantly struck by the great ironies of life.

On that last bid for freedom he'd been gone only a couple of months when his father had come after him. It'd been a huge backing down for B.B., who'd come as close to begging as that man ever could. After he'd had a chance to cool down, B.B. had seen the wisdom of not letting him go. For one thing, for B.B. to deny his own son would go down very badly in the Outback. Even he, Outback legend though he was, was afraid of that. And for another, B.B. knew that Cy was not only the rightful heir to the Bannerman empire, but he was *needed*. Cy's skills had been tested and proven. Many thought him the man of the future, serious, influential people who for years had muttered about B.B. and his ruthless practices. Things could be done right without throwing honesty and justice aside.

The conniving Robyn, though she was an excellent businesswoman and owned a very successful art gallery and a couple of boutiques in Darwin, couldn't hope to replace him. Though she'd try. Robyn *wasn't* a Bannerman, though she bore the name and fully took advantage of its clout. Robyn had a *real* father around someplace, but no one had heard of him for years. She was a year younger than Cy. She and Sharon had come to Mokhani two years after his own mother's death. Sharon had been sweet and kind. Robyn was anything but, though she trod very carefully around B.B. It was no big secret to insiders that Robyn's greatest ambition was to somehow usurp Cy and inherit Mokhani. He, the heir apparent, was the only obstacle in the way. Once, a good friend of his, Ross Sunderland, looking uneasily at Robyn, had suggested he watch his back. "Robyn likes shooting things, Cy," he'd said.

Cy had responded with a practiced laugh. The reality was he'd been watching his back for years. Right from the beginning, Robyn had been a strange one. Cy had divined even as a boy that in Robyn he had an unscrupulous rival.

But for once, he and Robyn had joined forces against B.B.'s decision to hire Ms. Tennant. His decision had been based on Jessica Tennant's age and inexperience, not her gender; his own mother, after all, had been a very creative woman. But Robyn was violently opposed to the idea of having another *woman* do the job she'd tried to convince B.B. she could do. She had reacted with the bitterest resentment not even bothering to conceal her hostility from B.B. A big mistake.

"Be careful, Robyn. Be careful." B.B. had turned on her coldly. "I have hired this young woman. I don't want second best."

Finality in action.

THEY WERE MAKING their descent into Darwin airport when the slightly tipsy nuclear physicist beside Jessica leaned into her to confide, "We're landing."

"Yes, I know."

"Darwin airport has one of the longest runways in the southern hemisphere."

"Really? I'm not surprised to hear that." She kept staring out the porthole. The guy had been hitting on her in an in-offensive way ever since they'd left Brisbane. At one point she'd even toyed with the idea of asking the flight attendant to move her, but the plane was full. In a few minutes she'd be able to make her getaway from Mr. Intelligence.

It was not to be. He followed her every step of the way into the terminal, making like an overzealous tour guide, pointing out areas already clearly marked. He topped it all off by offering to give her a lift to wherever she wanted to go.

"Thanks all the same, but I'm being picked up."

"You never said that." He turned to her with such an ag-grieved look the image of Sean floated into her mind.

"No reason to," she smiled. "Bye now." If her luck held…

It didn't. "At least I can help you with your luggage."

Drat the guy! He was as hard to brush off as a bad case of dandruff.

"So what say we meet up for a drink sometime?" he suggested. "I live here. I can show you all the sights."

"That's kind of you, but I'll be pretty busy."

"Doin' what?" He looked at her as though she were playing hard to get.

Irritation was escalating into her as much as the heat would allow when she suddenly caught sight of a stunning-looking guy, head and shoulders over the rest, maybe twenty-eight or thirty, striding purposely toward her.

It *was* to her, wasn't it? She'd hate him to change his mind. What's more, the milling crowd fell back as though to ease his path. How many men could carry *that* off?

"For cryin' out loud, you *know* Bannerman?" Her companion did a double take, his gravelly drawl soaring toward falsetto.

Bannerman wasn't Count Dracula surely? She nodded. "He's a *friend?*"

This was starting to belong in the too-hard basket. "He's meeting me," Jessica said.

"Well, I'm movin' outta here." Her annoying companion, a full six feet, all but reeled away. "I wouldn't want to get in *that* guy's way. Good luck!"

Jessica held her breath. So *this* is Cyrus Bannerman, she thought tracking his every movement. This was as good as it gets. The fact that he was so striking in appearance didn't come as a surprise. Broderick Bannerman was an impressive-looking man—she'd seen numerous photos. Obviously good looks ran in the family. What she hadn't been expecting was the charisma, the air of authority, that appeared entirely natural. Obviously Cyrus Bannerman was ready to take over his father's mantle when many a son with a tycoon for a father finished up with a personality disorder. Not the case here, unless that palpable presence turned out to be a facade.

He was very tall, maybe six-three, with a great

physique. The loose-limbed, long-legged stride was so graceful it was near mesmerizing. It put her in mind of the sensuous lope of a famous Pakistani cricketer she'd had a crush on as a child. Bannerman, as well he might be, given his lifestyle, was deeply tanned. In fact, he made everyone else's tan look positively washed out. He had thick, jet-black hair, strong distinctive features, his eyes even at a distance the bluest she had ever seen. "Sapphires set in a bronze mask," the romantically inclined might phrase it, and they'd be spot on. She knew instinctively she had better impress this guy with her professional demeanor. No contract had been signed as yet.

"Ms. Tennant?" Cyrus, for his part, saw a young woman, physically highly desirable, with a lovely full mouth and a mane of ash-blond hair springing into a riot of curls in the humid heat. Her tallish, slender body was relaxed. She had beautiful clear skin. Her large green eyes watched him coolly. Young she might be, but there was nothing diffident about her. She looked confident, clever, sizing him up as indeed he was sizing her up. They could have been business opponents facing each other across a boardroom table for the first time.

"Please, *Jessica,*" she said. Her voice matched her appearance, cool, confident, ever so slightly challenging.

"Cyrus Bannerman. I usually get Cy."

"Then Cy it is." Though every instinct shrieked a warning, she offered him her hand. It was taken in a firm, cool grip. Jessica let out her breath slowly, disconcerted by the thrill of skin on skin. "How nice of you to meet me."

"No problem. I had business in Darwin." The startling blue eyes continued to study her. She had already grasped the fact that, despite the smoothness of manner, he hadn't taken to her. Was it wariness in his eyes? A trace of suspicion? More the pity! Anyone would think she had coerced his father into hiring her. Not that it mattered. She didn't altogether like him. She did, however, like the *look* of him. A teeny distinction.

Baggage was already tumbling onto the carousel. He looked toward it. "If you'll point out what's yours, I'll collect it. I'd like to get away as soon as possible. We're going by helicopter. Hope that's okay with you. You're assured of a great view."

So much for the big dusty Land Cruiser complete with a set of buffalo horns she'd been expecting.

THEY LIFTED OFF, climbing, climbing, into the blue June sky, climbing, climbing. Jessica tried to stay cool even though her heart was racing. This was a far cry from traveling in a Boeing 747. Outside the bubble of the cockpit, a mighty panorama opened up. Jessica caught the gasp in her throat before it escaped. Below them was the harbor. The immensity of it amazed her. She hadn't been expecting that. Aquamarine on one arm of the rocky peninsula, glittering turquoise on the other. She knew from her history books that Darwin Harbour had seen more drama than any other harbor in Australia. The Japanese Imperial Air Force had bombed it during World War II turning the harbor into an inferno. Every ship, more than forty, including the U.S. destroyer *Peary* that had arrived that very morning, had been destroyed before the invaders had turned their attention to the small township itself, standing vulnerable on the rocky cliffs above the port. The invasion of Darwin had always been played down for some unknown reason. The town had been devastated again by Cyclone Tracy, Christmas Day 1974. Even her hometown of Brisbane, over a thousand miles away, had suffered the effects of that catastrophic force of nature.

Today, all was peace and calm. Jessica's first impression was that Darwin was an exotic destination. A truly tropical city, surrounded by water on three sides, and so far as she could see the most multicultural city in the country. The Top End, as the northern coast of Australia was right on the doorstep of Southeast Asia, and there was a lot of traffic between the two. She was really looking forward to exploring the city when she had time. The art galleries, she'd heard, particularly the galleries that featured the paintings of the leading Aboriginal artists were well worth the visit.

The helicopter trip was turning into probably the most exciting trip of her life. As they banked and turned inland— Mokhani was a little over 140 kilometers to the southeast— just as Cyrus Bannerman had promised, she had a fantastic view of the ancient landscape. Such empty vastness! So few people! She'd read recently, when she'd been researching all she could about Broderick Bannerman, that although the Northern Territory was twice the size of Texas, it had one percent of the population. She'd also read that the population of Darwin was less than eighty thousand, while the Territory covered over two million square kilometers, most of which lay within the tropics. The Red Centre, fifteen-hundred kilometers south of Darwin and another great tourist mecca, was the home of the continent's desert icons, the monolith of Uluru and the fantastic domes and minarets of Kata Tjuta, which had thrown such a scare into Brett and Tim. She realized in some surprise she knew more about overseas destinations, London, Paris, Rome, Vienna, New York on her last fabulous trip, than she did about the Top End and the vast interior of her own country.

That was about to change. She watched the rolling savannas and the vivid, vigorous pockets of rain forest give way to infinite flat plains, the floor of which was decorated with golden, dome-shaped grasses she knew were the ubiquitous spinifex that covered most of the Outback. The great glowing mounds made an extraordinary contrast to the fiery orange-red of the earth, and the amazing standing formations, she realized, were termite mounds. From the air, they looked for all the world like an army on the march.

Silvery streams of air floated beneath them like giant cushions. At one point, they flew low over a herd of wild brumbies, long tails and manes flowing as they galloped across the rough terrain. It was such a stirring sight, the breath caught in her throat. She wouldn't have missed this for the world.

"Camels dead ahead." Bannerman pointed. A very elegant hand, well-shaped, the artistic Jessica noticed. Hands were important to her. "Very intelligent animals." Despite himself, Cy was mollified by her high level of response to the land for which he had such a passion. She was young enough to be excited, and that excitement was palpable, indeed infectious. His own blood was coursing more swiftly in response. She didn't appear in the least nervous even when he put the chopper through its paces, whizzing down low. There was much more ahead for her to enjoy. Falling Waters, a landmark on Mokhani, looked spectacular from the air. He planned a low pass over the gorge. It would allow her to see the wonderful, ever-changing colors in the cliff walls.

THE FLIGHT INSIDE the magnificent canyon, carved by count-less centuries of floodwaters, was the ultimate thrill. Here below her was a verdant oasis in the middle of the desert. The colors in the cliff walls were astonishing. All the dry ochers were there, pinks, cream, yellow, orange, fiery cinnabar, purples, thick veins of brown and black and white. She felt a strong urge to try to paint them. Tier upon tier like some ancient pyramid was reflected perfectly in the mirrorlike surface of the lagoon. To either side lay broken chains of deep dark pools, but it was the main lagoon with its flotilla of pink water lilies that held the eye. It directly received the sparkling waterfall that cascaded from the plateau-like summit of the escarpment, littered with giant, orange-red boulders in themselves marvelously paintable.

"Beautiful, isn't it," Bannerman said, his voice betraying his pride in his Outback domain.

This was one lucky guy, Jessica thought. He appeared to have it all. Looks, intelligence, a vibrant physical presence, a rich if ruthless tycoon for a father, and one day all this would be his. Some three million glorious savage acres, and that was only Mokhani. She knew from her quick study of Broderick Bannerman's affairs that several other stations made up the Bannerman pastoral empire. It had to be an extraordinary experience to have millions of acres for a backyard, let alone a spectacular natural wonder like the gorge. Both sides of the canyon were thickly wooded with paperbarks and river gums; the lagoon and water holes were bordered by clean white sand.

"Can you swim there?" She pointed downward.

He nodded. "I have all my life. The pool is very deep at the centre. Perhaps bottomless."

A little frisson ran down Jessica's arms.

FROM THE AIR, MOKHANI STATION was an extraordinary sight, a pioneering settlement in the wilds. Bannerman's ancestors had carved this out, living with, rather than conquering, the land. Jessica, with her capacity for visualization, saw monstrous saltwater crocodiles inhabiting the paperbark swamps and lagoons that were spread across the vast primeval landscape. Not for the first time on this adventure did she consider the fate of Mokhani's governess who had vanished without a trace all those years ago. It was, after all, a haunting tale that had never found closure.

The station was so large it sent a shock of awe through her; miles of open plain interspersed with large areas of dense scrub, through which she could see the sharp glitter of numerous creeks and lagoons. It would be terrifyingly easy to get lost in all that. The table-topped escarpment that towered over the canyon and dominated the landscape was another major hazard. Although she didn't suffer from vertigo, Jessica was certain one could easily become dizzy if one ventured too near the lip of the precipice. It would be all too easy to topple over. Easier still to get pushed.

I've got an overactive imagination, she thought, a strange taste of copper in her mouth. Could it be that was what had happened? A young woman, too frantic to be afraid groping at thin air, skin ripped as she bounced off rock to rock. Did Moira go into the water alive? A body carried into the deep lagoon would make a succulent meal for a man-eating crocodile. Surely no one could say for sure that one didn't lurk there....

She was rather ashamed of her lurid thoughts. There were always suspicions when no body had been found. But if she'd been pushed, it would have been murder.

She longed to question Cyrus Bannerman about the unsolved mystery, but sensed she would only anger him. Such tragedies, though never forgotten, would have resonated unhappily down the years. He could well have been the butt of a lot of taunts in his school days. Like most Outback children, he would have been sent away to boarding school at around age ten. Looking at him now, she felt, boy and man, he had coped.

They flew over a huge complex of holding yards where thousands and thousands of cattle were penned. Probably awaiting transport to market by the great road trains. Clusters of outbuildings surrounded the main compound like a satellite town. The silver hangar with MOKHANI emblazoned on the roof was enormous. It looked as if it could comfortably house a couple of domestic jets. Two bright yellow helicopters were on the ground a short distance from the hangar, as well as several station vehicles. Up ahead, across a silver ribbon of creek, she could see the original homestead, very large as even large houses go, and some distance away what appeared to be a great classical temple.

Broderick Bannerman wanted her to furnish *that?* Hatshepsut, queen of ancient Egypt, no mean hand at decorating, might have called in the professionals. Should she, Jessica, return to ancient Egypt for inspiration or settle for pre-Hellenic? Smack-bang in the middle of the wilderness, either option seemed a mite excessive, not to say bizarre. Obviously Broderick Bannerman, like the kings of old, had built his temple as a monument to himself. She wondered what role his son had played in it. There was an elegant austerity about Cyrus Bannerman that suggested *none.*

Another employee was on hand to drive her up to the house.

"I'm needed elsewhere, but Pete will look after you," Cy said, his eyes resting on her with what seemed like challenge.

"Many thanks for such an exciting trip," she responded, giving him her best smile. "I feel like I'm starting a new life."

"And yet at the end of a few weeks, you'll return to your old life." He sketched a brief salute and went on his way.

THEY DROVE PAST THE MULTITUDE of outbuildings she had seen from the air, then topping a rise, she had her first view of Mokhani homestead. The original homestead that had withstood the fury of Cyclone Tracy, being miles from the epicenter. It was a most impressive sight, approached by an avenue of towering palms. Jessica wondered why Bannerman had wanted to build another. Two-storied, with a grand hip roof and broad verandas on three sides, the upper story featured beautiful decorative iron-lace balustrading. The extensive gardens surrounding the house no doubt fed by underground bores, were full of trees: banyan, fig, tamarind, rain trees, the magnificent Pride of India, flamboyant poincianas and several of the very curious boab trees with their fat, rather grotesque bottle-shaped trunks. Tropical shrubs also abounded. Oleanders and frangipani, which so delighted the senses, agapanthus, strelitzias, New Zealand flax plants with their dramatic stiff vertical leaves, giant tibouchinas and masses of the brilliant ixoras. The slender white pillars that supported the upper floor of the house were all but smothered by a prolifically flowering white bell flower.

She had arrived! It all seemed wonderfully exciting, dramatic really. And Cyrus Bannerman had had a considerable effect on her when she'd grown accustomed to distancing herself from any physical response to men, as it made her job easier.

As Pete collected her luggage, Jessica walked up the short flight of stone steps to the wide veranda. It was obviously a place of relaxation, she thought looking at the array of outdoor furniture. Low tables, comfortable chairs, Ali Baba–style pots spilling beautiful bougainvillea. A series of French doors with louvered shutters ran to either side of the double front doors, eight pairs in all. She hoped she looked okay, though she was well aware that her hair, which had started out beautifully smooth and straight, was now blowing out into the usual mad cloud of curls. She was wearing cool, low-waisted Dietrich-style pants in olive-green with a cream silk blouse, but no way could she put on the matching jacket. It was just too hot! Her intention had been to look businesslike, not like a poster girl for amazing hair.

Jessica hesitated before lifting the shining brass knocker with the lion's head. Wasn't anyone going to come to the door? They had to be expecting her. Just as she reached out her hand, one of the double doors with their splendid lead-light panels and fan lights suddenly opened. A tall, gaunt, ghost of a woman, with parchment skin, violet circles around her sunken eyes and as much hair as Jessica, only snow-white, stared back at her. The vision was dressed in the saffron robes of a Tibetan monk, an expression of dawning wonder on her face.

"It's Moira, isn't it? *Moira?* Where *have* you been, dear? We've been desperately worried."

The extraordinary expression on the old lady's face smote Jessica's tender heart. She took the long trembling hand extended to her and gave it a little reassuring shake. "I'm dreadfully sorry, but I'm *not* Moira," she explained gently. "I'm Jessica Tennant, the interior designer. Mr. Bannerman is expecting me."

"Jessica?" Recognition turned to frowning bemusement. "Absolutely *not.*"

"Lavinia, what are you doing there?" A young female voice intervened, so sharp and accusatory it appeared to rob Lavinia of speech. "Lavinia?"

Lavinia feigned deafness, though Jessica could see the little flare of anger in her eyes. She leaned forward, clutching Jessica's hand to her thin chest and whispering into her face, "Always knew you'd come back." She grinned as if they were a couple of coconspirators.

"Silly old bat! Take no notice of her." An ultraslim, glamorous-looking young woman, with her glossy sable hair in a classic pageboy, and the long, dark brown eyes of an Egyptian queen, came into sight.

"Silly old bat, am I?" the old lady shouted. "You just leave me alone, Robyn. I'm the Bannerman, not *you!*"

The young woman cast Jessica a long-suffering look. "Excuse us. You forget, Lavinia, Dad adopted me. I'm as much a Bannerman as the rest of you. Perhaps you could do us all a favor and retire to your room. I know how much you like to read. What is it now? Let me guess. Gibbon's *The Decline and Fall of the Roman Empire*?"

"Bitch!" the old lady muttered sotto voce.

"So nice to have met you, Miss Lavinia," Jessica smiled into the troubled old face. What was it, Alzheimer's, dementia? The bane of old age. So sad. Lavinia had to be well into her eighties, though she didn't look in the least demented. More an eccentric living in the past.

Lavinia kept hold of Jessica's hand as though unwilling to let her go. "You've not come near the house for years and years," she said, looking as though she were about to weep.

"I expect I had to wait for an invitation," Jessica whispered back.

"My dear, don't you care that you put us through such an ordeal?" The sunken eyes filled with tears.

"I didn't mean to," Jessica found herself saying. Anything to calm the old woman.

"Livvy, that's quite enough!" The young woman swooped like a falcon. Her long-fingered hand closed over Lavinia's bony shoulder. "You're embarrassing Ms. Tennant. I suggest you go to your **room** before Dad finds out."

Lavinia threw off the hand with surprising strength and adjusted her robe. "It was Broderick who brought her here," she said. "I've never liked you, Robyn, though I tried hard. You were a frightful child and you're a frightful woman. She pinches me, you know."

"Lavinia, dear." Robyn Bannerman smiled tightly, obviously trying to retain her patience. "If I've hurt you, I'm sorry. Your skin is like tissue paper. Now, Ms. Tennant is here to see Dad. He's not a man to be kept waiting."

Lavinia nodded fiercely, setting her abundant hair in motion. "Dear me, no."

Robyn Bannerman lifted beautifully manicured hands. "She's quite gaga," she told Jessica softly.

There was nothing wrong with Lavinia's hearing. "Not gaga, Robyn. Ask me who the prime minister is. I'll tell you. John Howard. I didn't vote for him. Ask me about the war in Iraq. I guarantee I'm better than you at mental arithmetic, let alone music, the arts and great literature. I speak fluent French. I had to give up on Japanese. I'm not reading *The Decline and Fall of the Roman Empire* by the way. And it's *The History of the Decline and Fall of the Roman Empire.* I'm reading *My Early Life* by Winston Churchill. Quite delightful!"

"I couldn't imagine anything worse," Robyn sighed. "Please go to your room, Livvy. You'll be happier there."

Looking quite rebellious, Lavinia spun to face Jessica who said in a soothing manner before the whole thing got out of hand, "I'm looking forward to seeing you later, Miss Lavinia. I hope I may address you that way?"

The old lady gave her a startlingly sweet smile. "You always *did* call me Miss Lavinia. I have trouble sleeping, you know. But you always come into my dreams. I've had no trouble remembering you. Until later, then, dear."

Lavinia moved off serenely, while Robyn Bannerman stood, rather inelegantly biting the side of her mouth. "I'm sorry about that," she said after Lavinia had disappeared. "Poor old dear has been senile for years. She usually stays upstairs in her room, rereading the entire library or listening to her infernal opera. Some of those sopranos know how to screech, or it could be Lavinia. She had a brief career on the stage. She only ventures down for dinner, thank God. I'm Robyn Bannerman, as you will have gathered. Come on in. My father is expecting you." Robyn's dark eyes swept Jessica's face and figure. "I must say you look absurdly young for such a big project."

Jessica frowned and was about to respond when Robyn continued, "What you want to do is enjoy yourself for a few days, then head back to Brisbane. My father rarely if ever makes mistakes, but there's a first time for all of us. Though I must say, I'm dying to hear what you come up with."

A lot better than *this,* I hope, Jessica thought, glancing around in surprised disappointment. Although opulent, the interior of the homestead did not so much impress as overwhelm. The furnishings were far too formal for the bush setting, the drapery, though hellishly expensive— Jessica knew the fabric—too elaborate. This was, after all, a country house. It didn't look lived in. In fact nothing looked even touched. There were no books lying around, no flowers, not an object out of place.

The air-conditioning, however, was a huge plus, utterly blissful after the blazing heat outside. Jessica felt that given what she had seen so far, she wouldn't be right for the job. Not if Broderick Bannerman wanted more of this.

Brett wouldn't be happy, either, unless Bannerman gave her carte blanche. The homestead had a vaguely haunted air about it, or so it seemed to her, but she could see how it could be brought back to life.

"I see you're admiring the decor," Robyn said, as though they were gazing at perfection. "I did it all a couple of years back. I hoped to do the new place, but I can't be expected to do *everything!* I practically run the domestic side of things here and I have businesses in Darwin that have to be looked after. If I do say so myself, I'm a hard act to follow."

Jessica managed a smile, but she couldn't for the life of her act impressed. In fact, she could hear Brett's voice saying, *Dump the lot!*

CHAPTER THREE

SHE WAS SHOWN INTO A LARGE, luxuriously appointed study. There was no one inside.

"That's funny. Dad was here ten minutes ago. I'll go find him," Robyn said, giving Jessica another of her dubious looks. "Take a seat. Won't be long. You'd like tea or coffee?"

"Coffee would be fine. Black, no sugar."

"Looking after your figure?" Robyn asked with a slightly sarcastic smile.

"I do, but I've grown to like coffee that way."

Alone, Jessica stared around the room, thinking how one's home environment reflected the person. It had to be the one place from which Robyn Bannerman's decorating talents had been banned. It certainly looked lived in. Going by the faint film of gray on the wall of solid mahogany bookcases, Jessica doubted if anyone was game to go around with a feather duster. Behind the massive partner's desk hung a splendid three-quarter portrait of an extraordinarily handsome man, *not* Broderick Bannerman, though the resemblance to Cyrus Bannerman was striking. He was painted in casual dress, a bright blue open-throated bush shirt the color of his eyes, a silver-buckled belt, just the top of his riding pants, the handsome head with crisp dark hair faintly ruffled by a breeze, set against a subdued darkish-green background. The eyes were extraordinary.

Because of her own deep involvement with art, she stood up for a closer look, wanting to study the fluent brush strokes, which she had the strangest feeling she'd seen before.

"My father," a man's deep, cultured voice said from behind her. He startled her, as she felt sure he had meant to.

She turned quickly toward the voice, surprised he was standing so close to her. She hadn't heard him come in. "It's a wonderful painting," she said. "I was just going to check on the name of the artist. I've a feeling I've seen his work before and—"

"You couldn't have," Broderick Bannerman cut her off, his appraisal of her intense, as though he wanted to examine every inch of her. "The artist was a nobody. Just a family friend."

"He may have been a nobody, but he was a very good painter," Jessica said, determined not to be intimidated by the great man. "Excellent technique."

"Would you know?" His icy gray eyes beneath heavy black brows didn't shift. Had he been a horse fancier, he might have asked to check her teeth.

"I think so. I have a fine-arts degree. I paint myself. I started with watercolors, which I love, but I've moved on to oils and acrylics."

"It's a wonder you've found the time," he said. "You're twenty-four?"

"Yes, but you already know that, Mr. Bannerman." Jessica held out her hand. "A pleasure to meet you, sir," she said, though aspects of the man had already started to worry her. His gaze was so piercing, she felt she needed protection.

Bannerman took the slender hand, thinking most people

had to work hard at containing their awe of him, but this chit of a girl showed no such deference. He stared into her large green eyes. Memories speared through him, for a moment holding him in thrall. "Please, sit down," he said after a moment, his voice harsher than he intended. On no account did he want to frighten her away. "Has Robyn organized some coffee?" With an impatient frown, he went around his desk, sitting in the black leather swivel chair.

"Yes, she has," Jessica answered, thinking intimidation was something this man would do supremely well. He had been born to power. Clearly, he took it as his due. Broderick Bannerman had to be nearing sixty, but he looked at least ten years younger. He didn't have his son's amazing sapphire eyes, but his icy glance was remarkable enough. His hair was as thick and black as his son's with distinguished wings of silver. All in all, Broderick Bannerman was a fine figure of a man with a formidable aura. Why in the world would a man like this choose her to handle such a big project? Brett would have been the obvious choice.

"Speaking of watercolors," he said, "my aunt Lavinia loves them. She's a very arty person, so you should get on well."

"I had the pleasure of meeting her momentarily," Jessica said, thinking it best to say. It would come out sooner or later.

"Really? When was this?" The frosted gaze locked on hers.

"She happened to be in the entrance hall when I arrived."

"Good. I don't want her to hide. Then you'll know she's somewhat eccentric?"

"I found her charming," Jessica said.

"She can be a handful," Bannerman said, with a

welcome trace of humor. "Most people think she's senile, but she's not. She likes wearing weird costumes. She had a brief fling as an opera singer in her youth. Still daydreams about it. You'll no doubt get to see the costumes. Tosca's my favourite. She's a Buddhist at the moment. She's actually had an audience with the Dalai Lama. Regretfully she has arrived at the point where we can't let her go out alone, though she managed to get to Sydney recently—but I'd sent along a minder for her and she stayed with relatives. Don't be too worried by anything she says. Livvy never really knows what time frame she's in."

Wary of his reaction, Jessica didn't tell him Lavinia had called her *Moira*.

Bannerman was still talking when a middle-aged woman in a zip-up pale blue uniform wheeled a laden trolley into the room without once lifting her head. Robyn was standing directly behind her, looking very much as if one false move and the tea lady would get a good rap on the knuckles.

"Thank you, Molly," Bannerman said. "This is our housekeeper, Mrs. Patterson, Jessica. You'll be seeing quite a bit of each other."

The two women exchanged a smile, Jessica saying a pleasant hello.

"I'll pour, shall I?" Robyn asked.

Bannerman looked back at her coolly. "This is a private conversation, Robyn."

Jessica felt mortified on Robyn's account. Was this his normal behavior?

Robyn colored, as well she might. "I thought you might need a little help."

"Thank you, no."

Not the nicest man I've ever met, Jessica thought.

In the end, she poured the coffee, which turned out to be excellent. To her surprise, instead of getting down to business, Bannerman began to question her, albeit in a roundabout way, about her family, listening to her replies with every appearance of interest. One might have been forgiven for thinking before matters progressed any further she had to establish her family tree. Surely he didn't talk to everyone this way, did he? Not everyone would expect to be quizzed about their ancestors, unless they were marrying into European royalty.

In the middle of it all, the phone rang. At least *she* was off the hook for a while, she thought wryly. Bannerman turned his intense pale gray stare on the phone as though willing it to stop. Finally he was forced to pick it up. "I thought I told you to hold the calls," he boomed into the mouthpiece.

He certainly has a way with the staff, Jessica thought. That sort of voice would make anyone gulp, let alone damage the ears.

"All right, put him on."

Jessica made to jump to her feet to give him privacy, but he waved her back into the seat, launching into a hot, hard attack on the poor unfortunate individual on the other end of the line. How people of wealth liked to make lesser mortals quake! Afterward, satisfied he had made himself clear and beaten one more employee into the turf, Bannerman centered Jessica with his lancing eyes. "Look, you haven't had time to settle in and I have to attend to some fool matter. You have no idea the amount of nonsense I have to put up with. Some of my people can't do *anything* on their own. What say we met up again at four? It will be cooler then. I can take you on tour of the new house."

"I'm looking forward to it, Mr. Bannerman," Jessica

said. He might be shaping up to be an ogre, but no need to call home yet.

"You're hired, by the way." He flashed her an odd look, impossible to define.

"Wouldn't you prefer to wait until I submit some designs or at least hear my ideas? They'd be off the top of my head, of course. Better, when I've had time—"

"No need," he said dismissively. "You'll do very well."

It was the first time she'd been given a commission on the basis of her looks and ancestors.

UP IN HER BEDROOM, Robyn paced the perimeter of the Persian rug, as a lioness might pace the perimeter of her cage. She was utterly enraged. For B.B. to humiliate her in front of a complete stranger left her wanting to kill someone. Though she had done everything in her power to fit into this family, she fumed, she would *never* be regarded as a true daughter of the house. Like that old witch Lavinia, who smiled so lovingly on Cyrus, had said, Robyn wasn't a *true* Bannerman. No unshakable bond of blood; the belonging was only on the surface. Scratch the surface and it was as clear today as it had been from the outset when she'd first come to Mokhani with her mother, she was an *outsider*. Her mother, not capable of getting both oars in the water, had nevertheless shochorned herself in, always sweet and unassuming, dutiful and deferential to her rich and powerful husband.

Their marriage had been a big lie. B.B. had married her mother, an old school chum of the incomparable Deborah, only to beget more sons. But poor Sharon couldn't rise to the challenge, though she had looked like "lust on legs," as a guy she knew put it. The sad reality was that Sharon hadn't been very fertile, and her marriage to B.B. seemed to render her completely barren. Her daughter, Robyn, her only child, was her sole achievement. Needless to say, B.B. was bitterly disappointed in her mother and had all but ignored her, unceremoniously bundling her out of the master suite and into a room on the other side of the house, causing Sharon to curl up and simply fade away. B.B. had wanted a long succession of heirs, not just Cy, the son of the only woman he had ever loved, that paragon Deborah who, for all the cups and ribbons she'd won, had gone hurtling over the neck of her horse.

Robyn had sensed quickly, as an animal might, B.B.'s deep-seated fear of his own son, as though one day Cy would overshadow him, and hell, wasn't it already happening? Though she hated to have to say it, Cy was remarkable. Cy was the *future*. She didn't know anyone apart from B.B. who didn't wholeheartedly admire Cyrus. As for how people regarded B.B., they mostly feared him, called him a *bloody bastard*—but never within B.B.'s hearing. B.B. would regard such a thing as a declaration of war, then order a preemptive strike.

But he *was* a bastard, nevertheless. A ruthless bastard. It was that more than anything that kept Robyn in line. In the odd moment when she choked up on memories of her mother—she really had loved her, or at least as much as she *could*, given Sharon's single-digit IQ—she realized with great bitterness just how badly B.B. had treated her mother. Sharon had had everything *material* she'd wanted, but she had missed out totally on what she really wanted—tenderness and affection. Sharon had realized from the beginning there was no way she was going to get love.

Ironically, this beast of a man seemed to inspire all kinds of women, from the innocent needy like her mother to gold diggers, to give matrimony with him their best shot.

B.B. hadn't married any of them, but he certainly hadn't been celibate since her mother's death. Lord, no! There had been various affairs, all very discreet. Even with young women, who found the sexiest thing about a man was his bank balance. The one thing Robyn hadn't been prepared for when B.B. had announced he was calling in an interior designer to decorate the mansion, was that she would be so young and ravishingly pretty. Attractive would have been okay, but not a bloody aphrodisiac for men.

The shock had been ghastly. She didn't think Cy had expected it either, nor had he been pleased. But here she was among them, this Jessica Tennant.

B.B. had first seen her on national television. Robyn had missed the program herself, as had Cy, so they'd had no warning. They knew only that she was shortlisted for some big prize, which meant she had to be good at what she did, but at twenty-four she couldn't have had much experience. Add to that, she was a bloody siren. Robyn had seen the look B.B. had given the woman. It had been as rapt as a sixteen-year-old boy's.

Robyn halted in her frenzied pacing, and her blood turned to ice water. What if B.B. had it in his head this time to take another wife? Why should that shock her? He had plenty of money, after all. So what if they were decades apart in age? B.B. was a secretive man, but he didn't do anything without a reason. No one had ever seen him make a false move. Now Ms. Jessica Tennant, in the guise of an interior designer. What had seemed incomprehensible started to appear perfectly clear.

I have to protect myself, Robyn thought. *I'm no loser like Mum.*

A FEW MINUTES BEFORE THE TIME scheduled for the grand tour, Jessica made her way downstairs. Best not be late, when Bannerman was famous for bawling people out. Robyn had dropped out of sight, no doubt slamming her palm against her forehead in mortification, but Mrs. Patterson, who turned out to be a very pleasant woman, had been on hand to show Jessica to her room.

There, she had changed her outfit, settling for something cool, cotton pants with a gauzy multicolored caftan top decorated with little crystals and beads over with tiny buttons down the front. Usually she did up just enough to cover her bra, but with the way Broderick Bannerman had been looking at her, she decided to do them all up.

The dazzling play of late-afternoon light falling through the beautiful leaded panes and fan lights on the front door held her immobile for a moment. The kaleidoscope of color unlocked some lovely fragment of memory from her childhood. Before she could move, the door opened, letting in a wave of hot air.

And Cyrus Bannerman. The look he gave her held her transfixed.

"Hi!"

"Ms. Tennant. We meet again."

At first glance, he could have been a particularly sexy and virile escapee from the TV show *Survivor.* His darkly tanned skin glowing with sweat and grimed with red dust gave him a startlingly exotic appearance. Red dust had thrown a film over his jet-black hair, which was tousled and fell onto his forehead. There was a stain of brownish-red—blood—across his bush shirt, and his eyes seem to blaze a hole through her.

They continued gazing at one another for what seemed an inordinate amount of time. Was it the atmosphere?

she wondered. The old homestead certainly had an air about it.

"Sorry," he said finally. "I must look a mess. One of the men took a bad fall off his motorbike. Head injuries. We didn't want to move him. I had to call in the RFDS. That's the Royal Flying Doctor Service, as I expect you know. God knows what we'd do without them. They didn't take long."

"Is he going to be all right?" Only now could she take a few more steps down the stairs, reassured that an injured employee so clearly mattered to him.

"We have to wait and see with head injuries. I'm worried about him." Cy's remarkable eyes made another sweep over her. "Meanwhile, what have you been up to?"

"Why, nothing." She stopped where she was on the stairs. "Change of clothes is all," she said sweetly. " Now your father is taking me on a tour of the new house."

"I see." He pulled at the red bandanna at his throat, exuding so much powerful masculinity she felt in need of oxygen.

"That's good. For a moment I thought you'd missed something along the way. Your father *has* hired me to handle the interior design."

"Indeed he has. Forgive me if it takes a little time to get used to it." He came close to her, so commanding a presence, Jessica remained where she was, two steps above him. A dubious advantage.

"You must be extremely clever, Ms. Tennant. Dad was compelled to hire you after seeing you for about ten minutes on a TV program? Have I got that right?"

He was suspicious of his father's motivation, she suddenly realized. It was emblazoned on his smug, handsome face. "You have. What's so amazing?"

"The pure chance of it." His eyes shifted to the little beads and crystals on her top and he gave a leisurely verdict. "Very pretty." He paused, then said, "Look, Ms. Tennant, I'll level with you. I'm concerned about this. I'm sure you're talented, but it doesn't automatically follow you should be given such a big commission. At this stage of your career anyway."

She leaned forward slightly, her voice mock confidential. "Be that as it may, it was your *father* who hired me, Cyrus. He's the man I have to answer to. Not you."

"Say that again." Suddenly he smiled into her eyes. Night into day.

"I'm sure you took it in the first time. Your father hired me—"

"Not *that!*" he scoffed. "The *Cyrus* bit. I really liked the sound of my name on your lips."

She knew she blushed, but she couldn't control it. "Calling you Cyrus *is* the easy bit. Getting on with you appears to be quite another. What exactly is it you and your sister—"

"I don't have a sister," he corrected.

"That's odd. I've met her."

"You've met Robyn," he pointed out suavely. "Robyn is my father's adopted daughter."

"Which surely means legally she's your stepsister?"

"Ah, you're turning into a hotshot lawyer before my very eyes. Robyn is my stepsister, forgive me. She must be. She lives here."

"Not your average loving family, then?" She forced her breath to stay even.

"Unfortunately, no."

"I'm sure there are reasons."

"There always are. Are you going to come down from those stairs?"

"Not for the moment. I like us to be on the same level." She was attracted to this man. *Powerfully* attracted. It was the very last thing she needed or wanted. She was here to do a job, not play at a dangerous flirtation.

"That would never be unless you grow a few inches."

"Or own some very fancy high-heeled shoes, which I do. Well, it's nice chatting with you, Cyrus, but I'm supposed to meet your father."

"I'm not detaining you, surely?" He made an elaborate play of backing off, his ironic smile putting more pressure on her. She felt slightly giddy as she descended the last two stairs to pass him. Something he undoubtedly noticed and chalked up as a small victory.

Her nerves were stretched so taut she actually jumped when Broderick Bannerman, a look of barely suppressed impatience on his face, suddenly appeared in the entrance hall. He looked from one to the other as though they were conspiring in a plot against him. "There you are, Ms. Tennant. I did say four o'clock, didn't I?"

"I'm so sorry—" Jessica was tempted to mention it could only have been a few minutes after four, but Cyrus intervened.

"She was chatting with me, Dad. Okay?" He lifted a hard-muscled arm and glanced at his watch. "How time flies! It's three minutes past."

"And you're back early," B.B. clipped off.

"Surely there's not a note of disapproval in that. I don't clock on and off, Dad. Eddie Vine took a bad spill off his motorbike. He's been airlifted to the hospital."

"I'm not surprised to hear that," B.B. said with a frown. "He's a bad rider."

"No." Cyrus jammed his hands into his jeans pockets. "*You're* the one we all have to get out of the way for, Dad. Now, I'm off for a good scrub. Enjoy the tour."

"We shall," his father replied curtly.

At that moment, a middle-aged attractive woman with soft gray eyes and long dark hair pulled back into a severe French twist hurried into the entrance hall. "Excuse me, B.B. I'm sorry to interrupt, but Mr. Kurosawa is on the line. I know you want to speak to him."

B.B. all but snarled. "Dammit!" Then, more mildly, he added, "Okay I'm coming, Ruth." He turned back to Jessica with a surprisingly charming smile. The many faces of Broderick Bannerman in less than half a minute she thought. "I'm sorry, my dear, this is going to take time. I'll have to postpone our tour until tomorrow."

In the background, Cyrus Bannerman spoke up. "If Ms. Tennant will give me ten minutes, I can show her around the place."

"I prefer to do it, thank you, Cyrus."

"No trouble, Dad," Cyrus insisted smoothly.

There was a silence as B.B. responded to what seemed like a challenge.

"Very well," he barked, turning abruptly on his heel.

Cyrus Bannerman stood, lean elegant frame propped against the cedar post of the staircase. "By the way, Jessica, you haven't met Ruth, have you? Ruth is Dad's secretary. Ruth this is Jessica Tennant, Dad's new interior designer."

"Pleased to meet you, Jessica." B.B.'s secretary gave Jessica a sweet, flurried smile, clearly anxious to follow her master. "I must go. B.B. might want something."

"Best not keep him waiting, Ruthie," Cyrus warned, his blue eyes full of mischief. "Now suddenly it's up to me, Ms. Tennant, to give you the grand tour."

"Why is it I'm thinking you're trying to score points in a competition with your father?"

"God, is it that obvious?" He shook his head. "Why don't you wait for me on the veranda? It's nice this time of day. I'll only be ten minutes."

"I beg you. Don't hurry on account of me."

"You should thank me for rescuing you," he said blandly.

CHAPTER FOUR

HE WAS BACK ON THE VERANDA in fifteen minutes flat. "Did you time me?" he asked. "I'm a bit late."

"Actually I'd forgotten you," she said casually, which was a long way from the truth. "I was breathing in the air and the exotic scents. It's another world up here. I've never felt so connected to the earth. It's rather a profound experience. Thanks again for the helicopter trip. It was a revelation, and one of the highlights of my life."

"I think you mean that." There was an appraising look in his eyes.

"How could you doubt me?" Jessica stood up, trying to hide the excitement he engendered in her.

"There's plenty more I can show you," he said. "How come you've never visited the Red Centre?" Something she had mentioned. "Or Kakadu, which is the jewel in the Top End crown—maybe a little off the beaten track—but Alice Springs? It's quite a tourist destination these days. Our desert monuments, Uluru and Kata Tjuta, are world-famous."

"Maybe when you have the time you can take me." She gave him a sidelong glance.

"Jessica, we don't know yet if you're staying."

"Why does it bother you so much? My staying, that is."

"I have my reasons."

"That sounds intriguing. So what are you going to do to frighten me off?"

"Whatever it is I have to act fast." He met her eyes, a gleam of mockery in his. "No. It's going to be your decision."

"Your father's, surely," she said. They walked down the flight of stone steps together, Jessica acutely conscious of his height and pure, animal magnetism.

"He's already made up his mind," he clipped off. "My father isn't an easy man to know." His tone indicated he wished things could have been different.

She gave him a wry, understanding smile. "I can see that."

"So you can see we're not the best of pals."

"Why is that?" she asked gently.

"Long story." He glanced away.

"I can listen."

"Not right now, Ms. Tennant. Seriously, apart from my dysfunctional family, you don't have the feeling this job might be too big for you? It's a helluva place. Helluva size."

"Your father has a helluva lot of money," she reminded him dryly.

"Doing things right takes a lot more than money."

"I know that. I'm good at what I do, and I can count on my Uncle Brett for all the help and advice I need. Brett's my rock. You mustn't be so skeptical of me. I have skills to put to good use. No job is too big to handle, given ability, time and money. You have to take one thing at a time not tackle it all at once. Then it *can* become too confronting."

He shook his head. "Trouble is, there seems to be more going on here."

"Meaning what, exactly?" She was truly puzzled.

"I'm damned if I know. It's just a hunch backed up by observation. This family has a haunted past. It makes people *different,* for better or worse. No way you're not going to hear about it, if you haven't already, though it's way before your time and mine."

"You're talking about the old Mokhani Mystery?" She headed him off. "The disappearance of the governess?"

There was a decided glint in his eyes. "So you *do* know."

She nodded. "Only because I did my homework." They were walking along a lush avenue of tropical palms and ferns, on one side bounded by a four-foot-high stone wall. Around the base of the ferns grew beautiful soft creamy lilies that gave off a perfume not unlike gardenias. *Exquisite!* She bent to pick one, twirling it beneath her nose.

"I suppose you'd have to," he conceded. "Have you met my great aunt Lavinia yet?" He held back a palm frond that partially blocked their path. "Livvy claims to have seen her, *heard* her around the place."

"The governess?"

"Of course the governess," he said shortly. "Her name was Moira. Livvy was dreaming or having one of her visions. Living in the past is so much richer for her than the present. She's got a fantastic imagination. She's always said Moira would come back one day, and we'd all have to fall on our knees in welcome. People think Livvy has gone around the twist, but they're making a big mistake. A lot of it she does deliberately. It's the thwarted actress in her. But in many respects, she's still as sharp as a tack."

Jessica laughed quietly. "I can believe that. I've met her. She greeted me at the front door. It must have been in the middle of one of her fantasies, because she called *me* Moira. I tried to assure her I wasn't, but I don't think she was entirely convinced."

He stopped dead on the path, forcing her to do the same. "Well maybe that's your trump card, is it, Ms. Tennant?"

"Trump card?" Anger rose. "You sound as though you've caught me out at something."

"I'd really appreciate it if you were straight with me," he said crisply, his gaze very direct. "You've never met my father before? Even fleetingly?"

She frowned and resumed walking. "I think I'd remember. He's not the sort of man you'd miss. *I* would have thought my trump card was the fact I'm in line to win a big award. No point in being modest. Not around you. That's quite an achievement in our business, especially for someone my age."

"Hell, I'm sure there's no question you'll win it." He was brusque. "But I'm not referring to your artistic abilities." He made a frustrated gesture. "As I said, Moira has haunted this family for over half a century. You'd swear she wanted to have some kind of vengeance for God knows what! For all the various articles and versions of events, I've never been able to find a photograph of her. The only one on record is a grainy one supplied by her parents, but then she was only a child. Someone in the family either destroyed what we had or whisked them out of sight. But I do know she was an ash-blonde with green eyes, which might explain my father's attraction to you. Livvy obviously was drawn to you, as well. My great aunt had a soft spot for Moira, so she took it very hard when she disappeared."

"Surely everyone did?"

"That goes without saying," he said tersely.

"I'm sorry. It must have been a bad time for the family," Jessica said. Suspicions, speculations, the police and newshounds coming after them.

"It's bad enough hearing about it all these years later," he said, pulling a sharp twig off a hanging branch and throwing it away. "Even her name causes distress. Can you understand that?"

"Of course I can," she said. "I'm not an insensitive person."

"I don't know yet what you are," he said. "I got hell at school until I was driven to shut my tormentors up. The entire family was badly affected. My grandparents in particular, Steven and Cecily. My dad, who was only a kid, and my dad's twin, Barbara. Aunt Barbara won't come near Mokhani except for the obligatory Christmas visit. She's married to a brilliant academic. Unfortunately no one can understand a word he says—we might if he threw in some normal everyday language now and again. They live in Sydney with a magnificent view of the harbor. No children. Barbara used to say she didn't want to pass on a bad gene, whatever the hell that means. Livvy divides her time between them and us."

"I see."

Brilliantly plumaged parrots flashing an array of the most beautiful vivid colors appeared above their heads, several turning somersaults like an aerobatics display before diving into a spectacular flowering plant with huge scarlet flowers and iridescent violet-striped leaves. Jessica looked up, engrossed and entertained. "Does Miss Lavinia haunt art galleries?"

"Yup," he said laconically. "I suspect you do, too."

"I *am* an artist. Would she have attended a Christie's auction lately?"

"Ms. Tennant, I wouldn't know. Why don't you ask her?"

"I will." Who knows where such a question might lead?

For a scary moment, Jessica felt as if she had entered a tortuous maze.

"What's with the *Miss* Lavinia?" he asked presently. "A bit quaint, isn't it?"

Jessica reached out to touch a prolifically flowering truss of bougainvillea somewhere between deep pink and cerise. "It just came to me. It seemed respectful, okay?"

"Respectful, certainly. Maybe contrived. I happen to know Moira called Livvy Miss Lavinia." Outright suspicion glittered in his eyes.

"Surely you don't think there's some kind of conspiracy going on here, do you?"she asked uneasily. "One wouldn't have to be the smartest person in the world to realize your family might have become a bit paranoid about Moira and her sad story. The fact I called your great-aunt Miss Lavinia means absolutely nothing. I'd feel a lot happier if you'd put it down to good manners."

"That's it, good manners?" He glanced at her as if he had considerable difficulty accepting that.

"Of course." Jessica met his gaze squarely. "I told you I came across the old mystery in the course of my research into the Bannerman family. It's been the subject of numerous articles on and off over the years. The mystery has never been solved. That alone would keep it alive."

"I hope you're not implying anything sinister there," he said, warming to the challenge.

"Certainly not." She shook her head. "It's exactly as I've told you. My desire to understand my commission led me into researching the Bannerman history. I'm sure your father had my professional credentials thoroughly checked out well before I arrived. He's since questioned me at some length about my family background."

"Obviously he wants to learn more about you," Cy said, his scrutiny, like his father's, too intense for her comfort.

"I admit I was surprised. I couldn't see what a lot of it had to do with my design skills. But I could say my family is highly respectable."

"Thank God there are a few of us left," he said acidly.

Jessica didn't bother replying. She knew he was seeking answers to what bothered him, but how could she supply them when she didn't even know the questions? But he had made her uneasy. *Was* there more to discover as to why Broderick Bannerman had chosen *her* for this project? Even Tim had found it hard to believe.

Jessica's ponderings were diverted as up several hundred yards ahead rose the soaring white edifice Broderick Bannerman had caused to be erected as a monument to himself and a celebration of his wealth.

"This is it!" Cy announced as if they'd arrived at a great circus tent. "Home sweet home! I might mention I had no input whatever so that gets me off the hook. My idea of Mokhani is the *ancestral* home of the Bannermans. I plan to keep the original homestead intact for my son. Families die out without sons. But my dad isn't circumscribed by those sentiments. He thinks Mokhani is his entirely. It isn't. A lot of my mother's fortune went into keeping it going during the hard times. We've had them like everyone else."

"It's quite extraordinary." She shielded her eyes with her hands, staring up.

"A masterly understatement. It's bizarre."

"Don't shut your mind on it altogether," she said, realizing the original homestead had great significance for him. Probably because it was not only the Bannerman ancestral home, but also the place his father had brought his mother to as a young bride. There had to be many reminders of his mother at the homestead, indeed all round the station. "You must miss your mother," she found herself saying.

He looked at her sharply, his tone cool. "At least I know what love is," he said.

"You've never been *in* love?" she asked, putting a hand to her hair as the wind gusted.

"Have you?"

"Sort of," she said smiling, "but no one I found irresistible."

"While you, no doubt, were adored."

She heard the sarcasm; responded to it. "The question is not whether I was adored, but given your need for heirs, why *you* at the very least aren't engaged?"

"Hey, ease up!" He threw up his hands. "I'm not going to do anything to jeopardize my bachelor state at the moment, Ms. Tennant, if that's what you want to know."

"I'm only making conversation." She shrugged, pausing to take in the magnitude of her commission.

"Wait until you get inside," he softly jeered. "If the Shah of Iran were still around, he'd love it."

"Good grief, it's immense." She was genuinely stunned.

"Well, I suppose it has to be big," he said carelessly. "B.B. does a lot of entertaining. He hosts many important overseas guests. Things quieted down a bit when Sharon, that's Robyn's mother, became so ill. She died two years ago. She was a good, sweet woman."

"Robyn doesn't take after her?" Jessica asked wryly.

"Well, I never!" He did a mock double take. "Are you saying Robyn's neither good nor sweet?"

She colored a little. "I only meant she isn't overly friendly. Shall we go in?"

"Of course. After you."

Just being with him was exhilarating. She felt as though she could go on talking to him forever.

They entered through a huge gabled portico supported by monumental Ionic columns that led directly to the twenty-foot-high double doors. Beyond, a space nearly as big as a football field culminated in an equally monumental staircase. After the first breathless shock, Jessica saw it as a wonderful multipurpose area. All the same, she didn't know whether to applaud or hoot. As a public building, it would have been splendid. As a private home it staggered the imagination.

"We had an army of builders and workers on site forever." Cy groaned at the memory. "They lived in row after row of tents just like on an archeological dig. Dad strode around like a pharaoh bullying and threatening. I'm only surprised he didn't carry a whip. An old quarry had to be reopened in North Queensland for all the marble—lots of columns, as you can see. B.B. loves columns. God knows what his mausoleum is going to be like."

"You're joking!" She turned to stare at him, relieved to catch a smile on his lips.

"Probably. But I can't entirely rule it out."

"This is fit for Prince Charles," Jessica said solemnly.

"Perhaps he'll come a-visiting. Do you wonder why I much prefer the old homestead? It's plenty good enough for *my* castle. It stood firm through Cyclone Tracy, though it has to be said we didn't bear the brunt of it. This place is apocalypse-proof."

"I guessed that." She stared up at the double-height soaring ceiling with its great cupola letting in streams of light. "I think I'm going to need a team."

"Around two hundred might be good," he said. "I hope

they enjoy living in tents. How come your uncle didn't get the commission? I don't want to hurt your feelings, but I had him checked out and he's the best. For that matter, how come he didn't want the job? From what I've seen no one is ever *too* rich."

"Isn't there something you're forgetting?" she asked, starting to pace round the huge area, staring up at the dome with its splendid yet restrained plaster work that bore the imprint of artisans.

"God, you're right. Dad wanted *you*. All we've got to discover now is why. Is it possible you remind him of someone? Someone dead these many, many long years?"

She drew a deep breath; slowly released it. She knew he was baiting her. "Oh come on, *say* it. Why beat about the bush? I made a mistake telling you your great aunt called me Moira."

"Well, she's never called anyone else that," he said, his voice flat. "Not in fifty years. Now, isn't that something that absolutely sets you apart?"

"It would seem so," she conceded. "It's certainly very unusual, but if there is a resemblance, it's sheer coincidence." Jessica walked quickly away from him to regain her composure, entering one of the huge reception rooms off the great hall. "Why don't we just stick to the grand tour instead of trying to figure out odd coincidences?"

"I thought we were doing both," he said blandly. "Perhaps you're Moira in another incarnation."

"Perhaps you're a reincarnation of the guy who chucked her in the lagoon," she retorted recklessly.

He frowned. "Is that wise saying something like that?"

"I usually give as good as I get." She felt anger and excitement in equal measure. "Why is it so difficult for you to accept me at face value?"

"Maybe that's it. The *face*." His tone was light, but with a sharp edge.

"I'm the interior designer your father happened to hire."

"And you haven't wondered at all why *you* in particular?"

"Maybe I have," she admitted irritably, "but unlike you, I haven't credited—or discredited him—with ulterior motives, whatever they might be. I know nothing of the situation between you and your father except what you've told me. So it's difficult? I sympathize, but don't bring me into it. As you pointed out when we met, I'm just passing through. I can handle this job. I know it's huge, but I'm not overwhelmed. If your father's ideas and mine don't mesh or he wants me to do it *his* way entirely, then I'm not the person for the job. He'll have to find someone else. While we're on the subject, why not your stepsister, Robyn? Why did he overlook her? I understand your father gave her carte blanche to refurbish the reception rooms of the old homestead."

"And have you ever seen such a disaster? If my poor mother were around she'd cry buckets." He didn't bother to keep the disgust out of his tone. "It was all done when I wasn't around. Downright sneaky, I call it. Robyn thinks good taste and wild extravagance go hand in hand. Dad gave her the go-ahead—maybe to get square with me for some imagined slight—then went away on a long trip. When he got home and saw what Robyn had done, can you image the furor? Bellowing by the hour. Even great men like B.B. make at least one mistake in a lifetime. I don't want him to make another."

"He won't with me!" she answered, her voice brisk.

"If only we could be sure." He stared at her. She was as beautiful as she was potentially a threat to life as they knew it. Not that that was all good. He knew his father too well not to intuit that B.B. had a consuming interest in this particular young woman, and it wasn't for her creative skills. He'd stake his life on that. Did she remind him of that sad little phantom of his childhood, Moira? There was no doubt his father had been deeply affected by Moira's mysterious disappearance. It was all so damned odd. Cy had all the proof he needed that Ms. Tennant had a certain fascination for his father. His father still had an eye for a beautiful women. But this one was way too young. Hell, she was five years younger than *he* was. Maybe his father's interest had been so captured when he'd seen her on that television program that he'd felt compelled to work out a way to get her here. He knew more than anyone that when his father resolved on something, it happened.

"Why don't we see what's behind this?" Her voice broke into his ponderings. She was waving a graceful arm toward the adjoining room.

"Why not?" He followed her in, both of them moving across the space of the room. Brilliant rays of sunlight fell through the tall windows, holding her as if in a spotlight. They illuminated her very feminine slender figure, the lovely face, the cloud of ash-blond hair, setting a-sparkle all the little shimmering ornaments on her emerald blouse. Beauty like that packed a powerful punch. He had never before seen anyone that beautiful *and* sexy. He could easily imagine what it had been like for his father. A man of strong sexual appetites. Cy was reaching in his deductions, of course. But over the years he had learned how to read his obsessively secretive father.

Jessica turned her head, giving him a small sidelong glance. He was as edgy as she was. Both of them were too aware of each other and showing it. "What are you thinking?" she asked. "You've gone quiet."

"I'm still in pursuit of answers," he said.

"Please don't continue to look at me," she begged. "The sort of answers you appear to be searching for are beyond me. I have no connection to the Bannerman past, even if I do have a passing resemblance to your father's governess."

"Which, like Lavinia, he would have seen immediately."

She reacted with an admonition. "That would scarcely prompt him to hire me to decorate all this. That's just plain crazy."

"Not just crazy, it's completely bloody insane. Look, it's entirely up to you and Dad if you stay or go," he told her. "I'm not asking to be your friend, Ms. Tennant. I've got too much else on my mind."

"When I would have treasured your friendship." She lifted her green eyes to his, not bothering to hide her interest.

He returned her gaze. "It's not mandatory to seduce the clients, is it?" he asked.

She shook her head, her cheeks flushed pink. "I'd have to be very foolish indeed to try to seduce *you!*"

He gave a cracked laugh. "You might enjoy it."

"It's a trap, isn't it?" she asked, her eyes narrowing. "You want me to make one big mistake."

"Damn, you're on to me," he said with a low laugh.

Then he shocked her. His arm snaked out to lock around her waist, sending streams of sensation into her body and down her legs.

"Think before you go any further." She couldn't keep back the faint tremble in her voice.

"Don't guys around you tend to lose it?" He gave her a taut smile, but he didn't take away his arm.

Unconsciously, she ran the tip of her tongue over her dry lips. "Some do. But you're just playing games."

"That's so." He pulled her in and put his mouth against her ear. "I don't get much fun around here."

She stiffened in his arms, alarmed at how easily he was thrilling her. "You're going to be difficult about this, are you?" she asked sharply. Something potentially damaging to her position in this family was whipping up between them. It was like being out in a yacht in a high wind.

"Just testing, Jessica," he drawled, though in reality he was having difficulty taking his arm away. Her body alongside his made him wonder what it would be like for them to become entwined.

"Well, I'm not about to fall into the trap." She pulled back and looked at him. He was so close, if she relaxed against him he could bring his other arm up and lock her in an embrace.

"Do you know how good you feel?"

"Stop it." She felt weak, her limbs swept by a warm languor.

"Hell, I *ought* to."

She thought he was going to release her, but instead he spun her right into his arms, bending his head and finding her mouth.

She saw stars. Other sparkling shapes. The whole world fell away to a roaring in her ears. Only sensation was left. Sensation so violent Jessica could barely stand. She had to cling to him as the only thing that wasn't moving.

When he finally let her go, she had to remain where she was, unable to move until her balance was restored. He *knew* how to kiss a woman. How many other women had he kissed? She put a hand on his chest and pushed.

"I can't believe you did that," she said.

His answer came right away, his tone not a lot different from hers. "I can't believe I did, either." His laugh held a trace of self-disgust. "I hope there aren't any hidden cameras around here."

She pushed tumbling locks of hair behind her ear. "Too bad you didn't have time to get them in place. You'd like to discredit me with your father, wouldn't you?"

He shrugged. "I'm not that kind of guy, Jessica. Truth is, you threw me momentarily off balance."

"Sorry, you're too smart for that. It's obviously much better for you if I get kicked out before I have a chance to get underway."

"Did you think I was counting on Dad turning up?"

"Weren't you?" Excitement turned to anger. She wanted to hit him.

Take that challenging look off his face.

"It scares me to tell you, Jessica, but I never gave my father a thought."

"I don't believe you!"

They were so engrossed in confronting each other, it took a few moments before the clack of boots across the marble floor penetrated. Cy turned immediately, while Jessica froze. "Talk of the devil and you conjure him up. That'll be Dad now. We both better cool down. You can bet your life he's come to check where we're at."

Her agitation increased. She was flooded by embarrassment and panic. "God, have I got any lipstick left?" She was forced to appeal to him. That kiss had been deep and prolonged.

For answer, he whipped a handkerchief out of his jeans pocket. "How could you? It's on *me*." He drew the white linen across his mouth, stuffing the handkerchief back in his pocket. "What are you waiting for? Go into the other room. Come on, *move*."

Jessica didn't need to be told twice. She'd only been on

Mokhani a day and already she was waist-deep in trouble. She bit down hard on her bottom lip—it was still throbbing from his kiss—in an endeavor to color it pink. Her heart was beating a rapid tattoo—which was fast becoming a routine around Cyrus Bannerman. She knew her face was flushed. She could still feel the *heat* of that clinch all through her body. It was the most explosive thing that had ever happened to her.

"Settle down, you look great," he reassured her, crossing the room swiftly on his long legs. He lifted his resonant voice so it rang around the empty space. "This is obviously intended to be the library. Of course you and Dad might have other ideas for it. An auditorium maybe? Dad loves giving speeches."

In another second, Broderick Bannerman appeared, his nostrils flared like an animal trying to pick up a scent. "I expected you'd be a bit further along than this," he said in an accusatory voice, looking from one to the other.

"I had no idea we had to rush," Cy responded, totally unfazed. "Surely Ms. Tennant needs *time* to take in all this magnificence."

Jessica felt as nervous as if Broderick Bannerman had caught the two of them in bed. "I had no real idea of the scale of the mansion, Mr. Bannerman," she said. "The great hall is awe-inspiring."

"My father loves grandeur," Cyrus told her.

Bannerman's smile came close to a snarl. "Thank you, Cyrus. I'll show Jessica the rest of the house."

"Glad to be of assistance." Cy sketched a brief, ironic salute. "See you at dinner, Ms. Tennant."

"Please…Jessica." She gave him a quelling glance. It was obvious he liked to get a rise out of his father, and she couldn't in all fairness blame him.

"Jessica. Thank you. Feel free to call me Cyrus," he invited.

"Don't take any notice of my son," Bannerman warned after Cyrus had gone. "All he cares about is goading me. It's not so surprising, I suppose. He's always lived in my shadow. Makes it hard for him to grapple with. Our relationship is far from easy. Now, what are your thoughts so far?"

The intensity of his gaze made her uncomfortable. She could only hope she wasn't betraying the turbulence that was inside her. How could she have let Cy Bannerman kiss her? Not that she could have offered resistance—he moved so fast. She had to assure herself that's all it was. "You've set me quite a challenge, Mr. Bannerman," she said, getting full control of her voice at last. "It's a massive job. These are great architectural spaces. We'll need to separate the public from the private. The great hall could be used for any number of purposes—functions that I'm sure you have in mind. I know you're looking for a sense of luxury and opulence in keeping with the building, but I see it through the framework of the environment. I don't have to tell you that's quite unique. What we're doing is reconciling classical architecture with modern sensibilities and needs. I don't know if you want to make the public rooms a showcase for art, some sculpture… I'm sure you'll want the latest technology. Equally sure you already have it at the homestead. Why don't we continue our tour? You can tell me your likes and dislikes along the way."

They walked into another room that could be used for banqueting. "What do you think of my son?" he asked with such harsh abruptness she almost jumped.

She knew she had to play it safe. "I haven't really had the time to form an opinion." What could she say? That he was as arrogant as Lucifer and, by the way, the best kisser in the world? That would go over well.

"He's quite a catch."

"I imagine he is," she answered in a calm, composed voice.

"*I'm* bigger," he told her, with what she could only describe as fierce triumph.

CHAPTER FIVE

AUNT LAVINIA CAME TO DINNER in costume.

"Tosca," Cyrus Bannerman told Jessica in a swift aside, an indulgent look on his face. It was obvious he was very fond of his great aunt. They had met on the stairs. Jessica hoped her face hadn't flamed, but his voice when he greeted her had been dead casual, as though absolutely nothing had passed between them. The best way to go, she thought, matching his nonchalance. Now they watched Lavinia, not without anxiety as she tottered down the staircase, one frail knotted hand trailing along the banister. Lavinia must have been beautiful when she was young, Jessica thought. She still retained glimmerings of it.

"Tosca. I guessed as much." Jessica, an opera buff, watched the old lady's gown swish around her ankles. The navy sneakers she wore only slightly detracted from the dramatic effect. In her copious white hair she wore an elaborate high-backed ebony comb studded with pearls and rhinestones. The bodice of her gown fell flat and low due to the fact her bust had diminished with age. Some underwear was showing. Around her neck she wore a shagreen choker from which was appended a great stone that had to weigh ten or twelve carats. It couldn't be a diamond, surely. Whatever it was, Jessica's eyes were dazzled by the bounce of light.

"Don't you look lovely, Moira!" Lavinia called, her watery eyes studying Jessica with pleasure before shifting to her great-nephew. "Good evening, my darling. Didn't I always tell you she'd come back?"

So this is what dementia is, Jessica thought sadly, feeling a prickle run up and down her spine.

"Like my dress?" Lavinia's expression indicated there was no possible answer but yes.

"Love it." Cyrus's smile was a little strained. "Not that I haven't seen it a million times. And it's Jessica, Livvy. Not Moira. Moira has ceased to be."

"Good evening, Miss Lavinia," Jessica spoke quickly to get over a sticky moment. Lavinia continued to stand on the bottom step, posing. "Don't tell me. You're Tosca."

A big smile covered Lavinia's face. "So you still love opera! That was one of the reasons I loved you. You *are* Moira, aren't you? There's no use Cyrus shushing me. Turn around, would you, dear? What a lovely, lovely dress." She smiled and nodded as Jessica twirled. "You always were ravishing."

"*Ravishing* is too tame a word," Cyrus said, his tone sardonic.

"Miss Lavinia, I'm not Moira," Jessica insisted, thinking she was becoming immured from further shocks. "I'm Jessica, remember?"

"Child, what's wrong with you?" The old lady, who had been executing a few dance steps, broke off to stare into Jessica's face, incredulous. "You can't have forgotten your name? Are we dealing with amnesia here?"

Cyrus intervened. "We're dealing with age and submerged grief. Come on, Liv. Give it up. It's a wasteland. Besides, you know you'll push Dad over the edge if you start this Moira stuff."

"His story and my story don't tally," Lavinia said.

"How could they?" Cyrus put a hand to his head. "Dad was a child."

"Broderick was *never* a child," Lavinia said, her voice sinking a whole octave. "And that's the truth."

"Oh, hell, Livvy, have a heart." Cyrus appealed to her. "Meal times are never easy, but we do have a guest. Two guests actually. Jessica and Robyn's boyfriend Erik Moore is here."

At the news, Lavinia began to beat her arms like chicken wings. "Oh, I don't like him!" she wailed. "Started up an affair behind his poor little wife's back. He always looks at me as though I should be locked away somewhere. I don't worry about that, though. If I'm so stupid, why do I know more than anyone else?" She danced a few more steps before tripping over her long velvet skirt. "Bother!"

Both Cyrus and Jessica came to her aid, each taking one of the old lady's arms. "Isn't that costume a little hot for this evening?" Cyrus inquired.

"So far so good." Lavinia gave a little laugh that turned into a cough. "I couldn't decide between it and *La Traviata*. I was such a success as Violetta." She turned her puffed white head toward Jessica. "I would have been a big name, like Sutherland. I could have had the adoration of millions, only the Honorable George Fairweather came into my life and wrecked it."

"At least you had the sense not to marry him," Cyrus comforted her.

"His dragon of a mother, a terrifying woman, insisted he break things off. His father really liked me, but he was no help at all. Mother had the power. I'm constantly astounded at the power of women."

"You can say that again!" Cyrus seconded. "A beautiful woman has all the power in the world."

THE OTHERS WERE ASSEMBLED in the opulent drawing room Robyn had spent so much of her stepfather's money on. As Cyrus, Lavinia and Jessica entered, those waiting looked up with varying expressions. Broderick Bannerman's intense scrutiny gave Jessica goose bumps. She thought he might have been seeing *through* her, then shook her head in dismay; this Moira business was getting to her. Robyn, looking very glamorous as she perched on the side of her boyfriend's armchair, showing off her long elegant legs, said, "Hi!"

Erik, so unpopular with Lavinia, smiled pleasantly and stood to attention. He was good-looking, slightly overweight, a full head of thick brown hair, hazel eyes, well-dressed. A lot older than Robyn. Married *and* divorced? Jessica wondered if he had children. Robyn wouldn't make the sweetest stepmother in the world.

"Sorry to keep you waiting," Lavinia trilled radiantly. "Don't worry. I'm safe with these two." She bestowed her sweet smile on first her great-nephew, then Jessica. "And you needn't look at me as if I've gone mad, Erik," she chided. "I love to keep my heyday alive."

"Tosca," B.B. informed Erik briefly. "You're all having a drink before dinner? Jessica, what would you like?" Again his rapier gaze swept over her face and body, taking in her cool, very pretty minidress, in layered swirls of deep pink and mauve. *Surely he can't have any sexual interest in me,* Jessica thought. If so, she might have to abandon a marvelously challenging commission. *And,* she was forced to admit, getting to know Cyrus Bannerman better.

When she glanced briefly in Cy's direction, she found his expression a touch severe. Had he recognized the sexual component in his father's stare? If he had, he bore *no* sympathy for it. Jessica shifted her gaze to Robyn, who was nursing a half-empty champagne flute.

"Champagne, if I may. That would be lovely."

"Cyrus, would you mind? Sherry for you, Liv?" B.B. asked.

Lavinia reacted with the little trill that fell so softly on the ears. "I'll join Moira in a glass of champagne," she said happily. "After all, it's a celebration. She's come back."

"'Struth!!" Robyn groaned, putting one expensively shod foot to the floor. "That's *Jessica,* Liv. Jessica Tennant, Dad's new interior designer." She'd raised her voice, perpetuating the myth Lavinia was stone deaf.

Lavinia remained oblivious to Robyn's scorn. "Why must you screech, Robyn? No one in the world yells at me like you do. That includes Broderick. I know what I'm talking about, thank you very much. *You* know, too, don't you, Broderick?"

Jessica felt herself go cold, but Bannerman's stare directed toward his aunt didn't waver. "I know you're talking nonsense, my dear," he said suavely. "That's a bit of a worry."

Oh, dear, Jessica thought. *He can't be implying Livinia is due for a nursing home, can he?*

"Ignore that, Livvy," Cyrus instructed, returning with two glasses of sparkling champagne. He gave one to Lavinia, the other to Jessica. "There's no worry. Trust me."

"Oh, I do, my darling." Lavinia's eyes flew to his after a few seconds of rapid blinking. "Every day you're alive is a miracle. The angels are looking after you."

Behind them, Robyn gave another protesting moan. "For God's sake, have we got to listen to this stuff, Dad? What Liv's got packed inside her head isn't entirely harmless. Why did you give her that glass of champagne, Cy?"

"Mind your own business, Robyn," Cyrus answered pleasantly enough. "Livvy has a perfect right to say what she likes."

Broderick Bannerman, who was standing in a cloud of preoccupation, now collected himself. "You must forgive us, Jessica. It's always a circus around here. Belatedly, I present a friend of Robyn's—Erik Moore. Erik's a property developer. I've no doubt he'll want to tell you all about his latest project. Erik, meet Jessica, who has come to take over the job of furnishing the new house. She's young, but she has a great deal to offer. I was very impressed with her ideas as we were touring the house. Off the top of her head, too, but first class."

"Delighted to meet you, Jessica." Erik didn't approach her, perhaps fearing Robyn might kick him in the shins. Instead, he executed a smooth Euro-style bow.

"Well, drink up," B.B. said briskly, throwing back his handsome head and draining the last of his drink. "My afternoon tour has made me hungry."

THEY ATE IN THE FORMAL dining room, occupying one end of the long polished table.

It was beautifully set and Jessica commented on it.

"Molly," B.B. said. "She's so much better at it than Robyn."

"I don't have to prove myself setting a table, Dad." Robyn's voice betrayed no resentment, but her eyes reflected her hurt. "The fact I'm a very successful businesswoman says all that needs to be said about me. Isn't that right, Erik?"

Erik answered the only way he possibly could. "Indeed it is, my love. You're going from strength to strength."

"She'd have been going nowhere without my support,"

Broderick Bannerman cut in like a master stroke. This evening he looked very distinguished at the head of the table, his jacket emphasizing his broad shoulders. Although Jessica hadn't taken to Robyn—the woman had scarcely been friendly—she was starting to feel sorry for her. It couldn't have been easy growing up in such an intolerant household.

It had been the very helpful housekeeper who had knocked on Jessica's door earlier in the evening to inform her with a smile that Mr. Bannerman liked everyone to dress for dinner. There was no slacking on Mokhani.

"Not *formal,* dear. You know what I mean. A pretty dress."

Jessica had thanked her for being so thoughtful. She had an ally in Molly if not in Robyn, who had probably been hoping she would turn up in a T-shirt, shorts and thongs. She had, in fact, laid out a simple yellow dress cut like a slip, but had quickly changed it for something a little dressier. One wouldn't want to offend B.B.'s sensibilities.

All three men were wearing lightweight linen jackets. No ties, but fine-quality shirts open at the throat. A concession to the heat, though the air-conditioning kept the house at a constant twenty-four degrees Celsius. It had to cost a fortune, Jessica thought. But what was a fortune to ordinary folk would probably be B.B.'s notion of small change.

Given the deep undercurrents, dinner went off well. The food was delicious—Jessica vowed there and then to get Molly's recipe for the baked barramundi for which the Territory was famous. Chili obviously, lemongrass, coriander, Kaffir lime peel…and what else? Thai shrimp paste, coconut cream and some other spices she couldn't name. The bouquet of the superb chardonnay mingled with the light scent of the bowl of white, cerise-veined Asian lilies. At one time, B.B.'s hand touched hers where it lay on the tablecloth of starched white damask. Inside, Jessica froze, but tried extremely hard to convey unawareness.

Cyrus continued talking—it seemed to Jessica the conversation eddied around him—but from the blue flash in his eyes he had seen the touch and continued to draw his own conclusions. Robyn, thankfully, was staring across the table at her stepbrother, apparently totally focused on what he was saying. Something about Jabiru, one of the four major mining settlements in the Territory, the other three, Ranger, Kabiluka and Koongarra, all uranium mines, all within Kakadu National Park, World Heritage listed. Although the Commonwealth government imposed a high level of environmental regulation, the issue of mining versus environment was one of bitter controversy. It was clear from what Cyrus was saying that he was firmly on the side of environmental preservation. Robyn, apparently, wasn't. Neither was Broderick Bannerman, with his extensive mining interests. Erik Moore sat uncomfortably on the fence. Australia, the most ancient continent, was an incredibly rich repository for valuable minerals, polarizing both sides.

"What do you think, Jessica?" B.B. asked, putting her on the spot.

No point in shirking it or trying to be diplomatic like Erik. "I'm on the side of the environment," she said quietly.

"Don't go to Jabiru and tell the miners and their families that," Robyn said, happy to entangle Jessica in the controversial issue. "Don't go to the Tasmanian forests either, and tell the forest workers to pack up their chain saws and go home."

"I understand both arguments, Robyn," Jessica said,

"but I believe preserving the great wilderness areas of the world is far more important than the short-term fueling of the economy. Take Greece. Do you think farmers of ancient times realized that their olive crop, their liquid gold, was undermining a fragile ecology and turning their once-lush land barren? They didn't, but I've read that their great writers delivered stern warnings. Sophocles for one. Most trees have a branching network of roots that hold the topsoil, but olive trees don't. It has a taproot that burrows deep. Once the topsoil has gone, it can't be replaced. That was Greece's tragedy."

"That's all news to me." Robyn brushed it aside. "The olive crop is still of great commercial importance, surely."

"Of course. But what was not known *then,* or largely disregarded, is known now. We have to act on the mistakes of the past."

"That's all very noble, Jessica," Broderick Banner said. "But people and governments live in the present. Mining in the Territory is overtaking cattle. *I* should know. Now, why don't we put the subject behind us?"

"With that attitude, Dad, nothing will change," Cyrus said quietly.

Lavinia, who had over-imbibed under cover of the conversation suddenly piped up with, "Mining isn't the *worst* thing Broderick has done."

"Thank you for that, Lavinia." B.B. turned his striking profile toward her. "You'll need help to get up the stairs."

If that wasn't a dismissal, what was? Jessica thought.

Only, Lavinia wasn't going to be deflected from speaking her mind. "What did you do with all the old photographs, Broderick?"

B.B. threw down his damask napkin. "What old photographs, my dear? There are scrapbooks all over the house."

"None of Moira," Lavinia snapped back like *Take that!*

"That's ancient history, Livvy." Cyrus touched his grandaunt's arm in a gentle warning.

Lavinia swept on single-mindedly. "Where are the paintings? The paintings Hughie did."

B.B. smiled at her. "I have emptied the homestead out myself, Liv—which hasn't stopped *you* from foraging around all these years. There *are* no photographs. No paintings. Do you think I wouldn't know?"

Cyrus took a long hard look at his father. "But you *would* know, Dad. You know everything. By your own admission."

"Please don't try to annoy me, Cyrus," B.B. returned. "You do it so often."

"Hear, hear," Robyn raised her wineglass, her rivalry with Cyrus springing to the fore.

"You can't hide things forever, Broderick," Lavinia warned, seemingly unaware of Cyrus's continuing warning touch.

Broderick Bannerman set his two palms down heavily on the table. "Listen and listen carefully, Lavinia. You've had too much to drink." The piercing gray gaze moved on to Robyn. "So have you, Robyn, for that matter. In my view, women should stick to one drink. No more. They have no head for alcohol. I want all this Moira business stopped. If you can't or won't stop, Lavinia, I'll have to speak to your doctor about it. He might well want to put you into a nursing home for a spell."

"You call a doctor and I'll *kill* you, Broderick." Lavinia bunched her frail, knotted hands into fists.

"All right, that's enough!" Cyrus stood up. "Why bait her, Dad?"

"I'm serious," his father said. "She's getting much worse."

Any sense of shyness in Jessica, amid such a family, had to be cast aside. She understood, like Cyrus, that Lavinia had to be protected from B.B.'s wrath. "Would you like to go upstairs now, Miss Lavinia?" she asked, rising to her feet, too. "I'm feeling a little tired myself. That was a beautiful meal."

"Molly is an unsung heroine," Lavinia said. "I *am* a little tired, dear. Don't think I don't know you want me to keep my trap shut, Broderick." She shot a glance at her nephew. "There's always been too much to hide." Unsteadily, she rose to her feet, wincing a little as the blood returned to her legs.

Cyrus took her arm. "Think you can make it up the stairs, Tosca?"

Lavinia giggled like a schoolgirl. "I may be a bit slow."

Erik Moore, who looked as if he'd been hoping against hope it would all blow over, rose courteously to his feet. "Good night, Ms. Bannerman. Sleep well."

"Good night, Erik," Lavinia replied graciously. "You seem like a nice person. Unfortunately I can't seem to like you. Oh, Moira, dear, aren't you sweet! You're coming, too."

Broderick Bannerman wasn't going to suffer that. "Stay here, please, Jessica," he said, gray eyes cold.

Dared she disobey? Jessica thought she could. She stepped forward, hoping her guardian angel was right behind her. "I'll only be a minute or two, Mr. Bannerman."

"Love to you all," Lavinia caroled wickedly over her shoulder, giving Cyrus a woozy smile before Jessica came to stand at her other side.

IT WAS JESSICA WHO HELPED Lavinia undress, while Cyrus waited in the adjoining sitting room. This was more like it, Jessica thought, looking around the beautiful, slightly theatrical bedroom and what she could see of the sitting room beyond. Robyn had no hand in decorating this. It truly expressed the essence of Lavinia, even if she *had* lost much of her substance. The color scheme was the blue and white of Chinese porcelain. Filmy white draperies adorned the large four-poster bed. Beautiful blue-and-white fabric was used for the curtains at the French doors, the upholstery of the daybed and the two armchairs. An exquisite blue Venetian writing table—Timmy would love it—stood proudly in a corner. There were two lovely flower paintings on the walls, a collection of miniatures, and dominating one wall, a full-length portrait of Lavinia in her heyday dressed in an extravagantly beautiful white ball gown, clusters of pure white camellias tucked behind her ears.

Violetta, the Lady of the Camellias.

Jessica took a long, admiring look. Just as she thought, Miss Lavinia had been a beauty.

"Yes, that's me," Lavinia confirmed. "I was *glorious* in those days. No big fat diva about me. And my soaring voice! I could hit F above top C no trouble at all. Don't know where I got it from. No one else in the family had a voice unless one counts good speaking voices. We all have those. Come back in, Cyrus, darling," she called. "I'm decent."

Cyrus reentered, vibrantly male in that ultrafeminine room. "That's news to me."

"Don't be naughty, darling." Lavinia was tucked up under the covers now, her abundant white hair pulled back in a plait.

"If I had some watercolors handy, I would paint this lovely room," Jessica said. "I adore the portrait."

"Of course the artist was in love with me," Lavinia said.

"Of course," Cyrus smiled. "That was to be expected."

"You'd really like to paint my room, Moira?" Lavinia asked, motioning to Cyrus to come sit on the side of her bed. "I didn't think young artists did that anymore."

"I do," Jessica smiled. "I took it up in my student days. My uncle Brett encouraged it. I've had quite a few commissions."

Lavinia patted Cyrus's hand. "Get Moira some watercolor paints when you're next in Darwin," she said.

"No problem." The sapphire eyes moved to Jessica, standing beneath Lavinia's portrait. "You'll have to come with me to get exactly what you need."

No second invitation needed, Jessica thought.

They were almost at the door when Lavinia said, "Don't go away again, Moira. Promise?"

Jessica appealed to the formidable man at her side. "What do you want me to say?" she whispered.

"This whole bloody thing is totally insane," he retorted quietly with intense irritation. Then, "Make her happy."

"You don't think I should stop it right now?"

"Do you *want* to?" he asked tightly.

She tried to rein in her temper. What game did he think she was playing? And how could it possibly be an advantage to her? Jessica turned her head over her shoulder. "I promise, Miss Lavinia," she said.

Cyrus lifted a hand and turned off the light. "It doesn't matter, anyway. She's asleep now. Bizarre as it may seem, Jessica, your chance resemblance to our resident ghost has brought shock waves into our already disordered lives. Time has stopped for Lavinia. Even my father seems suspended in a past only he can see."

"Well, let me assure you yet again this has nothing to do with me. We don't even know if I actually do look like Moira or if it's simply a matter of coloring."

"What I should do is conduct a hunt of my own," Cyrus muttered, almost to himself. "There are a million places to hide old photographs, even large paintings."

"But your father has denied their existence. Rather strenuously, I thought."

"Which doesn't mean he's not lying. The hell of it all is no one *knows* what happened to Moira, and your resemblance to her is keeping the whole bloody thing alive."

"Has anyone ever thought about reconstructing her last days? The last days she was seen alive?"

"For God's sweet sake, of course they did," he said, none too politely.

"Only making a suggestion. No need to bite my head off."

His eyes flashed. "Jessica, don't expect anyone around here to keep calm on the subject of Moira. She's been dead for a half a century, yet sometimes it seems like only fifteen minutes ago. Now we've had a visitation—you." His eyes rested on her face. "Can you blame me if I'm suddenly very anxious about what it all means?"

CHAPTER SIX

THE NEXT MORNING in her bedroom, Jessica had a long conversation with Brett on her mobile phone, conveying her excitement while answering his many questions. She carefully refrained from saying anything that would make him in the least bit worried, such as Great-aunt Lavinia's memory playing tricks and making her believe she was Moira. She'd rung Brett briefly the moment she'd touched down in Darwin as promised, but a scant, incident-packed day later there was so much to talk about that her side of the conversation continued nonstop.

"Then you think you can cope?" Brett asked when she took a breather. He might have been sitting in a Darwin office rather than his office more than a thousand miles away, Jessica thought. Darwin was, in fact, closer to Asia than it was to any other Australian capital city.

"I'll need help," she told him. "A lot of help. I can't carry it all. It's an immense project. Far bigger than we anticipated."

"You'll get all the help you need on this, Jass. Take plenty of photographs. I need to know the layout."

"I'll draw up floor plans. That should keep me busy. I'll need to ask Mr. Bannerman's secretary, a nice woman called Ruth if I can load them onto one of the office computers. They have all the latest technology here."

"A man in his position, with his vast interests, would need to," Brett said. "How are you supposed to get around?"

"I'm sure I'll be provided with something. A nice spirited horse, maybe a camel. There are thousands and thousands of them roaming around. Kangaroos by the millions. I never knew it but there are twice as many kangaroos in Australia as people. That means roughly forty million."

Brett laughed. "And to think I've never come face-to-face with one. Don't get burnt in that tropical sun," he warned.

"I won't. I've bought lashings of sunscreen. There are plenty of station vehicles, by the way. Helicopters, a Beech Baron and a Lear jet."

"When you're filthy rich, nothing is unobtainable," Brett said dryly.

"I prefer to think *some* things are."

"What is that supposed to mean?" Brett picked up on her tone.

"Nothing. B.B. has his own pilot, but I understand he and Cyrus are licensed to fly the jet. He goes over to New Zealand a lot. He has interests there. Apparently the jet can fly to Auckland without refueling."

"Marvelous! What else does it do?"

"I'll tell you when I'm in it."

"The son, what's he like?"

Jessica twisted a long curl around her finger. "Very lordly. His father's manner veers more to severely autocratic. Cyrus is the only one who doesn't jump at his father's command, anyway."

"Princes are like that," Brett said. "Just don't become his willing subject. What's the father-son relationship like?"

Jessica eased back on the bed. "Not good. I think they've had some terrible clashes in the past."

"That's awful!" Brett sounded appalled. "You be careful, Jass," he warned. "Enmity between father and son is not to be dismissed. Whatever you do, don't get between them. You're there in a strictly professional capacity. Don't let the heir-in-waiting turn your head. Sounds like Tim will play a role in this. He can take a few quick overseas trips if necessary. Source out antiques."

"Good idea. Has Timmy found out anything more about the portrait he bought at Christie's?" she asked.

"Not as yet."

"She looks so much like me. Don't you think that's odd?"

"It *is* odd, but it's not like it doesn't happen, Jass. Remember the portrait we had of the woman in the red dress? She was the spitting image of the Lady Mayoress. What about the governess who disappeared? Any mention of that?"

Brett always had been on her wavelength. "The subject is taboo."

"I guess so," Brett said in a somber voice. "Can you imagine what it must have been like for Bannerman growing up? At least he had an alibi," he quipped sardonically.

"Why would he need an alibi? Why would anyone need an alibi?" Jessica felt an icy finger down her spine.

"Bannerman's father might have had an obsession with the girl, for all we know. He could have seduced her. The wife found out. The kids found out. The servants were agog with gossip. If I were writing a movie script, it would be a life-threatening situation. Listen, I have to go. Becky is signaling me. Clients have come in. Ring me every day and take care."

BRODERICK BANNERMAN INSISTED on coming with her while she took her photographs. Surely, she thought, such a high-pressured tycoon would have something more important to do. But no. It seemed nothing would suit him better than to walk around with her while she shot off hundreds of photographs of the exterior and interior of the new homestead, although *homestead* was far too modest a word for this modern palace. There were six guest suites contained within the main building, all with their own private porch. She would have a lot of fun decorating those. She took shots of the surrounding garden, well-nurtured by bores: sweeps of lawn like a vast green plain, towering palms and banyans, the boabs and poincianas, native frangipani that had grown into huge trees, the mango, coconut and the giant tree ferns that formed such a lush oasis in an arid land.

"We could do with a water feature," she said, removing a memory stick from her digital camera and inserting another. "The sight and sound of water is very cooling. I'd make it a focal point. Keeping to the classical idiom would be crucial. Who was your landscape gardener?" They might have to call him or her back.

"A fellow called Alan Jensen," B.B. answered, his sunglasses making his piercing gaze unreadable.

"I knew it had to be someone good," Jessica said, instantly recognizing the name. Jensen was very highly regarded in the field.

"I only deal with the best."

She took her shot, then smiled. "Then you're taking a chance on me."

"I don't think so." His deep voice was very measured, very sure.

"Well, I'm very happy about it, Mr. Bannerman."

"Broderick. Call me Broderick," he said with a smile. "I don't want B.B. or Mr. Bannerman from you. Broderick is my name. I liked the look of you, Jessica, and the way you expressed yourself on that program. I liked your beauty, your polish, your style. I like grace in a woman. My first wife, Deborah, had it in abundance. I lost her far too early. I was beside myself with grief. Then I had to put her firmly out of my mind. The Bannerman empire had to come first. The fact you're in contention for a big design award helped. The young should be given every chance."

Jessica's mouth quirked. "I'm firmly behind that." She was touched by the way he had spoken about his wife. It showed a more sensitive side of him. It was all so sad. "Thank you for your faith in me. I'll do everything in my power to make you happy you chose me."

He looked at her standing there, flashing her lovely smile and brimming with life. The sun made a glory of her cloud of ash-blond hair, her green eyes shone like jewels, and her skin was shimmering. For a moment, he thought he was dreaming. In this young woman's presence, nothing seemed normal. "I'm not used to happiness," he said, and abruptly turned away.

Jessica stood rooted to the spot for several moments, staring after him as he headed down the path. His progress was unhurried but purposeful. There was a lot of darkness and misery in Broderick Bannerman, she thought, relieved she could now continue on her own. She didn't feel comfortable with the man. She doubted anyone would. She realized, too, Cyrus wouldn't like her calling his father by his Christian name, taking little account of the fact that she, too, preferred not to. But having been *told* as opposed to *invited* to call him Broderick, she would be giving offense if she didn't.

Robyn wouldn't like her calling her father Broderick

either. Both son and stepdaughter were seeing concerns further along the track. Broderick Bannerman was still a handsome virile man. He had obviously taken a fancy to her, which was the very last thing she'd expected. Surely they all knew that. She was making her own way in life. The old rule about never mixing business with pleasure had its history in experience. Her position had already diminished, simply by allowing Cyrus Bannerman to get under her guard. She should have known better. Sexual attraction swept away good judgment. What she needed was a good shot of self-control.

Slowly, she walked back into the house, filled with a desire to capture and send just the right images back to Brett and Tim. She had already made her request to Ruth, B.B.'s secretary, for the use of a computer.

"Whatever you want, my dear, B.B. has given me my instructions."

It was abundantly clear Ruth craved her boss's approval. Jessica also had a strong sense Ruth secretly craved a lot more.

She spent until lunchtime, which Molly had told her was one o'clock sharp, getting her feel of the dimensions of the various rooms and their outlooks. She made some quick sketches of floor plans for her own benefit, having already asked Broderick—why was it such a hurdle to call him that—if she could make copies of the original house plans. The architect, not surprisingly, was of Greek extraction currently living and working in Brunei, no doubt building more palaces.

They were in fact waiting for her when she finally made it to the informal dining room situated at the rear of the homestead. It could be, and probably had been at one time, a lovely room, floor and ceiling dark gleaming timber with contrasting chalky white walls crying out for decoration. Paintings, mirrors, surely they had them? Probably Robyn had had them stored away. The hard question was, if Robyn owned an art gallery, what made her shun putting paintings on her own walls? Jessica had seen lots of superb antique silver, fine china and beautiful glittering crystal, but the house was devoid of artworks and some fine pieces of antique furniture. She wasn't thinking of all that many, but certain focal pieces from China or Japan.

Entering the room, her eye carried to the huge turquoise swimming pool in the garden beyond. She had already taken a quick look at the intricately carved ceiling of the pagoda covering it, which Robyn had told her had come from an Asian temple. It struck her, not for the first time, that the original homestead with its wonderful high-hipped roof and deep overhangs was far more appropriate to the climate and its extraordinary setting than the palatial new building, which would have looked great among the mansions of the very rich rising above Sydney Harbour.

"So sorry," Jessica made a quick, smiling apology. "The time simply flew."

Ruth, who ate with the family during the working day and sometimes at night—she had her own self-contained bungalow on the grounds—acknowledged that with an empathetic smile. Robyn remained silent. Her friend Erik Moore gave Jessica a smile full of interest. Very daring of him, with Robyn sitting by his side. B.B. gestured Jessica into the empty chair to his right. "Wondered what kept you," he said, as though that now she was present they could get underway.

No sign of Lavinia.

No sign of Cyrus. Big disappointment. Again her powerful attraction to him hit her like a blow.

Lavinia would be in her room listening to her favourite CDs of Tebaldi and Callas. Cyrus would be working hard around the station. Being a cattleman was a tough seven-day-a-week job. His father, having done it all in his time, presided at the lunch table.

"So what *were* you doing with yourself?" Robyn was in interrogation mode. She started to help herself to a very small portion of coconut chicken salad sprinkled with toasted sesame seeds and piled high on a large lime-green-and-white platter.

It looked good. Jessica found herself hungry.

"Taking photographs, mostly," she replied. "I've e-mailed a lot of them back to my uncle. He's taking a great interest in the project, which as you can imagine is a considerable coup for our firm."

"Why does everyone go in for designers?" Robyn's voice was laced with scorn. "*I've* never seen the need for calling them in. Obviously a lot of people lack self-confidence and taste."

"For which you qualify on at least *one* count," her stepfather commented in a level voice that sat oddly with the barbed remark.

Naturally Robyn protested. Jessica didn't blame her. "Oh, Dad, that's a bit cruel. *You* mightn't have been entirely happy with what I did a couple of years back, but most of our friends love it. *You* do, don't you, Erik?"

"Well, he would, wouldn't he?" her stepfather retorted before the embarrassed Erik could speak. B.B. inclined his handsome head in thanks as Ruth, having piled a plate with the delicious-looking salad, rose and set it before him.

Now that's service, Jessica thought. Ruth was not only the loyal devoted secretary; she was the hired help.

"Robyn and Erik are in partnership building an indigenous art gallery and adjoining boutique hotel on the coast a few miles out of Darwin city," Bannerman said, turning to Jessica. "At least Erik had the sense to call in a good architect, a very clever young Malaysian. Construction has only just started, but there's a chance for a good interior designer." He patted her hand.

For one shocking moment, Jessica thought Robyn would explode; instead, she threw down her fork, which bounced off the table and fell to the floor. "Ms. Tennant will have more than she can possibly chew trying to meet the challenge of the Big House, Dad."

Ruth, whose blush at being thanked by the great man still hadn't subsided, now sat so still and so quiet she might have been trying to make herself invisible.

"I hope you weren't thinking of doing the job yourself, Robyn," Broderick Bannerman said, again in that mild tone. "If so, I have to tell you, if Erik won't, you're not competent."

Robyn flushed but fought back gamely. "That's what *you* say, Dad."

Inside, Jessica applauded. *Good for you!* The nicest person in the world would have been adversely affected by a lifetime with the hypercritical, acid-tongued Broderick Bannerman.

"If you don't want to listen to good advice, Robyn," he replied, "Erik will have to. Remember, I have some stake in this."

Ah, the iron fist in the velvet glove. Jessica watched Erik surreptitiously rub Robyn's back to calm her. "You're being a little hard on Robyn, aren't you, B.B.?" he asked, keeping his tone respectful. Clearly it didn't pay to get on the wrong side of Broderick Bannerman.

B.B. suddenly looked bored. "Well, *you* can't risk the truth, Erik, can you? Erik is hoping to marry my step-daughter," he turned his head to inform Jessica, who, had she been Robyn, would have run from the table, having first slapped B.B. over the head with her napkin. "It isn't particularly good news. Erik made his first wife—a very nice little thing—extremely unhappy. She could have had her revenge for that, but she didn't."

"Actually, B.B.," Erik spluttered, his affable face turning brick-red, "she finished with more than her fair share. Elizabeth deliberately tried to turn our friends against me. She wanted to protect her own reputation."

"Which was blameless." Bannerman gave his judgment. "God knows why Robyn is determined to have you. You won't make her happy, either." He broke off to examine Jessica's plate. "You're not eating?"

She contemplated the chicken dish before her. "Yes, I must start. This looks delicious." Dutifully she picked up her fork before she was force-fed.

"I've organized a vehicle for you to run around in," B.B. told her presently. "A four-wheel drive. You can take it out anytime you like. But unless you have company, I'd like you to keep in sight of the outbuildings and the airstrip. It would be very easy for someone like you, a city girl, to get lost. There's no need for you to spend all your time on the job. I want you to enjoy your stay on Mokhani."

He threw her another one of his rare charming smiles. If only the man would lighten up a little! Even the odd kindly word seemed to exhaust him. If only he'd show some loving kindness toward his son and his stepdaugh-ter. Maybe kindness wasn't in his disposition, and his wealth no doubt had played a large part in solidifying his autocratic manner.

"Thank you…Broderick," Jessica murmured, keeping an eye on reactions around the table.

If looks could kill, she would have been dead in her chair.

"That's a bit presumptuous calling Dad by his Christian name, isn't it?" Robyn spoke emotionally, blindly ignoring Erik's hand at her elbow. Even the deeply reserved Ruth looked shocked.

Bannerman's voice was as dry as ash. "The fact is I *asked* Jessica to call me by my Christian name, Robyn. She isn't taking liberties. I don't hear my name enough. In fact, I don't hear it at all."

Everyone fell silent, embarrassed. Robyn, dark head bent, lifted her eyes just long enough for Jessica to see their glare.

How to make friends and influence people, Jessica thought.

CHAPTER SEVEN

JESSICA FOUND HERSELF working so feverishly on the layout of the Big House, as the family called it, she had little time to go exploring on her own or indeed with anyone else. B.B., too, was extremely busy, for which she was grateful. The very last thing she wanted was that he should follow her around. She couldn't help but be aware that she had captured his eye. Approaching sixty or no, the libido had definitely not been drained out of the man. Besides, he was very rich, and Jessica's experience of rich people told her they thought nothing impossible. Courting and capturing a woman young enough to be one's daughter might be viewed as a piece of cake.

The only time all of them met up was at dinner. As the weeks passed, Jessica had come to think of it as the time that really counted. She got to see Cyrus. Cyrus with his brilliant, mocking eyes resting lightly on her, his attentions friendly but in no way sexual. Yet when he was around, the very air sparkled, her perceptions intensified. It might have been champagne running in her blood. Only, with his punishing workload, she didn't get to see him half often enough. He was up and away at dawn, only returning to the homestead at dusk. His absence *should* have kept her in check, but it didn't. She felt him there even when he wasn't, which she concluded was one of the side effects of such attraction.

Erik Moore had long since returned to Darwin, inviting Jessica to look over his and Robyn's latest development whenever she came to town. Needless to say, Robyn wasn't there at the time he issued the invitation. Aunt Lavinia kept mostly to her room, out of harm's way. Probably that bit about the nursing home had frightened her. Which was cruel. Robyn continued to be unfriendly to the point of being rude. She seemed quite unable to say a single thing with grace. Jessica realized Robyn had convinced herself there was some mischief afoot that included her stepfather's designer. Not that Jessica could blame her when B.B. persisted in treating her, Jessica, with a gentleness and attention he bestowed on no other. Jessica might well be thought to be a rival for Robyn's stepfather's affections. Perhaps a mistress in the making? Whatever the thinking, Jessica was becoming more and more aware that her arrival at Mokhani had produced much the same effect as a bomb going off.

She tried not to let Robyn's manner upset her. Robyn clearly had problems. Although she was by all accounts a successful businesswoman, a mega-rich man's stepdaughter, Jessica had come to appreciate that Robyn's life wasn't easy. Accepted though she was as a Bannerman, she wasn't by *birth*. Jessica could quite understand how Robyn had struggled with that all her life, since blood was so important in this family. So much of her prickly manner could have its basis in insecurity. Odd she had never sought complete independence. Obviously money was the key. Robyn might find separation from the *money* unbearable. Money compelled people to stay when they really wanted to run.

Overnight, Mokhani had become the center of Jessica's world. She felt a powerful affinity with it. Every day she rose with the birds, awakened by the stupendous outpouring of song. A veritable opera she had come to think of as an homage to the sun. She lay in bed each morning, her arms stretched above her head, enthralled. The legions of birds lent the choir great power. She supposed the rest of the household was used to having the world's greatest orchestra in the backyard, but she found the depth and the volume of sound quite impossible to sleep through. And who would want to?

She longed for the weekends to come, for then she had her best chance of seeing more of Cyrus. Neither of them could turn their backs on that kiss. She supposed that's what kisses were for—to bring an attraction right into focus. Not all kisses left one with a feeling of falling into the unknown. Falling into *love?* Sometimes something he said or the way he looked at her built on her own yearnings. Other times, she told herself she was dreaming. Or simply she was far more impressionable than he was. She had never been so impressionable before.

One Saturday when she was well into her second month at Mokhani, Jessica lingered at the breakfast table, saying she'd like to pay Aunt Lavinia a visit afterward. B.B. had left the table only a few minutes before to take an urgent phone call, leaving Jessica and Robyn together. Not a comfortable situation when Robyn was in one of her abrasive moods.

"I wouldn't bother if I were you," Robyn told her shortly. "Livvy likes her own space." She raked her nails over some little bump on her arm, leaving a red weal. "Why the heck are you so bent on ingratiating yourself around here?" she asked, making no effort to hide her resentment. "Don't you think you're exceeding your brief?"

Jessica had been waiting for some sort of attack; still, she was taken aback. "Gosh, I'm certainly not ingratiating myself with *you,* Robyn. Can't we be friends? It would make life so much easier. I can't overlook your rudeness anymore. I know I don't deserve it."

"Well, you'll damned well have to put up with it," Robyn said, a glimmer of tears in her eyes.

Immediately, Jessica backed off. "You're upset. Please tell me why. I want to help."

Robyn didn't answer, but bit down hard on her lip.

"Do you see me as some kind of threat, Robyn?" Jessica persisted, trying to clear the air. "I'm no possible threat to you. How could you think it? I'm here to do a job, then I'll be gone. Out of your lives."

Robyn snorted. "As far as I'm concerned the job is simply a ploy. You're like every other female Cyrus or B.B. meet. They've all got getting bedded on their minds. Who knows? Getting bedded could be a first step to marriage."

For a moment, Jessica saw red. She counted to ten, tempted to bop Robyn in the nose. "Don't be so ridiculous," she said crisply. "If you believe that, you'll believe anything. No wonder our friendship is doomed. You couldn't be more wrong. In fact, you're downright insulting. I'm here in my capacity as interior designer. You must have missed it, but I've been working extremely hard."

Robyn gave a brittle laugh as she demolished a piece of a freshly baked roll in her fingers. "Look, Jessica, I'm the victim here, not you. Dad is paying you so much attention it's sad to see. I wouldn't care if you were one of his old girlfriends, his own age. But you're not. You're a bloody love goddess. Cyrus thinks so, too. Both of us are convinced you have a far bigger coup in mind than pulling off the Big House. *I* haven't seen anything you've done so far."

"Robyn, you haven't shown the slightest interest."

"Why should I? All the money Dad's paying you, I would have done it for nothing."

"I'm sorry, Robyn, but it's not as easy as you think. I have a lot of training behind me."

"Big deal!" Robyn returned rudely. "There's something wrong with this whole thing. Are you going to tell me?"

Jessica sighed. "Robyn, there's nothing *to* tell."

Robyn studied her with narrowed dark eyes. "Obviously, you remind poor old Livvy of that dreary skeleton in the closct, Moira. That being the case, Dad must see something of her in you, too. Maybe *that's* the big fascination. Seeing you on that television show freed up a lot of stuff in Dad's head. Moira still stands for something in Dad's life. *I* rate a lot lower than her. I don't really matter to him, however hard I try. I'm not his blood, after all. I'm not a bloody Bannerman, I'm a lousy stepdaughter. I've been trying to get his attention all my life, yet you sashay in with your blond hair and your big green eyes and you get it right away. It must be a pleasure for men just to look at you. I see Cyrus taking his fill over the dinner table. Dad can't take his eyes off you, either. I've never seen that before. Ever! And I've been watching him for most of my life."

Jessica, staring with a mix of dismay and sympathy into the other woman's eyes, saw genuine fears. "Look, I'm sorry for all this and your problems with your stepfather, but you've just said, they started long before I came on the scene. Don't blame me for being blond, either, or for a chance resemblance to your stepfather's childhood governess, which could be very slight. What you're saying is wrong and damaging to me. Your fears are quite without foundation. Your stepfather is old enough to be my father. Don't you think twenty-four and sixty is a no-go?"

Robyn stood up so violently she sent her chair flying.

"Try twenty-four and sixty million!" she cried, curling her lip in scorn. "You're no different from any other female. Your big dream in life is to land a millionaire. The older the better! You won't have to wait that long to get the money."

Jessica pushed her plate away. "Speak for yourself, Robyn. I'm not another version of *you*. I haven't got anything against Erik, but isn't *he* middle-aged? You could well be chasing a father figure."

"Bitch!" Robyn smarted.

Jessica, too, stood up. "You're not the only one who can take cheap shots, Robyn. I'll go and see Lavinia now. Unlike you, she enjoys my company."

JESSICA TAPPED LIGHTLY on Lavinia's door. Her little spat with Robyn had upset her. Her hands were shaking. She needed to calm down.

"Miss Lavinia?" She hoped the old lady would speak to her. She'd missed her, although Molly had assured her Lavinia was perfectly well. Her meals were being taken to her room, Molly always returning with an empty tray. A surprise, considering Lavinia looked as though she hadn't eaten in more than a half century!

No sound inside. Disappointed, Jessica was about to withdraw when she heard a scurrying on the other side. The door opened a fraction, a tiny face covered in thick white makeup peered out, then on seeing Jessica, the door opened right up.

"Moira, dear." Madame Butterfly showed her pleasure. "I was wondering when you were going to come and see me."

Jessica was so enchanted, she forgot to correct the old lady. "I've been very busy, Miss Lavinia, but I've been asking about you." She smiled, her eyes ranging all over the elaborate costume so completely different from Violetta's ball gown. No wonder Lavinia could stay in her room, never bored.

"Well, come in, come in," Lavinia invited happily, adjusting the wide red silk obi that had slipped from her waist to her nonexistent hips. Her kimono, red and white silk, was exquisite, the scarlet panels embroidered with white peonies. Lavinia, the purist, had arranged her hair in a loose puff with a thick topknot, various gold and pearl baubles holding it in place. "Shall I send for tea?" she asked. "I know exactly how to perform the tea ceremony."

Jessica would have agreed, only there wasn't time. "That would be lovely, Miss Lavinia, but perhaps some other time. I've just had breakfast."

"Of course you have." Lavinia tottered on her wooden clogs into the sitting room, and Jessica followed.

"Well, sit down." She waved Jessica to a comfortable armchair, taking one herself by falling back into it. "Tell me what you've been doing. I've been keeping to my room out of harm's way. I've found I can only take Broderick in small doses, anyway. As for Robyn! All she does is torment me. She was such an unhappy little girl. Never laughed, always glowering. She wants Mokhani, you know." The faded eyes, set in their violet sockets, were shrewd.

"But Cyrus is the heir?"

Lavinia wriggled in her chair. Jessica, familiar with such wriggles in the elderly, got up to push a little cushion behind her back. "Better?"

"Thank you, Moira, love." Lavinia patted her arm. "Everything fell apart in this house when Deborah was killed. Even then Broderick was a hard, strange man, but he had a horrible time trying to get over Deborah's death.

He neglected Cyrus terribly. I used to think it was because Cyrus is so much like her. Not in looks, so much. Cyrus is a Bannerman, with his grandfather's blazing blue eyes, but his nature. Cyrus is a very fine young man. He's caring and thoughtful and everyone loves and respects him. They *fear* Broderick. Quite a different thing. Since he's become a man, Cyrus has shown his own brilliance. He could take over from his father any day. That's not just me saying that. The people who know agree Cyrus is *The Man*. That hardly makes Broderick happy. It must be a terrible thing to be jealous of your own son—jealous of his *youth*. Aging isn't easy, Moira." Lavinia shook her head dolefully. "Someone said—I just forget who—it was a whiplash in the face of the human spirit. I totally agree."

Jessica felt very disturbed by Lavinia's insistence on calling her Moira, but equally she felt powerless to do anything about it. "Why does Cyrus stay?"

Lavinia shrugged. "His father can't last forever. Broderick can dispose of all his other assets as he pleases, but Mokhani and the ancestral home belong to Cyrus. Even Broderick knows he has no right to deprive his son of that. Cyrus is standing in line to inherit just as Broderick inherited from his own father, Steven. My God, there was a man! But tormented, too, just like poor Broderick."

"I've admired his portrait in the study."

"Doesn't do him justice!" Lavinia delicately snorted. "As *you'll* know." She looked sympathetically into Jessica's eyes. "Madly in love with him, weren't you?"

"Oh, Miss Lavinia!" For an instant Jessica had a powerful attack of vertigo. She lowered her head until the dizziness passed. She despaired she would never get the old lady to recognize her for who she was, but she had to continue to try or slip into a similar kind of madness. "I'm Jessica, remember?"

But Lavinia's brain had an infinite number of interlocking caverns where the past and the present flowed together. She laughed softly. "It's all right, love. I was so worried about you, but now you're back. I'm not mad, you know. I know I make a lot of people uncomfortable, even my darling Cyrus. He doesn't like me talking about Moira."

I don't blame him, Jessica thought. She was feeling spooked herself.

Lavinia's tiny face contorted. "Any talk of Moira always has started such a *fuss!*" Her thin knotted hands began to twitch. "Do you know how many years have passed since you've been gone, child?"

"Moira's been gone over fifty years," Jessica said gently, leaning forward in her chair. "I must look like Moira. That's why you've made the mistake."

"Shh!" Lavinia said, holding a finger to her lips. She didn't look in the least grotesque with the white theatrical makeup plastered all over her face and her lips painted a bright red. The fine wrinkles on her face covered, she looked an echo of her far-off heyday when she had stolen an English aristocrat's heart. "Just between you and me, I think I know where Broderick hid your portrait," she whispered, as though her nephew were standing listening just outside the French doors. "Always said he destroyed it, but he tells lies. Have you ever been into the big storeroom?" she asked.

Jessica was galvanized by that piece of information. "The attic?"

Lavinia shook her head vigorously, setting her pearl-and-gold baubles dancing. "No, the big storeroom is a separate building. You must know it. It's at the rear of the kitchen complex, the old servants' quarters. It's where Robyn, bless her, emptied out all Deborah's things. Graceless creature! Shoved them in there. The nerve of her!" Hostility burned from Lavinia's eyes. "If you manage to get in there—it will have to be when Broderick is away— you can do a search. I failed, but *you* won't."

Suddenly a light went on in Jessica's head. "Have you seen another portrait of Moira lately?" she asked. "At an art auction, maybe? When you were in Sydney?"

Lavinia frowned, at first looking as if she didn't understand but then she responded indignantly, "Some bloody man bought it. Needless to say he was not a gentleman, because he wouldn't let me have it. I thought he would if I offered him a lot of money, but he wouldn't be persuaded, waffling on about how it was the image of a dear friend. Of course I didn't believe him."

Jessica was shaken. Very shaken. So it *was* a portrait of Moira. Moira who had disappeared in 1947. Moira, who had, in fact, looked very much like *her.* It was an incredible coincidence, the resemblance, but the sudden appearance of the portrait after half a century's obscurity surely wasn't. Was someone pulling strings and for what purpose? Had B.B. put it on the market? Maybe even his twin, Barbara?

"Did your niece, Barbara, go with you to the auction?" she asked.

"Skipped off without her," Lavinia said confidentially. "Ferris, their driver, took me in. Babs doesn't like sitting around auctions like I do. As it turned out it was a great blessing she didn't come. She'd have been tremendously upset to see the portrait, and I simply couldn't tell her about it."

No, but it set you off, Jessica thought, appreciating that the portrait had had a considerable effect on the old lady. "Do you know the name of the artist?" she asked.

"Of course," Lavinia's jet-black brows, painted in a high arch, rose farther toward her hairline. "Why are you asking me? It was Hughie."

"Hughie, of course." Jessica murmured, piecing the story together.

"He had a great deal of talent," Lavinia said, sunken eyes gazing into the past. "He painted that wonderful portrait of Steven that hangs in Broderick's study. But Hughie never had a chance. He was a pansy, you know, poor old Hughie. He tried to kill you, didn't he?"

Brilliant sunlight poured across the veranda, but Jessica felt so cold she might have been caught in an icy draft. "Why ever would you say that?" She had to force the words out.

"He was in love with Steven, of course," Lavinia tutted, "but unable to ever speak of it. There was something utterly shameful about being homosexual in those days. A man's reputation would be stained forever if he was suspected of being one. You would never pick him. Looked perfectly normal. But what did F. Scott Fitzgerald call it? An aberration in nature, that's it. Cecily was terribly cruel to Hughie, though they were cousins. Perfectly understandable. Steven was her husband. She worshipped him. People said it was the war, but I think it was poor old Hughie's forbidden love that made him drink. Killed himself in the end. I know I saw the body. I believe he intended to hurt you, Moira. He couldn't stand the fact Steven loved you. It laid him waste."

BY THE TIME HER CHAT with Lavinia was over Jessica's brain felt fried. She crammed a sun hat on her head, shoved on dark sunglasses, then took a brisk walk around the homestead and the extensive gardens. It might calm her, though she'd gotten into the habit of taking a walk every morning after breakfast. Moving about the main compound also gave her a better feel for what she was doing. The landscaper would have to be contacted again. His work on the complex of gardens had been completed before the Big House had gone up. Now a new layout would be required to complement the classical lines of the house. She had in mind a broad expanse of fine gravel the length of the portico bordered by white marble, with perhaps a few of the wonderful upright plants, such as miniature date palms, planted into the gravel. For comparison, perhaps some rounded cushion plants. The contrast would work well.

She had no idea when she would get the opportunity to check out the old servants' quarters. She'd circled the building many times with only a passing thought as to what it was used for. Now that she *knew,* she had a mission. To find another one of Moira's portraits. What she had learned about Hughie had shocked her. Not that he was homosexual, scarcely that, but that Lavinia had thought he had wanted to kill her. For God's sake, kill *Moira,* she berated herself. Lavinia's habit of calling her Moira was really getting to her, the way a role, if taken very seriously, got to an actor.

When she returned to the homestead some forty minutes later, she found Ruth, who didn't appear at weekend meals, bustling about in the great hall. Several pieces of very expensive luggage were stacked at the foot of the staircase.

"Oh, Jessica!" Ruth's furrowed brow cleared. "B.B. asked me to find you. He's been called away unexpectedly. We're off to Hong Kong until at least the end of next week. A development B.B.'s involved in. I'm going with him. I'll be needed."

"Is there anything I can do to help?" Jessica asked. "You look a little flustered."

"I am," Ruth freely admitted. "I've often had to pick up and go at a minute's notice, but I didn't foresee this. How do I look?"

"You look fine."

"Sure?" Ruth's insecurities were deep.

Jessica smiled. "You always do." Jessica guessed Ruth was a very efficient woman to remain in B.B.'s employ, yet she seemed so vulnerable otherwise.

A little distance off, they heard B.B.'s voice, raised in anger. Did the man ever relax? He was a prime candidate for a heart attack or a stroke. "No, Robyn. I won't let you come with me. I want you here."

Robyn's voice, wonder of wonders, sounded young and beseeching. "But why, Dad? I want to do some shopping. You've taken me at other times."

"You'll be company for Jessica," B.B. snapped. "I don't want her here on her own."

"Cyrus is here," Robyn protested. "So's Liv. And Molly. She's not alone. *Pl...ee...ze,* Dad," she implored.

"I don't want to talk about this!" B.B. strode into the entrance hall, a little startled to see Jessica standing there. "Ah, Jessica!" He recovered quickly. "Ruth's told you the news."

"Yes, she has." Jessica spoke with respectful regret, though in reality she was thrilled the household would be out from under for a few days. "I hope everything goes well for you. I'm quite okay. I have so much work to do I'll be kept very busy until your return. I couldn't help

overhearing you were concerned I might feel lonely.
Thank you for that, but there won't be enough hours in the
day for all I've got to get through. I'm not surprised Robyn
wants to do some shopping. Hong Kong is a wonderful
place to do it."

For the first time since they'd met, Robyn shot Jessica
a friendly look. "See, Dad? I won't take a minute to get
ready." She was, in fact, already prepared, hoping for the
ride but never sure of her stepfather and his unpredictable
moods.

At that moment, Cyrus strode through the front door,
his tall, lean body outlined against the brilliant sunshine.
"Got your message, Dad," he said. "I thought I'd come in
and drive you down to the airstrip."

"Very thoughtful of you, Cyrus," B.B. answered in his
habitually sardonic tone.

"Think nothing of it." Now it was Cyrus's turn to be sarcastic, though initially he had spoken as a devoted son
should. What deep rifts lay between father and son resided
within Broderick Bannerman's complex personality,
Jessica thought.

"Well, Dad, what's the decision?" Robyn asked eagerly,
only to be admonished by an emphatic, "No!"

A lot of friendships must have crumbled around Broderick Bannerman. Jessica felt Robyn's disappointment.
Who knew? Robyn might have become a pleasant person
had B.B. been a different kind of stepfather.

"No, what?" Cyrus asked, looking from one to the other.

Robyn turned to him, desperate to enlist support. "I'm
trying to cadge a ride on the jet. It's ages since I've done
any real shopping. I love Hong Kong."

"So?" Cyrus shrugged. "What's the problem? There's
plenty of room."

"The problem *is,* Cyrus," Bannerman said testily, "I've told Robyn I don't want her along."

"So much for optimism!" Cyrus gave a lopsided smile. "That's a bit mean, isn't it? It's not as though she's going to bother you." He was watching his father closely, long used to picking up on hidden motivations. "We'll look after Jessica if that's what you're worried about."

It was Jessica's chance to step in. She caught Cyrus's eye. "I've already told…Broderick—" just the slightest hesitation "—I have a big job to grapple with. I don't need looking after."

"That's wonderful news," Cyrus said suavely. "Your work is your pleasure. So, Dad, can Robyn go?"

Any other father, no matter how grumpy—including even Jessica's father, not the easiest man in the world—would have said, after a beat or two, "Oh, very well!" But Broderick Bannerman was in many ways the father from hell.

Robyn on the other hand, pleasantly stunned by so much support rushed toward him to peck his cheek. She wasn't going to give him the chance to refuse. "Thanks, Dad. I'm all packed."

For a moment B.B. looked as though he would explode, but Cyrus laughed. "There's something you can do for me, Robyn, if you would. Drop in on my tailor and get me a stack of shirts. You know, smart, casual kind of thing. They know what I like by now. I'll attend to the bill at this end."

"No problem," Robyn said quite cheerfully for her, and danced off.

It was a wonder she didn't blow him a kiss, Jessica thought sardonically.

WHEN CYRUS RETURNED to the house thirty minutes later having seen his father off, he found Jessica, Lavinia and Molly sitting out on the rear terrace enjoying morning tea.

"When the cat's away the mice will play," he observed dryly.

"Want some tea, darling?" Lavinia asked in a wonderfully jovial mood. She had changed out of her Madame Butterfly costume into her monk's habit. Traces of white paint lingered around her ears.

"Why not?" Cyrus pulled out a chair and sat down beside Jessica. "And how's our lady interior designer?" he inquired, looking into her eyes.

He seemed to have a hundred different expressions when he looked at her, each more heart-stopping than the last. She commanded her pulses to stop racing. "Fine," she smiled. She had expressions, too.

"I'll make fresh tea," Molly said, jumping up.

"Goody." Lavinia clapped her hands. "You can bring back some more of those lovely cookies. Cyrus will enjoy them."

"Will do." Molly smiled, as happy as a kid let out of school.

"You're not thinking of working today, are you?" Cyrus asked Jessica.

Excitement soared. Hadn't she wanted and waited for this? "I should."

"Nonsense!" Lavinia broke in. "What is the weekend for if not to relax? Broderick's gone." She grinned. "Why else would I be sitting here? Robyn's gone with him. Something I was counting on, so there's just you two. And me, of course. And Molly. But we old girls don't count. Show her around the place, Cyrus. There's so much that's new for her to enjoy."

Me or Moira? Jessica thought, but dared not ask.

"Do you ride?" Cyrus asked, looking a shade doubtful.

"In a fashion," Jessica answered, resting back in her rattan armchair. If she levered herself forward a little, she could brush his throat with her lips. She knew how warm his skin was. She knew the touch of his mouth. It seemed an awfully long time since he had kissed her and in doing so changed her life.

"Perhaps we should take the Jeep then," he said, continuing his own exploration. "I was planning a fairly long trip, and if you're not a seasoned rider you'd finish up very sore and sorry."

"No, we'll go riding tomorrow," she said blithely, rather enjoying keeping him in the dark. She was, in fact, an excellent rider, but it was plain he had branded her a city slicker.

"Don't go near the escarpment," Lavinia suddenly moaned.

"Now, now, Livvy." A flicker of irritation was in Cyrus's eyes.

"When I go there I always hear her cries."

"It's the waterfall," Cyrus clipped off in a way meant to shut Lavinia up. "I've told you that."

But Lavinia thought she had something important to say.

"Never!" She shook her snow-white head. "It could never be the cry of falling water. It's a woman. The sound haunts me, it's so piercing."

"Oh, for God's sake! If you're going to start, Livvy, I'll have to bolt."

"No, no, sit there." She reached out to detain him. "Have your cup of tea. You understand, don't you, Moira?"

"Miss Lavinia, please let it go," Jessica urged gently, and caught the old lady's trembling hand. "It's all in the past."

If only it would stay there.

CHAPTER EIGHT

IT WAS UNLIKE ANY OTHER day trip Jessica had ever taken, one filled with tumultuous fun and excitement. It seemed a marvelous thing to have Cy's company, and she wondered if her happiness showed. The breadth and grandeur of the landscape was enthralling. The sky above them was a bewitching peacock-blue, the arid earth supporting little vegetation but the ubiquitous spinifex, colored a bright rust-red, which made a brilliant contrast with the sky. The heat haze ran before them in shimmering parallel lines of silver-blue, suggesting far-off lagoons. She could readily understand how the early explorers had been fooled into thinking the mirage was real.

The vibrancy of the colors—the burning reds, the bright yellows, the dark greens and all shades of the color purple—had been captured wonderfully by the great Aboriginal artist Albert Namatjira. To Jessica's artistic eye, too, they were an extravagance of inspiration. This was *her* country, too. She felt a great urge to paint it with the substances she loved: indigo, cobalt-blue, vermilion, lapis lazuli, cadmium, gold. An artist could create any color by blending the three primaries, red, yellow and blue. The whole world *was* color when touched by the miracle of light. She felt saturated in it.

They stopped many times so she could get a closer

view of a particular natural feature. Once, they stopped to watch the antics of a joey only a few days out of the pouch, bounding about ecstatically on its supercharged pogo sticks of legs while its mother kept a gentle eye on it. It was like a frolicking lamb, only on a far more dynamic scale.

"Kangaroos have to breed when they can," Cyrus told her, leaning indolently against the Jeep, yet managing to convey hair-trigger alert. "They can't depend on water in the Dry. That mother has the little fella, another in the pouch and probably an embryo, as well."

"Have you ever seen such joy!" Jessica, charmed by the joey's antics, laughed aloud. Easy to see how kangaroos had evolved in a land where they had plenty of room for their fantastic bounding!

"At certain speeds, kangaroos are far more efficient than horses," Cyrus told her. "There are so many of them they're a damned nuisance, but so much part of the land-scape you have to love them. They can go without water for a while, but they don't stray too far from it. There are billabongs nearby. And all those standing 'monuments' you see around us are termite mounds."

"They're extraordinary." Jessica looked out over the vast terrain where termite mounds sprang up like ancient build-ings. Wide at the base, very narrow at the tip, many of them were nearly twenty feet tall. "Can we take a closer look?"

"Of course. We might even catch a piece of action."

Jessica soon found out what he meant. Fierce little lizards with forked tongues were trying on burrow their way out of one mound, almost twice Cyrus's height.

"Oh, goodness!" Jessica jumped back as several foot-long monsters clawed their way to the surface of the termite walls and clambered eagerly down their length.

"Won't take them long to reach six feet or more," Cyrus told her, amused by her reaction. "Goannas are harmless to man though I'd steer clear of the big fellas. They grow to more than eight feet and have very powerful limbs. I wouldn't want to try outrunning one."

"So they incubate in there?" Jessica asked, moving back cautiously, expecting more to emerge.

Cyrus nodded. "All goannas lay eggs. They've been in there around nine months. The mounds are the perfect protection. By the same token they present a formidable barrier when the newly hatched babies want to get out. Those walls are rock hard."

Jessica stretched out a tentative hand. She had seen the newly hatched goannas formidable claws.

"It's June now." Cyrus raised his face to the cloudless sky. "In another five months, when the monsoon comes, probably the most powerful weather system on the planet, all this—" he waved his arm "—becomes a very different place. The Wet has a dramatic effect on the landscape. Rain falls so hard our creeks, lagoons and billabongs fill to overflowing and inundate the plains. Falling Waters, the waterfall I showed you when we flew in, becomes a mighty torrent. As the rains subside, we have a glimpse of what ancient Gondwanaland—the supercontinent— looked like. Wildflowers bloom in exotic profusion, quite different to the floral carpets of the Red Centre with their endless vistas of paper daisies. These are tropical flowers. This part of the Territory, the Top End, lies in the torrid zone. And abundance of native fruits and vegetables ripen. The land turns lush and green. You get a real feel for the prehistoric past. There's a plentiful harvest for all— humans, animals, birds. We've got more species of animals, most of them unique, than Europe and North

America put together. That happened when Australia broke away from Asia. The water birds have to be seen to be believed. They arrive in their millions. It's an incredible sight. The crocs don't have to swim about in lagoons fast turning to mud or do their extraordinary overland gallop to find a pool that hasn't dried out. It's paradise while it lasts. A few months. Then the dry southeast trade winds arrive. By July, the plains will have started to dry out and all the waterways shrink. We have a few lagoons with deep permanent water like the lagoon at the foot of Falling Waters. By October, every living thing is waiting for the return of the Wet."

"Are we going to the escarpment?" She lifted her gaze to his, feeling the familiar surge of pleasure.

"If you want. We'll drive some more, then have to go by foot." He glanced up at the table-topped mesa. It wasn't particularly high, but the flatness of the giant landscape lent it considerable impact. From this distance, it glowed amethyst. "Tell me, is all the interest because of what Livvy said?" His look was very direct. "Livvy has never been exactly *normal*. Even, I understand, when she was a young woman. She has her own way of seeing things. She gets muddled up between past and present—as you know by now."

"What's normal?" Jessica shrugged.

"I suspect one can't talk to long-dead people to qualify," he said very dryly.

"I suppose not. Has she always talked about Moira?"

He sighed as though bored to death by the whole subject. "Not until *you* arrived, which in itself is quite extraordinary, don't you think?"

"I didn't plan it, Cyrus," she said, not for the first time, aware of his suspicions. "It's quite scary to be confused with someone who disappeared off the face of the earth."

"But she *didn't*." His tone was softly vehement. "Somewhere on this land, in some crevice, in some cave, lie Moira's bones. The number of deaths in the Outback by misadventure is quite frightening. Moira wasn't a good rider or an experienced one. She had, in fact, learned on the station. The horse came home as horses do eventually. Moira didn't." His face hardened. "I find this whole business of Moira, tragic as it is, phenomenally upsetting. For a while, my entire family was under suspicion, despite the proud Bannerman name. My grandfather was a war hero. He flew Spitfires in the Battle of Britain and reached the rank of squadron leader. He was decorated. How would you like it if your grandparents were thought capable of murder?"

"They say we're all capable of murder, given overwhelming circumstances," Jessica said bleakly.

He flinched. "Let's start again. My grandparents were fine people. Highly respected all over the Outback. Everyone was fond of Moira. She loved being on Mokhani. According to Lavinia, a thousand times she said she didn't want to go home."

"Who exactly was Hughie?" Jessica asked abruptly. "What relation?"

"Look—" His brilliant blue eyes flashed.

"Cyrus." She grasped his arm. "I don't want to upset you, but this whole business, the Mokhani Mystery, has never been laid to rest. It haunts Lavinia. It haunts your father. It haunts *you*, fifty years later. There must be something more to it than the tragedy of someone becoming lost in the bush and perishing. I know it's happened many, many times over the years, but with Moira there appear to be so many suspicions. That's why journalists can't leave it alone. Now by some truly bizarre twist of fate, I'm involved in it."

"I don't disagree with that," he said somberly.

"Simply because by some freak of nature I look extraordinarily like her," Jessica went on to say.

His brow furrowed in puzzlement. "But how would you actually *know* that? You can't rely too much on what Livvy says."

"I'm not," Jessica answered quietly, turning her head away. It was about time she told him about the portrait Tim had uncovered, no doubt increasing his lack of trust. "You still haven't told me who Hughie was."

The question did nothing to ease his somber expression. "He was Hugh Balfour, my grandmother Cecily's cousin. Livvy told you about him?"

H.B., of course. "She told me Hugh liked to paint Moira."

"Maybe he did," he answered curtly, "but I've never seen anything he did outside the portrait of my grandfather."

"You're certain?"

"Of course I'm certain." Cy's temper flared. "Finding a portrait of Moira would be a major discovery."

"One has been found," Jessica said, watching him snap to full attention. "It was bought at a Sydney auction by my uncle's partner simply because it reminded him of me."

Cyrus's strong hands grasped her shoulders. "What the devil are you talking about? I think you'd better level with me."

"I'm trying to, if you let me. Tim attended a Christie's art auction a short time back. So did Lavinia, apparently without your aunt Barbara's knowledge. Tim's interest was captured by the uncanny likeness. Lavinia would have recognized it right off. Who knows seeing the portrait after all this time hasn't disturbed the balance of her mind? She didn't tell your aunt because she thought it would upset her greatly. According to Tim, he had a confrontation with Lavinia afterward. She offered to buy if off him, but he refused. Lord knows what she intended to do with it. Probably confront your father with it for reasons of her own. At the moment, it's hanging in the foyer of our design studio in Brisbane."

Cyrus's hands dropped away. He wheeled to calm himself. "What's the time frame here?" He turned back to face her, looking quite daunting. "When did this mysterious portrait turn up? Before or after Dad hired you?"

She reacted to the hard flare in his eyes. "It would have been put up for auction some time before your father offered me the job. Please don't take your anger out on me. I know nothing about any behind-the-scene machinations, if indeed there *are* any."

"Of course there are. You're not stupid." Stern blue eyes stared down at her.

She shrugged. "I admit it all seems very odd. My uncle and I were discussing the project the same day Tim returned from Sydney with the portrait. At that time I had absolutely no idea who the subject was. Why should I? None of us did. It was simply a portrait given to Christie's for auction. Tim only bought it because it reminded him of me."

"And there's no connection?"

"Absolutely not!" She reacted sharply to his tone. "I wonder you ask. Lavinia hasn't laid eyes on Moira for over fifty years. It's coincidence, the whole thing. Chance rules our lives after all." So why, then, was she so perplexed and confused?

"Lavinia's brain might be a little skewed as to time, but she obviously recognized Moira. She would have known it was Hugh Balfour's work. *Who* put it on the market. Can you find out?"

"Tim tried, in fact, but got nowhere. A solicitor handled it for a client. The solicitor is not saying."

"I suppose we've all got a double," he said doubtfully.

"So they say. But the portrait gave us all a shock. It would shock you if you saw it."

"Oh, I will see it," he said grimly, beginning to walk toward the Jeep. "All right, I've had about enough of Moira for today."

JESSICA WAS GLAD SHE WAS FIT and took regular exercise, because they had to walk up the track, which was tough going but infinitely rewarding. To one side of them lay rugged bushland, to the other magical glimpses of the lagoon and the multicolored walls of the canyon. By the time they neared the high plateau, her hair was damp with sweat and her pink cotton shirt stuck to her back.

"You okay?" He stretched out a hand to her. The spark where their hands touched wasn't just a physical thing.

"Fine."

"You're doing well. Pretend a dingo is chasing you."

"I think I can make it under my own steam, thank you."

He looked back at her. The flush of exertion in her cheeks only served to enhance the flawlessness of her skin and the clear green of her eyes. She was a beautiful woman. He had to assume her lookalike Moira had been beautiful, too. Hadn't his grandmother Cecily been a little naive bringing a beautiful young woman into the household? The family had lived in such isolation, but paradoxically in close proximity to one another. Beauty made waves. It disturbed the very air. He reached down with fluid ease and lifted this maddening young woman up the rest of the way.

"We're here!" he announced, finding it nigh on impossible to release his hold on her. Her head had sunk against his left shoulder and she was moaning softly at the exertion.

"It better be worth it." Jessica straightened, laughing, until she saw the expression in his eyes. Was it desire?

The raucous cry of a bird broke the spell of the moment.

"I should have brought my camera." She busied herself retying the lace of her shoe, shocked at how quickly he could stir her body to arousal.

"We've got hundreds and hundreds of photographs."

"I'd love to see them."

"And so you shall. We can fit in quite a bit before Dad gets home."

Jessica let out a shaky breath. She started to move off toward the edge, feeling slightly light-headed.

"Jessica, *no!*" His voice cracked out, loud and urgent. He caught her up swiftly, pulling her back. "The lip could crumble at any time. Those rocks and boulders down there in the canyon have come from up here. Never, ever go near the edge."

"It's okay." She tried to soothe him. "I wasn't going to. It's a pretty vertiginous drop, anyway." His cry of *no!* had had the velocity of a bullet. "I just wanted a better look at the lagoon."

"Stay with me." He drew her back against his chest.

"You're the boss." She could have remained there forever. "It must be wonderful to preside over your own kingdom," she murmured, filled with a piercing exhilaration. "This is fantastic. It's like we're on another planet. It's daunting, too, all that empty vastness without end. It would be so easy to die out there."

"Just you remember it," he said, the harshness still

evident in his voice. "Don't go wandering off on your own. We've had seasoned bushmen get lost."

"So not everything's a mystery." The remains of the little governess could be anywhere out there in the wilderness. Moira could have been injured; thrown from her horse, lying helpless, vulnerable to the attack of wild animals. She had heard the dingoes howling at night. The deadliest snake in the world, the taipan, had its home here; marauding camels, wild horses, foxes, wild boar, feral cats as fierce as miniature lions. A massive search for Moira had been mounted. Jessica had read that in all of the articles she had sourced on the computer. The search had revealed nothing. Today, looking out at the ancient land spread before her as far as she could see, she didn't find that so strange.

Her eyes dropped to the deep lagoon. It looked so beautiful, the vegetation fresh and green even in the Dry. The waterfall, which apparently would become a deafening roar in the Wet, was tranquil today, spilling its crystal purity from the top of the escarpment whence it flowed to the water's edge. The lagoon was surrounded by aquatic reeds and grasses of a lush emerald green. The glittering water floated its cargo of magnificent pink water lilies holding their heads high above huge pads. Around the base of the escarpment grew a luxuriant tangle of exquisitely colored creepers that climbed into the stands of pandanus palms decorating their spikes. It was like looking down into an earthly paradise.

"The view from here is magnificent, but is it possible to walk the length of the canyon?" she asked him, eager to try.

He nodded. "Yes, but let's take one thing at a time. There are grottos at the base of the cliffs sculptured by the water over thousands of years. In the Wet, the high waters drown out everything down there."

"So there could be a crocodile still in residence, you're suggesting? Perhaps with a mate or two?"

"No one has sighted one," he answered, frowning at the thought. "Which doesn't mean one isn't there. Aboriginal stockmen take dips in the lagoons—those are the guys with the crocodile totem. We haven't had a fatality at Falling Waters."

One you know about, at any rate, she thought. "But elsewhere?" she asked.

"We've had a couple of stockmen taken over the years. Working dogs. Cattle. Kangaroos, of course. They never learn. This is the Territory. We have to live with the crocs. We respect them."

"No matter how great your detestation?"

"I don't detest them," he said. "I don't trust 'em either. The trick is not to stand near the edge of a river or lagoon where they're known to be. We're not that far from Kakadu National Park and the Alligator Rivers system. The person who named the East and South Alligator rivers thought the prehistoric beasts he saw lining their banks *were* alligators. Of course they were crocs. The rivers should have been named the East and South Crocodile rivers. Kakadu inspires reverence. The Aborigines worship the place. If you're lucky, we could take a trip in. It's only accessible— and then only parts of it—in the Dry. In the Wet, enormous stretches turn into water-lily-covered lagoons supporting phenomenal birdlife. A white mist hangs over the dripping canopy of the rain forest, adding to the primeval look. Waterfalls thunder. Our waterfall is a trickle compared to them. You'd swear you were back at the beginning of time."

"So why can't we pack up and go tomorrow?" She knew they couldn't, but her heart swelled at the very thought.

"Tomorrow's out, I'm afraid."

"I was only joking," she said, shaking her head. "I have a ton of work to get through."

"You've done sketches, that kind of thing?"

"Plenty," she said. "I'm getting close to what I want to achieve. I've designed quite a number of pieces that will be custom-made. The rooms are so huge, but the six guest rooms will be a piece of cake. As will the other bedrooms. I have a good idea what Broderick—"

"Did he ask you to call him that, or was it your own idea?" he cut in.

"Left to myself I'd be calling him Mr. Bannerman for the rest of my life," Jessica retorted crisply, moving away from him a little. "He asked me to call him Broderick. *Ordered* really. Arrogance runs in the family."

"You should be flattered," Cy said. "Dad's a different man around you."

"What are you implying?" Her voice rose.

"I'm not implying anything. It's a simple statement of fact. My father is a different man around you."

"Maybe you should be grateful." She shrugged. "I find calling him Broderick rather embarrassing, but I can scarcely disregard his wishes."

"Of course not," he agreed suavely.

She chose another tack. "The great hall is the biggest challenge. I have to get that right. I have a good idea what your father wants for the conference room and the tele-communications room. I'm in constant contact with my uncle Brett. Nothing will go ahead without his say-so."

"Something wrong with your judgment?" he inquired.

"Not at all. But this is an important project. I work for my uncle, as well as your father. Uncle Brett taught me all I know. Eventually, we'll need a team of people up here, as I've told you. Before that happens, I have to work it all out in my head and on paper. That includes color schemes. I work from the floor up."

"Isn't that a lot to deal with for a relatively inexperienced twenty-four-year-old?"

She knew he was baiting her. "It is. But someone's got to do it. It may seem like heresy, but I prefer the original homestead. Please don't tell your father that."

"Not unless I want to stop your winning streak," he told her with a mocking glance. "I prefer the old homestead, too, as I've said. It looked a million times better before Robyn was let loose on it. Notice the minimalism on the walls? She solved the problem by shoving the paintings my mother had put there away. The Oriental screens and rugs were next. All the touches of Southeast Asia my mother loved and so suited the house. The porcelains and big fishbowls on carved stands. The fishbowls used to be filled with orchids. They stood on either side of the staircase. Robyn removed every vestige of my mother from the house. And my father let her."

"Perhaps he found it too painful," Jessica suggested, hearing the bitterness in his tone. "Didn't you make your feelings known?"

He grimaced. "I did, but it made no difference. I'm biding my time. I could at some time in the future have the mausoleum razed to the ground."

"Oh, don't do that," she advised. "It will have its uses. If not as a residence, than as a conference and business centre. I'm assuming you will take over your father's extensive business interests?"

"You're assuming a lot." He spoke very dryly. "My father is an extremely unpredictable man, a strange man in anyone's judgment. He's become increasingly hard and aloof as he's grown older. You've brought with you a troubling sea change. For all I know he could be planning to start another family. Sire a new heir. He could have met a woman he'd risk his soul to possess. I know he'd like to be young again. He makes no bones about it. He wants to be my age again, wants his life all over again. Dad won't ever be content with his allotted portion. He wants life everlasting. Maybe he thinks a young woman would bring it to him."

She couldn't control a shiver. "That's quite Faustian. I hope to goodness you're not looking at *me* for the job?" Jessica felt the shock break over her.

He stared into her eyes. "A lot of women, young, good-looking women, would fight to the death to marry Dad. Money is the perfect aphrodisiac, didn't you know?"

"Not for *me* it isn't." Jessica said emphatically.

"Really? That's heartening to know. So tell me, what is it you want, Jessica? *Love?*" His blue eyes were melting not only her limbs but her brain.

"Don't you?" she parried. "I thought love is what we all want. And *need*. Why is it every time you mention your mother I can hear the grief? Your father suffered from the loss, too. He'd made a powerful emotional connection with your mother, Deborah, then she was cruelly taken away from him. A man could become very bitter from that experience. Your father is a very rich man, but no one could describe him as at peace, much less happy."

"God, no. His life has been difficult. There's no denying that. The tragedy in his childhood—the invasion of privacy the family suffered—was the start of his misery. He never got over his governess's disappearance. His twin, Aunt Barbara, was adversely affected, as well. Both of them were almost twelve before they were ready to be sent away to boarding school. My grandmother taught them herself. I went to boarding school at ten. Even then the Mokhani Mystery was still alive. I guess we'll never be free of it."

Her answer came out unconsidered and of its own accord. "Maybe that's about to change."

"Why do you say that?" He turned on her.

"Just a feeling I have."

"You're psychic, then? That explains it?"

Tense moments ticked over. "Don't you sense that, too?" she responded to the challenge.

His expression was dark and brooding. "All I know is, when the past intrudes on the present, there can be unwanted consequences."

CHAPTER NINE

JESSICA REMINDED HERSELF SHE had to work even on Sunday. She would have to have something fairly impressive to show Broderick Bannerman when he returned, so she sat at her desk working away, though with perhaps not her usual serene efficiency. Her emotions were in a kind of turmoil. So many things were happening that her life had taken on new dimensions, some thrilling, some ominous and strange. Added to that, she had discovered within herself a certain recklessness and a taste for danger. Infatuation, falling in love, was an extreme state, after all.

Violent delights could have violent ends.

Hadn't Shakespeare said it all? She was in daily communication with Brett, speaking to him each morning on the phone, then sending him reams of sketches and information by e-mail. When she was ready, she would make watercolor renderings of her proposals. She needed to take that trip into Darwin to stock up on her art supplies. She supposed she could make the two-hour journey on her own in the four-wheel drive B.B. had put at her disposal. There were bound to be plenty of readable signs, preferably the ones not featuring a skull and crossbones. There was something very daunting about a dead straight road that ran through endless uninhabited miles of shifting red sand blanketed with spinifex.

Over dinner, Cyrus relaxed, his heart-melting smile much in evidence as he and Lavinia recounted stories from the family's past—mercifully without the complications of the family ghost. Molly, the housekeeper, joined in, displaying her own puckish sense of humor. Cyrus and Lavinia treated Molly as one of the family; B.B. and Robyn treated her like a programmed robot. There was no question of Molly's sitting down to join them either for a cup of coffee or a meal when Broderick Bannerman was in residence. Servants had their place as far as B.B. was concerned.

Afterward, Lavinia, in high spirits, brought some of her favourite CDs downstairs for the occasion, comparing this soprano against that, turning up the volume so high the station staff in their bungalows and dormitories probably had to shout at one another to be heard. Cyrus indulged her, with only a mild "Turn it down a bit, Livvy," as criticism, but soon Lavinia was up and away, reminiscing about her career.

"I do believe I could have been as great as Sutherland," she told them, not for the first time. "Marvelous voice, marvelous technique, but oh, there was something about poor tragic Callas I adored. The *passion* in her voice! I miss that. No one else has it. I can't hear her without the tears coming to my eyes."

Occasionally, she astonished Jessica, but not the others, who had probably heard these performances many times before, by belting out a top note along with the diva on the CD. Of course Lavinia's voice was being supported by the voice singing with her, but Jessica realized she was hearing however briefly, little patches of what once had been a brilliant coloratura soprano. Molly, having produced another one of her delicious meals, poured more wine. Both ladies sat sipping contentedly while Cyrus and Jessica excused themselves for a short stroll before turning in.

That, too, proved intoxicating, though Cyrus made no move that could have been construed as romantic. Nevertheless, an exquisite tension vibrated between them as if neither knew where or when or even how the tension would manifest itself in action. Jessica looked and listened as he pointed out the stars in the night sky and their spiritual significance to the Aboriginal tribes of the Top End. That in itself provided an element of the romance she was starting to crave. In Aboriginal life over countless thousands of years, when the people slept out beneath the stars, the moon and the stars had assumed great significance.

"They know every star in the sky," Cyrus said, his tone full of appreciation. "There's a legend to explain every origin. Such beautiful myths and legends, too. No matter how many times you hear them, you don't mind hearing them again. I used to find them enthralling when I was a kid around the campfire listening to a stockman—who also happened to be a tribal elder—telling them so soulfully. Aboriginal gods and goddesses are all too human. The sun is a woman—a beautiful woman who spreads light and warmth. The moon is a man. All the stars and planets were at the time of creation, men, women and animals. They flew up to the sky when times were bad on earth. The sky was their refuge. The Gagudju people of Arnhem Land believe a shooting star is a spirit canoe transporting a soul to its new home."

"You were blessed with a childhood out here," she said.

He nodded. "I don't know what I would do if it were taken away. Mokhani is my life."

She could hear the love and pride in his voice. She thought, as she did so often these days, how difficult it must have been for him growing up without the love and support of his mother, especially given his father's unyielding nature. He must have been wounded over and over in the past. Probably continued to be to this day, though he had grown an extra skin. B.B. seemed to be hell-bent on having control and mastery over everyone, but in his son he had chosen the wrong man to try to dominate.

"Home is where the heart and the soul find their most comfortable place," she murmured into the starry night. "I've never seen such a glorious night sky." Her eyes were on the blue-white scintillating broad river of diamonds across the sky. The Milky Way. It shone with great brilliance and luminosity in the pure air of the Outback.

"No pollution," Cyrus explained. "No buildings, no glass and concrete towers, just the timeless land. There's the Southern Cross sparkling over us. It couldn't be clearer. The star furthermost to the south is a star of the first magnitude. It's said the ancient Greeks and Babylonians were able to see it. They thought it was part of the constellation Centaurus, so that's how much the Crux has shifted. The night sky in the Red Center is purported to be the most beautiful sky on earth. There again, it's rarified desert air and our isolation. We might be able to fit in a trip there."

"That would be wonderful." Jessica felt like a plant fast unfurling its fronds. But like tender new fronds exposed to sizzling heat, she could get burned. She had divined that the moment she'd laid eyes on Cyrus Bannerman at Darwin airport.

TO EVERYONE'S DELIGHT, Cyrus returned to the homestead for lunch. Something he rarely did when his father was there, which was perfectly understandable considering the two men were often at loggerheads.

"Darling boy, how lovely it is to have your company."

Lavinia sat up straight in her planter's chair. She and Jessica had been sitting companionably on the front veranda enjoying the brilliant display of strelitzias in the garden. Now Lavinia jumped up, surprisingly spry in the legs when her once-elegant hands were knotted with arthritis. "I'll tell Molly you're here. She'll be so pleased. Broderick could stay away forever, as far as we're concerned."

"Don't go to any trouble," Cyrus called after her, pitching his Akubra into a chair. "Coffee and a sandwich will do.

"So, making progress?" he asked, pulling out a chair and settling into it "You'll have to have lots to show Dad." A lock of crow-black hair fell over his forehead and he put up a hand, raking it back. Jessica let her eyes rest on him. He was wearing his usual working gear, an open-necked pale blue bush shirt, jeans, dusty high boots, a red bandanna knotted carelessly around his throat.

He looked marvelous, so intensely vital he took her breath away. How could any woman ignore a man like that? It took a moment or two for her to answer. "You'll be pleased to hear I've been at my drawing board all morning. Mostly sketching designs for the custom-made furniture I told you about. Regardless of size and scale, the pieces must represent intimacy. It's a private residence, after all. I want to stick to the classical idiom, but obviously with a twenty-first century twist. The furnishings need to be elegant, functional, with pure, clean lines, if you know what I mean. The architecture speaks for itself."

"You're able to do that?" He looked at her as if she might have bitten off more than she could chew.

"Sure. My goal is to push myself to the limits. I have talent. I'd like to do more furniture designing down the track. My uncle Brett has won awards for furniture design. He's been my mentor."

"I'd like to meet him," Cyrus said. "He sounds a very talented guy, and obviously you love him."

"I'm sure it could be arranged. He's gay," she tacked on casually.

He cocked an eyebrow. "So? I'm not looking for a relationship."

"Just thought I'd mention it. Uncle Brett is a very clever, multitalented man. He trained as an architect, which has been an enormous help with his work."

"Tell me, do you see something embarrassing about his being gay?"

"Not at all!" She shook her head "I wanted to see your reaction, cattlemen being such macho types. I love my uncle dearly. He's been very good to me, but he's suffered in his way."

"I daresay," he answered, letting the *macho* bit go. "One can't afford to be different. But tell me about *yourself,* Jessica. I'm all ears."

She found that electrifying. "What do you want to know?"

"Everything. Go on. Give it to me. I know you're beautiful and gifted. You certainly don't lack confidence. You think you can conquer the world. I like that. I've got big plans of my own. Tell me about when you were a little girl. I bet you were adored, with your big green eyes and your blond curls."

She looked out over the garden before replying. "It wasn't quite like that," she said wryly, by now used to the way life really was. "I'm an only child. My father is a high-profile lawyer, senior partner in a firm started by my great grandfather. I think he felt betrayed when my mother couldn't give him a son. Mum always says so, anyway. There was just curly-headed me. To make it worse, I don't look at all like him or that side of the family. I was a good student, at least, so he expected me to follow him into law. Show some ambition. Instead, I opted for a fine-arts degree, which I gained with honors. But it wasn't a degree my father thought much of. He's made no bones about the fact that as far as he's concerned I've let the family down. Especially as I went to work for Uncle Brett. The *different* factor came into play there. Dad is a great one for civil liberties and the rights of minority groups, but he's actually ultraconservative at heart. Needless to say, Brett and my father don't get on. In fact, they avoid one another, which makes it hard. Practicing law in my family is considered by all to be far more important than practicing art of any kind."

"Poor Jessica." He reached out, his palm briefly cupping her cheek. It was a gesture so unexpected, so *tender*, it nearly washed away her hidden tears. "I didn't expect to hear that. You certainly *look* very loved."

"Well, I am." She didn't fully understand why she had told him so much, but he affected her on all levels. "Don't get me wrong. Maybe it's just not in the way I'd choose. I was very close to my maternal grandmother, Brett's mother. Closer even than to my own mother, who likes her own space. Nan was my haven when my teenage world went mad. Sadly, she died some years back, but her memory will always remain with me. A lot of the time I feel she's looking out for me. Brett and I have the same coloring, the same family face. Both of us take after Nan."

"She didn't, by any chance, have a Moira in the family?" Cy's voice had a sardonic edge.

"Good grief, no." Jessica shook her head. "Don't you think Moira would have been mentioned in passing? Especially given what happened to her? Had Moira lived she would have been a couple of years older than my nan. Someone like that would have haunted my family as much as she's haunted yours. Left alone to die—"

"We don't know *what* happened to her," he cut in, his voice hardening slightly. "I'd very much like to see that portrait of yours."

"That can be arranged. I'll ask Tim to e-mail a photograph first. Tim is Uncle Brett's partner in life and business. Once you see it, it'll be your turn to be astonished. Did you ever find out what Moira's parents had to say after she disappeared?"

He sighed deeply. "Jessica, I missed all that, not having been born. Moira belongs to another time, another world. I just wish she'd stay there. My *father* was only a child."

"But you must have heard *something* over the years," she persisted. "I mean, they couldn't just paper her over or abandon her to a deep watery realm. Moira is part of your family's history."

"I assure you there's no need to constantly remind me. All I know is her parents journeyed up here to see for themselves. I believe they were an older couple. Moira was a child of their middle years. Naturally they were filled with grief but compelled to accept, as everyone else did, that Moira had died by misadventure. Either she'd become lost in the bush, fallen from the escarpment or even drowned. Despite an intensive search, she was never found. Have you spoken to Livvy about any of this?"

"Not for now. She knows about the existence of the portrait, of course. She told me about her confrontation with Tim. She claimed he wasn't a gentleman because he didn't give it to her. I didn't tell her of my connection to Tim. Neither did I tell her I'd actually seen the portrait. She thinks there should be others, or at least one, here at Mokhani."

He groaned. "Well she would. Livvy is a creature of the theatre. She loves dramas. My father denies it."

"I recall you said he tells lies."

"Jessica, please."

She searched his face for a moment. Blazing blue eyes. Enigmatic. Maybe a little hostile.

"That's no answer." She knew he didn't trust his father. For that matter, neither did she.

"Perhaps you should ask Dad yourself," he suggested dryly. "Where exactly do you stand with my father?"

Hot color bloomed in her cheeks. She swiped her long beautiful hair over her shoulder. "I scarcely know him— he isn't an easy man to know. As for me, what you see is what you get. Why can't you accept that?"

"Too many coincidences along the way. What do you suppose was my father's first thought when he saw you on that television program? Hey, this is a young designer who could bring off decorating my mausoleum? What could be more B.B. than going with his instincts? They're so sharp they're feral. Or did the image of his former governess block out every other consideration? He may have been a child at the time of her disappearance, but that image has been kept alive. Something has to be feeding it. It's like a fairy tale by the Brothers Grimm. Maybe Hugh's paintings of her were hidden away, but given my father's temperament and his excessive persistence, he would have gone hunting for them. He's the best hunter in the world. Maybe it was *he* who put the painting you've got on the market? It would have been too beautiful to destroy. Maybe it was a member of Hugh's family. Who the hell knows? Maybe one day Dad stumbled upon the hiding place— 'Nice to see you again, Moira!'"

"A bit melodramatic don't you think?" Though she didn't disagree with any of it.

"Hell, Jessica, we're all experts on melodrama with Dad and Lavinia playing the leads." He leaned toward her, unconsciously emanating tremendous male allure. "We could go on a treasure hunt together."

"We should." She was quick to agree.

Lavinia chose that very moment to stomp back onto the veranda in her monk's habit worn with gym boots. Jessica found herself wondering when Lavinia would come down to breakfast in a pink tutu. "What are you two whispering about?" she stared at them with deep satisfaction.

"I've asked Jessica to marry me," Cyrus said calmly.

"When?" Lavinia asked delightedly, turning her head to peer at Jessica, who was past being surprised by anything, however outlandish, that was said.

But shouldn't that *when* been an astonished *What!* or a *Wow!* "I've had to tell him no," Jessica said. "I won't be crowded by proposals. I'm not ready to tie the knot for years yet."

Lavinia hurried over to touch her shoulder. "But darling girl, you have to get on with your life," she protested. "You've wasted so much time already."

Jessica caught Cyrus's searing glance. "You went too far with that one," she muttered.

"You're worried I wasn't serious?"

"To be serious a man has to get on his knees."

Lavinia beamed at him. "*Do* it, Cy! Don't let her get away again."

When he moved, Jessica jumped up, placing her chair in front of her as a barrier. "This has gone far enough, thank you, Cyrus. We're joking, Miss Lavinia. Just fooling around."

Lavinia made a little birdlike cry of pain, tears welling

up in her eyes. "But you're *perfect* for each other! You don't doubt that, do you, dear?"

"Miss Lavinia, I'm Jessica. Moira hasn't come back again."

Lavinia's chin wobbled. "No, of course not."

"You understand that, Livvy," Cyrus said, drawing a great sigh of relief for that chink of sanity. He regretted the fact, however, they had upset her.

"Yes, I do, darling. It's just that…" She turned and stared beseechingly at Jessica. "You *are* Moira, though, aren't you?" she whispered as though Cyrus couldn't hear.

"I'm planning to take you out riding this afternoon, Jessica," Cy intervened in an endeavor to head Lavinia off. "We should be able to find you a nice quiet horse."

"Thank you, thank you," she said sweetly sardonic. "I'm so grateful. This is the happiest day of my life."

"Yes, indeed. It's not every day a girl gets a marriage proposal," Lavinia said, yanking on her saffron robe. "Just wait until Broderick hears about it. He won't be pleased. He wants you for himself." She cackled as though she'd said something very funny.

"The most useful thing about growing old is you can get away with saying anything," Cyrus observed, his tone a little harsh. "Although in all fairness I have to say there's been something to Livvy's revelations in the past."

"Oh, stop. Livvy's revelations are way off this time," Jessica said tartly.

"Just teasing, Jessica," he said. "I really don't fancy you as a stepmother."

"Which part of *stop* don't you understand?"

"I told you I jest. Though deep down—"

Jessica couldn't restrain herself any longer. She picked up a plush cushion and began belting him with it.

Molly, eyes bright with pleasure, came out on to the veranda at a brisk trot. "You're a one, Jessica, so you are!"

"So she is!" Cyrus put his hand very gently around Jessica's wrist and took the cushion from her, throwing it back on the chair. "I'm not used to women who play rough."

"That's hard to believe," Jessica said, "when you're the most infuriating person I've ever met."

"Now, now, my darlings!" Lavinia intervened. "It's only an excuse to kiss and make up. You were doing great, Moira. I think you scared him."

"So there it is!" he declared. "You've become one of Lavinia's incurable hallucinations."

"If you're hungry, and I hope you are, I've set up lunch on the rear terrace," Molly intervened, her cheeks flushed with pleasure.

"Oh, goody, hurray! If only there were more Mollys in this world." Lavinia executed a little pirouette, holding her arms aloft for balance. "If it weren't for you, Molly, we'd all starve."

IT WASN'T UNTIL LATER in the afternoon when the heat was less oppressive and the fiery exposure to the sun lessened that Jessica made her way down to the stables, where Cyrus had arranged to meet her. He was running a little late, so she had the Aboriginal stable boy, Seth, saddle up a lively looking filly called Chloe. Jessica had taken to the filly, one of obvious good blood, on sight. Chloe in turn appeared to like the smell, voice and touch of Jessica. They made friends over a couple of oatmeal cookies.

"That's pretty damn good." Seth grinned his approval. "Most people have to watch themselves around that one. Chances are she might throw ya."

"I don't think so, Seth." Jessica continued to stroke the filly's sleek neck, making soothing clicking sounds at the same time. Chloe was jet-black, well-groomed, with a white blaze on her forehead.

"She got speed and she got spirit." Seth spoke with love and pride. "A real high stepper and a natural jumper, but she ain't an easy ride." He gave her a black liquid glance. "Threw Miss Bannerman, but then, Miss Bannerman got bad habits."

"Robyn?" Jessica turned to stare at him.

"Yes, ma'am. Chloe here don't like to be pushed around. She's a beautiful sweet girl when you know how to handle her right, but when ya don't…" Seth pulled a face. "Miss Bannerman don't treat the horses right. She think she got to be in control all the time. Thing is, she don't really like horses and they don't like her. Tell you the truth, the boss won't be happy you picked Chloe. He told me to saddle up Manny. A nice sedate horse. I gotta do what I'm told."

Jessica had already met Manny, a bay gelding, as she'd entered the stables. Manny was friendly, extending his silky muzzle to be stroked. She had fed him an oatmeal biscuit before leaving him in peace. "That's okay, Seth. I'll explain to him that Chloe was my choice."

"Manny is the nicest, quietest ride we've got." Seth tried to persuade her.

"I'm not surprised." Jessica smiled. "Manny's just about due for retirement. Chloe and I are a better match. Don't worry. I know how to ride."

"Thought so, seeing how you are around 'em, but Chloe can be full of mischief. Skittish, I call it. Why she has days she gallops off in all directions."

"Don't you worry," Jessica repeated. "It won't take me long to get Chloe to trust me."

JESSICA WAS TROTTING the responsive Chloe around the yard when Cyrus arrived. He stood stock still for a moment watching the proceedings. "Okay, so you can ride," he observed dryly. "Why didn't you tell me?"

"I thought I'd take the mickey out of you," she responded sweetly. "I've been riding since I was a little girl."

"I can see that." He had checked her out automatically, his mind processing all the information that told him she was perfectly at home on a horse. In fact, she looked great, a good seat, well balanced, straight back.

She brought the filly to a halt beside him. "Your automatic assumption I would sit like a sack of potatoes piqued me."

He gave a faint smile. "Oh, well, you are a city girl."

"This city girl lived on acreage. My nan, Alex, bought me my first pony when I was six. My parents didn't really want me to have it, but I was thrilled out of my mind. My father saw to it I was well taught. I joined a good pony club."

"What a piece of luck." He turned back as Seth led out his horse—a gleaming, silver-gray Thoroughbred, clearly no workhorse, but a horse reserved for pure pleasure.

"What a beautiful animal," Jessica said with appreciation. She had an excellent eye and instinct for good horses. The gray was superb.

"Monarch," Cyrus pronounced. With a nod to Seth, he took charge of his horse. "So named because there's nothing comparable in our stables. So don't bother racing me."

"I'm not that foolish. You've got the superior horse. Monarch must be a good sixteen hands high, but then, a tall horse for a tall man. Chloe is only a filly, but I can outwit you."

"You can't. I know this land like the back of my hand." He stared up at her. She had bound her long hair into a thick plait, revealing her very pretty ears. For a moment, he thought he could taste the creamy lobes in his mouth.

"So what are we waiting for?" She didn't know it, but her face was lit with such exuberance, that feeling was transferring itself to him. "Come on," she urged. "You've stared at me long enough. Let's get going. Tallyho!" She clicked her tongue, lightly kicked the filly's flanks and the spirited animal spurted into action.

She was off and away before Cyrus had time to swing into the saddle.

What a surprise packet Jessica was turning out to be! he thought with a mix of amusement and admiration. She even put him on his mettle. She was scooting across the back paddock in a genuine gallop, approaching the white post and rail fence where a short distance off, a glossy-flanked chestnut mare was pacing with her beautiful foal.

No! For God's sweet sake, no! His heart rose to his throat as he saw Jessica lean forward, rising in the saddle as she gave the filly the signal to jump.

"God almighty!" High spirits were one thing, but you had to have nerve and confidence galore to attempt that fence. Robyn always stooped to unlatch the gate. So did most visitors to the stables.

Jessica had both confidence and nerve. Horse and rider soared, clearing the top rail with maybe an inch to spare. That the filly showed a surprisingly clean pair of rear hooves was brought to his attention. Chloe could make a show jumper. He could hear Jessica whooping with delight. He knew the incredible feeling of exhilaration and power, but his moment of fear was legitimate and had its roots in the tragedy that had taken his mother. Yet risk appeared to be a state Jessica happily embraced. Risk, to the point of recklessness. His mother had been reckless. Her dying in a riding accident had left a deep wound that would never heal.

Suddenly he felt mad as hell. Why hadn't he insisted she wear a hard hat? Because she had let him believe she was a novice who could only travel at a sedate pace.

He took off after her, urging Monarch into a gallop before he, too, flew over the fence. At least he knew what Monarch could do and what lay on the other side.

Jessica glancing back over her shoulder, saw him pursue her at a gallop. She took in a lung full of air, almost light-headed with exhilaration. Across the plain to the left of her, a great herd of prime cattle were strung out. She needed fresh territory. This was glorious! She had proved Chloe was a natural jumper. In fact, to her very pleasant surprise, the filly was flying like she was on steroids.

"That's it! Go, girl!" Cyrus would have that much more of a job to catch them. God, she loved racing!

By the time he caught up to her, he was fairly seething with anger. He came alongside, his eyes flashing. "What are you trying to do?"

"That's easy," she called back. "Beat you." Her lustrous green eyes brimmed with life, which in his agitated state he interpreted as having no sense of danger.

"Slow down, Jessica," he thundered.

"Why?"

"If you don't, we won't continue on to the canyon."

Immediately she started pulling the filly back to a fluid bounce, muttering her resentments at the same time.

When the two horses were back to a walking pace, he said tersely, "That was pretty damned risky taking the fence."

She raised her eyebrows. "I know what I'm doing. Chloe was traveling well. She *wanted* to jump the fence. She didn't take much urging."

"If her back legs hadn't cleared it, you'd have taken a tumble."

"I've taken plenty of tumbles in my time. The trick is to get right back up. Whatever is the matter with you, Cy? Why are you so upset?" Now she noticed a definite pallor beneath his deep tan.

"While you're on Mokhani, you're my responsibility."

She was a little startled by the sternness of the rebuke. "Okay, I'm sorry if you got a fright. It was stupid not telling you how experienced I am, but you're being far too cautious."

"That's the way I am." He tried to lighten up, but found he couldn't.

"Oh, God, oh no, how insensitive of me!" Jessica flushed as she belatedly recalled the great tragedy of his childhood. "I am so sorry."

He fixed his eyes on the purple escarpment that dominated the flat landscape. A pulse beat in his temple. "My mother was reckless. Just like you."

Jessica quietly protested. "You could have that wrong, Cyrus, though I do understand how you feel. Your mother could look after herself. So can I. Freak accidents happen. No one can prevent them. For a fatalist that means your number is up." She reached across to briefly touch his hand. "You promised me we'd ride into the canyon. I hope that wasn't a ruse because I looked like giving you a run for your money."

"You'd be still nursing the disappointment." He relented enough to smile slightly. "Okay, Jessica, we'll go explore the canyon."

CHAPTER TEN

WITHIN HALF AN HOUR, they were deep inside the canyon, parts of which had been hidden from Jessica's eyes when she'd viewed it from the escarpment. No matter how beautiful the canyon had appeared from the escarpment, it was pure magic when seen from the ground. An idyllic place lost in time. The walls glowed with such intensity, the very air was shot through with rainbows of color; all the deep terra-cottas, the russets, the rose and pink, the dark purples. What was extraordinary was the way the ubiquitous, indestructible spinifex clung to every crevice in a spray of gold. Cascades of icy cold water tumbled down the tiered rock face supplying moisture to the lush profusion of plants that grew in the shade and shelter of the towering walls. Jewellike greens, tangles of blue-flowered vines, gorgeous little native hibiscus, ferns that could be quite rare, secreted as they were in this far, far away ancient canyon that few people or animals had penetrated. It was so wonderfully unspoiled. A belt of small red-barked trees with shining green foliage lined both sides of the ocher walls, interspersed here and there with what must have been some species of wattle—glowing masses of fluffy yellow puff balls gave off the all-suffusing scent of her childhood, when the lovely Queensland wattle lit up the hills surrounding her home.

Jessica walked slowly, noticing everything. The color effects and the natural beauty of the scene touched every artistic nerve. She and Cyrus scarcely spoke, but they frequently threw smiling glances at one another, each content to be in this wild and beautiful place. Small shrubs were ablaze with a heavy crop of scarlet fruit the size of cherry tomatoes.

"A bush delicacy?" she called to Cy.

"Yes, you can eat them. They taste a bit like loquats."

Jessica popped a couple in her mouth, her taste buds coming alive. They were sweet, a little bit tart. They had a sweet, tangy smell, as well. She knew there were any number of native fruits and vegetables highly prized by the Aborigines and bushmen alike. To her sensitive nostril, everything was so clean and fresh. The sand of the canyon was a radiant white in stark contrast to the deep lagoon, with its tall humming reeds and flotillas of pink water lilies, the sort Monet would have loved to paint. The waters of the lagoon were a milky lime-green in the shallows, deepest cabochon in the center where the spirit of the Aboriginal girl lived. In such a place, if one were listening, one could almost feel her presence, perhaps even hear her voice.

Jessica wandered near the edge of the pool, wondering if long ago Moira had met her fate here. No matter how beautiful, the lagoon had treacherous depths. Here, too, some prehistoric monster could have found its way through the neck of the canyon and into the lagoon to make its home. This was the Dry. What would this place look like in the full swing of the monsoon? This glittering stretch of water, at absolute peace today would the next fill the entire canyon, pounding against the rock walls and carving out the grottos before inundating the valley beyond. The beautiful pink water lilies would be torn away, scattered for miles. Falling Waters would grow and grow, immeasurably wider, thundering down the escarpment. A striking picture began to form in her head. It would be an incredible thing to see from the air, a sight never to be forgotten. She envied Cyrus his wilderness home. There was freedom to think here, to glory in nature, to get a profound sense of oneness with it. Mokhani was having such an effect on her it was difficult to believe she had another life in the city.

A shadow fell over her. Overhead, coasting low, was a powerful blue-gray peregrine falcon with its distinctive blackish-brown bars. Probably it had its nest on a shelf of the cliff face. She knew it was the fastest of all birds, able to swoop in on its prey at incredible speed. Even as she watched, guessing the predatory bird was ready for the kill, it plunged into a patch of thick vegetation and made off with its prey in a matter of seconds.

"Poor little thing!" She saw it was a small bird with azure-blue-and-black wings with flashes of bright yellow. It was slightly unnerving, the speed and accuracy of the attack, but that was nature, after all.

Much later, Cyrus called to her, pointing to the cooling blue of the sky. "Had enough?" He was a short distance down the canyon, picking up and examining some curiously shaped stones.

Jessica shook her head. "I could stay here forever. What about a swim? I'm game if you are." Of course she was teasing. Soaring on horseback over fences was one thing. Sharing a swimming pool with a crocodile was suicidal.

To her amazement, he began unbuttoning his shirt. Jessica gulped for air. This wasn't an ordinary guy from the suburbs. This was a Territorian, probably used to going skinny-dipping. She ran toward him, grasping his arms. "I was fooling, you know."

"What are you worried about?" His blue gaze was deeply teasing. "It's been many years since anyone sighted a croc around here. You feel like a dip. I feel like a dip. What's stopping us?"

She felt herself blush yet again. "I don't have a swimming costume with me."

"So you can swim without one. *I* don't care."

"Sorry, but *I* do."

"I'm amazed to hear that, Jessica, you being such an adventurous girl." He smothered a laugh. "Okay, but hell, it was definitely worth a try."

His skin in the sunlight was enriched to a warm amber. A light mat of hair, as black as the hair on his head, tapered to a narrow V dipping into his low-slung jeans. Her heart catapulted into her throat. The sight of him aroused her like nothing she had known in her life. She could feel the vital heat off his body. Her fingers ached to touch him, to stroke him, to lick the fine beads of sweat that glistened at the base of his throat…

His head snapped up. He leveled her with a blazing blue stare. Sexual tension stretched to the breaking point between them. "You want to touch me, don't you?"

"I was thinking about it," she said slowly, knowing there was a lot of ammunition in her hands. A single move on her part could lead straight into a sexual encounter.

"So what stopped you?" he asked.

"Good old common sense," she said wryly. "I have to obey the red light."

"I thought you liked risk." He covered her shoulders with his hands. Warm, light, but enflaming.

"You're too risky for me," she said in a low voice.

"Also contrary to what you might think, risk hasn't been part of my life."

"It is now," he pointed out. "The two of us are quite, quite alone. No one around for miles and miles."

"Look, I'm shaken enough already!" Her laugh trembled. "What are you trying to do to me, Cy?"

"Charm you, maybe."

"You're succeeding."

His fingers caressed the fine bones of her shoulders. "Is it fate that threw us together, Jessica, or planning?"

She gave a deep sigh. "You won't let it alone, will you. Okay, it *was* planned, but not by me." She was struggling against a need so intense, nothing in her experience had prepared her for it.

"So we all dance to Dad's tune?"

"*I* don't and from what I've seen you don't, either." She tried to step free of his hands, but he preempted her movement, locking his arms around her, trapping her in a cocoon of sensation.

"No, Jessica. You're not going to get off that lightly. The last kiss we shared was so intoxicating, it left me with a driving desire for more."

She abandoned any thought of resistance. At that moment being in his arms was what she wanted most in the world.

Time stood still as he kissed her. Caution was suspended. Desire ran ahead like a flame to a keg of dynamite.

Their kiss was passionate, openmouthed, sumptuous, as though they both wanted as much as they could get in the shortest possible time.

Jessica brought up her hand, breathing hard, to sink her fingers into his black glossy hair, loving the feel of it. Her entire body clutched for his—her breasts, her stomach, her groin, hot and tingling now, her legs.

Still holding and kissing her, he moved them back into the shade of the towering cliff walls. His hand sought her breasts, pulling at the buttons of her shirt until it fell loose and he pushed it off. Immediately, he lowered his head, tonguing each sensitive nipple through the delicate fabric of her bra, so it became wet and the engorged buds strained against it.

"God, I'm *mad* for you." His free hand moved to unsnap her undergarment. He inhaled sharply as her small breasts sprang free. "So beautiful!" His hands moved over her bare skin, his lean fingers, calloused on the pads, positioning themselves over the pale creamy contours.

"Jessica!" he cried softly, and the sound was so erotic her breaths came shorter and quicker. Her heart hammered. She brought up her hand to press his over it. Couldn't he feel how her heart beat for him? His touch was exquisite, nothing rough or insistent, but masterful, and meltingly tender and loving. He took hold of her long hair to release it from its plait, wrapping it around his hand. His mouth tasted of salt. From her flesh?

When finally he lifted his mouth from hers, they were both breathing as if they'd just run a marathon. "Is this a good time to stop?" he muttered, perversely holding her closer to him so she could feel his hard arousal. "If we don't, I mightn't be able to stop later."

"So don't!" She clung to him, afraid of the ease with which he had dismantled all her defenses.

"But is it a safe time for you?"

She hid her face against his chest, but her voice didn't falter. "Yes."

"Then I'd be a saint if I resisted you." He made her lift her head, his blue eyes glowing. "And I'm no saint, Jessica. Lord, you're so beautiful it *hurts*. I should warn you I'm the kind of guy who wants it *all*. *All* is something I've never had in my entire life. I guess you could say some part of me has been deprived. I find myself wanting to drown in your body like a man might drown in waterhole out there in the desert."

"But is it *me* you're seeing?" Jessica asked, desperate to be sure he saw her as a *person* rather than the object of his sexual desire before their lovemaking went further.

"Of course it's you." He shook her slightly. "I've had to put up a struggle against you since the moment I laid eyes on you. I'm still not sorted out. Sex isn't all I want, Jessica, if that's what's bothering you. There are worse wants. I want to know everything about you."

"That will come," she said gently. "Everything I've told you about myself is true."

He relaxed his grip slightly, pulling her head back. "Except you haven't told me everything, have you?"

Her expression broke into pieces as if in pain. "Oh, Cy, will I ever have your trust?" At last, she found the strength to step away.

"You have to admit strange things are happening," he countered, "and you're the catalyst. Dad got you here for a lot more than decorating the Big House. What's his real motivation?"

"I don't know." Her voice was very tight. "Ask him."

"I'm sorry. I'm spoiling things."

"You are."

His gaze was intense. "Because you have the power to change my world, I want desperately to believe in you. Surely you know that." He reached out a hand to her, but she drew farther away. "Why does Dad follow you around? It's been a real eye-opener for Robyn and me. What's his plan for you? A portrait of a young woman who disappeared over fifty years ago suddenly turns up in an auction room. Your uncle's partner buys it, though Livvy wants it, too. Livvy claims there are more paintings. When she looks at you, she sees Moira. She calls you Moira and you call her *Miss* Lavinia. Why should that be? Do you wonder I want to know what the hell is going on?" He stood there, gloriously handsome and very troubled.

Jessica lifted her head to stare into the brilliance of his eyes, as her own ripples of anger and confusion washed over her. "You're not the only one who's desperate for a few answers. I'm as much perturbed by your father's attentions as you and Robyn. I came up here to do a job. My expectations in life don't include marrying a man old enough to be my father. And I think there's something evil about too much money—it's such a powerful force it can start wars. I'm genuinely amazed Lavinia calls me Moira, though I have to admit Moira and I share a remarkable likeness. When you see the portrait, you'll agree."

"I can't wait," he said tersely.

Jessica's eyes were very green. "You're right about one thing. I mightn't be here long. You say you want me, yet it will probably be *you* who drives me away." To her horror, she felt like bursting into tears.

"I might have wanted to at the beginning, but I don't now," he protested. He'd been so high a moment ago, and now was plunged to the depths.

"Is that supposed to make me feel better?" The electric tension in him whipped up an answering tension in her. "Because it doesn't." Angry and suffering a feeling of humiliation, she shrugged into her shirt, fumbling with the buttons. "Let's drop this, shall we? All we've got going for us is sexual attraction."

He leaned closer, as if pulled by an unseen hand.

Jessica, too, felt herself swaying into him. She might have been a stringed instrument strummed by a master.

"It's okay, Jessica." He felt the trembling that went through her body, the warring emotions that were in her. "The day isn't ruined. There's no need for you to feel threatened. I'll keep a respectful distance. That way we won't be led directly into temptation. It's not going to be easy, though, when we cued in to each other on sight. But what the hell!" He winced and moved away from her. "Shall we call a truce?" His voice had more than a lick of mockery in it.

"I've no choice," she answered, still fumbling with her shirt. "My job is at stake."

"Dad's your boss. Not me." He shrugged, watching her. Then said, "You do realize you've forgotten your bra. I know how you like to be modest."

"What? Oh, blast!" It came out in a staccato burst.

"Why don't you just leave it off?" he suggested, plucking the scrap of polyester and lace off the bush where it had landed. "You're in no further danger from lustful old me." He twirled the undergarment around his finger. "This'll fit neatly in my pocket."

"Why don't you just give it to me?" Her green eyes flashed as she stretched out a hand.

"In the old days a lady, if she were romantic, allowed an admirer to keep her handkerchief."

Jessica snatched the bra from his finger and stuffed it in her pocket. "Well, I don't have a handkerchief on me right now," she said jaggedly.

His blue eyes burned into her. "Despite that feisty rebuff I'll be seeing you in my dreams. Tonight, Jessica. I have to tell you, I think you'll be seeing me in yours."

Arrogant bastard!

IT WAS MOLLY WHO TOOK the news that B.B. and Robyn would be returning at the end of the week.

"All good things come to an end," Lavinia lamented. "I do so love it when they're not here."

Jessica had to throw off her fluctuating moods and get motivated. Because there was no time to make the trip to Darwin, all the art supplies she'd ordered had been flown in. She had Cyrus to thank for that, but when they came together, the atmosphere between them was so far removed from companionable she never did get a thank-you out. She had no excuse now for not creating a whole portfolio of sketches enhanced by a sensitive wash of watercolors. The last thing she wanted was strong color. The vast landscape was ablaze with it. For the interior she wanted a cool tranquillity. Pristine white with accents of aqua, turquoise, harmonizing greens and maybe a shot of fuchsia-pink in the huge living room. She and Brett had discussed antiques, rugs and artwork over the phone. She had the large, well-equipped office at her disposal, and e-mails and faxes were going back and forth daily. Brett had vetted most of her proposals coming up with some excellent suggestions of his own, which was something she had counted on. Everything was going well. It was a great comfort to know her clever uncle had such confidence in her judgment.

Lavinia took great interest in what Jessica was doing, poring over the sketched interiors brought to life by watercolors. "There's some marvelous stuff Robyn had stored away," she told Jessica, frowning. "You should get over to the old servants' quarters and have a look while you can. It's a very interesting place. Haunted, of course, but that's not going to worry you. Once Broderick and Robyn get back, they'll be following your every move. Robyn is terribly jealous and it shows. I remember some priceless things, Persian rugs, *big* rugs, dear. None of your little silk prayer rugs. Incredibly beautiful, glorious colors and patterns, a couple of floral Herats of the Isfahan type. Deborah knew how to display things. Coromandel screens, porcelains, furniture and paintings galore. Lovely mirrors in gilt frames. Robyn didn't even leave them up—she has no taste whatever, but I'm fascinated by your vision. It's most sophisticated, Moira, very polished. I had no idea you were such a wonderful drawer. Exciting things going on! We'll leave these out, shall we?" She indicated the many sketches spread out all over the table. "Cy will want to see them when he comes in. It's so wonderful to see the pair of you together. But don't forget. The two of you have to face Broderick when he gets home." She leaned forward and chucked Jessica under the chin.

Talking with Lavinia was like being detached from reality.

Towards late afternoon on the Wednesday, Jessica decided to take a great leap into the unknown. She knew the old servants' quarters were locked, but only ten minutes before Lavinia had crept up on her as she was working, dangling something hard and cold against her cheek.

"Oh, goodness!" Jessica gave a start, not knowing anyone was there.

"Sorry, dear, did I startle you?" Lavinia asked, gentleness surging into her voice. "This will solve the problem of how to get in." She twirled the large brass key, blinking coyly. "I found it in Broderick's study. I actually stole it. Oops. Did I really say that?"

"Yes, Miss Lavinia, you did, you brazen thing! Mr. Bannerman probably doesn't want anyone to go in."

"I don't care a fig for what Broderick wants," Lavinia

snorted, drawing the gypsy shawl that topped off her Carmen costume around herself. It reeked of naphthalene, but it went wonderfully with all the gold medallions hanging around her neck. She passed Jessica the key. "Now push off," she said behind her hand as though someone was hiding behind the curtain. "I'd come and help you, only dust affects my sinuses. Don't say anything to Cy," she warned. "What's biting you two, anyhow? The air sizzles when you're together." Her voice dripped with interest.

"Nothing," Jessica assured her. "Cy likes to bait me, that's all."

"Works both ways, dear," Lavinia chortled. "You know, Cy hated what his father let Robyn do to the house. You never saw a boy love his mother so much. Broderick, of course, was jealous of his own son, even in those days. He craved *all* Deborah's attention, but she was a mother who loved her son. A mother, I think, before a wife. Broderick couldn't take that. He's such an extreme person."

Jessica wasn't about to argue with that.

INSIDE THE STOREROOM, it took a while for her vision to adjust to the gloom after the brilliant sunlight outside. She had never done anything like this in her life before. In truth, she could have been about to open a Pandora's box, so nervous did she feel. Why hadn't she waited for B.B. to come home and ask permission? To answer her own question, she wouldn't get it. She couldn't for the life of her think of him as Broderick, and calling him that was a jarring note. If a man, however rich and powerful, was starting to develop warm feelings toward her, she'd have to start praying those feelings would fizzle out. She had no ambition whatever to become a rich man's trophy wife, even if he covered her in diamonds, rubies and pearls. It was so embarrassing and so totally unforeseen she couldn't bring herself to tell Brett.

There were several rooms, she discovered. One very large, all of them crowded with a great collection of things covered in dust sheets. She turned away to work at a catch on a window to let in more light. There! It was oppressively hot and still. All these unmoving things towering over her, and right up the walls gave her the willies. Despite the size of the main room, which she suspected had been several rooms knocked into one, she felt strangely claustrophobic.

She nervously looked under a couple of dust sheets. The whole place was drenched in an atmosphere one could almost call ghostly.

Settle down, girl!

"Drat it!" she said softly as she stubbed her toe on what was the leg of a heavy mahogany chair. She could see a stack of what looked like pictures in frames behind a gray dust sheet. She'd probably have a heart attack on the spot if one turned out to be another painted image of Moira. Sad little Moira belonged in the past but it seemed she wouldn't stay there. She lifted the sheet and was confronted by a magnficent oil on canvas of exotic fowl in the Dutch style. A glorious peacock its iridescent tail spread, its hen, a pink flamingo, a crane with a golden tuft on its head, several pheasant, and a bird she couldn't identify nesting in a branch of a tree. Such a painting had to be extremely valuable. What was it doing here in the heat? Didn't these people care? It was so big and so heavy, it was difficult to see the paintings behind it. Not portraits. Landscapes. More paintings. Chairs, marble-topped side tables. Cabinets. High up, rolled rugs. Probably rotting the whole damned lot. This was frightful! Broderick Bannerman had turned his back on what had to be a large family collection going back generations. In doing so, he surely had turned his back on his wife and son.

There was an instant when Jessica thought she heard a whispering behind her.

Mice.

What else could it be? She stood perfectly still, listening.

When the whispering became a little louder, she swung around to face it. "Is anyone there?" She moved on again, treading warily.

You feel guilty, that's what's wrong with you. You shouldn't be here.

Even that was ridiculous. Why should she feel guilty? She was absolutely certain there was a treasure trove for the Big House beneath all these dust sheets. Why buy expensive antiques, paintings and artworks when you already possessed a valuable collection? she rationalized. She ventured into the other rooms, flinging dust sheets this way and that. Why, they'd scarcely have to buy a thing outside the custom-made sofas, armchairs and soft furnishings. She didn't intend to use draperies at the double-height French doors, but white, brass-bound shutters fitted on the inside.

The whispering started again. Either she could bolt or pay it no heed. Was she going to allow a little family of mice to send her away? Even so, she felt nervous.

Her shoulder bumped against something that turned out to be a splendid eight-panel coromandel screen decorated with birds and flowers and studded with ivory and jade. What a find! She could easily place that and the two majestic baluster vases standing on the floor—both green and gold, with brilliant enameling—without any protection to the right of it. She supposed Robyn would be furious with her for entering the storerooms without permission. But she in turn was furious with Robyn for her wilful disregard of the correct storage and preservation of beautiful and valuable things. Why was such a place made inaccessible?

She patted the curly head of a life-size white marble statue of a little girl carrying a basket of flowers. "At least *you* won't fall apart."

The whispering continued.

"Go away!"

Her words had no effect. She walked toward the sound, thinking she could better cope with an apparition than a gang of scurrying mice.

After a while, hot, dusty, dry in the throat, her toe aching, she'd had enough. She recovered one of a pair of superb tall cabinets veneered with panels of marquetry and turned to leave. Still, she lingered and looked around as though something further was required of her. Finally she made her way between the mounded dust sheets, heading for the main storage room.

As she did so, the whispering increased in volume. It wasn't mice. It was more like a frantic murmur. Something was trying to get through to her. She could feel it in the very air. "Is there anyone there?" she called out again.

Nobody was. She was quite alone, her heart knocking madly. She looked back the way she'd come. Just for a moment she thought she saw a curling *shape* swirling in the dusty air. Suddenly she felt ice cold. The sudden drop in temperature raised gooseflesh on the skin of her arms. She even put up a hand to cover her eyes.

"Jessica!"

She reacted by collapsing against one of the tall cabinets.

A tall figure emerged from the gloom. Cyrus. "God, you scared me."

He walked toward her. "What the hell are you doing here? Dad says this place is off-limits." After the brilliance of the daylight outside, Cy could just make out her cloud of ash-blond hair. As he drew closer, he took in the rest of her, pale face, huge glittering eyes. "Are you okay?" He reached out to her, holding her arm as she slowly straightened up. "You look like you've seen a ghost."

"Frankly I think I have," she said raggedly. "There's something skulking around back there."

"Mice," he said shortly, continuing to stare at her, doomed to be fascinated.

"Mice whispering secrets in my ear? I don't think so."

"What are you talking about?" he asked impatiently.

"God knows! I'm not a nervous person. I don't panic easily—until today. There are bloody ghosts back there."

"Right. Let's go and take a look," he said with some decisiveness. "What's the matter? Chicken?"

"Not with you around. Even a ghost won't want to mess with you."

"Give me your hand." His tone was brisk, at odds with the way he was feeling.

"You know what happens when we hold hands."

"Any excuse will do for me," he told her dryly. "But ghosts are definitely out, Jessica. There's no such thing."

"Tell that to the people who've entertained uninvited guests. Tell me, if there's an afterlife and hundreds of millions of people believe there is, why can't a few souls go missing? For one reason or another, their travel home has been interrupted. They still have business to attend to before they can move on."

"I'm not buying it," he said firmly.

"You haven't got a spark of imagination."

"Whereas you have too much. What exactly did you hear?" He led her through the spectral dust sheets. "This is one of the earliest buildings on Mokhani. The timbers creak."

"I'm not hearing anything now," Jessica said, starting to feel a little foolish. "What are you doing here, anyway? Checking up on me?"

"I might just be," Cy said, staring around him. "I'm really angry with Livvy for encouraging you and giving you that key."

"Why shouldn't she?" Jessica retorted, standing up for herself and Livvy. "What's the big secret about this place? It's jam-packed with beautiful and valuable things. No way should they be here. Certainly not the paintings. Fine paintings should be stored at a certain temperature. I can't imagine why *anyone* would banish the treasures I've seen to a storeroom. They must have rocks in their head."

"Yeah, well you won't get any argument from me."

"Don't you *care?*"

He leaned heavily against a sideboard, giving into sheer need and pulling her taut body alongside. "Oh yes, I care," he said bitterly. "But when I was a kid, after my mother died, when I cared about something my father disagreed with I got whipped."

"You didn't!" The expression on her face mirrored her shock.

"I've still got a scar on my back. Want to see?"

"Yes." Suddenly she was extremely angry. Broderick Bannerman, what sort of man *was* he? She hated physical violence. Abuse of any kind. And on a child, a motherless boy? That was a sin!

Cy released her, pulling his denim shirt out of his jeans, one hand lifting the hem of his shirt.

His skin, even in the poor light, gleamed a dark bronze. She could see the play of muscles across his back. And the long scar that ran from one shoulder blade almost to his waist.

"Oh, Cy!" She couldn't help herself. Tenderly she traced the faintly depressed line. "This should never have happened! I'm so sorry." His pain lacerated her. On an impulse, she leaned forward and pressed her lips to the deepest part of the scar. "I'm kissing it better," she explained huskily.

He took a deep jagged breath. "Then could you do it again? You're turning my legs to jelly."

"We're starting to forget how we decided it should be."

"Relationships are like that," he said, his voice very dry.

"So we've got one?"

"You know we have. Next thing you know, I'll be back to kissing you."

"I might get in first." She slipped her arms around him, pressing her mouth to his puckered skin.

The flame of desire, ever present in him, leaped higher than the rafters. He turned about swiftly, the muscles of his arms quivering, as he caught her face between his two hands. "Abstinence isn't working for me, Jessica." His voice was harsh with emotion.

She stared back at him. "Don't you think I know what it's like to be sick with longing?"

"So what are we going to do about it? I have to tell you sexual frustration is weighing very heavily on me."

"Me, too," she sighed, determined not to say a word out of place.

"I get the feeling you're not on the pill?"

"No." She shook her head. "I wasn't expecting any sexual encounters when I came here," she said wryly, "but boy, has everything changed."

"Maybe we'd better take a trip into Darwin," he said tautly. "Meanwhile I've got protection. I want you but you have to come to me of your own free will. I would never put pressure on you."

She raised her head, giving him a dreamy smile. "You put pressure on me every time you look at me!"

"You've been pretty good at hiding it these last few days."

"I wasn't being my true self. Anyway, you're conceited enough."

"I'm not conceited at all," he scoffed. "This week has been pretty much a torment."

"You wanted pulling into line."

"What I want is to pull you into my bed." His hands ran caressingly down her back.

"Oh, I like that," she murmured. "Your father won't take too kindly to…us." She had a grim picture of what might happen.

"I can imagine," he said. "So what's more important to you? Your relationship with *him* or your relationship with me?"

She looked up to meet his eyes. "I don't have a relationship with him, Cyrus. So quit trying to extract a confession. It's *you* I care about."

"Good." He bent his head and kissed her fiercely. "Because you've got a choke hold on *both* of us," he muttered, as they paused for breath. It was incredible, Cy knew, that he could say such things to her, but the rivalry between himself and his father had been going on for years and years.

Instantly, Jessica felt animosity enter into their passion. "Don't make me another point of conflict between you," she warned. "Lavinia told me there was rivalry between you and your father for the love of your mother."

There was a distinct edge to his voice. "The rivalry was always on Dad's side. I couldn't even recognize rivalry at that stage. I had a wonderful mother. She loved me, Jessica, but she loved my father, too—or she must have at one stage to marry him. He's a striking-looking man now. How much more so in his youth? He couldn't always have been a monster, but the monster began to appear early. God knows what Dad's true nature is. I've given up trying to find out."

"I can understand that." She looked at him with sympathy. "But please don't direct any bitterness toward me. I may have some effect on your father—an aging man's fantasy—but the deep attachment I've formed is for *you,* so don't give me a hard time."

"Blame it on the difficulties of our situation," he said laconically, hauling her back into his arms. "Kiss me."

She reached up to draw down his head.

They kissed with such hectic passion, the very air around them throbbed and whirred and both of them wound up disheveled. Finally, he wrenched back. "We Bannermans are a tortured lot. You have to sleep with me, Jessica."

It was like being offered a passport to heaven. "One day I want you to talk to me about your childhood," she said. "Your precious memories of your mother. I can't imagine what else you're going to tell me about your father, now that I've seen that scar."

"Don't make too much of it." He shrugged the injury off. "I don't think he meant to go as far as he did. Dad was severely depressed for quite a while."

"Yet he remarried quite soon?" There was a subtle look of disapproval in Jessica's eyes.

He drew her down on an old Victorian settee with beautiful but threadbare upholstery. "Dad wanted more sons. One maybe more like him. It was no whirlwind romance with poor Sharon. He didn't love her, but she, incredibly, loved him. Can you beat that? Years of being treated like a piece of furniture, yet Sharon continued to love him."

"It's a wonder he didn't beat *her*," Jessica said, deeply disturbed by what she had learned that day.

"Good God, nothing like that." Cyrus shook his head. "He'd never raise his hand to a woman. *I* was his mark. It made me grow up fast. By the time I was fourteen, I told him I'd kill him if he ever touched me again. I must have sounded like I meant it. By the time he got over the shock, he never tried it again."

"What an awful story!" she sighed with sick disgust. "How am I supposed to work for a man like that? I feel like throwing in the towel."

He replied instantly, "The only problem is, Jessica, you signed the contract, remember?"

"He pressed me into it."

Cy stroked her cheek with his finger. "You can't fight Broderick Bannerman and hope to win. Scores of people could tell you that. Dad has control of everything while he lives. I know the priceless stuff that's here. I know it shouldn't be here. This is my inheritance, too, but sometimes I think my father would like to see me miss out. This can all crumble and decay. He's not dedicated to preserving it for me. He's one of those people who think only of themselves, their own pride and place in the world. Other people aren't important."

"No wonder he's a deeply unhappy man," Jessica said. "Caring about other people brings its own fulfilment." She waved an arm around her. "I'm going to speak to him about all this when the moment is right. All these treasures lying neglected. There's a magnificent painting in the other room. The light was too bad to see the name of the artist, but I wouldn't mind betting it's a Dutch master."

"It is," he confirmed. "One of my mother's family— English originally—worked for the Dutch East India company. He lived in Batavia for many years. He acquired it there."

"So it's yours through your mother."

His expression was grim. "My mother died without a will. Anyone so young and beautiful was meant to live forever. Her premature death was never foreseen. She often pointed out what things were mine. The paintings, the jade collection, the porcelains—all her family stuff. The one time I mentioned it to Dad, he told me to go to hell. He was drunk and in a brutal mood. It was all *his* until he died, and he had no intention of dying before he reached ninety."

"Then he better start looking after himself," Jessica said. "He must have a problem with high blood pressure. He's like a pressure cooker threatening to blow the lid."

"Maybe, but he's never had a sick day in his life. Probably the bad stuff will happen all at once. He survived a plane crash, did you know? Walked away from it with only a few lacerations. The pilot was killed. Dad thinks he's invincible. He thinks he's going to go on forever. Maybe take another wife. Rupert Murdoch fathered a child in his seventies. Men do."

"Lucky old them!" Jessica said tartly, staring toward the back of the room. "Listen…"

"The mice again?" He dropped a kiss on her hair, inhaling its freshness.

"The whispering has stopped. I swear it was real enough. It was like someone trying to contact me."

"Not get rid of you?" he asked, rising and pulling her to her feet.

"Joke all you like." She shook her head. "This place has a strange aura. There's not enough light around here, either. It's dangerous in a way. Any of that stuff up there in the rafters could fall."

"Except there's no wind to move it." He lifted a dust sheet that covered a very pretty writing desk. "My mother's." The expression on his face had grown more intense. "You didn't come across another painting of our resident ghost?"

She shook her head. "It would take a month of Sundays to sort through all this. It should have been catalogued. If there were such a painting, it could be anywhere, even up there." She pointed high up on the wall to what could have been covered paintings secured by an iron brace. "I can't explain it, but I can't help thinking there is one. There are a lot of shadows around your father. It seems to me that the more strident he was when denying the existence of anything relating to Moira, the more I thought he wasn't telling the truth."

"That's a state of affairs that's been going on a long, long time. We'd better go," he said. "And don't say anything about being inside or Livvy giving you the key."

"Of course I won't," she said indignantly. "I'll try to find another way to get in. Your father's tough, but he's not that tough."

"Not when he's in the middle of creating a fantasy." He picked up the white marble bust of a young girl. "Mignon," he read the inscription. "My mother's."

"It's beautiful." She realized just being in here and seeing his mother's things was upsetting him. She was about to turn back when a voice clearly said:

Don't go.

She almost couldn't breathe, stumbling back against Cyrus. "Did you hear that?"

"What? I didn't heard a thing, but I have to say it's a little weird in here."

She caught his hand, holding tightly to it.

He laughed, looking down at her. "I'm starting to see another side of you, Jessica."

"You're not too happy here yourself."

"Then let's get out."

They were almost at the entrance to the main room when there was a blast of wind that rushed at them with surprising force. Then a loud crash.

"What the hell!" Cy swore.

"It has to be the window I opened."

Cy strode into the main room, looking quickly around him. "That makes no sense. No wind has blown up." He crossed to the door. "It's perfectly still outside. The fronds of the palms aren't moving."

"No glass shards on the floor, either." The window Jessica had opened was still on the hook, intact. "So what crashed?"

"Must have been the other room. We must have disturbed something. It could easily have been a pedestal or a lamp." He said it matter-of-factly to counteract the strangeness of the occurrence.

"Time to take our ghost seriously, wouldn't you say?"

"Big girl like you believing in ghosts." But he, too, felt edgy without knowing why. "That's the cause," Cy said when they saw how half a dozen paintings had come down from the wall. "The strap must have broken."

"The ghost got to it," Jessica said stubbornly.

"Doubt it." Cy dropped to his knees.

Jessica joined him, the two of them pulling the pictures

from their coverings one by one. No portraits. A couple of good still lifes. A flower painting Tim would have loved, a beautiful storm scene by a famous Australian artist— Jessica didn't need to see the signature to recognize the work—a forest scene and an abstract that could have represented a star being born. The canvas had come away from the gilded frame in the fall.

"Something has to be done about these," Jessica, the artist and lover of all beautiful things, said. "Leaving them like this is a crime."

"Okay, so we *will* do something about it," Cy said, pierced by her criticisms, which were warranted. "I try to avoid major blowups with my father, but one's long overdue."

"I guess so," Jessica said, rewrapping the flower painting. "He's afraid of you, you know."

"No way!" Cy was startled.

"Oh yes he is," Jessica maintained. "You're everything he's not."

"That deserves another kiss." He put his arm around her neck and kissed the sensitive spot behind her ear.

"You're kiss deprived, that's your trouble," she said.

"I've had hordes of girls chasing me," he said, then continued his inspection of the paintings.

"You never married one. I'll leave you to rewrap the abstract, although it really should be reframed. What do you think?"

"Let's have a look," he suggested. "It's getting dark in here." He broke off abruptly, his fingers slipping down behind the canvas. "There are two paintings here," he said, sounding intrigued.

"What?"

"Take a look for yourself. There's another canvas here."

Cy rested the large painting against himself while she looked.

"Push the canvas backward."

"Right out of the frame?"

"Yes. It'll be okay."

Cyrus obliged while Jessica separated the two paintings. One filled up Jessica's vision.

She rocked back on her heels in shock. "How is it possible this has been hidden for so long?" Momentarily she looked away from the newly revealed painting to stare into Cyrus's eyes. "It's Moira." She started to tremble.

"Who else!" he said in a hard, considering way. "And horror of horrors, a nude!"

"God, yes," Jessica whispered.

Moira was reclining on a couch covered in green silk, her back and shoulders propped by cushions covered in rich fabrics. Her beautiful long hair fell over her shoulders and her white, pointed breasts. She looked extraordinarily vivid yet fragile. Her skin was luminescent. Her eyes glowed. One slender leg was discreetly raised, blocking the pubic area. One lovely hand rested on her stomach, the other was twisted in her hair.

The artist in Jessica bowed low before the artistry, even if she was shocked Moira, the little governess, was the subject of such an erotic painting.

"Poor old Hugh must have been madly in love with her," Cy said, hit by a wave of arousal that had at its center the extraordinary resemblance Jessica bore to the painted image.

"That's Hugh Balfour?"

Cy bent for an inspection. "There's an *H.B.* in the right-hand corner. How did he get an innocent young girl to pose for him nude? I'm not getting any of this."

"It's a tough one all right. It opens up a whole new area

of investigation. At the heart of the Mokhani Mystery, was there a love triangle? A crime of passion?" It stuck in Jessica's throat, but she had to say it. "Yet Lavinia claims Hugh was gay."

He swung his shoulders her way. "Livvy should be arrested," he said with quiet vehemence. "It's best not to believe anything Livvy says. She's outrageous, sometimes even mad. I've never heard anything about Hugh being gay."

"It was probably a big secret."

"Nonsense!" His tone was clipped.

"People were scared to admit being gay in those days. Wasn't it against the law then?"

Cy's expression was disturbed. "Look at this painting, Jessica. Doesn't it look a wee bit erotic?"

"It looks bloody marvelous," she said, suddenly wondering if the artist had painted from life or simply drawn on a fevered imagination. He could have done it from numerous seemingly innocent sketches. Would Moira, fresh out of convent school, really have posed for this? Today it mightn't have been so shocking, but fifty-odd years ago it would have been considered scandalous. And where did that leave Lavinia's claim that Moira and Steven had fallen in love? Conceivably that, too, was nonsense. Perhaps Lavinia made up stories so life wouldn't get boring. One could expect something like that after life on the stage. "Hugh Balfour was really a very fine painter," she said. "Maybe that, too, was frowned on. Painting wasn't considered a serious career, perhaps? Hugh was probably expected to do great things. Lavinia says—"

Cyrus broke in. "No one, absolutely no one, including Dad, has ever been able to get Livvy to shut the hell up." He took a calming breath, still reeling from the stunning resemblance between the painted Moira and Jessica. Of course the longer he looked, the more he could see differences. Moira appeared more fragile, a vulnerable young person. Jessica was a thoroughly modern young woman, very fit, confident, with a promising career. But the coloring, the small features, the full mouth, the luminous skin. It would appear to anyone looking from the painting to the living woman they were somehow related.

Were they? He had to wonder. More to the point, did Jessica know and was keeping it from him for some reason? Was there a conspiracy at work here? Was his father part of it? Someone had taken a punt by putting the other portrait of Moira on the market. To what end?

"Just listen quietly to what I have to say," Jessica began cautiously, anticipating an explosion. "Don't shut your mind to it. Lavinia said Hugh loved your grandfather, Steven."

He coolly scrutinized her. "My darling Jessica, I *know* that. Everyone knows that. Hugh damned near worshipped him—for what he was, for what he'd done. He was a war hero, you know. He remained Hugh's friend from the first to the last. Hugh's own family deserted him. Many men came home from the wars alcoholic. They needed alcohol to deaden the pain of their terrible memories. The world can be a pitiless place. Hugh committed suicide. He wasn't very old at all. I don't suppose anyone told you. He died here on Mokhani. My father was there when they found the body."

Jessica drew in a sharp breath. "I didn't know that."

"It's not the sort of thing one wants to talk about. No wonder Dad grew up the way he is. The events of his childhood permanently scarred him. That's why I occasionally feel pity. I don't know how Livvy came to believe

Hugh was homosexual. Livvy's such a drama queen! She's known for telling howlers. God knows what she'd say if she saw *this!* The poor devil was in love with her. She disappears. Years later, after silently grieving, Hugh finds a way out of all the pain." His voice took on a harder edge. "You'd tell me, wouldn't you, if there's a connection between you and Moira?" He lifted a hand as she rushed into speech. "I know you've denied it, but you could have your reasons. I want honesty between us."

"Of course, honesty. That's all important. I've told you nothing but the truth. There's no connection whatever. Past or present. I expect you to believe me, Cyrus, otherwise what have we got?" She touched his arm briefly. "It's as my uncle says. We all have a double somewhere. If *I* look like Moira, then so does Brett. My grandmother, Alex, looks more like this Moira than I do. But there was no Moira in our family." Her hand dropped away as, acutely attuned to him, she felt a residue of resistance.

He might want her. He might long to have her. But he wasn't *sure* of her.

CHAPTER ELEVEN

B.B. RETURNED MUCH THE SAME as he'd gone away. A difficult, domineering man, surrounded by shadows and given to long bouts of moodiness. At least the trip had gone well. His partners in whatever venture it was—he didn't explain—had come to heel, no doubt with words of contrition. He was, however, generous in his praise when Jessica submitted her conceptualizations for the main rooms of the Big House. He didn't go so far as Cyrus, who on seeing them had remarked they were good enough to be framed, but his opinion was highly favorable.

They were in B.B.'s study with the drawings spread out across the desk. "So you like the idea of rendering the columns that support the dome lapis lazuli?" she asked.

"I can see they'll be striking." Bannerman stabbed a finger at the excellent architectural drawing. "Who is supposed to do the fresco on the cupola?" Jessica had meant to represent a heavenly blue sky with dazzling white puffs of clouds, the edges touched with gold and pink as if from the sun. Had this been glorious Italy, she could have added cherubs for good measure, but they would have looked out of place in such a setting as Mokhani.

"I know just the man," she said. "He's Italian, classically trained. He's never out of work."

"You can't do it yourself?" His glance beetled beneath his heavy brows.

"I suppose I could, but I wouldn't have the time and I'm not as good as Primo anyway. I had been thinking that instead of paintings for the hall, we could use panels. They would go here." She quickly began to draw in several long rectangular panels. "Blue on gold. They would pick up the blue of the columns. There's so much white we need a contrast. It's a pity when the marble floor was laid the architect hadn't thought of a central design. But never mind. Do you like the library?"

"Very impressive," he nodded. "But where are we going to get the leather-bound books in those particular colors?"

"Well, we can't," she smiled, "unless we have the covers specially done. That would cost a great deal of money. Or we could have *some* of them done in order to pick up the turquoise blue. I felt the carpeting should be this very soft pinkish-red. Inviting, nurturing, but not too warm. We'll need a big important painting here." She pointed to the pale ocher wall above her rendering of an antique writing desk flanked by two splendid chairs.

"This is all very palatial," he said, his body a large physical barrier between her and the door.

"Isn't that what you wanted? A modern palace. I had to strike a balance between sumptuousness and classical purity."

"Well then you've succeeded, Jessica," he said, making no attempt to disguise the admiring scrutiny he bent on her. It went well beyond the aesthetic, Jessica thought. In fact, he was thoroughly unnerving her.

"I have some ideas for the front court," she quickly added, beginning to sketch a plan for the landscaping immediately in front of the house.

"We used to have an artist in the family," he commented, staring down at her slender flying fingers. "Name of Hugh Balfour. Ever heard of him?" He lifted his handsome head, shooting her the now-familiar piercing glance. This wasn't a man who indulged in idle conversation. He was pushing her to declare what she knew. Moreover, who'd told her.

Calmly she lay down her pencil. "Lavinia mentioned him. I think in connection with the portrait of your father up there. She's interested in art."

"Not that she knows anything about it," he scoffed.

Again she wondered if he had, through his agents, put Moira's painting on the market. To what purpose? She couldn't figure it out.

The silence stretched, uncomfortably for Jessica, during which time he continued to stare at her. Jessica thought she held up rather well. How many people actually could? Oddly, she had the impression he was not so much staring *at* her, as *beyond* her. As though Moira lived in *her* body and the two of them had metamorphosed right in front of him.

"You got to look around the station, then?" He finally shifted position, moving around the massive desk.

She could see where this was leading. "Not as much as I wanted. I needed to have these drawings ready for you. That was my top priority. I did, however, get to the top of the escarpment and later explored the floor of the canyon for a while. It was a marvelous experience, like seeing a surviving pocket of Gondwana. Before I go home I want to take lots of pictures. This is another world, the Top End. The plant life is unique. I used to think a lot of our tropical plants had their origin in the South Sea islands. Apparently it's the other way around."

He shrugged off the information as of little interest. His

whole life had been addressed to making money. "You didn't go by yourself. Cyrus took you?"

She had already anticipated the question. "He was kind enough, yes," she said with a smile. Broderick Bannerman was indeed in some sort of conflict with his son, conflict that had deep roots in the past. For all she knew, Bannerman could have had problems with his own father, Steven, the man Cyrus resembled so closely. Many factors in Broderick Bannerman's early life could have been in play.

"It must have been really hard work escorting a beautiful young woman around Mokhani," he said, openly sarcastic.

Had he ever appeared in another guise, this severe, controlling man? "There was something I was going to ask you, Broderick." For the first time, she uttered his name with ease. "I understand you have many beautiful things from the family collections stored away in the old servants' quarters."

He smiled, the sort of smile that was almost alarming. "You can't use those," he said.

"I had hoped you would allow me to see them."

Bannerman leaned back in his chair, interlocking his hands behind his dark head with its distinctive silver wings. "I can't have any of my wife's things back in the house," he said.

An aura of pain was suddenly around him. Jessica stared at the handsome features drawn taut. "Oh, I'm sorry! I didn't mean to upset you." Who could begin to understand this complicated man?

"It appears I still haven't dealt with my wife's death," he said. "Perhaps I never will."

"A tragedy like that does strange things to people's lives."

"What would you know about tragedy?" he said.

"I lost the grandmother I adored."

"Ah, yes, the grandmother!"

"Why do you say it like that?" She frowned.

"You resemble her greatly?"

"Well, yes. How do you know? I don't believe I mentioned it at our first meeting, or since."

"I think you did and you've forgotten. Maybe I *will* let you take a look at what's in storage. As an artistic person, you must love beautiful things."

"That would be wonderful. Thank you. I was told there are beautiful paintings. Forgive me, but it's not wise to store them in the heat. Even the furniture will buckle. I had thought there might be a possibility of placing some pieces in the Big House. They could look quite different in such a very different setting."

He looked at her with such a strange expression on his face. "I understand what you're saying, Jessica, about the heat and humid conditions. I can see you *care*." Then, the words rolling like drumbeats, "Who's been talking to you?"

"It's been more my asking questions!" She laughed. "You must understand, I've never been anywhere remotely like Mokhani before. Do you wonder I'm fascinated?"

He seemed to relax, if indeed a hunting hawk ever relaxes. "It pleases me to hear that." He reached out, spreading his large elegant hand over hers. "Speaking of fascination, there's some magic about *you*." His resonant voice dropped low. "I'm already feeling your influence about the place. I enjoy talking to you. In fact, I've so looked forward to coming home. I haven't done that since I can't tell you when."

Jessica made no comment, not daring to inch her hand away. Well, not immediately. It wasn't the first time a male client had become attracted to her. She had begun to look on it as an occupational hazard. But this was something else again. She knew women married men old enough to be their fathers—certainly if they had several-odd million stashed away—but she thought she'd rather remain unmarried for the rest of her life than play on the soft underbelly of an aging man's weakness. Broderick Bannerman, with his formidable energy, bitterly resented growing old. He may have come to the conclusion marriage to a young woman could accomplish the impossible and keep him eternally young.

Jessica swallowed her dismay. Was it possible he was seriously considering *her?* Dear God, if true, it was a nightmare, particularly when she was head over heels in love with his son. Gently she withdrew her hand, starting to put all her sketches together.

"There's no word yet about your award?" he asked, a faint flush in his cheeks.

"I expect to hear any day now." She hugged the rolls of sketches to her. "I don't expect to win. It was an honor to be short-listed."

"So modest when you're so clever. I like that. The painter in our family wasn't a success. He was a great failure." His eyebrows jutted in a frown.

"Hugh, you mean?" Jessica's mind was racing. *Had* Balfour been gay? The family would have known. Could a gay man paint such an erotic nude? Silly question. Great painters had done it in the past.

"Rumor had it he was gay," Broderick said with a harsh laugh. "But if he were, he was very discreet. Hell of a thing to be homosexual. Maybe that's why he topped himself."

"Poor man. So he couldn't have been in love with Moira?"

The handsome, heavy head shot up. "Whatever are you talking about?"

She was almost welcoming a confrontation, but backed off. "I did a lot of research on Mokhani before I came. Many articles have been written about the Mokhani Mystery."

"I expect there'll be lots more," he grunted. "The press is conspicuous for dragging up all the old unsolved mysteries."

"They said Moira was beautiful. Was she?"

"I was only a child, my dear."

"So you never saw the paintings Hugh Balfour did of her?"

He smiled like a man who had nothing to hide. "If I did I've forgotten. I have to tell you I'm not used to being interrogated, Jessica. I can tell you Moira had your coloring. She was tallish like you and exceptionally slender."

"So you do remember some things about her?"

He studied her very gravely. "I suppose, now that I think about it. Few women in my experience have been as beautiful as Moira, though my boyish memories can't be entirely accurate. My wife was a very beautiful women with skin like a pearl. You, too, are beautiful. When I first saw you on that television program, your chance resemblance to my governess stunned me."

"Is that why you hired me?"

"You sound very anxious to know."

"Well, of course I am."

"Let me set your mind at rest," he said suavely. "I paid far greater attention to your qualifications, Jessica. You don't know me if you think otherwise."

I don't know you at all, Jessica thought.

"By the way, Robyn's boyfriend—ridiculous word,

particularly as he's been married and divorced—is giving her a birthday party Saturday night at his home. I'd like you to come."

"Shouldn't I wait for an invitation?" She gave him an uncertain glance.

"You're getting one from me." He spoke as if that was all that was required. "Dress up."

"Is that an order?" On her way to the door, Jessica turned to ask.

There was a flare of amusement in his eyes. "Of course not. I confess I'm looking forward to seeing you turned out for a party. Formal is what Robyn wants. She spent a fortune in Hong Kong. That way no one gets to see her in the same thing twice."

WITH THE MASTER OF THE HOUSE back in residence, Lavinia didn't come down to dinner.

"I've told Jessica about the party on Saturday." B.B. threw the remark at Robyn as though daring her not to catch it. "She says she won't come without an invitation."

"But she must come. Please come," Robyn said as though the invitation had been lost in the mail. "I'm so sorry, Jessica, I was getting around to it. It's going to be a big night."

"She's thirty now, you know," B.B. told Jessica. "Thinking of matrimony. We'll have to make sure there's a prenuptial agreement. No way is Erik getting his hands on my money."

"He's got money of his own, Dad," Robyn was moved to protest.

"Let's face it, my dear, Moore wouldn't have given you the time of day if you hadn't been my stepdaughter."

"I'm truly amazed someone hasn't bumped you off,

Dad," Cyrus drawled. "Erik isn't the only man to notice Robyn's attractions. With or without your money."

"I'm not a very nice person, as you know, Cyrus," Bannerman said.

Cyrus lifted his wineglass in a dubious salute. "Actually I'm not all that keen on going. I think you can do better than Erik, Robyn. He ran out on his wife. He could run out on you."

"He promised me he would never leave me." Robyn was bristling and very much on edge.

"Hell, you couldn't exactly call you a loving couple. My bet is you're desperate to leave home."

Robyn gasped. "How can you say such a thing? Dad has given me a marvelous life. It's as he says, I'm not getting any younger."

"Check with Erik, he wants children," Bannerman slipped in smoothly, turning his head to capture Jessica's gaze. "Robyn could be barren like her mother."

Jessica felt herself flinch. Could Robyn be that desperate to inherit her stepfather's money to tolerate all these cruel, cutting remarks? But it was Cyrus, not Robyn, who came to Sharon's defense. "Sharon wasn't barren, Dad. She had Robyn. That, of course, was long before she met *you*."

"How you love to set me straight, Cyrus," his father answered, brushing that fact aside. Once more he addressed Jessica. "I have a little something for you, Jessica, I bought in Hong Kong. I'd like you to wear it Saturday night."

It was a startling statement that left Jessica greatly worried.

"I really think you should tell Jessica what it is first," Cyrus suggested. "Some things a girl has to refuse on principle."

Jessica felt Robyn's gaze locked on her, but her answer was weighed and controlled. "Goodness, I don't need a present, Broderick. You're paying me extremely well."

"Of course I am," he smiled, "but it gave me pleasure to buy it. I'm sure you're going to enjoy wearing it. I have it in my study. You can take a look after dinner."

"It would be so nice if Robyn and I were invited along, too," Cyrus said, contemplating Jessica's face, a decided glint in his eyes.

"This is *private,* Cyrus," B.B. said. "You and Robyn will just have to wait."

"How do you know you haven't made a big mistake?" Cyrus sat back with indolent grace.

"About what?" B.B. asked in his most aggressive fashion.

"Jessica's mother will have told her not to accept presents from near strangers," Cyrus pointed out.

"I don't think sarcasm is the answer, Cyrus," his father said.

"Of course it isn't. Jessica is shocked, in case you haven't noticed."

"That's not true, is it, Jessica?" B.B. turned to her.

She swallowed, not wishing to insult him but determined to find a way out of it. "I *am* surprised," she said.

"And a little nervous. Don't be, my dear," Bannerman patted her hand. It was getting to be a habit.

WHAT B.B. HAD REFERRED TO as "a little something" turned out to be a pair of platinum earrings, each set with a half carat round brilliant cut lemon diamond and two brilliant cut white diamonds from which was appended a beautiful golden South Sea teardrop pearl of at least fifteen millimeters. Pearls of that size and shape were relatively rare, and so were much sought after by collectors. Jessica knew this from her love of pearls and her own mother's collection. Luster, the single most important factor in determining the value of a pearl, was well in evidence. The nacre was very rich.

It was quite out of the question to accept a gift like this. It was too valuable and too personal. The sooner she made that clear, the better. "Broderick, I can't possibly accept these," she said as courteously as she could.

His piercing gaze rested on her. "That alone makes you different from most women of my acquaintance." Dinner was over. They were alone in his study.

"It's extremely generous of you, but I've done nothing to warrant such a gift."

"Try them on, anyway," he said, pointing to a mirror. Broderick Bannerman hadn't gotten where he was without putting down opposition. "At least let me see them on you. They say pearls are in again."

"They should never have been out." Jessica didn't want to offend him, but she couldn't give him leverage, either. Broderick Bannerman's inch was another man's mile.

"*Please.* I don't often beg." He turned her by the shoulders, looking directly into her eyes.

Yes, she thought. Begging would be grotesque in such a man.

"If you see yourself wearing them, you might want to keep them," he said, reaching for the jewelry box.

"They must have cost a good deal of money," Jessica said. She had a fair idea how much; she looked in the windows of jewelry stores often enough. She would have thought a gift costing a hundred dollars too much, but these earrings had to be worth many thousands of dollars. There was no way she could accept. In her embarrassment, she saw it as a form of prostitution.

"What's money?" he asked, as only a rich man could. "I have all the money in the world, but it hasn't made me happy. Since you've been here, Jessica, I've felt a lifting of the spirit. Do you know what I'm saying?"

She kept her head down, not needing to feign sweet confusion.

"Put the earrings on," he urged, looking as if he wanted to do it for her. "At least give me the pleasure of seeing them on you."

She relented. "Very well." She removed her own earrings, the peridots Tim had bought her, and inserted the pearl drops. "It was very nice of you to think of me, but I know you'll realize I can't accept such a valuable gift—the skin on the pearls appears flawless."

"Would I select pearls with the slightest imperfections when your own skin is flawless?" He came to stand behind her, an imposing-looking man. "I suggest we take one thing at a time."

Jessica vowed he wasn't going to override her decision. "Which I've done. I've shown you what they look like on."

"Perfect!" he breathed, like a connoisseur. "Push your hair back," he instructed.

Though the air-conditioning was working efficiently Jessica felt stifled. He stood back studying her, then he moved to lay a hand on her shoulder. "You can't refuse me."

To her horror, his voice had taken on what seemed to her an ardent note. This was the worst thing that could possibly happen. It would change everything, make her job untenable. With no encouragement whatsoever, Broderick Bannerman had become infatuated with her.

Patches of color stained his prominent cheekbones.

"It's clear to me you're not used to accepting presents, Jessica. A beautiful young woman like you should be showered with them."

The intensity of his expression altered abruptly when a knock came at the door. The next moment, without waiting for an invitation, Cyrus entered the room, his blue eyes flashing over the fixed tableau: his father's hand on Jessica's shoulder, Jessica, her head averted, her face as pale as his father's was ruddy, her cloud of ash-blond hair pushed behind her ears to reveal exquisite drop-pearl earrings.

It was *exactly* what Cyrus had feared. His father had been struck by Cupid's arrow. A man couldn't avoid it any more than he could avoid dying. Approaching sixty—even if he didn't look it—his father was now young at heart. For once, B.B. wasn't thinking with his *brain*. He was endeavoring to romance a woman young enough to be his daughter. He should know better. That's if any man would know better with someone like Jessica around.

Jessica fell back from the blazing contempt in Cy's regard. He was so judgmental! Anyone would think she'd been caught in some odious act.

"So this is the present." Cyrus reached Jessica, standing before her. He put a finger to the beautiful drop pearl, setting it swinging. "I expect you've promised Dad never to take them off."

"Why should she when they suit her so beautifully!" Bannerman exclaimed in a mix of anger and triumph. "Is there something you want, Cyrus?" he demanded. "It's customary to knock and wait for an answer before you barge into a room."

"Sorry about that, Dad," Cyrus said. "I had a rough

childhood. No mother to teach me manners. I just wanted to know if Jessica wanted to go for our usual after-dinner stroll, if that suits her?"

"It suits me," Jessica said, already removing the earrings one by one and laying them back in the satin-lined, polished walnut case. "These are much too good to wear around the garden. They're perfectly beautiful, Broderick, but I can't accept them."

"And I can't take them back. Not *now*." A deep crease appeared between Bannerman's brows. "You've worn them. Pierced ears and so forth. As I've said you'd make me happy if you'd wear them Saturday night, Jessica. I'll leave them in the safe for you. You probably didn't bring much in the way of jewelry and the other women will be dressed up. There's quite a bit of money in Darwin."

JESSICA'S KNEES WERE TREMBLING as they walked down the front steps of the homestead. Cyrus was striding ahead as though he wanted to lose her.

"What's your hurry? Are you so desperate to get back inside?"

Immediately he stopped, swinging around to face her. "What the hell was *that* all about?" He towered over her.

Her temper rose to match his. "Might I remind you we're still within spitting distance of the house?"

"I'm seething, that's why." He grasped her arm, hauling her along the path. They had rounded the end of the veranda, though the exterior lights shone over the path and into several feet of the garden, ablaze with huge birdlike heliconias. "Well?"

"Well, nothing!" Jessica jerked her arm away. "Absolutely nothing. You have a very suspicious, not to say, dirty mind."

"No one has accused me of that before." He swung her back to face him. "There are certain rules of behavior—"

"Never stopped you," she reminded him sharply. "Look, Cy, I don't want to get into an argument with you. It's really your father you should be speaking to. If he sees nothing wrong in wooing a woman young enough to be his daughter, I *do*. It's so damned embarrassing."

"I agree. I told you to tread carefully around him."

"What do you think I've been doing? I've given him no encouragement at all—it simply didn't occur to me. Why put the pressure on me anyway? Go tell your father to lay off."

He laughed, though he was obviously upset. "Hell, I mightn't be seen or heard of again."

Tentatively she reached out to him, trying to read the expression on his face. His striking features, which for all the bad feelings between them bore his father's stamp, were tense. "It can't be that bad." She had a fluttery sensation in her chest as though her heart were missing beats.

"A slight exaggeration," he said in self-mockery. "I've learned how to defend myself." He walked on. Jessica followed, increasing her pace to keep up. "Dad's cracked the whip for so long, he thinks there's nothing and no one he can't get. He could exhaust any woman with his persistence and his money. Dad's not coming to the end of his sex life. It's still all systems go."

"Not with *me*, it isn't, as I've told you a dozen times. What do you think I am, an adventuress?"

"Maybe more of a temptress."

Jessica smarted. "I'd watch it if I were you. Men are all the same. Always bemoaning a woman's power over them. *She made me do it.* Rapists have sworn on their mother's lives that their victims seduced them. It all started with Adam."

"What are you going to do about those earrings? He clearly expects you to wear them."

"He can take the bloody things back. And I don't care if my swearing offends you."

"Don't worry, I'd be swearing, too. I *hated* to see my father's hand on your shoulder."

"Jealous?"

"Yes. That's what you wanted me to say, isn't it? Jealous, angry, sad, embarrassed, deeply concerned, as well. My father is a dangerous man, Jessica. A predator. It would be very foolish to trust him."

"I don't need *you* to tell me that. A little bird told me on day one—he's very cruel to Robyn. I can't help feeling sorry for her."

"So do I, now and again. Only, Robyn has picked up a few too many of Dad's traits, haven't you noticed? She reveres him like some people revere dictators. Like Dad, I don't think she'd have any difficulty resorting to drastic measures. If she could get away with it, she'd push me off a cliff."

"Are you serious?"

He forced a laugh. "If she could get off scot-free. Poor old Robyn craves Dad's love and attention. In that way *only* is she like her mother. Robyn suffered from being adopted. She's never believed she *belonged*."

"Hardly surprising!" Jessica cried. "No one acts as though they like her. Even her husband-to-be."

Cy made a little clicking sound of disgust. "They're a pair all the same. Erik's just as mercenary as she is. Dad's right when he says Erik's real interest in Robyn is the family connection. Being Broderick Bannerman's son-in-law would be great for business. Which is why I don't like him. In fact, I despise him, though he always tries to be pleasant.

As for Robyn, don't think I didn't try quite hard to be friends with her when we were kids. Sharon was a nice woman who deserved better than what she got. Livvy tried hard to be good to Robyn, as well. Neither of us got anywhere. She didn't want us. She wanted Dad. Robyn is her own worst enemy. I've gone way past trying to connect with her, especially when she'd like to see me out of the way."

Jessica's whole body tingled with a sense of danger. "That's a terrible thing to say."

He shrugged. "I'm afraid it's true. Robyn believes that with me out of the way, everything would be perfect. Of course, she couldn't be more wrong. My father and I might be mostly at loggerheads, but he'd scarcely be happy if anything happened to me. At some level, in some deep dark cave, he's buried his love for me. But it's there. He's a tormented, moody, restless man. Robyn could *never* take my place. That's what she can't seem to understand. Dad never gives me a word of praise or gratitude, but he knows and I know he can't do without me. I run Mokhani these days and I've inherited his business brain. It was my mother who gave me the gift of a *soul*. Dad might have had one, but he doesn't own it anymore."

JESSICA WAS IN THE OFFICE reading through a long fax from Brett, which included an architectural drawing she found very helpful, when Robyn came in search of her.

"Hi! Thought I'd find you here." Robyn actually smiled, looking a totally different person in the process. She had beautiful white teeth that showed up well against the pale gold of her skin.

What had caused this huge sea change? Since Robyn

had returned from Hong Kong, she was acting much more human and likable.

"I'm so looking forward to my party!" Robyn laughed excitedly, perching on a desk and placing the envelope she had in her hand beside her. "It's going to be great! I'm very much in love with Erik."

Jessica tried her level best to look as if Erik were among the most desirable of suitors. "I'm happy for you, Robyn. Is there going to be a surprise announcement?"

"Gee, I don't know." Robyn put her elegant, manicured hands to her blushing cheeks. "Erik loves surprising me. Whatever Dad says, Liz wasn't a good wife to him. She never wanted children. Erik is a man who should have children."

"Have you discussed it with him?" Jessica's instinct told her Erik might have been lying.

"Heavens, it's understood. The truth is, I don't want to rush into motherhood. After a couple of years of marriage, maybe. Dad would adore a grandchild."

Jessica couldn't for the life of her fire off a quick answer. She tried hard to see B.B. through Robyn's eyes, but had to leave off. Broderick Bannerman would make her own crusty grandpa seem like a Boy Scout.

"What I wanted to ask you…" Robyn frowned for a moment, considering. "Have you a suitable dress? It's formal, you know."

"Your father told me," Jessica nodded. "I do have one dress I think might do."

Robyn removed some photos from the envelope. "Look, here are some possibilities. I'd like to help. You know I own a boutique in Darwin. Exclusive designer wear. I can tell you're a girl who knows clothes."

"Why thank you, Robyn. You have beautiful taste." It

wasn't a white lie, for strangely enough, Robyn did—with her dressing. She always looked very glamorous, nothing over the top. It was when she had attempted to be her own interior designer she had gone adrift.

Robyn passed the photographs to her. A lovely Eurasian model was wearing a collection of party dresses, all in the height of fashion.

"These are beautiful!" Jessica said with genuine enthusiasm.

Robyn leaned forward. "I had Selina put them on to give you a better idea of what the garments would look like when worn. So much better than showing you something on a hanger. Selina is your size." Her dark eyes ran over Jessica's tallish slender figure. "What do you think? If you like one, I could have it ferried in. Evening shoes to match. What would you be? Size thirty-six, European?"

"Yes." Jessica was starting to feel a little more kindly towards Robyn. "This is very thoughtful of you, Robyn, but—"

"Dad wants you to look your best," Robyn said as though that clinched it.

"That would be my goal in any case," Jessica answered with faint irony. "But you're the guest of honor, Robyn. Not me. My own dress is very pretty."

"As glamorous as these?"

"Maybe not." She smiled. "I didn't come here expecting to be at the ready for formal parties."

"I have a faultless eye," said Robyn, obviously thinking there was nothing to be gained from false modesty. "You'd be pleasing me very much if you would pick one out. You've got a good figure, and a good back—the dresses are cut low at the back. There'll be a lot of beautifully dressed women there. All showing off. The husbands have money coming out their ears. The wives fly off to Hong Kong and Singapore all the time to do their shopping. Some have the most gorgeous jewelry. Hope I'm not boring you. You've heard of Paspaley pearls?"

"Who hasn't? They're the most beautiful pearls in the world."

Robyn gave a throaty laugh. "I know Dad called into their Darwin showroom fairly recently. I happened to run into a friend who let it slip. I suspect he chose something to mark my thirtieth birthday. Dad knows I adore jewelry. He bought my mother a few nice pieces, which I inherited, but I can't get my hands on Deborah's stuff. Deborah died without a will, but her jewelry goes to Cyrus's future wife. That's sure to be Roslyn Newman. They've been on and off as an item for years. Not Roz's fault—Cyrus won't commit. No one measures up to the adored Deborah. That's pretty much it. Cy never got over losing his mother."

"I can understand that," Jessica said.

Robyn's mouth tightened. "I lost my own mother a couple of years back. I've had to get over it. You learn to pack your feelings away in a box. You can't let them influence your thinking."

"Easier said than done, Robyn," Jessica said quietly.

"Some of us are more strong-minded than others." Robyn snapped her fingers. "So what's the verdict? I thought the green myself as you've got green eyes."

"The green is beautiful. I'm a little nervous about the price…"

Robyn laughed. "It would be a pleasure to *give* it to you, Jessica. Good advertising for me, too, if you could just drop the hint it came from my boutique. You're bound to be asked."

The fact Broderick and Robyn wanted to shower her with presents Jessica found more disturbing by the minute.

"I wouldn't dream of taking it for nothing, Robyn, though it's very generous of you to suggest it. How much is it?"

"You'll accept a discount, surely?" Robyn named a price that was practically a giveaway.

"Not *that* much of a discount," Jessica said, looking adamant.

"All right!" Robyn named a price Jessica had never yet spent on a party dress. "But it's worth it."

"Done." Jessica wanted to look beautiful for just *one* man. She put out her hand, but instead of shaking it, Robyn slapped it in a bit of fun. "I'll get on the phone right away. What about evening shoes?"

"I think my own will do."

"There'll be dancing." Robyn executed a few dance steps.

"That's great!" A sexy lambada with Cyrus, Jessica thought.

At the door of the office, Robyn turned, her gleaming pageboy falling in close on her cheeks. She really was very attractive when she managed to unwind. "We must go riding one day. I'd love to show you around. You *can* ride?"

Obviously no one had told her Cyrus had taken her riding on Chloe. "Yes."

"Good," Robyn said, sounding pleased. "I don't imagine you're an expert, but I'll be able to give you a few tips. I'm sorry we didn't exactly hit it off when you first arrived—the fact you're so young was a shock—but if Dad says you know what you're about, who am I to argue? I'll leave you in peace now. Wait until you see *my* dress. It's terrific! I want Dad to be really proud of me."

Jessica was left feeling sad. Robyn measured all her triumphs and failures against what her stepfather thought. A pity when no one could call Broderick Bannerman a kind man.

CHAPTER TWELVE

THE DAY OF THE PARTY Cyrus flew them into Darwin. A stretch limousine was waiting at the airport to drive them to their city hotel. The same limo would be on call to deliver them to and from the party that evening, as Erik's house was a few miles outside the city. It was eight-fifteen before they were ready to leave, although Robyn was the guest of honor. Lavinia had kept them waiting, trying to manage her freshly washed hair. Now it stood out from her head in a pure white pompadour decorated on the crown with a great jewelled brooch. Around her neck she wore a necklace that could have adorned the neck of Queen Nefertiti: multiple strands of turquoise beads caught at intervals with diamond arrows with a large open square of diamonds as the center piece. Lavinia, Jessica had noted, was not short of stunning vintage pieces. Tonight she had abandoned her arresting operatic wardrobe in favor of a classical turquoise toga. Turquoise-and-amethyst pendant earrings circa 1930, now the rage, dangled from her ears, dragging down the delicate lobes.

"Magnificent!" Jessica applauded when they met up in the lobby. "I'm wild about your necklace."

Lavinia advanced regally, putting her arms around Jessica and kissing her with real affection. "How I wish I'd had a granddaughter like you, Moira. If you find my necklace attractive, it's yours. But you must keep your hands off it until I'm safely with the angels. You look glorious. What it is to be young, beautiful and in love. I've never seen you made up. Those *eyes!* Where did you get all your beautiful clothes from? I don't remember seeing any of them." Her eyes swept Jessica from head to foot.

"You know how it is. One always finds something," Jessica joked, forced to accept the fact Lavinia would always confuse her with Moira.

Looking up hadn't she been anticipating this very moment?—she saw Cyrus quickly descending the stairs with easy male grace. He looked so stunning she thought he would take any woman's breath away. Clothes hung the way they were supposed to on his tall, lean, wide-shouldered body, but in a white dinner jacket with black tie he was so sexy it *hurt!*

"Nothing like a family party, is there?" he smiled, his blue gaze moving from his great-aunt to Jessica, where it stayed.

She bewitched him. Her exquisite evening dress clung to her, molding her body before it tapered to her delicate ankles. Her beautiful eyes glowed sea-green. Her hair was even more abundant than he had ever seen it. Magnificent hair, that rare ash-blond!

His heart bucked beneath his ribs. She filled him with such pleasure. All he wanted to do was pick her up and run away with her. Far, far away from his father, who was starting to act like Count Dracula. Of all the scenarios he had calculated had lain ahead when Jessica had first arrived, he had never considered he and his father might want the same woman. It was crazy.

"So where are the others?" he asked, managing to sound relaxed when the sight of Jessica in her finery had nearly robbed him of breath.

Jessica's own light tone covered her heightened emotions. "Your father *was* here, but he went off again with Robyn." She wanted to put out her hand to caress him. It was getting so bad she didn't think she'd be able to hide her depth of feeling for him much longer.

Look at me Cyrus. Look at me in my beautiful dress. I've never had a dress as beautiful as this. And it's all for you.

"I HAD TROUBLE with my pompadour," Lavinia was explaining to Cyrus. "I washed my hair. It was so soft it kept falling down, but Moira loaned me some spray. I never knew spray made it so easy. I must get some."

"Well, you managed in the end, Livvy," he said, kissing her cheek. "It looks marvellous. You both look marvellous. I'm glad you decided to come, Livvy. I find it impossible to believe you're in your eighties."

"I know. I look splendid in my dotage," Lavinia said complacently, rearranging a fold of her toga.

"Indeed you do. Just remember one thing."

Lavinia understood perfectly. "Be on my best behavior." She rolled her eyes. "I ask you, would I embarrass you, my darling?" She turned to sweep an admiring glance over Jessica. "Doesn't Moira look beautiful?"

"*Jessica* does," Cyrus stressed, relieved beyond words Jessica wasn't wearing his father's golden pearls. She was wearing, instead, the very pretty peridots he had seen before. They were almost hidden in her cloud of hair.

"That's a seriously sexy dress, Jessica," he said, the note in his voice sending exquisite little shivers up and down Jessica's spine. "I'm extremely impressed." He made a little twirling gesture. "Turn around."

Jessica joyfully obliged. She wanted to remember *everything* about tonight. Her silk chiffon dress, strapless, in a lovely shade of mint-green, was draped closely around her body to the hips, from where the tapering hem floated from mid calf almost to her ankles. Her evening shoes—she had brought them with her on the off chance—were sexy gold heels, which gave her extra height. The plunging back of the gown showed an expanse of youthful skin as smooth as cream.

"Delightful. Delectable. Delicious." His mouth curled into a rakish grin.

"Sounds like an ice cream."

"Tell her you want her to have your children," Lavinia burst out, a tender smile on her face.

Long used to her outbursts, Cyrus didn't even blink. He replied gently, "Livvy, dear, if I come on too strong I'll frighten her off."

"No, no, no. She feels safe with you. This family made one dreadful mistake. We can't make another."

Jessica intervened quickly. Although she was pleased Lavinia was coming to the party, she was concerned about what Lavinia would say in company. It was becoming increasingly apparent Lavinia dwelled in the realm of fantasy. She had never *once* called her Jessica. Why should she start now? She touched Cyrus's arm, her heart in her eyes. "*You* look wonderful."

"Thanks." He gave a little bow. "Especially as it took me several hours to fix this blasted tie."

Lavinia gave him a tap on the hand. "It did not. When do you suppose we'll have the pleasure of seeing Robyn in her birthday finery? Pity she's got such a flat chest. Poor little Sharon was just the opposite. Top heavy. I must say Broderick looks very distinguished in black tie. Such a shame he's got a manner one wouldn't wish on a rott-weiler." She smiled at them happily.

Cyrus shot her a near-despairing look. "Livvy, I hope this isn't a case of your starting out the way you mean to go on. It's very rude to criticize Dad. You've just promised me you'd behave."

"Ah, yes. I did say that. And so I shall. It's just that I'm too old to worry about a lot of things."

Jessica couldn't help wondering how long it was going to take before Lavinia's thunderbolts came down on the party.

ERIK MOORE'S HOUSE was very much one built to survive the elements. Darwin had suffered terribly in Cyclone Tracy of 1973, so the architectural firm that had designed the Moore house had made sure it could withstand the most severe cyclonic weather. The massive two-story concrete structure was elevated high on piers to protect it from floodwaters and topped by a broad, sheltering hip roof. The piers, surrounded by beds of agapanthus, gave the impression the house was floating. Jessica looked around her with great interest as they walked to the glass-enclosed stairway, which was the entry to the house. Its solidity and clean lines were complemented by a splendid garden full of lush and fragrant tropical plants, trees and shrubs, including four floodlit soaring date palms with the trunks bent at an interesting angle.

"Elizabeth was a great gardener," B.B. informed Jessica, sensing her interest. As usual, he didn't even bother to lower his voice. Indeed it bounced off the glass walls. There were guests both in front and behind them, rich, solid, substantial-looking people with a fair sprinkling of very beautiful Eurasian women, all spectacularly gowned. "She was responsible for all this."

"That's so unfair, Dad," Robyn protested, holding up the skirt of her sleek black, silver-trimmed creation. "Erik had considerable input."

"Without actually doing any of the work," B.B. replied with a thin smile. "Erik is a firm believer in not getting his hands dirty."

Jessica cringed in case anyone overheard him, but she realized by now Broderick Bannerman simply didn't care. Such was the fearful power of having a great deal of money.

The plant-filled central atrium was crowded with people who acted absolutely delighted by their arrival. There were lots of beaming hellos, calls of admiration and an outbreak of clapping for the guest of honor, Robyn. The general opinion may have been Robyn was a vain self-centered creature who could turn nasty when threatened, but what the hell! She was B.B.'s stepdaughter and his good will had to be preserved at all costs. It was the way societies all over the world played the game. No one was going to be completely honest. Honesty didn't pay.

Many smiles even came from people who had never forgiven Broderick Bannerman for doing awful things to them in business, but the instant Bannerman passed by, the smiles changed to expressions of bitter envy and in some cases open rage.

What *had* he done? Jessica wondered. Obviously not enough to come under investigation like a couple of mul-timillionaires currently in the news, but then, an investigation would take a lot of digging.

It was odd, therefore, to witness the way Cyrus worked the atrium. If he'd been running for the top position in the Territory, he surely would have been elected. The women loved him, and why not? The men gripped his hand, the smiles apparently genuine. On the one hand a Bannerman who was held in some awe and deep-running hostility, on the other a man who appeared to be universally liked and admired.

The living room was so vast there were still empty gaps between large groups of people. Erik immediately broke away from his circle, coming toward them, his expression so full of warmth it could have melted the polar cap.

"Now the party can begin!" he cried expansively. "Darling, you look sensational!" He kissed Robyn on both cheeks. Lavinia grandly extended her hand; Jessica was welcomed to his "humble abode" and the men shook hands. "I know this is going to be a wonderful night," Erik continued jovially, the picture of prosperity in a double-breasted, beautifully tailored black dinner jacket that hid his slight paunch.

"Ever the optimist," said Broderick Bannerman.

The truth was, Broderick couldn't control the anger that prowled around inside him like a wild beast. Anger seemed to be destroying him these days. Was that inevitable as one progressed into old age? He hated the thought of growing old. There was so much more he had to do. So many future possibilities! An opportunity to redo the past and get wider meaning to his life. He had come to think of it as his second chance.

But she hadn't worn his gift of the earrings.

That affected his self-esteem, his whole view of himself as a winner. He'd been absolutely sure she would. Ferociously ambitious all his life, as well as enormously successful, he couldn't grasp the possibility he couldn't buy anything he wanted. Now the fact that he felt thwarted, *worse*, scorned, did nothing to soothe his jangled nerves. So many forces were at play. He was aware Jessica and his son had reached some kind of an understanding. That manifested itself in ways that caused him anxiety. What was more natural than a young woman turning to a young man—only, no one was going to be allowed to get in his way. Cyrus, especially, who these days only served to remind him his best days were over. *Unless* he could form a new intimate relationship. The fact Jessica so closely resembled Moira would allow him to put the past to rest. Perhaps make amends to a stern God. Ever since he'd laid eyes on Jessica, the possibility had presented itself. He thought of it as his time of *transformation*. He could construct a new identity.

The experiences of his childhood had shattered him. Years had passed in a kind of terror, but he had survived. Not only survived, he had raised the family fortune to new heights. As a prime mover he was a superstar. If he had an eye for a woman, he didn't worry too much about getting her—his money pulled her in. His mirror told him he was still handsome, fit, virile. People called him a dynamo even if these days they didn't fully realize how much Cyrus propped up that image. He was *exactly* the sort of rich man who deserved a beautiful young wife. Fate had robbed him of Deborah. But by God, it wasn't going to rob him of his second chance.

Bannerman felt the hot beating urgency of his own plan. He wasn't in love with her. Nothing so sentimental. Love had little place in his life. But he *wanted* her as an avid collector wanted a centerpiece for his collection. Yet her refusal to accept his gift had left him with a dreadful aching emptiness. And goddammit, his head ached, as well. It ached a lot these days. He put it down to a high level of stress, even if he *had* lived with stress all his life. And he'd forgotten to take his blood-pressure medication.

It was Moira who had brought destruction on his whole family. So beautiful, so full of innocent allure. His father, the war hero, respected by all, had totally lost his head over her, though he had never doubted his father had put up a fight. Loving Deborah as he had, Broderick understood the power of passion. The two of them had simply been carried away. But they would never have run off together. His father had been master of Mokhani. His poor betrayed mother should have sent Moira away. Sometimes his son's resemblance to Steven, his father, turned him inside out. Then there was Hugh Balfour, so tortured and torn he had to escape life.

He had always thought Moira had deserved to die for what she'd done to all of them. But now?

Jessica Tennant was her *blood.* He'd known that instinctively the instant he'd seen her on TV. She might as well have admitted it with her own lips. And she was *real,* not a ghost. That he'd even seen the program was a miracle, and he came to recognize it as fate. He remembered the instant of recognition as an explosion in his head. Then gradually he had begun to see how he could rewrite history. It wasn't difficult for a man in his position to have had gathered for him every scrap of information on her and her family. Families always had secrets. Even from one another. He hadn't been too shocked to find out theirs. After that, everything had fallen into place.

Everyone was a slave to fate. In reaching out to Jessica, Moira's kinswoman, by making her his wife and showering her with all the gifts money could buy when Judgment Day came—he still believed in one, for he'd been through hell, so correspondingly there had to be a heaven— mightn't he be judged less harshly? For a time, after Deborah had been taken from him, he'd been seriously suicidal, but he hadn't been able to go through with it for fear of what lay on the other side. Deep down inside him was a very frightened man. As frightened as a child whose mother had to leave a night-light burning in his room.

JESSICA, SMILING BRIGHTLY as expected, was introduced to a lot of people as the clever young woman B.B. had chosen to decorate the new mansion. She could almost hear the speculation ticking in their heads. No matter how gifted she was as a designer, wasn't she too *young* to have won such a commission? Was it sheer chance she was good-looking, as well? Some reached out to her in a warm, friendly fashion; others, older, shrewd-eyed women probably one-time girl-friends of the great man, appeared cynical. The men looked at her rather too long. She might as well have arrived hanging off B.B.'s arm for all the interest she was creating. Tonight would start a lot of malicious rumors, she thought dismally, and in turn jeopardize the blossoming relationship between her and Cyrus. That *couldn't* be allowed to happen.

Robyn wouldn't like what was happening, either. Robyn in her ultrasophisticated, one-shouldered gown with a gleaming silver trim across the neckline and on the gathered hip, was wearing glittering two-carat diamond studs in her ears. She clung to Erik, who rested his hand for the most part on her taut rounded bottom. Jessica knew she would have asked him to remove it, but Robyn obvi-ously didn't mind.

Hours on, with the party in full swing and many whispers of a possible engagement announcement, Jessica found herself worried Robyn could be in for a bitter disappoint-ment.

She was standing briefly on her own, waiting for Cyrus to return with champagne when Robyn, smiling brilliantly, came up to her. "Oh, Jessica, this is a dear friend of Cy's and mine. Roz Newman. She's just arrived. She had to call in on a family party."

"Hi." A very pretty, dark-haired young woman wearing an absolute knockout of a red dress, made the more so by a push-up bra, held out her hand. "It's lovely to meet you, Jessica. Robyn has told me how clever you are."

"Lovely to meet *you,* Roz," Jessica responded, looking into doe eyes that were warm and friendly. "I'm glad to hear I've done something right. It's an important commission."

"Don't I *know!*" Roz made a moue of her luscious mouth. "Everyone thought Robyn would be handling it. She did such a great job renovating the homestead, but then, she has her businesses to look after. Love your dress. One of Robyn's?"

Jessica did what was clearly expected of her. "Yes." She smiled, holding out the lovely floating skirt.

"That's Robyn. She only caters to the young and lovely."

"Make that *rich,* young and lovely," Robyn said, looking around her. "Where's Cyrus?"

"He'll be back in a moment." Jessica realized that Robyn was moving her friend right into position.

"There he is!" Roz's eyes suddenly glowed like lamps, and her smooth cheeks flushed with pleasure. "I must talk to him. We haven't seen oneanother since Mum and I took off for New York, my favorite city in the whole world. Cyrus!" she caroled, as though Cyrus walking directly toward them holding two glasses of champagne was visually challenged.

"I'll leave you to it," Robyn said. "My beloved is jealous of every minute I'm away from him."

"Robyn must have rocks in her head to even consider him," Roz muttered sotto voce as Robyn moved off.

"Really?" Jessica's ears perked up.

"We all loved Liz," Roz said, becoming aware Jessica was vaguely shocked. "She had it pretty tough with a philanderer like Erik. But Erik will do anything to get onside with B.B. Ah, here's my darling Cy," she said eagerly as Cyrus joined them.

Roz stood on tiptoe and kissed him full on the mouth.

Where there's smoke, there's usually fire, Jessica thought.

"Oh, boy! That was just what I needed!" Roz enthused, tweaking his tanned cheek. "It's *sooooo* wonderful to see you! I missed you like you wouldn't believe. You haven't returned my calls." She cast him a wickedly flirtatious look.

"I fully intended to get around to it," he apologized. "But you know me, Roz. I'm always working."

"Too hard, if you ask me. Are those drinks for us?"

"Roz you look too young to be drinking," he teased, handing one glass to Jessica before giving the other to Roz.

"You know exactly how old I am," Roz said, taking a sip. "Oh, that's glorious!"

"And damned expensive," Cyrus said dryly.

"Erik wants to impress B.B.," Roz gurgled.

Jessica stared at them with a near-disembodied sensation. What did she know of his life, after all? "Look, you two have a lot to catch up on," she said brightly. "I'll see you later."

"You'll be sure to," Cyrus retorted as Jessica all but flew away.

It was the opportunity for Broderick Bannerman to move in. He reached out to grasp Jessica's arm. He was infuriated with his son. So jealous, the heat of it consumed him.

"You've met Roz," he said, powerfully proprietorial in his manner. "Scatty little thing, but she's always been wild about Cyrus. Her mother and father are here. You've probably met them. Max and Sonia Newman of Newman

Industries? Max and I sit on various boards together." He drew her toward the upper balcony, which looked out on the midnight-blue harbor scattered in the moonlight, with a billion sequined dots. "Your dress is beautiful, but the earrings you're wearing spoil the effect."

"I'm sorry. I thought they went well," Jessica said lightly. "I loved the earrings you picked out, Broderick. You have perfect taste, but no way am I deserving of such a valuable, *personal* gift."

"Don't be ridiculous," he said impatiently, fighting to keep his anger under wraps. "If I think you are, you *are!*"

With her instinct for people, Jessica was aware of the terrible tensions that were tearing him apart. He was very flushed in the face. "Do you feel okay?" she asked with concern, staring into his face.

"I'm fine when I'm talking to you." He dropped his hand to close it over hers, an action Jessica was certain was seized on. "This party and the people here are boring me stiff. I don't know what Robyn sees in Erik. He'll never make a tender, loving husband."

"Maybe she's desperate for love," Jessica suggested, withdrawing her hand under the pretext of checking a stray lock of hair. "She seems to be missing out on it."

He laughed roughly. "You amaze me, Jessica. No one else says things like that to my face."

"You were wondering, and I tried to supply a probable answer. Why *does* Robyn persist if she knows you don't approve? I don't think she's in love with him, either."

"Mostly because she's turned thirty," he said dryly. "She's no different from other women. She wants a man. She wants to be married. She's had plenty come courting. *I* didn't send them away, in case you're about to blame me. *She* did. She lost every one of them with her lack of charm. Now, would you care to dance?"

"That would be lovely."

What else could she say? She had to handle this situation as carefully as she'd handle a hive of hornets.

THINGS DIDN'T GET BETTER, they got worse. Roz Newman set about making up for lost time. Time and again, she attempted to chain Cyrus to her side, though to Jessica's immense relief she was far from successful.

"Ever tried saying no?" she suggested sweetly when Cyrus groaned. They were dancing.

His embrace tightened. He was a terrific dancer. "You might try doing the same with Dad."

Broderick Bannerman had continued to pay his strange court to Jessica. Already it had set tongues clacking like knitting needles. Was B.B. looking for a trophy wife? Would she be the one? As the night wore on, B.B. wasn't the only man who made a pass at her. Serious, solidly respectable types did, too. It was as Jessica had come to accept. Men behaved badly around blondes.

There was no engagement announcement before or after the sumptuous supper featuring the superb seafood of these tropical waters. Didn't Erik Moore see that's what Robyn had pinned her hopes on? Didn't he care? Did he think B.B.'s disapproval would in the end work against him? Who could tell? Robyn's rigid expression revealed that Erik had taken a massive swipe at her ego. Jessica sincerely hoped she would dump him and afterward seriously consider charm school.

It was Lavinia, who was having a fine old time catching up with all the gossip, who brought the evening to a spectacular end. She was seated on a comfortable sofa with a few older ladies, stately stalwarts of Darwin society, when she called to Jessica from halfway across the room.

"Moira, dear! Yoohoo!" There was little hope no one heard her even in a very large room. Lavinia's voice was her splendor. It had been big enough to project to the bleachers in her prime. To add to it, she held up her hand, setting several antique bracelets tolling like temple bells. "Come and meet my friends."

The whole area took a collective breath.

Moira?

The laughter, the animated conversation turned off like a tap. They might have all been waiting for a cataclysmic announcement.

"Funny old thing!" someone said, giving a nervous giggle.

"Moira, did you hear me, dear?" Lavinia raised the decibels as if she wanted to crack glass.

Another woman muttered an obscene word beneath, her breath and her husband looked at her in astonishment. "Carole!"

"What the hell am I supposed to say?" Carole retaliated, although she wished she hadn't been shocked into a swear word. "That Lavinia frightens me to death."

"It's Alzheimer's," another woman said sorrowfully. "The family is in for a tough time."

Farther away Broderick Bannerman looked up from a discussion with a couple of his business cronies, the hectic flush on his face deepening further.

"That's just dandy," Cyrus muttered in Jessica's ear. "Frankly I don't know how we got through this much of the night."

"I better go to her," Jessica said, horrified to be the focus of hundreds of eyes. "She'll only persist."

"Yes. I guess they can hear her at city hall." Cyrus realized with a jolt that his father looked furious. But, hell, wouldn't it be fair to say it was on their own heads, bringing Lavinia? Without question, she was suffering some form of dementia, but why should she be condemned to stay at home? She was *family,* even if she was border-line nuts.

Cyrus and Jessica walked toward Lavinia as one. "Livvy, dear, perhaps we should consider making a move," he prompted gently, leaning over the sofa and clasping Lavinia's bony shoulder. "It's well after twelve. You must be tired."

"Just a teeny bit." Lavinia laughed, fighting to get up before someone helped her. "Josie, you remember Moira, don't you?" She addressed a very smart septuagenarian with beautifully coiffed platinum hair.

"Jessica Tennant," Jessica smiled at the woman.

"She's all grown-up," Lavinia said. "I've waited over fifty years."

Josie patted Lavinia's cheek. "You aren't supposed to talk about Moira anymore, dear," she chided affectionately, herself forcibly struck by Jessica's extraordinary resemblance to the missing girl. "She's dead, darling."

"No, *no!*" Lavinia's voice took on a soaring wail. "She was just hiding. Weren't you, Moira?"

"Why don't you find Robyn and Erik? Tell them we're leaving," Cyrus suggested to Jessica in a low voice, quickly getting an arm around Lavinia.

"Robyn looks so damned unhappy," Lavinia moaned. "He might have been toying with the idea of marrying her, trying to work out if it was the right move, but he won't now. Broderick is against it. Probably the kindest stand Broderick's taken in his whole life."

"We'll say our good nights." Cyrus flashed the group the charming smile that worked miracles. He expected and got their understanding. It wasn't until the very last minute the woman called Josie caught Jessica's hand.

"Poor old Liv! No wonder she's confused. You're the very image of Moira, my dear. Is there any connection? I can't help wondering."

"I'm sorry, none." Jessica said. She could see that the woman didn't quite believe her.

B.B. GESTURED FOR THEM to meet him in the central atrium, which was diplomatically cleared in seconds, though the partygoers were dying to stay and watch. Everyone knew the Bannermans weren't like anybody else. And old Lavinia, bless her, was good for a laugh at any time. She was what Darwin society thought of as a real character, a welcome eccentric.

"You can't be trusted, Lavinia, can you?" B.B. bore down on her, his deep voice thin with anger.

"About what?" Lavinia demanded to know, turning fearlessly toward that hard face and glittering eyes.

"Please leave it, Dad." Cyrus had an authority all his own. "At least until we get out of here. I'll take her back to the hotel. I won't be coming back to the party. Robyn and Erik won't mind."

"You don't intend on leaving, as well, do you, Jessica?" Bannerman whipped around to ask, his tone oddly vulnerable.

A strange sense of sympathy flowed through her. She could hardly claim to like him—he didn't allow anyone to like him—but she was trying hard to understand him. "I'm only in the way, Broderick. People are talking. Robyn won't want me around."

"Don't worry about *her,* Moira," Lavinia advised, opening her evening bag and putting away her glasses.

"You always were a tender hearted little thing. It will all pass like a nine-day wonder."

Robyn rushed out from the living room in a fury. "God, I swear I'm going to scream! Lavinia isn't eccentric, she's barking *mad.* I told you, Dad, it was a mistake to let her come. She's made a show of us all."

"And you're about to make another one." Broderick shrugged a powerful shoulder as though he couldn't care less.

Cyrus, however, spoke to Robyn in an undertone. "Hey, the biggest mistake is your hooking up with Moore. Leave Livvy alone. She can't help what's happened to her mind. Jessica *is* the image of Moira, after all."

Jessica's heart skipped many beats. In her ear came a long, soft sigh. She wondered where it'd come from.

Broderick Bannerman stared at his son, his formerly flushed face now drained of color. "And how would *you* know?" he asked.

"By checking. Just like you, Dad." Cyrus locked eyes with his father. "What did you think you were doing, putting a portrait of Moira on the market? What did you hope to achieve?"

Bannerman's handsome features went slack for a few moments, then he laughed harshly. "I don't have to explain myself to you."

"Maybe you could explain it to *me,* then, Broderick," Jessica said, her sympathy evaporating. "It upsets me you didn't hire me for my professional skills. I could have been puttering away in my office earmarked for failure, for all you cared."

"That's not true." Broderick looked momentarily off balance. He searched Jessica's face for understanding. "I hired you because you've achieved recognition in your profession. Look, we can't argue here. You'd better go. Please remember, Jessica, that you signed a contract. You're obliged to finish the job. If you doubt it, you should have devoted yourself to reading the fine print."

Robyn stabbed a finger at Lavinia. "I could kill you," she cried emotionally. "You're a real witch."

Lavinia trilled aloud. "Takes one to know one," she retorted, quite unmoved.

A nerve twitched near Robyn's eye. She continued to accompany them down the stairs. "You have no business being allowed out, Lavinia."

"More of us out than in, Robyn," Lavinia told her sweetly.

"It was all destined," Broderick muttered.

"More like planned." Cyrus gave a short, angry laugh. "You've got a lot to answer for, Dad. You might have been only a kid, but you didn't escape it all. I think you know— or you learned—what happened to that poor girl."

"Yes, who did it?" Lavinia, showing her vocal range, toned her voice down to a whisper. "Did she die from a fall? Was it an accident?"

"Hello, you're *with* us, are you?" Broderick asked of his aunt, not without humor.

"Livvy, please stop." Cyrus spoke so firmly Lavinia responded by zipping her fingers across her mouth. "This conversation has to continue at another time."

"Trust me, it *won't!*" Broderick whipped out a snowy handkerchief and mopped his broad brow. "And don't take that tone with me, Cyrus." It was obvious he was barely keeping himself in check. "I *forbid* you to take Jessica."

"That's a pity, because take her is what I intend to do," Cyrus returned curtly. "It's what Jessica wants, after all. Let's finish this right now." He grasped both Jessica and Lavinia by the hand, then inclined his head toward the living room. "They must be just loving it inside. The feuding Bannermans. Have you heard what they're up to now?" He exhaled in disgust. "Let's face it, Dad. You don't inspire trust."

This charge suddenly reminded Robyn of her dearest role in life. She linked her arm through her stepfather's, chin up, eyes flashing, the picture of loyalty. "*I* know Dad better than *you* do, Cy!" she exploded. "I love him, unlike *you*. You don't deserve to be his heir. You're staying, aren't you, Dad?" She turned, imploring eyes on her stepfather, though he was standing stock-still, seemingly unaware of her. "Don't abandon me."

"Quit sucking up to him, Robyn," Lavinia advised. "It does no good at all."

That brought Broderick out of his semi-trance. "I'll stay for another hour," he said, his face impassive. "In my opinion, Erik humiliated you tonight, Robyn. But don't worry, he'll pay."

"That's right, make 'em pay, Brodie," Lavinia crowed as Cyrus and Jessica led her away. "You should get on with your own life, Robyn. The *D*-word comes around quicker than you think."

"What's the *D*-word?" Robyn frowned in perplexity.

It was possible there was great sadness in Broderick Bannerman's answering voice. "*Death,*" he said.

CHAPTER THIRTEEN

THEY WALKED TOGETHER along the waterfront with the trade winds blowing in off the Timor Sea. The great copper moon of the tropics hung over the vast expanse of the harbor cutting a bright orange path from the glittering water to the sky. It was a beautiful night with a lovely breeze that strengthened into intermittent gusts. It caught at Jessica's long hair and silk chiffon skirt, ruffling the surface of the water into peaks that broke in white ruffles on the shore.

Their minds, still frazzled by the events of the evening, they were just trying to relax. They had finally got Lavinia to bed—she'd been overexcited, difficult to calm—and now both Jessica and Cyrus recognized that either this thing mounting between them had to stop, or become a serious commitment. Nothing this desperate stood still.

"How did you know your father had sent Moira's portrait to auction?" Jessica asked, watching a pair of lovers blend into the night. "You didn't tell me."

"I *didn't* know," he said wretchedly "Dad just fell into the trap." Cyrus cursed himself for what he had to say. "You know you can't remain on Mokhani, Jessica, no matter what threats my father makes. I'll take care of all that. If you *don't* go, we're headed for an almighty showdown."

They were her own thoughts; nevertheless, she was

devastated to hear him put them into words. "Hang on a minute. I've scarcely arrived." The fact he was urging her to go, with good reasons or not, sliced into her like a knife. She had fallen crazily in love with him. She was ready to take her chances. Now he wanted to see her off.

Cyrus caught her into the half circle of his arm, so attuned to her he knew what was running through her head. "I know. It's one hell of a mess, but it's just too explosive. You *know* it is." There was a ragged edge to his voice. "I'm worried about you and I'm worried about my father. I've never seen him like this before. He's getting like Livvy. Mixing up the past with the present. Did you see how flushed he was tonight?"

She nodded, not trusting herself to speak, she was so agitated. "He lives under such pressure," she managed to say after a while. "It can't be good for him. Now there's this problem of *me*. Something *new* is driving him."

"You don't have to be Einstein to work it out." Cyrus's voice grated. "When Livvy looks at you, she sees Moira. It seems Dad does, too, in a way. Obviously, he's never been able to forget her. Maybe he's trying to bring Moira back. God, I don't know, but I don't like it."

Jessica shook her windblown hair from her face. "Do you suppose Moira could have been murdered all those years ago?"

Cyrus's groan was eloquent of unhappiness and confusion. "She disappeared, Jessica. This mystery will never go cold."

"Is that a yes?"

"It's a *no!*" He turned her to him almost desperately. "We're talking about *my* family, remember? *My* blood."

Tension was crackling like the flames of a bonfire. "I'm sorry."

They walked on, reaching a moon-washed clearing like a small park. Her stiletto heels dug into the grass as they moved off the pathway into the deep sapphire gloom. Colors of flowers came out of the darkness. Color and heady tropical scent. She could see timber benches.

"Jessica?"

She lifted her face to him with breathless urgency, her feelings for him invading every part of her, wiping out anger. "What?"

He stared down into her shimmering face "*You.* Just you." In his world gone mad, she seemed to be the only thing he could hold on to. He bent his head, kissing the side of her satin cheek, burying his face in her neck. "You smell like a field of flowers."

The way he said it was so seductive, so utterly thrilling it went a long way toward restoring her badly shaken confidence. She wanted to beg him to make love to her, furious with Broderick Bannerman for pursuing her and thus ruining everything....

"Hey." He lifted his head. "Are you getting shorter or what?"

She held on to him with a little shaky laugh. "My high heels are digging into the grass. I'm sinking. There's a bench around here someplace." She felt she had to sit down. *Lie* down. Her breathing had changed—short, faintly panting.

"So there is." Without warning, he lifted her high in his arms as if her weight were insubstantial. The bench was set on a concrete block. He lowered her gently onto it, keeping his arms around her. "You should wear that dress always. Though if I had you to myself, I'd peel it off you."

"When will that ever be?" she asked mournfully, aware the parameters of her world had shifted. She was so much in love with him she was ready to do things perhaps she shouldn't. Cyrus Bannerman was her one great leap into the unknown.

"Can't be soon enough," he said fervently. "I want *you* no matter how much baggage keeps getting in the way."

"Why should we let it?" That golden moon hovered over them, like a pathway to heaven. She lifted her arms, drew down his dark head.

Why indeed!

When he finally stopped kissing her, it was only to mutter, "I think we should finish this in your room—or *my* room?"

"What happens when your father comes looking for us?" she asked in a voice verging on edgy laughter. "God knows he's capable of it."

"We don't answer." Cyrus was almost afraid of what he might say and do if his father pushed him too far. The idea of his father wanting this young woman he had come to love drove him crazy. Clashes with his father were one thing, but this was so dreadfully inappropriate. "Kissing you is wonderful," he murmured. "You weave such a spell. Look at this hair!" He speared a hand through the pale moonlit tresses in wonderment. "I want to see your hair spread out on my pillow. You can wear your earrings—they're very pretty, after all, but nothing else." He twisted a long coil of her hair around her throat. "You'll make an exquisite bride."

Jessica's heart rocked in her breast. "Is that a proposal?"

"Why would someone like you want to marry into my family?" he asked with near despair. "Mokhani isn't a safe place for beautiful young women. Beauty seduces. Just as in the fairy tales, it can also carry a curse."

"Don't *say* that!" She put her fingers against his mouth.

He caught them and kissed them. "A world lost for love! I see nothing. I hear nothing. All there is, is *you* all around *me*."

"I might use the very same words," she whispered.

"I never want to let you go. I *won't* let you go." He stood up, pulling her to her feet. Their hunger for each other swept all before it. Tonight they were on the crest of a wave....

AS THEY HEADED BACK to the hotel, cars whizzed back and forth, couples strolled arm in arm or came out of restaurants, laughing, ready to go on to nightclubs.

"So much we have to get to the bottom of," Cyrus said. "Dad knows a lot he's not telling."

"Why don't you try to speak to your aunt Barbara again?" Jessica hugged his arm, thinking for all that was happening she had never been aware of such happiness.

He sighed deeply. "My aunt finds the whole subject of Moira and her disappearance too painful. Not that she'd know anything. Whatever happened would have been kept from the children."

"Unless your father saw what happened with his own eyes," she found herself suggesting, albeit in a fuzzy way. Certainly she'd made no decision to say it.

"God, no!" A convulsive shudder went through Cyrus's lean body. "He *couldn't* have been there. Dad was only seven. He would have been able to ride, of course, but he'd have been forbidden to venture too far from the main compound. From all accounts, there was a bad thunderstorm that day, as well. I've gone over and over this, Jessica. Dad couldn't have been out there."

"Could he have gone with someone who was?" The compulsion to ask these questions was worsening. She couldn't contain them.

He flinched, his arm tightening around her. "My grandmother or my grandfather?" he asked bitterly.

"I know how upsetting this is for you," she said quickly. "It was only a suggestion."

"I want a life *free* of the past, Jessica. You've affected us all so much. But we now know your coming to Mokhani was planned by my father. The great irony is I have to thank him for that, otherwise our paths would never have crossed. Dad's getting you to Mokhani had little to do with decorating the mausoleum. I don't want to offend you, but he probably didn't care if you turned out to be the worst designer in the length and breadth of Australia. He hired you to rework his *life* in some way. It's almost as though he's trying to rewrite history. But nothing makes sense. I can't begin to understand his motives. I'm horrified Dad has become fixated on you. He doesn't want *me* to get in the way.... Oh, hell, what's the use of talking about it? I don't want to talk. I want to make love."

"You shouldn't have to be in conflict with your father over me. It's not *meant* to be that way," Jessica cried. "I love *you!*"

WHEN THEY ARRIVED BACK at the hotel, they found Broderick waiting for them in the lobby. The minute he saw them, he heaved himself to his feet.

Cyrus swore beneath his breath. Jessica felt she could swim an ocean to get away. The unthinkable was becoming a daily occurrence.

Broderick approached, his shoulders hunched. "All right, so you're back!" He glared at his son, so cruelly young and handsome. God, if he had his time over again! he thought. Aging was a whiplash across a man's back. Jessica appeared to float, a lovely fluid motion to her skirt, her eyes brimming with emotion.

But not for *him*.

She was Moira, only different. Stronger, far more confident, knowing her place in the world. The tears would never dry for Moira. Moira lying so secret, so hidden away from the world.

"Don't do this, Dad," Cyrus muttered, between clenched teeth. "How can you sit here waiting for us like we were children?"

"I'll remind you, Cyrus, Jessica is *my* responsibility," Broderick said aloud, in a hostile voice.

Jessica noticed several other hotel guests looking their way. She squirmed inside. "You must excuse me," she said in haste. "I'm tired. I'm going to my room." She didn't fancy getting her picture in the noon papers.

"We'll all go up," Cyrus said briskly.

Broderick didn't say another word until they were in the elevator. Just the three of them in a claustrophobic space. "It may seem an odd thing for me to do, Jessica," Broderick said, apparently in an effort to apologize to her. "But your well-being is important to me."

"It's highly unlikely I'd come to any harm with Cyrus, Broderick," she said. "Besides, I can take care of myself." She didn't want to say another word, sensing they were on the brink of a terrible argument. It couldn't be good for Broderick. His color wasn't good. In the space of a few hours, he'd aged ten years. All the virility had seeped out of him.

"You know Cyrus is involved with Roz Newman?" he announced abruptly. "Am I wrong, Cyrus?" he challenged. "I rather think she's expecting an engagement ring sometime soon."

"And she's as likely to get one as Robyn." Cyrus issued a humorless laugh. "What are you on about, Dad?"

"You know damn well!" Broderick snarled. "It's for Jessica's own good."

"I'm sorry. This is my floor." Jessica took quick steps forward. "It's best if I say good night."

She wasn't swift enough.

"Not yet!" Broderick grasped her bare arm, restraining her. The door closed while they all stood arrested. "I want you to come up to my suite."

"Oh, Dad!" Cyrus groaned, shaking his dark head. His formidable father, always cold reason, seemed to be disintegrating right before his very eyes. "What's going on with you?" He began to wonder if dementia was going to overtake the entire family.

"What do my actions possibly have to do with you?" Broderick said through gritted teeth.

"I'm your son, remember?"

"So maybe I want your support, not your opposition."

"To do *what?*" Cyrus appealed to him. "Can you let us know what's on your mind?"

"I don't trust you, Cyrus," his father snapped.

"Around Jessica, is that what you mean?" Cyrus watched the high color flare into his father's face. "I take it that's a yes," he said quietly.

They had arrived at the top floor where Broderick had his suite. Still clutching Jessica's arm, he stepped out into the empty hallway, Cyrus right behind. Broderick turned Jessica to face him. "I thought you liked me, Jessica." Incredibly he spoke like a suitor who having been led on, was left bitterly confused and disappointed.

"Of course I like you, Broderick," Jessica said, sick with pity and embarrassment. "But first and foremost you're my client."

Their voices were hushed, but the atmosphere couldn't have been more intense.

"That's the only reason I got you to Mokhani," he explained, never taking his eyes off her. "So we could get to know one another."

Jessica dropped her head, quite unable to meet his gaze. He had placed her in a terrible position. "I can't talk about it anymore. I had no idea your thoughts were running on those lines. You actually got me to Mokhani under false pretenses, Broderick. I was so excited to get such a commission, too. I've done so much work already. All for nothing! Cyrus is right. I must go home."

"Go home?" Broderick's eyes flashed with shock and rage.

"You don't leave her with much alternative, Dad," said Cyrus. "There can't be any relationship between you and Jessica." He stretched out his hand to his father in sympathy.

But Broderick ignored the gesture. "You envy me, Cyrus. Envy fills your heart. Envy of one's father is a terrible thing."

"It's the other way around in our case," Cyrus said with weary sadness. "I don't envy you at all. You may have achieved a great deal in your life, but you're not a happy man. You've given everyone, including yourself, such a hard time. Let's end this discussion. Call it a night. You can't expect Jessica to want to stay on when you're starting to harass her."

"Harass her?" Broderick spat. "How dare you!" He shook his head like some sovereign of old, ready and able to put his own son's head on the block. "How dare you say such a thing! It's not *right!*" He twisted his body, shaking his head from side to side.

Tears were forming in Jessica's eyes. "Please stop, Broderick," she begged, laying a restraining hand on his arm. "You don't look at all well. You must see I can't stay."

Arrogance flooded Broderick Bannerman's expression. "My son is acting like he's trying to protect you. He really just wants you for himself."

"And you have a big problem with that, don't you, Dad?"

"You've always hated me, Cyrus."

Cyrus's handsome face contorted in distress. "God, Dad, we're *family*. The wonder is I *don't* hate you. You've always treated me like the enemy even when Mum was alive. You seemed to see me as a rival for her love and attention, isn't that right? You turned your back on me when I was just a kid. You didn't change even after she was dead."

Broderick's head shook as though he had palsy. "You can't know how desperately unhappy that made me."

"You could have turned to me, your son." Cyrus got a grip on his father's shoulder. "But that didn't cross your mind. You set out to bring me to my knees. I might have been another man's son. That really worried me when I was a kid, do you know that? I seriously considered I might have been a bastard. That would explain your behavior. But I look like you, don't I? I also look like my grandfather, Steven. I'm the Bannerman you rejected."

His father looked a bit mad. "With good reason. You're the—"

"Broderick, *stop*." Jessica put herself between the two men. "Somewhere deep down, Broderick, I think you hate yourself."

It was a statement that seemed to strike Broderick Bannerman like a blow. He closed his eyes as though he were in terrible pain and slumped as if pierced through with a sword. "I do. You're right, I do," he muttered.

"Let's go, Jessica." Cyrus reached for her.

But like a man possessed, Broderick changed suddenly from passive to violent.

"Cyrus!" Jessica shouted the warning, but it was too late.

With a look of savage hatred in his eyes, his fist clenched, Broderick Bannerman launched himself at his son, screaming, "Do you understand what you've done to me? *Do you?* Treason—"

Almost without volition, Cyrus swung a defensive punch. It sent his father sprawling back against the wall, from there to the floor, where he slumped into a posture of defeat.

Immediately Cyrus felt an overwhelming disgust for himself. He stretched out his hand. "Get up, Dad. I shouldn't have done that. Neither should you."

His face marred by a look of terrible bitterness and defeat, Broderick allowed himself to be pulled to his feet. "Damn you to hell!" he swore.

"I'm sorry I hit you." The words were flat.

"We've got nothing to say to each other," his father snarled. "Take her if you want her. She's not who she says she is, anyway. She's Moira back from the other side."

It was meant to be a deadly parting shot, only Broderick staggered, clutching at his head with his two hands.

"Aaaaaaaah!"

"Dad!" Cyrus cried in alarm.

"Go to hell," Bannerman said, still clutching his head.

Cyrus turned to Jessica. "Call an ambulance," he said urgently, moving to his father to physically support him.

She needed no prompting.

CHAPTER FOURTEEN

OVER THE NEXT FEW DAYS, the family fielded innumerable questions from the media about Broderick Bannerman's condition. Finally Cyrus had to take the phone off the hook. Their stock answer had been the same as the spokesman's for the Royal Darwin Hospital. Mr. Bannerman was resting comfortably. He had not suffered a heart attack or a stroke. He would be in hospital a day or two, undergoing tests.

A media crew drove all the way from Darwin to the station, but got turned back by stockmen acting as security guards. A media helicopter flew over the main compound, taking aerial shots, but the pilot wasn't about to risk landing. This was the Territory and strangers didn't come onto a man's land without an invitation. B.B. especially had to be treated with respect.

What Broderick Bannerman was really suffering from was a tumor growing in the right posterior temporal region of his brain, dangerously close to the brain stem. This information was not released to the press. The tumor would most certainly paralyze him, cause deafness, blindness, in short, kill him if not removed or treated by chemotherapy, which he refused. Broderick Bannerman had elected to take his chances with an operation. His doctors gave him only a fifty percent chance of survival.

It seemed the family had found the explanation for the patriarch's frenzied behavior.

"So this is when we say goodbye to Broderick," Lavinia announced, crossing herself in a rare moment of religious fervor. "Who would ever have thought I might outlive him? I'm old, old, old. A nuisance to everyone, including myself. He was a beautiful little boy. Steven's heir. We all thought he was going to be fine. It's what happened to Moira that tore the family apart. Even now Barbara won't come to Mokhani, although she visited the hospital." Lavinia was seated in her favorite planter's chair on the front veranda. Jessica had taken a chair near her, holding the frail hand with its knotted fingers. The skin around the contours of Lavinia's eyes was a murky violet, but the eyes themselves were bright. Jessica had the idea Lavinia played a lot at being batty. "You should ask him before it's too late," Lavinia said.

"Ask him what, Miss Lavinia?" Jessica tried to smile into the old lady's face.

"What they did with you, of course."

That blew the notion of not being batty out of the water.

A little distance off in the trees, a bird sang one beautiful heart-piercing note.

Jessica stood up. "I think I hear the phone. It could be Cyrus." Cyrus was in Darwin meeting with the eminent neurosurgeon who was to head the team to perform the very difficult and risky operation on his father.

It wasn't Cyrus. It was Brett, saying he couldn't leave until the weekend, but he and Tim were coming up to join her and take her home.

"You need to be looked after, Jass," he told her, his voice filled with concern. "You sound unhappy."

"I seem to have been through a lot." A lot she hadn't told him.

"It's scarcely your fault, sweetheart." Brett tried to console her. "The tumor has probably been growing for years. Cyrus will probably want to continue the project at some point, but that will be the last thing on his mind with his father so ill. And right in the middle of it, you win the award. You have to show up for the ceremony, you know. Life goes on, no matter what. We have to celebrate it. I'm very proud of you."

ROBYN WAS TAKING her stepfather's illness very badly. In fact, she looked like she was coming apart, lost in silent, secret, desperation.

Jessica no longer doubted Robyn loved her stepfather. She was not prepared, however, for Robyn's anger. "He doesn't want to see me anymore!" she screamed at Jessica, having sent Lavinia rushing to her room as though she couldn't lock the door fast enough. "I'm nothing to him. *No one.* I never have been."

"He doesn't want to see Cyrus, either," Jessica tried to point out. Facing death, Broderick had turned in on himself. "He's not clear in his mind."

"No, he's not." Abruptly she changed topics. "So who are you really?" Robyn stared at Jessica with her deep-set dark eyes.

Jessica sighed. "Not a ghost, Robyn. It's all gone far enough, this Moira business. Your stepfather has an excuse. He's been diagnosed with a brain tumor. Lavinia's excuse is—"

"She's mad as a bloody hatter," Robyn interrupted bitterly. "God, why doesn't the old bat die? Oh no, she's got plans to stick around for Cyrus's wedding when it's just possible he won't get married for years he's so bloody choosy. Look, I've got to get out of the house. Why don't we go for a ride?"

"If you want to," Jessica agreed, not really wanting to, but realizing Robyn was suffering in her own way.

WHEN THE STABLE BOY led out Chloe, Robyn turned abruptly. "I don't like that horse. It's bad-tempered. Take her back."

"It's for Miss Jessica," the boy said. "She rides him."

Robyn stared at Jessica with something like outrage. "Since when?"

"Since Cyrus took me to the escarpment," Jessica said, having second thoughts about accompanying this volatile young woman. Robyn delighted in baiting Lavinia about her eccentricities. Was it possible Robyn was bipolar? She certainly had huge mood swings. "It was when you were in Hong Kong."

"Congratulations. So how did you manage to stay on?" Robyn gave a twisted smile, laced with challenge.

"She's better than you," the stable boy piped up, digging his hands into his jeans.

"Oh, shut up." Viciously Robyn flicked her whip at him but he moved out of range with natural agility. "Who's asking you?" she growled.

"Only tryin' to help." Unperturbed, the boy gave Jessica a big white grin.

"Don't worry, Robyn, I'll keep up," Jessica said. "I don't think we should go all that far. Cy is due home late afternoon."

"You're involved with him, aren't you?" Robyn swung her leg over her mount, a big gelding. Her tone was despairing, as though she could prevent nothing.

Jessica turned the question aside. "Cy's thoughts are only for his father."

AN HOUR AND MORE LATER, they were lost in the vastness that was Mokhani.

"Somewhere around here that blasted Moira's life came to an end." Robyn sat her horse, one hand on the reins, the other indicating the primal wilderness surrounding them. "I suppose if the truth be known, someone killed her. I can just see it happening. She was very pretty, from all accounts."

Jessica shuddered. "Do you really believe someone in your family was capable of murder?"

"Not *my* family!" Robyn gave a bitter laugh. "I have something to be grateful for, it seems. My poor mother was a saint. She put up with Dad, who treated her like dirt, just a possible brood mare Dad could never get his adored Deborah out of his memory. He even turned on Cy, his own son. I ask you, is that crazy or what? Anyway, there's been some haunting in this family. The legend of bloody Moira has survived the test of time."

"She ought not be *bloody* Moira, Robyn. She was a victim and so young!" Jessica stared out over the immense primeval landscape. Its extraordinary mystique was palpable. It wasn't just the wonder of nature, the vastness or the savage beauty. It was the *antiquity* of the Timeless Land, the oldest continent on earth.

They were taking shelter beneath the branches of the loveliest of all the Outback trees, the slender white ghost gums. A grove of six or more were growing luxuriantly out of the sand, highlighting the rust-red of the soil, the golden grasses that sprung out of it and the burnt siennas of the boulders strewn about like discarded devils' marbles. To the northeast, the purple escarpment stood out ruggedly against the brilliant cobalt sky. She marveled that she had actually been right to the summit. She'd walked the length of that magical canyon with its rainbow walls, caught the spray off the waterfall, pondered the mysteries of the deep dark green lagoon where the spirit of a beautiful *lubra* had made her home.

"It's easy to see how Moira could have disappeared." Jessica spoke her thoughts aloud. "Someone who didn't know the bush would be in a lot of danger out here."

Robyn's expression was chilling. "Easy to bury the body. We have cases of disappearance right now in the present. That English tourist—they'll never find him."

"What a great grief for his family." Jessica drew a deep sigh. "Moira's family must have been devastated. I don't think they could have faced the notion she might have been murdered. They had enough of a nightmare to contend with. I've never asked you about what happened to *your* mother, Robyn. You must have loved her dearly."

Robyn hunched forward in the saddle, frowning. "I did. She comes to me in my dreams. But when she was alive, she was little use to me. She was completely dominated by Dad."

"How did she die?" Jessica asked again, very gently.

Robyn's face, inexplicably, became distorted by anger. "Curious, are you?"

"I'm sorry." Jessica hastened to apologize. "I was actually trying to help. Sometimes it lightens the load if you can share it with someone. You haven't had an easy time, Robyn."

Robyn's eyes brimmed. "Don't feel sorry for me. Feel sorry for yourself. Cyrus is only using you. You're nothing in the scheme of things. Just a passing affair. He doesn't give a damn about you, really."

"I don't think you're in his confidence," Jessica said. She trusted Cyrus. She knew she was right to trust him. This was a clumsy attempt to undermine him.

"I know this much." Robyn looked at Jessica, hard-eyed. "He's going to marry Roz Newman. He doesn't need you. He needs Mokhani . He's there in Darwin pouring out filial love, but he's too late. Dad will see I get what I deserve."

"You can't be implying he'll make you his heir?"

Robyn gave a convulsive laugh that petered out. "Cyrus hitting on you was a disastrous move. It upset Dad greatly. From that moment, things started going well for me."

"I thought you wanted to marry Erik Moore." Jessica endeavored to follow Robyn's reasoning.

She shrugged. "Dad was right. He isn't worthy of me. Liz did try to warn me."

Jessica shook her head. "Don't you think it strange your stepfather doesn't want to see you now? Perhaps he was building up your hopes, Robyn, only to knock them down. A tumor affects the sufferer's behavior, sometimes in a disastrous way. I would say even before that, your stepfather liked to pull the rug out from under people."

"He's famous for it," Robyn confirmed. "People have warned me a thousand times but I was blind. Dad seemed like a god to me when I was a kid. My judgments were all wrong. I picked the wrong Bannerman to be my champion." Robyn sank in the saddle as though all the air had gone out of her body. "Cyrus tried to bond with me, God knows he got precious little love from his dad, but I shut him out. You know why? There's something dread-fully wrong with me. I'm even *happy* in a way that Dad's dying—put him out of his misery. He's said some rotten things to me. If there is a heaven, which I seriously doubt, Mum will be there. Dad, I'm thinking, is heading straight for hell."

THE SUN SANK IN A BLAZING BALL of fire toward a horizon brushed with great sweeps of pinks, golds, indigo and grape. The mauve dusk settled in quickly. They didn't seem to be getting anywhere. How was it possible for Robyn to get lost? She'd grown up on Mokhani. The horses were tired and sweating, especially the filly, Chloe.

Robyn ripped off her Akubra and smoothed her shiny black hair in agitation. "Listen, I have to go for help. You stay put. You'll just be holding me up."

"You don't expect me to stay here by myself, do you?" Jessica looked nervously around her, amazed that the Outback-bred Robyn seemed as disoriented as she was.

"You're not scared, are you?" Robyn taunted.

"I think anyone in their right mind would be. It's pitch black at night. There's no water. We haven't seen any dingoes, but I'm sure they're about. What about snakes? Are you sure you're not doing this deliberately? You want to punish me for some reason? You said yourself there's something wrong with you."

"Don't be so bloody stupid," Robyn snarled. "Cyrus will be home. He'll be expecting us back. All you have to do is stay put. That's the first rule in the bush. When someone knows the area you're in, you stay there. You don't move off. I'll ride back as fast as I can. I can cope a lot better without you and the filly tagging along. She's tired. She doesn't have the stamina of the gelding. Cyrus will be only too happy to come back for you. You might even rate a night under the stars. Make the most of it. It's all you're going to get."

ROBYN ARRIVED BACK at the homestead to a very hostile reception.

"Explain yourself, Robyn. And fast." Cyrus's voice

carried the strain of their wait. "You rode out together. Where's Jessica?" Cyrus generated such anger it was like a fire had been lit inside him.

"Yes, where is she?" Lavinia ran at Robyn raining blows on her. "Don't lie to us, you wicked girl. Where's Moira?"

Robyn ground her teeth with fury. "It's *Jessica*, you crazy old bat. You should have been locked up long ago. Jessica is where I left her. It's all her fault, wanting to wander around on her own, taking no notice of the time. She could easily have ridden back with me if she'd tried, but she's just a soft city girl. She's out by Wirra Creek. At least that's where I left her. I told her to stay put."

"You better not be lying to us, girl." Lavinia stared up at Robyn, wild-eyed.

It *was* a lie. Robyn had long felt she was under no obligation to tell the truth. All her efforts these long years, her bids for love and respect proved futile.

"Why the hell would I? You're nuts!"

Lavinia shook her head grimly. "You're not so sane, either."

Cyrus's voice cut them off like the crack of a whip. "Livvy, you'd better go up to your room. I'll come and see you the minute I get back with Jessica. Robyn, I'd advise you to leave Livvy well alone or you'll answer to me."

"I will, will I?" Robyn shouted, her face twisted with bitterness. "Let's have it. Dad's told you you're his heir?"

"He hasn't said a word." Cyrus regarded his stepsister with contempt. "And if I am, that's as it should be. You're not going to get anyone to disagree with that. But take heart, you won't be left out. I'll take the helicopter. You made Jessica understand the importance of staying where she was?"

"What do you think I am?" she asked with weary disgust. "Of course I told her. She mightn't have listened."

"You'd better be telling the truth." Cyrus was nearing the end of his tether.

"Yeah, yeah. Go to her," Robyn yelled. "It's pretty damned dark out there."

OVERHEAD, WATERFOWL, myriads of them, were flying in formation, squadrons of them at various heights, darkening the already fading sky. Jessica kept looking until they disappeared from sight. They were heading for water. Without water, all creatures died.

I can't sit around waiting for help, she thought. *I have to get myself settled in case I'm stuck here for the night.* In her saddlebag she had a canteen of water, a couple of teabags, two crisp Granny Smith apples, and a few little packets of dried fruit—sultanas and apricots. She had even found a box of matches right at the bottom of the saddlebag, though she hadn't put them there. Maybe one of the stable boys stealing a quick smoke while he was out exercising the filly.

Food and fire, at least. A cup of tea. No milk. No sugar. She didn't care. Her throat felt parched, a combination of heat and panic. Hot during the day the desert, she knew, could turn freezing at night. What could she use for warmth? She was wearing jeans and a cotton shirt, a bandanna around her throat. If the worst came to the worst, there was Chloe's saddle blanket. She didn't fancy that around her, but then it was still light and the temperature was only beginning to drop.

She found herself a stout stick just in case a couple of dingoes came calling. Beautiful-looking animals, she knew they could and did kill humans. She had to be ready for that sort of violence.

What a fool you are trusting Robyn.

Robyn had big problems, which she frequently demonstrated. Like today.

Jessica felt a bursting sensation in her chest. She had the dismal feeling she had walked right into a trap. But what had Robyn hoped to achieve? Had she simply wanted to give her a good fright? A miserable night spent alone in the wilderness, communing with the guardian spirits. With Moira perhaps? Poor little Moira, who had disappeared without trace. Jessica had no fear of Moira's shadowy ghost. Moira didn't threaten her. Moira was a friend.

You are, aren't you Moira?

She spoke exactly as if the young governess were standing near her. One needed a friend at such times, even if the friend existed in another dimension.

As she worked to collect enough firewood, Jessica cast her mind back over Broderick Bannerman's parting shot. *She's not who she says she is.*

Had he found out something about her family? Something no one else knew or about which no one had ever spoken? It had nothing to do with her beloved Alex, her nan. Virtually every minute of Nan's life had been well documented. Nan had been the only daughter of a prominent family.

Yet it was such a strange thing to say. If not Nan, who? Someone who had handed down the family face. Her great grandmother, Margo. Margo had gained quite a reputation for being "difficult." She had run off to Europe at one stage and her parents had had to go chasing after her. She'd been at that time engaged to an upstanding young man who'd been devastated when she'd taken off without a word of explanation. The miracle was he'd taken her back and married her. Nan always told that story, an odd expression in her eyes.

Jessica got the fire going without too much trouble. Fire was beautiful and terrible. Tonight it was beautiful, wonderfully comforting. She made herself a cup of tea. Again, absolutely delicious, and she wasn't a tea drinker; it slicked the dry patches in her throat. She was hungry, so she started on a packet of raisins. Good source of iron.

In no time at all, it was dark, except for the orange-gold flames of her fire, which, as she piled on the kindling, rose higher and higher. She couldn't let it go out. She'd collected a good amount of fallen branches, dried leaves and grasses. Ordinarily, she wasn't frightened of the dark, but then, she'd never spent a night in the vast desert where nocturnal animals were on the prowl. She had Chloe to protect her. Or maybe she was supposed to protect Chloe, she wasn't sure. Chloe wouldn't be hungry, at least. She'd had her fill of the golden grasses, and Jessica had given her some of her own water.

All they had to do was sit tight and wait for Cyrus.

Cyrus!

Just to say his name sent a thrill of warmth through her. Images of her other loved ones kept coming.

If you're up there, Nan, now's the time to make the stars come out.

They did.

As she watched with bated breath, the stars came out in all their glory, spreading their brilliance across the sky. There was Orion, the mighty hunter striding across the sky, his faithful hunting dogs at his heels. The Southern Cross beamed its magic down on her. Even the night wind sang a song to her. Not mournful but shivery sweet. The rapidly cooling air was incredibly fragrant as the desert plants released their aromatic oils which blended subtly with the perfume of a little carpet of wild flowers, like a mauve mist that covered the sand nearby.

One by one, several kangaroos approached the fire. They remained there, standing upright on their powerful back legs, ears pricked, their large soulful eyes seeming to ask her what she was doing there and was she all right? It was clear they meant her no harm and expected no harm from her, but when Chloe wheezed, they bounded off into the night, their great sinewy tails pounding the earth. She was sad to see them go.

Time went slowly. The cold air acted like a drug on her tired body. It was almost possible to nod off....

At one point, she thought she heard a whirring sound. It grew louder. Had she really dozed off? She must have. Her eyelids were heavy and she was freezing! Her fingers encountered gooseflesh all over her arms.

She leaped up, staggering a little.

It was a helicopter.

"Cyrus!" she yelled like a madwoman, a loud melancholy wail. She began to leap around the fire like a dancer at an Aboriginal corroboree. Something skittered across her vision. She peered across the mounting flames where someone who looked very like her had joined in the dance. How was that possible? She had to be hallucinating. She fought to reassert logic. The cold had sapped her brain. "Is that you, Moira?" she cried confusedly. "Do you know this place?"

Moira disappeared with a little wave.

Jessica told herself everything would be okay. She

was being protected. She didn't know how she knew that. She just did.

And now, she could see the welcome lights of the helicopter beaming over the rough terrain, coming over.

HAD ROBYN LIED? Why? But then Robyn basked in lies, Cyrus told himself, even now scarcely crediting she had done such a seriously twisted thing as abandon Jessica in the desert. He could be heading miles in the wrong direction given that it was Robyn who'd told him where Jessica was. Nevertheless, he made a low pass over the area around dried-up Wirra Creek. It was as he was circling he spotted the glow of a fire several miles off.

Thank God.

His relief was enormous, sweeping from his head to his heart.

I'm coming for you, Jessica. Hang on.

All he wanted in this world was to gather her in his arms. To tell her how much he loved her and wanted her to be with him forever.

SO, IT WAS TIME TO FACE the music, was it?

Robyn heard the helicopter before she saw Cyrus put down on the home grounds. Him and his easy skills. Not a bloody thing he couldn't do. She stood at the French doors watching the rotors slow to a stop before he jumped out, disappearing around the other side of the chopper from where he emerged into the strong wash of exterior lights with a bundled-up Jessica tucked in his arms. He loved the bitch, Robyn realized now. She had seen the very real fear in his eyes when she had returned to the homestead alone.

He hadn't trusted her to tell the truth, of course. Never had. Very wise.

Her head ached. Her stomach cramped with nausea. She couldn't do a goddamned thing right. The bitch was back. Not that she'd really believed Cyrus wouldn't find her. Cyrus knew she'd been lying her head off since she was a kid, hell-bent on trying to get him into trouble. But what choice did she have, then or now? Nobody loved her. Well, her mother had, but her mother had passed through life without causing a single ripple. By rights, she should have hated B.B. if only because of the callous way he had treated her mother. Instead, in accordance with her perverse nature, she had singled him out as the one person in life from whom she wanted love and attention. That longing had taken on obsessive proportions. But then, she'd been an extraordinarily distressed and needy child. She had been drawn to Erik because he was something of a father figure.

"I'm a natural born victim," she said aloud. "It's bleedingly, blindingly, bloody obvious!"

Her head spun. Why not? She was drunk. Her poor mother had turned into a real lush.

Robyn pulled back the opulent covers on her bed—fit for Cleopatra—then slipped beneath them. Turning groggily to look at her bedside clock, she was startled to see it was only seven-thirty. Little kids stayed up later than that!

But what the hell! She wasn't going to endure any tongue lashing from Cyrus, so madly in love with Jessica, who looked like bloody Moira…pardon me, *Moira*. There was always the chance Jessica and Moira were somehow related. If they were, B.B. would have found it out, B.B. the super sleuth. She'd locked her bedroom door. Cyrus could pound on it all he liked. Her entire existence could be summed up in one word.

Failure.

Robyn pulled her iridescent violet nightgown around herself. She'd shelled out a fortune for it. She'd intended to wear it on her honeymoon. Turn Erik on, though it would've been blood hard, damn pansy. Yawning helplessly, Robyn allowed her troubled spirit to sleep.

CHAPTER FIFTEEN

IT WAS A SILENT HOUSE they returned to, although enough lamps were blazing for a Christmas party.

"Robyn's not here, waiting for us," Cyrus commented, his tone grim. "I bet she locked herself in her room the minute she heard the chopper. Her pitiful little scheme— God knows what she hoped to achieve—foiled. It's about time Robyn was forced to stop and take a good long look at herself and what she's become. Dad was a terrible influence on her."

"Not tonight, Cyrus," Jessica begged. "I don't think she meant any real harm."

"How little you know her," Cyrus said. "How are you feeling now?" He looked down at her anxiously. She had stopped shivering. He had given her a brandy at the rescue scene which had quickly warmed her, then had wrapped her in the mohair rug. At the very least, he had expected and wouldn't have been surprised by a few tears. It was a pretty scary experience for anyone who wasn't used to the wilderness to be left alone in it. But she had been aglow with welcome, literally dancing into his open arms, wanting no fuss, even if she was chilled to the bone.

"What you need now is a hot bath," he told her. "I'll run it for you. Then I better tell Livvy you're safe and sound. I know she'll be worried."

"We'll both tell her," Jessica said, feeling utterly warmed by his embrace. "I can wait another few minutes. But I *am* hungry."

"I'll take care of that, as well." He dropped a kiss on her upturned mouth.

LAVINIA THREW OPEN HER DOOR at the sound of Cyrus's voice. She emerged in a crumpled pink nightie and a magnificent brocade full-length evening coat fit for Boris Godunov. "My darlings!" She threw her arms around Jessica and kissed her. "We couldn't lose you a second time. That bloody Robyn! She's a criminal. We ought to turn her in to the police."

"Have you had something to eat, Livvy?" Cyrus asked quickly, anxious to get Jessica settled.

"Molly brought me a tray. She's such a comfort. I hope Broderick has left her a tidy sum in his will."

"He's not dead yet, Livvy," Cyrus reminded her bleakly.

Lavinia sighed and touched his face. "It has to happen, my darling. What other ending can there be? Now, why don't you take Moira off and feed her? She must be hungry stuck out there in the bush, though I suppose she's accustomed to it by now. Good night then, my darlings." She made to shut the door. "You've got no chance of waking up Robyn. She's quickly falling a victim to the wicked booze like poor Sharon. At lease *she* had an excuse. Only, Sharon liked vodka, I think."

JESSICA TOOK A LONG TIME over her bath, letting the warm, scented water ease the tiredness and take the chill out of her bones. Afterward she didn't bother getting dressed again. She slipped on a nightdress, then covered it with the silk robe her mother had bought for her on her last trip to Hong Kong. It wasn't as magnificent as Lavinia's rich brocade coat, but it was very pretty. Pretty enough to wear out, considering some of her friends attended functions in what looked like their underwear.

She found Cyrus in the kitchen giving his attention to a meal.

"Omelets?" His blue gaze enveloped her.

"Sure you can make them?" She smiled. She went to him and slid her arms around his waist, resting her head against his broad back.

"Of course!" He stood perfectly still, in case feeding her didn't get off the ground at all. His heart was on fire. "You sure you're okay?"

"I'm finc. Don't fuss." Even now she was reliving the blissful moment when he had found her, swooping her into his arms, holding her so close their hearts had thudded as one.

That's what a man's arms were for, she thought. To hold a woman. To make her feel cherished. She had felt all that and more. She had felt a profound sense of homecoming.

"So come on," he said lightly, holding himself on a tight rein. "I'm going to feed you and *then* we're going to bed together."

"Sounds like the most wonderful destination in the world," she murmured.

He lifted her hand and pressed it to his lips.

HE CARED NOT AT ALL if they ate but tried not to show it. "Two eggs or three?"

"Three please. You need three for a good omelet." She sat down at the table, watching Cy with a sense of wonder. There were oranges, lemons, grapefruit in a bowl. She picked up a lemon and put it to her nose savoring the smell.

"Where's Molly?" she asked belatedly. She had expected Molly to be around.

He picked up a handwritten note and passed it to her. "She's gone over to stay with Ruth for the night. Ruth is tremendously upset."

"I know. She loves your father." She read the note, put it aside.

"Some women love men who treat them badly. Probably some syndrome. She's worked for him for twenty years, but he's never noticed her as a woman. Poor Ruth, wasting her life like that! She should have gone off, met the right bloke and had a family."

"The right bloke isn't easy to find."

Their eyes met and clung. "Then isn't it nice you've found him?"

ARM IN ARM, HER HEAD RESTING lightly on Cy's shoulder, they went around the house turning off the overhead lights, leaving only a few wall brackets glowing.

"Thought about what room?" He kissed her light and fast, setting up all sorts of aching expectations.

"I'm too distracted."

"Then mine." He wrapped her closer. "I've dreamed about you in my bed."

"Have you?" She was fathoms deep in love with him and falling farther.

"Oh yes. I was drawn to you from that very first moment. Now I'm absolutely sure you're the woman I want to share my life with."

OUTSIDE THE OPEN FRENCH DOORS, millions of stars patterned the sky. He carried her to his bed, her hair spread over his shoulder, his head bent, his lips kissing and tasting her lovely soft skin.

Cy lay on the midnight-blue quilted silk, poised over

her, an arm to either side. She was so beautiful. The most beautiful thing in his loveless life. He could never let her go. He could never allow anyone to hurt her.

A combination of soap and body lotion wafted up to him, deliciously citrusy and fresh. There was a trifle of lace showing at the neck of her robe. Slowly, he pulled the silk sash and the robe parted.

"Jessica." He was trying to steady himself, not give in too soon to the tremendous weight of desire. "I'm going to undress you, okay?"

She looked up at him with tender, trusting eyes. "You'll have to. I don't think I could get my fingers to work."

"Allow me."

The robe came off first, falling from her shoulders. Ever so gently, he turned her, tugging a little so it slithered out from under her. His breath was coming shorter and deeper. Hunger for a woman could be an agony. He had to hold her up so he could pull her nightdress over her head like a child. A groan came from the back of his throat as he saw her for the first time naked.

Her skin seemed to radiate light, and blood shot to his head. He had to regain his composure just to go on. His hands caressed her shoulders, silky skin and delicate bone, moving slowly over her, deepening his sense of touch and heightening his pleasure. His hands moved back up to her breasts, so beautiful, so perfectly formed, dusky-pink-tipped. It was a kind of agony just to look at them, hold them, take their tender supple weight.

Jessica let herself go with it, excitement roaring through her bloodstream like the most potent drug. The more he caressed her, the more she needed. Sensation ran so high she had to press back against the pillows, her eyes closed against the galvanic surges, like sails caught in a high wind. Didn't he know he tore the heart from her? His min-istrations continued, unhurried but intense. She had to clamp her lips shut so her little rasping breaths wouldn't escape her and turn into moans.

Cyrus understood perfectly the feelings that racked her. He was astonished at the depth of passion between them, long imagined, now finally being delivered. He was en-tranced by the slender perfection of her body, the curves, the long lines, the creamy whiteness of her skin. He let his mouth travel her body as though following a map that utterly absorbed him. Her little moans were both agonized and joyous, urging him on. Once, in a bout of intensity, her whole body bucked, then fell back onto the softness of the bed. She was reaching for him, inflamed into taking action.

She tugged at his shirt. Tore it loose. Next the waist-band of his jeans, thrusting her hand inside, giving him so much pleasure he cried out.

"I want you right next to me," she commanded. "Your skin touching mine."

He stood up, stripping off his clothes, a lean, powerful living sculpture of a man, his skin in the glow of the lamps a dense gold.

The sleekness and strength of him! Jessica sat up in the bed reveling in his manhood. She thought she might catch fire when he touched her. She threw out an imploring arm, secure in the knowledge she had made it her business to start on the pill for protection. "What's keeping you? I *want* you."

"How much?" He approached the bed, the planes of his face taut with passion.

"Let me show you." She was maddened by even the smallest distance between them. "I never knew it was possible to feel like this."

He wanted to cover her right then and there. Bear down on her. Make her his. Instead, he rose above her bracing his weight on his arms. "Then we have to do something about it."

"Let *me* start." This time she did the seducing. Her hands took hold of his fully erect shaft, scorching him with pleasure. She stroked and stretched the velvet skin until he grew too weak to withstand her.

"What are you trying to do to me?" He grasped her head to kiss her beautiful mouth. She tasted of white-fleshed peaches. It was amazing!

"Don't talk," she ordered. "I want to make you *feel*. I want you to experience the same rapture I do."

She moved over him and he covered his eyes with his hand, drawing in the ecstasy.

The intimacy between them continued to gain pace and intensity, the tenderness changing to the faint violence of passion bent on release. Delirious tears streamed down her cheeks. She and Cyrus were coiled around one another like vines, one ascendant, then the other, anything permissible between them because of the love they felt for each other.

"It was meant to be like this from the beginning." He pressed his mouth to hers, rapidly approaching his climax but waiting for her to catch up.

"I love you. Cyrus, I love you." She knew such a thing only happened once in a lifetime.

"Then come with me." He was determined to hold back until her climax seized her.

She held on to him for dear life, pressing her mouth to his shoulder tasting salt. Her body was filled with such heat….

And then it began. Ripples gathered in the pit of her groin. They gained strength, spreading to all levels of her body like molten lava. Her eyes were tightly shut so she could lock in the incredible sensations. She reached down to where their bodies joined. He was moving against her, very slowly like a sleek, powerful big cat. Up and down. Deep. Deep. Her whole body seemed to be quaking, as though something inside her was about to gush open.

"Now!"

Did she shout it? She was beyond caring.

ROBYN DENIED EVERYTHING. Her head was pounding from a hangover. She looked so ill that Jessica, despite everything, felt very concerned. Jessica herself was looking as radiant as a bride on her day of all days, still trailing the glory of the previous night. She was ready to forgive anyone, anything. Even Robyn, who undoubtedly would never be her friend.

Cyrus wasn't feeling anywhere near so magnanimous. He was deeply perturbed by what his stepsister had done. Robyn needed help and he came straight out and said it.

"Are you talking about a shrink?" she gasped, looking panic stricken.

"I'm angry enough to tell everyone what you did unless you make an appointment to see one."

"But everyone knows me," she protested. "I'd be the talk of the town."

"Don't be ridiculous! You know all about doctor-patient confidentiality. I'm serious, Robyn. It's important you get professional help. It could be one of the smartest things you've ever done in your life. Obviously we can't discuss this any further today. You're hungover. You can count your lucky stars I didn't believe you, and Jessica found matches in her saddlebag and was able to start a fire, otherwise this could have ended rather differently."

"Whereas it ended just the way she wanted," Robyn responded bitterly, hell-bent on driving everyone away. She jumped up precipitously, winced as her head threatened to split. "I don't know why I'm sitting here. I should be in Darwin with Dad."

Cyrus sighed. "If you're determined to go, Robyn, why should I stand in your way? You'll be better there than sitting around the house plotting some fool mischief. You're welcome to go to the hospital. I happen to know Dad's given instructions—no visitors. That means us. Bad sign in a man, don't you think, when he doesn't want to see his family?"

Robyn gave a snort. "Maybe I can get him to change his mind."

"Good luck, then. You might as well stay in Darwin while you're at it. The operation is scheduled for 9:00 a.m. Friday."

That got Robyn's full attention. "Dad would have made sure his will is in order?"

Cyrus's voice was dry. "I'm sure you've been well looked after."

"Well, I *am* his adopted daughter. Can I get Bill Morris to take me in the chopper? I can't face the long drive."

"Sure." Cyrus nodded his permission. "I'm going out to have a word with the men so I'll tell him now. When do you want to leave?"

Robyn fixed her stepbrother, then Jessica, with a hard stare. "As soon as possible. I'm sure you two lovebirds don't want me around. Say, eleven o'clock? I have to do a few things first."

"Like sober up?" Cyrus grunted. "I'll tell him." He looked across at Jessica, who had sat silently through the exchange. "What about if I come back for you then, Jessica? We can spend the day together."

"I'd like that," she said quietly. Despite what was happening, joy that would not be denied welled up in her heart.

"Course you would!" Robyn's laugh cracked. "With Dad out of the way, we'll have to drop to our knees and worship at Cyrus's feet."

"Dad's not dead yet, Robyn," Cyrus reminded her. "Now, I'm out of here." He turned away, crisply businesslike. "Be ready at eleven sharp, Robyn. I actually need Bill today, but I recognize you're in no state to drive into Darwin."

"Thanks a bunch." Robyn suddenly scooped up the delicate cup and saucer that held the rest of her morning coffee and flung them to the floor. They shattered into pretty pieces, the black coffee staining the rug.

BRODERICK BANNERMAN HAD BEEN on the operating table for four hours.

They all sat in the waiting room, Cyrus, Lavinia, Jessica and Robyn, their backs aching, their expressions betraying their strain. Robyn stared fixedly and, Jessica suspected, sightlessly, at the television, though Cyrus had insisted it be turned down. Robyn actually looked like she needed a hospital bed herself.

They all looked up as Barbara Nicholls, Broderick's twin, who had arrived from Sydney, came back into the room carrying a cup of coffee and a cell phone. "Nothing?"

"Nothing," Cyrus confirmed. "Babs, why don't you take Livvy back to the hotel? You're only ten minutes away. This could go on for hours yet. I'll call you the minute we have news."

Barbara Nicholls, with the same handsome features as her twin, but much less severe, stylishly confident, beautifully dressed, sank into a chair and sighed deeply. "I don't feel good about this."

"Better to die than finish up in a wheelchair or lying in a nursing home, Babs," Lavinia said. "That wouldn't suit Broderick at all."

Barbara shook her dark head. She had the same distinctive silver wings as her brother. "No," she agreed quietly. "Don't feel bitter, Cyrus dear, but he let me see him for a time." She laid a comforting hand on her nephew's. "Please don't hold it against me. Probably I'm the only person who can get inside Broderick's head. I'm his twin, after all. Broderick has always been his own worst enemy. Keeping you away from him, especially at this time, is part of his defense mechanism. You must understand that. You're so much like our father, Steven. For some reason that has always upset him. It takes him back in time. Then there was the damage left in Moira's wake. Of course, Broderick being Broderick found out I put that portrait of Moira on the market."

That hit Cyrus with stunning force. "*You* did? I didn't even know you had it. You've never said. I thought it was Dad."

They were all focused on Barbara now. Jessica reached out to take Cyrus's hand, seeing his agitation. Even Robyn dragged her eyes away from Oprah Winfrey for a moment, even though an extraordinarily slim Oprah was offering everyone in the studio a free car.

"I've had the painting in storage for years and years," Barbara said. "It was too beautiful to destroy and too upsetting to display. No, I was the one." Barbara looked at her nephew. "Your father never told you?"

Cyrus shook his head. "I accused him of it. He didn't deny it."

"That's Broderick all right," Barbara said heavily. "I did it on impulse. It was Hughie's anniversary. I always feel badly around that time. I feel cleaner, freer, bringing his portrait of Moira out of hiding. The tragedies of our childhood left terrible wounds. Wounds that were concealed, but never healed. I knew Broderick would find out what I'd done. There's nothing much that happens inside the family—and out—he doesn't know about. He knew how I felt about the portrait. He knew I had it. He knew I unravel around Hugh's anniversary—he does, too. I suppose he was waiting for me to let it see the light of day. He's uncanny like that."

Cyrus's handsome face was baffled. "What else have you and Dad been hiding all these years, Babs? We found another portrait, Jessica and I."

"Where, in the storeroom?" Barbara made an informed guess. "One could hide anything there. So much was concealed, you know. My mother could't bear to hear Moira's name. It was all so very painful. Brutal as it sounds, making all trace of Moira disappear was the only way we survived as a family."

"Oh man!" Cyrus turned away, sighing deeply.

"Hugh was a wonderful painter," Barbara said. "He could have made a name for himself, only his whole life ran off the rails. What was this painting of?" she asked.

It was left to Jessica to reply. "A nude. A very beautiful rendition."

"*What?*" Barbara gasped. "No, no, that's impossible."

"Nothing's impossible, dear," said Lavinia, looking worldly-wise.

Robyn sat as if struck dumb by all they were saying.

"A very erotic portrait," said Cyrus, searching his aunt's face.

"Moira didn't pose for it." Barbara spoke with absolute certainty. "Okay, I was only a child, but I *know*. A portrait of Moira in her prettiest dress was one thing. My parents allowed that. Moira nude would never have happened."

"No, it wouldn't!" Lavinia shook her forefinger energetically.

"Hughie must have seen her like that in his *mind*. An erotic fantasy as it were. He was an artist, after all."

"Bloody odd, if you ask me," said Lavinia. "Wasn't he a pansy?"

Barbara was thoroughly rattled. "No, he was *not*, Livvy. Where did you get that idea? Look, I don't know how this happened, but there was nothing between Moira and Hugh."

"As far as you know," Lavinia piped up.

Barbara flushed. "Of course he could have fallen in love with her, but Moira certainly didn't love him. All Moira could see was—" She broke off abruptly, dropping her gaze.

"Steven," Cyrus supplied grimly, as if this were the piece that was missing.

Silence from Barbara, but a look of extreme gravity.

"We're all human," Lavinia pronounced. "Human beings fall in love." She reached out to pat Jessica's hand. "That's what Cecily was afraid of. He loved you."

"Livvy, will you stop that?" Barbara exclaimed in horror, rising to her feet. "This is *Jessica*, for heaven's sake. I have to admit, I got a great shock when I first saw her. The resemblance is uncanny, but sheer coincidence. We were talking about Hugh. I've always thought something terrible happened to Hugh. Something he would never talk about."

"Unrequited love?" Cyrus suggested, continuing to regard his aunt closely.

Lavinia frowned at him. "No, no, my darling, Hughie was in love with Steven. Not that Steven had a clue."

Barbara was visibly trying to keep control. "Livvy, sometimes you sound quite mad."

"And sometimes I don't," Lavinia returned darkly.

"If Hugh had been in love with anyone, it was Moira. I'm sure Hugh wasn't gay."

"Gay?" Robyn's voice came out so loudly it made everyone jump.

"He was, too." Lavinia stuck to her guns. "It explains everything."

Cyrus held his head in his hands. "If it does, I'm missing it."

"*Everything* has to do with what happened to Moira," Lavinia insisted. "I expect if Broderick doesn't die, the police will come and arrest him."

Robyn gave a contemptuous snort. "If anyone should be arrested, it's you, Lavinia. You're long overdue for the giggle house."

"And you should be coming with me," Lavinia told her tartly.

Barbara acted. "Darling Livvy, I think we should go back to the hotel for a while. You need to lie down."

"You'll stay with me?"

"Of course." There was great confusion in Barbara Nicholls's gray eyes and the glint of tears.

SHORTLY AFTER THEY'D LEFT, Erik Moore made an appearance.

On seeing him, Cyrus straightened, his gaze challenging. "What are you doing here, Erik?"

"Yes, tell us." Robyn actually switched off the TV. "After my lousy birthday party, I vowed never to speak to you again."

Erik searched her face, looking for understanding. "You've no idea how I've missed you, my darling."

"That's the reason you came, is it, Erik?" Cyrus stood

up, towering over the other man. "To tell Robyn you've missed her?"

"That and to find out about B.B." So confronted, Erik sank strategically into a chair. "It was B.B. who warned me off, Robyn. He let us get to the stage of talking marriage, then right out of the blue he told me to butt out of your life. That was the very night of your birthday party, when we should have been deliriously happy. I had the ring. I still have it."

"You didn't dump me?" Robyn stared at him, apparently poleaxed by the disclosure.

Cyrus exhaled in wonderment but never said another word. His conscience was clear. He'd tried all he could with Robyn. None of it had worked.

A look of dawning wonder put life into Robyn's pale face.

"Would I dump the love of my life?" Erik asked, apparently always at the ready no matter what life dished up.

Robyn's look of shock had been replaced by hope. "Dad did that to us?"

Erik nodded, letting his head drop as in deep regret.

Obviously he was smart enough to know when actions spoke louder than words, Jessica thought cynically, not taken in by what she saw as a performance.

"Why didn't you tell me?" Robyn went to him, half kneeling so she could get a closer look at his face.

"Why bother?" he said forlornly. "B.B. means everything to you. I knew you wouldn't go against him in the end."

"The *end*? Now that, I think, is highly relevant," Cyrus cut in. "Your goddamn brain is always ticking over isn't it, Erik? Dad mightn't pull through. I bet you've got your sources inside the hospital who gave you a complete rundown on his condition. Many people survive brain tumors, however."

"Of course they do!" Erik heartily agreed. "I'm hoping and praying that will be the case with B.B."

"So who told you it was a brain tumor? We never gave out that information. It could be stomach cancer, for all you know."

Robyn was thoroughly roused from her stupor, apparently dead set on standing by her man. "Erik is a highly regarded member of the community, Cyrus." She ran a loving hand down Erik's cheek. "It would be easy for a man like Erik to be given certain information. After all, everyone knows we're as good as engaged."

"Really? I thought it was all over Darwin you'd broken up," Cyrus said with weary sarcasm. "So if Dad doesn't survive, Robyn will never know if you're telling the truth, Erik?"

"Robyn knows her father." Erik shook his head ponderously.

"Her stepfather," Cyrus corrected curtly.

"Robbie, would you like to have a cup of coffee in that little place across the street?" Erik said quickly, rising to his feet. "The coffee here is deplorable."

"I'd love to!" Robyn all but sprang to the door.

"Is that okay with you, Cyrus?" Erik asked before joining her.

"Sure," Cyrus drawled. "Thanks for coming."

Erik totally missed the sarcasm. "No worries. We'll be back."

THEY SAT IN A STUNNED SILENCE for a few moments after Erik and Robyn had gone.

"Sweet Jesus, can you believe that guy?" Cyrus sighed.

"She fell for it, hook, line and sinker."

Cyrus nodded. "He got the inside story. He knows just how bad Dad is. Obviously with Dad out of the way, he's home free. He can control Robyn and her money. And I'd say we're talking a lot of it."

"Reparation for not treating Robyn very well?"

"Probably." Cyrus shrugged. "I don't mind. Dad did adopt her when she was only a child. She's entitled. Erik is prepared to take his chances. That's how he runs his businesses."

"He's in big trouble if your father pulls through."

"I don't think the world holds any more appeal for Dad," Cyrus said, an expression of resignation on his face.

BRODERICK BANNERMAN DID NOT pull through, however great the combined skills of his surgical team.

As the neurosurgeon, Dr. Jung, who headed the team came toward them, Cyrus and Jessica stood up, their hands clasped tightly together for mutual support.

Something in the surgeon's expression alerted them the news was far from good.

"I'm so very sorry," he said, looking first at Cyrus, then Jessica. "Mr. Bannerman has gone. We did all we could, but we lost him. Please, let's sit down a moment."

Dr. Jung sat with them, explaining the various reasons why everything had started to go haywire. "I think your father had already decided he didn't want to live," he told Cyrus gently. "He was such a strong personality, such a powerful and influential man, he found it extremely difficult to consider the possibility of a greatly changed life. We had discussed every possible outcome of the operation, of course. He went into it with his eyes wide open. If there was a chance, he was going to take it. I wish things had turned out differently. I understand how deeply distressed you are. We did all we could."

But it hadn't been enough.

"So who WAS THE LAST PERSON in the family he saw?" Cyrus asked after the surgeon had gone. Despair and a deep hurt were in his voice. "Whose face did he light on last? Not me, that's for sure. Not poor unwanted Robyn. But Babs, his twin. Sons and adopted daughters don't count. You, the young woman he became so infatuated with. In the end he shunned you, as well."

"In his mind, I betrayed him," Jessica said. "He was living a fantasy. I was no *real* part of it, Cyrus. Barbara was his twin. She loves you and she knows much, much more about your family's history than she's ever let on. Except maybe to her brother."

"That's obvious," Cyrus said harshly, pulling out his cell phone to start making the necessary calls. "Well, it doesn't matter now. Dad's gone. The secrets he'll take to the grave are probably too shattering to know, anyway."

LATER, AS THEY WERE about to leave the ward, a tall distinguished-looking man in his late fifties came toward them. He was wearing a clerical collar.

"Mr. Bannerman, Cyrus Bannerman?" he asked, putting out his hand. His voice had a soft Irish lilt. "I'm Father Brennan. I was with your father last night. I've just been told he passed away. I'm so sorry. Please accept my deepest sympathies."

Though stunned by the revelation—his father had been anything but a religious man—Cyrus responded courteously, shaking the clergyman's hand. "Thank you, Father. This is my friend, Jessica Tennant."

"Miss Tennant." The priest's dark eyes wandered to her distressed face.

"You're a Catholic priest, Father?" Cyrus asked, trying to grasp what the man was saying. Clergymen had freaked his father out.

"Yes. I heard your father's last confession," the priest said in a perfectly calm voice.

"But we're not Catholic, Father." Cyrus forced himself to speak quietly when he was agitated and upset. Just when he'd been thinking there were no surprises left, up popped a Catholic priest.

Father Brennan smiled. "Your father and his twin sister, Barbara—is that right?—were baptized in the Catholic Church. I understand there was a tragedy in the family many long years ago and the faith lapsed, but your father called for me, as a matter of fact. He wanted to see a priest."

Cyrus shook his head as if to clear it. For the moment, he had to rely on the man's word, but he saw nothing but truth and dignity in the clergyman's eyes. "Father, I have to tell you I'm stunned."

"I can see that, Cyrus. May I call you Cyrus?"

"Of course." Cyrus stared into the quiet, focused face.

"If it gives you comfort, I can tell you your father was a peaceful man at the end. Strangely happy, accepting of his fate."

"You gave him absolution?" Did a man automatically get it? Cyrus wondered.

"Certainly," the priest confirmed gently. "You probably have some clergyman in mind for the funeral service. If you haven't, if I can be of help to you, you have only to let me know. I'm at St. Mary's. God bless you both." He lifted a hand in a gesture that was both a blessing and a salute.

CHAPTER SIXTEEN

BRODERICK BANNERMAN WAS LAID to rest according to his wishes in a closed ceremony with only his family and a handful of lifelong associates present. Because of his status in life, a memorial service was to be held in Darwin at a later date when it was expected a huge crowd would attend.

Like most great Outback stations, Mokhani had its own cemetery. The graves of five generations of Bannermans were arranged within a large enclosure bounded by a tall black wrought-iron fence and double gates, and shaded by massive banyan trees that spread their long weeping branches over the graves. In a far corner, removed from the intersecting concrete pathways, was a species of cassia in gorgeous display. It caught Jessica's artistic eye. It was the only bright spot in that quiet place; the spent golden blossom covered the built up mound beneath it.

How beautiful! The long perfumed sprays moved like floral arms, even though there was scarcely a breath of air. Cyrus had spoken to Father Brennan, who presided at the service in the calm dignified manner Jessica remembered. If Broderick Bannerman had called on a priest at an extreme moment the same priest ought to bury him, Cyrus had decided when the family had discussed it. He'd met with no opposition from anyone. From now on, everyone would defer to him as head of the family.

Broderick Bannerman's last will and testament had already been read. Overnight, Cyrus had inherited the bulk of the Bannerman fortune, making him one of the richest men in the country—and thus one of the most eligible, though no one, not even Robyn, made reference to it. Robyn might have been cut out of all Bannerman business operations, including the pastoral empire, but what she did get was splendid enough for her not to rock the boat and had Erik Moore talking wedding dates.

Barbara, already a rich woman, was made a whole lot richer, not that she cared, and that was that. For a notoriously tight-fisted man, B.B. had been extremely generous. His longtime secretary, Ruth, who had loved him from afar and was crazy with grief—she'd had to be sedated when she'd been told of his death—wouldn't have to work another day for the rest of her life. A godsend for most people, but looking at Ruth, anyone could see she would much rather have had Bannerman back. Handsome bequests were made to various longtime employees, including Molly, who had gone so far as to burst into tears and start planning to join her widowed sister in Tasmania. Charities had a bonanza. Hospitals, medical research centers, an educational institution to be set up in Darwin, also a park— B.B. had owned the land—bearing his name. A huge monetary gift was made to the city. The list went on and on. No mention whatever of Jessica, for which she was greatly relieved. She couldn't have handled even a tiny bequest. Nothing about her stay on Mokhani had been *normal*.

After the funeral, Jessica had made the decision to go home and give Cyrus breathing space. She had thought about it long and hard. Cyrus needed time to clear his mind and focus on his future. Whether in the light of momentous events she was going to be part of it, she still had to give him space. For all the bitterness Broderick Bannerman's behavior had engendered in his son and nigh on everyone around him, Cyrus *was* grieving.

Brett and Tim were due to arrive on Saturday, which was two days off. They would take a look around Darwin, make a quick courtesy visit to Mokhani to meet the new master and take a look at the great folly Broderick had caused to be erected in his honor. Indeed a mausoleum. It was up to Cyrus now to decide what would be done with it. Had it been a timber structure, Jessica thought Cyrus would have burned it down. Her own idea was it should be turned into a huge conference center with every facility. As Cyrus was to take over all of his late father's business concerns, which spread to Southeast Asia and New Zealand, such a center made sense.

They hadn't discussed it. Broderick Bannerman's death and the events leading up to it had cast Cyrus into an inevitable state of depression. He wasn't immune to grief, sadness for what might have been, and quite starkly, the knowledge that at the end he had been met with rejection. What extraordinary place he had held in his father's mind. His heir and, quite simply, his *rival*.

It was late afternoon before everyone left after a subdued reception at the homestead. Barbara couldn't avoid staying over at the homestead even if she wanted to. Her husband was at a conference in London, where he was a guest speaker, and had been greatly relieved he wasn't required to return home. Barbara had been staying at the same Darwin hotel the family favored. It was obvious Lavinia was very fond of her niece—after all, Barbara had had Lavinia stay for years on end—so to humor the old lady and offer some comfort to her nephew, Barbara had agreed to stay over at Mokhani, the Bannerman ancestral home where Barbara felt she no longer belonged. She didn't think she would ever get over the desolation of her childhood, she'd confided to Jessica. The *loneliness,* the internal struggles. Hitherto inseparable, overnight her twin had been shut off from her. Her mother had changed into someone else. Her wonderful father had never been the same. After Moira had disappeared, they hadn't worked as a *family.* For years, her mother had gotten all choked up if anyone so much as mentioned Moira's name. Her father had looked as though he had lost something irretrievable. Uncle Hughie, who was the nicest man in the world, had killed himself on the station. Something had caused him so much pain, he couldn't go on living.

Small wonder Barbara seldom visited her old family home.

Strangely, Barbara didn't appear to have those feelings now that her twin was gone. Was it because there was no more Broderick with his stinging tongue? Broderick, always trying to wrong-foot everyone. And his secrets? Broderick had been her mother's favorite. Their mother, Cecily, had loved him far more than she had her daughter. Broderick had been on the receiving end of all Cecily's attention. That had incensed and alientated Barbara right up until the time she had married and made a new life for herself.

Because everyone felt terribly sorry for Ruth, the woman was pressed into staying, instead of going back to her own comfortable bungalow.

"You don't need to be alone, Ruth," Cyrus told her kindly. "We all know how devoted you were to my father."

"Head over heels in love with him more like it," Lavinia the irrepressible piped up.

"What of it?" Ruth countered, distraught. "I'm not ashamed of it."

Barbara's voice was soft and sad. "You have no need to be, Ruth. Loving someone can never be wrong."

"What about Moira?" Lavinia asked, adjusting her monk's robe, which she had worn to the funeral, along with blue socks and sandals. "I mean, loving the wrong man must count as one of the worst things you can do in the world."

"Certainly one of the most painful." Barbara put a hand over Lavinia's in an effort to quiet her. "I told you, Livvy, dear, I didn't want to talk about Moira."

Lavinia did a double take. "But she's sitting right opposite you, love."

Robyn threw down her linen napkin. "The only bloody difference between Lavinia and Zelda, the mad old bag lady in Darwin no one seems to do a thing about, is occasionally the authorities have to lock Zelda up."

"How unjust," said Lavinia. "She does no harm, but she does go on a bit about *sin*. The reason you don't like me, Robyn, is that I see through you. I think Broderick's leaving you all that money was a dreadful mistake. Erik will only glom onto it, mark my words!"

Barbara's eyebrows shot up like birds' wings. "Livvy, it's scarcely the right time for all this."

"There are only two kinds of times," said Lavinia. "The good times and the bad. Let's drink to Broderick. He up and died on us and left my darling Cyrus with all his problems."

For the first time in days, Cyrus laughed. "Don't worry about me, Livvy. I can handle it."

"That's right, my darling!" she encouraged him. "Build a new life with Moira." Her bright eyes moved to Jessica.

"I don't know that there's any better color for a beautiful ash-blonde than black. No news, I suppose, but that's my expert opinion."

IT WASN'T UNTIL MUCH LATER in the evening that Ruth came out onto the veranda to speak to Cyrus. He and Jessica were sitting out there talking quietly.

"Sorry to interrupt!"

"No problem, Ruth. Can I help you?"

Ruth's eyes filled up again with tears. "You're so good to me, Cyrus. I must thank you." She shifted her gaze to Jessica. "Don't think I don't appreciate how nice you've been to me, Jessica, since you arrived." Although she was obviously sincere, Ruth spoke in a flat monotone. She was clutching a padded bag in her hand. "Your father asked me to give this to you, Cyrus, should anything happen to him," she said. "I've been so desperately upset, it all but slipped my mind, so I'll give it to you now."

"What is it?" Cyrus made no move to take it.

"A video." Ruth passed the package to Jessica, who was nearest, and Jessica in turn passed it to Cyrus. "Your father wanted to speak to you."

Cyrus stared down at the package. "He could have done that very easily, Ruth," he said, making no attempt to extract the video from the padded bag. "I waited for hours on end at the hospital."

Ruth shook her head. "You know your father was a very strange man, Cyrus, but in his own way he loved you. Remember, I knew him well. He suppressed so many of his true feelings."

"Wouldn't it have been easier for all of us if my father could have shown a shred of appreciation, let alone affection?"

Jessica could feel Cyrus's tension. The knuckles of his lean, tanned hands were white.

"I don't believe he knew how to, Cyrus. That was the cross he carried. You should thank God you're like your mother."

"I do, Ruth. I do." Cyrus slowly withdrew the video. "You have your job, Ruth, if you still want it. I'd never find anyone else as good as you. For that matter, you know more than I do."

Ruth looked amazed. "You're serious, Cyrus?" The flatness in her voice turned into an emotional quiver.

"Perfectly," he said. "My father found you indispensable and he was a hard taskmaster. Of course you'll need time to think it over. Time, too, for a holiday. Something to look forward to. Let me know."

Ruth pressed her hand to her agonized breast. "Where else would I go, Cyrus? I'd be honored if you'd give me a chance."

Cyrus leaned forward. "Get some confidence in yourself, Ruth," he said gently. "Somehow my father stole it. You're absolutely first class at what you do. I'll *need* you."

He couldn't have hit on a more powerful argument if he'd tried.

"Oh, thank you," Ruth said in a heartfelt voice and fled back into the house.

"So what am I going to do with this?" Cyrus asked Jessica, looking down at the package in his hands.

"What do you suppose it is?" Jessica felt a bit fearful.

He sighed. "You can bet your life it's not to tell me how much he loved me. The strange things he was doing—the intimate connection he was trying to make with you, Moira's double, calling in a priest, making his confession, I'd say it was an extension of all that. I don't think I want to know."

"I don't blame you. Still, it would be unthinkable to

throw it away. You've lived through bad times. You can handle it. Perhaps at the end he wanted to explain himself. He could even be asking forgiveness."

"So." Cyrus let out a sigh. "Where do we see it, in the study? Somewhere private anyway."

"Are you sure you want me?" Jessica asked, very sensitive to his grief. "These are probably your father's most private thoughts. I wouldn't blame you in the least, Cyrus, if you wanted to see it on your own."

Cyrus stood up drawing her to her feet. "You love me, don't you?"

Her voice broke a little at the expression on his face. "With all my heart."

"Then from this moment on we do everything together." He cupped her face in his hands, looking directly into her eyes. "I've been waiting for you my whole life, Jessica. I can't let you go. All right, you can leave with your uncle—I'm looking forward to meeting him—but that's only to go back and see your family. I'll need to meet them. They'll want to look me over. I love you, Jessica. I want to marry you. Not at some hazy time in the future. I want it to be right away, but that would be seen as too soon. Besides, I want our wedding day to be wonderful. I want to see you as a bride. I want the memory of that day to stay with us forever. Say you'll marry me?"

"You've got it all planned?" She smiled through her tears, believing herself to be truly blessed.

"Within seconds of meeting you," he confirmed.

"The miracle of love at first sight." Her eyes luminous with love, Jessica put up her arms and drew his dark head down to her in a long, loving kiss.

Cyrus was her life. Mokhani was her home.

Together they would bring it back to the light.

CHAPTER SEVENTEEN

BRODERICK BANNERMAN WAS SEATED somewhere that looked like a law office because of the legal tomes in the bookcase behind him. He was directly facing the camera. Just for a moment both Cyrus and Jessica forgot he was dead. He looked very much alive. He addressed himself to his son: "The best son a man could wish for!"

"Dear God!" said Cyrus. "I actually heard that, did I?"

Jessica, seated close beside the man she loved, held his hand, understanding Cyrus took great comfort from her presence. All that passion with tenderness and need, besides! Sublime sex wasn't all that connected them, but rather the *depth* of their connection, the perfect matching. They were truly meant for each other.

There were points along the way when Cyrus had to stop the video to get up and pace around the room. Jessica sat, head bent, appalled by Broderick's tale told in such a matter-of-fact tone. *Some people put more emotion into reading a grocery list,* she thought with some wonderment.

Bannerman's voice never faltered, not once, during the telling of his harrowing story.

Uncle Hughie and I followed Mom and Moira at a safe distance. They didn't keep to the usual trails like we thought they would. They ventured out into the wilderness, heading toward the escarpment. The weather was terrible, hot and thundery with the sky piled up with clouds. I knew Uncle Hughie was worried. He didn't have to say anything. I just knew. Once or twice, I'd overheard a couple of the stockmen sniggering about Dad and Moira. The father I worshipped and my *governess?* It didn't seem possible. Babs and I really liked Moira.

Mum was mistress of Mokhani. But Moira was a servant. There was a huge gulf between the two.

Uncle Hughie and I waited until Mum and Moira reached the top of the escarpment, then we followed using the scrub for cover. Mum began speaking angrily to Moira. My mother could be really scary when she got angry. Moira fell to her knees. Mum told her to get up. I remember every word like it was yesterday.

"Adultery is a sin, Moira. A terrible sin. No decent young woman in her right mind would allow herself to be seduced by a married man. Unless she's the sort who seduces men. And what about Hugh? You want him as well?"

I've never believed, like poor old Livvy, Hugh was homosexual. Maybe he did have a sexual encounter with Moira. Who would know? Lovely little Moira turned out to be a slut anyway. She had to be guilty because she did nothing to defend herself even when my mother began to hit her. Mum sounded like she was going out of her mind. That's when Uncle Hughie broke cover, yelling at Mum to stop. Maybe Hugh did love Moira, but it was my father Moira had set her sights on.

Mum was shocked when she knew we were there. The words she threw at Uncle Hughie were so ugly I had to cover my seven-year-old ears. I didn't even know Mum knew words like that.

"Sins have to be paid for, Hugh."

That's when Moira asked very quietly, even sorrowfully, "Is love a sin then?"

Mum whirled about and slapped her, struck her so hard Moira went reeling.

"Marriage is sacred, you wicked little bitch. Sacred, you hear? You'll never break up my family. Destroy my marriage."

That's when I knew what I had to do. A son fights for his mother's honor even if he's only seven years old. I was big and strong. We were all standing close to the edge. What could be easier than pushing Moira off the cliff? She deserved what was coming to her. No way was she going to be allowed to break up my family. So I ran, propelled by hate and the need for action, my mother's agonized cries ringing in my ears: "No, Broderick, no! Stop!"

It was impossible to stop. I evaded Uncle Hughie easily. Poor Hughie, he was sobbing like a woman. Moira just stood quietly with her face turned toward me as though accepting her fate. She only had time to get out a few words, but I've never forgotten them.

"I'll always be here, Brodie. You'll see me."

Sure enough I have.

Appalled and in thrall Cyrus and Jessica listened as the voice droned on with the same peculiar lack of emotion.

Afterward, wrapped so tightly in my hysterical mother's arms she could have broken bones, we watched as Uncle Hughie went down into the canyon. There wasn't the remotest chance Moira could have survived. We all knew that. But surely no one would blame me? A child of seven couldn't be held responsible for the outcome of his actions. It was a terrible accident. I hadn't meant to push her so hard. Except I *had*. I knew precisely what I was doing. I was the Bannerman heir. The family honor was at stake. I had chosen to send Moira to her death.

Of course the whole business turned Uncle Hughie's mind. That and the booze. He buried Moira under cover of night. "Out of sight, but in a sacred place," he told us, not that Mum and I ever wanted to know. Poor man! It was my mother who locked him and me into living a lie. She was the strong one. *She* made up the story. We had to get it straight. Moira had gone out riding alone. It had been drummed into Moira not to venture too far from the main compound. For some reason she had anyway. The horse came home. Moira didn't. She was never seen again.

My father turned into a madman instigating a mighty search. My mother aged overnight, but she never broke her silence. All that mattered was that I be protected. No one thought to question me. Not my father, not the policeman who traveled from Darwin to the station. I was a child, heir to Mokhani. My family was powerful, well respected. The mysterious disappearance of our governess joined Outback lore. Another tragedy of the bush, people said.

Only as it turned out no one could protect me from my memories or the apparitions. They ruined my life, twisted my soul. The whole story should have come out at the beginning. Perhaps the truth might have saved me. They could have locked me away in a home for the insane, and I wouldn't have cared. But my mother insisted I could never do anything so dangerous as to tell. My father would never understand.

"He would hate us, Broderick. Could you stand that? Your father would hate us. It was never your fault. How many times do I have to tell you? It was Moira's. She got what she deserved."

Did Moira really deserve such a terrible fate? These days, of course, I'd say, no. She was so very young and love is madness. Of late I've contemplated making my confession to a priest. My mother had been born into the Catholic faith. Babs and I had been baptized. What I so desperately need is absolution. God knows I've long repented yet, I often dream of the gates of Hell opening for me, then shutting me inside.

There was more. Jessica knew there had to be more. She placed a hand over her mouth as Bannerman explained the rest of the secret he had unearthed. There had been no stopping him once he'd laid eyes on Jessica's face in that interview. It was Moira's face. They had to be related by blood. Such a resemblance was too uncanny to be mere coincidence, though such things happened.

Before her marriage, Broderick's image said, Jessica's young and beautiful great-grandmother, Margo Townsend, had had an ill-fated affair that resulted in the birth of a baby girl. Her parents, knowing Margo was engaged to another, had been shocked out of their minds. Such disgrace would taint the whole family. Something had to be done and done quickly. Word was deliberately put out that Margo had gone off alone to Europe, and her parents were obliged to go after her. In fact though Margo spent her confinement on a remote farm in central Queensland. Her baby daughter was given up for adoption hours after the birth to two good people—he was a doctor—who hadn't been able to have children of their own. They named their baby Moira, never speaking to her of her adoption. Margo and her mother waited until Margo was fully recovered before they returned home. Margo's fiancé, genuinely puzzled by it all, still wanted her, and they were married a few months later. A year after that, their daughter, Alexandra, Jessica's grandmother, had arrived to a fanfare of joy.

JESSICA AND CYRUS were still sitting stunned in front of the television long after the tape had come to an end and this extremely tragic story had sunk some way in.

"So it turns out Moira was murdered, after all," Cyrus groaned, and passed a hand over his eyes.

"Could anyone hold a seven-year-old child responsible?" Jessica asked, as appalled as he was. "It must have been unbearable for a small boy watching his mother so furious, hitting out at Moira, screaming that she wasn't going to be allowed to break up the family. Her actions incited the child. Cecily would never have meant what happened to happen, but what your father did on that day tortured him for the rest of his life. It made it impossible for him to like himself. He was right. It all should have been brought out into the open. Brodie should have had counseling."

Cyrus shook his head. "My grandmother would never have allowed that, for Moira would have *won*. The marriage would have broken up. She took on the responsibility. Only, they all suffered, no one more than her own son. Even Hugh found a way out."

"I feel strongly that Hugh *did* love Moira," Jessica said.

"Those paintings surely lent credence to that." Cyrus's eyes leaped to the portrait of his grandfather. "God knows where Livvy got the 'pansy' bit from."

"She mistook the nature of Hugh's love for your grandfather. Probably Hugh had never found a girlfriend. But who knows what goes on in Lavinia's mind?"

"She was right about implying Moira's disappearance was not an accident," Cyrus pointed out bleakly. "How could my poor father show love when he believed himself a murderer? I won't accept that he was, no matter what he says. He couldn't have understood the full consequences of his actions."

"I think I know where Hugh laid Moira to rest." Jessica stared down at her clasped hands.

"A sacred place? That could be anywhere." Cyrus was in despair. He began thinking of all the Aboriginal sacred sites on the station. "That poor girl was hardly more than a child herself."

His words brought tears to Jessica's eyes. No wonder she had felt such a bond with Moira; the bond of blood was impossible to ignore. "Hugh buried her in the family cemetery," she said with an amazingly clear belief in what she had said.

Cyrus's face betrayed his shock. "Jessica, sweetheart, how could you say that? There's nowhere—"

"Yes, there is," Jessica said in a quiet sad voice. "Beneath that beautiful golden tree, the cassia, in the far corner. I was drawn by the way it captured all the light. I'm sure that's where Hugh buried her, then planted the tree. Sacred ground, not out in the wilderness—he loved her too much to do that. Cecily must have begged Hugh to keep quiet, probably appealed to him on bended knee. Hugh must have thought lying about what happened was a gift of mercy to his cousin and to his lifelong idol, your grandfather. They were protecting Broderick and the family. Only, Hugh couldn't live with the lie. The guilt and the grief were always there."

"Poor Hugh," said Cyrus, not wanting to think of the anguish that had led to his suicide. "So how do we lay Moira's ghost to rest? Start the whole sorry business up again?"

"Why don't we ask her?" Jessica said. "We'll go out there together and call to her."

"Jessica!" Cyrus stared at her, his love and need for her spilling out of his eyes. He stood and drew her into his arms. "Out of all this suffering, I have to bless my father for bringing you into my life."

Jessica lifted her head to kiss the sculpted line of his jaw. "I think all Moira wanted was for us—you and I—to know what really happened to her. She wasn't looking for vengeance, but recognition. I acknowledge her as my great-aunt. I am happy to do so. We can turn that area of the family plot into a garden of remembrance with a seat beneath the tree where one could say a prayer. I'd like that. Instead of living inside our heads, Moira can be set free."

Cyrus's somber expression brightened. "I'll say a simple amen to that, and goodbye to all the heartbreak." He bent his head and kissed her long and lovingly. "I'm almost afraid to be so happy with you, Jessica. I'm not used to such happiness."

She smiled up at him radiantly. "Well, you'd better get used to it, because we're going to have a lifetime of it ahead."

Cyrus enfolded her in his arms, speaking into her beautiful cloud of ash-blond hair. "Everyone I have, everything I am, is yours!"

EARLY THE FOLLOWING DAWN, they walked hand in hand to the family cemetery, paying their respects first to Broderick Bannerman, who finally lay at peace, before moving to the corner of the enclosure where the cassia bloomed in all its glory.

"It blooms for months," Cyrus murmured gently as the tree spilled blossom and soft perfume on them like wedding confetti. "Like a beacon."

"We'll think of it as Moira's tree," Jessica said.

It might easily have been a trick of the rising sun dappling the light green leaves and the pendulous branches of bright yellow, but looking up, Jessica fancied she glimpsed a smiling young face. A face very much like her own.

An illusion or Moira bidding farewell?

0306/02 V2

MILLS & BOON®

Live the emotion

Tender
romance™

MEANT-TO-BE MARRIAGE *by Rebecca Winters*

When Jarod Kendall met beautiful Sydney Taylor he faced the hardest decision of his life. He was a priest, and any relationship was forbidden. After a year of Jarod hiding his feelings, Sydney left town, believing her love wasn't returned. Now Jarod must persuade her that against all the odds their marriage is meant to be...

THE FIVE-YEAR BABY SECRET *by Liz Fielding*

Fleur Gilbert and Matt Hanover married in secret, believing their love could end a family feud. They were wrong. Matt has never forgotten Fleur. And when he discovers that their one-night marriage created a son he never knew he had, he's determined to claim his child – and his wife...

BLUE MOON BRIDE *by Renee Roszel*

Roth Jerric may be drop-dead gorgeous, but he's Hannah Hudson's ex-boss, and the last person she wants around. Now they are no longer working together, Roth can't understand why they're clashing more than usual! He's not looking for any romantic entanglement, but Hannah is one woman he can't ignore...!

MILLIONAIRE DAD: WIFE NEEDED *by Natasha Oakley*

Nick Regan-Phillips is a millionaire whom the world assumes has it all. But he's also a single dad, and his daughter has come to live with him. Little Rosie is deaf, and he's struggling to communicate with her. Is beautiful journalist Lydia Stanford the only person who can help Nick forge a bond with his daughter?

On sale 7th April 2006

Available at WHSmith, Tesco, ASDA, Borders, Eason, Sainsbury's and most bookshops

www.millsandboon.co.uk